FRACTURED MIND

by Sheridan Lee

ISBN: 978-1-956654-95-0

For Jeanette

Thank you for believing in me when I struggled to believe in myself.

ACKNOWLEDGEMENTS

Fractured Mind would not be what it is without Jeanette Cameron. While our working relationship transitioned with your career shift, I'm indebted to you for still being involved with Tara's story. You're an overqualified BETA reader, but I wouldn't want to travel this path without sharing "the fun stuff" with you.

Thank you, Cynthia Hickey and Winged Publications, for your encouragement and support. I'm glad to be part of this tremendous team.

Squishy hugs and cheesy grins to the gorgeous readers who've devoured my books, written reviews and shared your excitement over the characters in my head. You're amazing!

Special thanks to science teacher extraordinaire Mr Gerges (wherever you are in the world, my girls miss you!) for breaking your leg in style, and Jay-Maree for inspiring certain details in the wedding-related scenes. I'd rewrite the past for you if I could.

Thank you, Breakthrough Church, for loving me and my family despite our craziness, my parents and in-laws for your support, and over-the-top PDA for Mr Wonderful and our five remarkable girls. I love you all more than chocolate (truly!).

And, Heavenly Father, thank You for Your grace-filled love. I couldn't do life without You.

GLOSSARY OF AUSTRALIAN WORDS AND PHRASES

Bitumen – a tarred road surface
Chuck a wobbly – to throw a tantrum
Clucky – A sentimental wish for a baby
Exxy – expensive
Fossicked – searched or rummaged for something
Hungie – a hundred dollars
Kerbless – without a kerb (raised edge)
My shout/my treat – offer to pay the tab, usually for a meal, drinks or entertainment
Not the done thing – not socially acceptable
Noughties – the decade from 2000 to 2009
Squidgy – squashy and soggy

PROLOGUE

Tara Roberts whimpered in the dank, darkened room, the constant screams inside her skull her sole company. Fire blazed along her raw skin where taut wrist-and-ankle tethers chafed. Uncontrollable chills shuddered along her exposed body. She pressed into the warmth of the scratchy linen under her slight figure, desperate to escape the onslaught of body shivers.

When would this end? Her right shoulder still throbbed from his rough grabby paws, and the unceasing sting of his firm slaps pulsed her left thigh. The moist gag stretched her jaw to soreness, the corners of her mouth aching. Tara's painful, swollen throat struggled to perform basic functions and hold in precious fluid. And her neck thumped from his repeated stranglehold. He had slid his weapon down her neck and nipped the sensitive skin below her left ear on his last visit. Would he wield the cold knife along her throat next time? Useless, silent tears pricked her eyes and overflowed her temples, tickling her ears.

She sniffed, blinked, and grimaced at the latest gadget dangling from the rusty oversized hook bolted above the four-poster bed. A storm of shivers coursed down her spine, curdling in her gut. What possessed a man to treat another human like a soulless instrument?

A click resonated in the soundless room, and the portable oil heater awoke at the foot of the bed. Treasured heat radiated against Tara's toes, igniting goosebumps along her legs, kickstarting her pulse. Her breaths laboured. She squeezed her eyes shut, her palms numb from constant clenching.

He would return soon.

The hallway floorboards creaked behind the heavy, locked door of Tara's prison, and she stiffened. Beads of perspiration dotted her brow and dampened her armpits. She gasped for air, her mouth dry. Nausea eddied her empty stomach, and she wiggled her toes against the sudden yet familiar sensations racking her body.

Someone bellowed.

Tara snapped her gaze to the door.

Clomping footsteps and another shout arrested her attention. Glass shattered and a blood-curdling scream pierced what little hope she had shrouded within.

Tara's heart pounded. She wrenched her arms and legs against the tethers, her movements frantic despite the building inferno of agony consuming her extremities. Her irritating long blonde hair matted across her eyes and against her damp neck. The screams in her head intensified.

Something slammed against the wooden door. Had he snapped? Would he finally break her in two?

Tara kicked with her cramping legs and yanked her weak arms, chest heaving and tears tracking down her face.

Voices shouted. Someone buffeted the door. Once. Twice. Three times.

Tara's chest squeezed, her lungs airless and her heart siphoned of all hope. Were the other monsters back to play?

The fourth resounding impact splintered the door open.

Tara gurgled around the gag.

Uniformed officers invaded the room. A young woman covered Tara with an oversized coat. She removed the gag, freed Tara's hands and feet, and assisted her into the warm jacket.

Tara sobbed against the woman's shoulder.

The officer whispered and slipped an arm behind Tara's back.

When Tara's legs steadied, she padded along the creaking hallway with the help of the officer. Out to freedom.

CHAPTER ONE
Relapse

My head thudded like a speaker box at a death metal concert. I opened my eyes and groaned. Who detonated a bomb inside my skull?

I squinted and twisted my neck. Where the heck was I? Had I stumbled into one of the newly renovated rooms at my bestie Diana's place and slept in the wrong bed? I hoped this was the other spare room and not the main bedroom. Last thing I wanted to tell the newlywed Mr. and Mrs. Harris was I had christened their brand-new bed. Ew.

I narrowed my eyes. Was that a bathroom vanity attached to the ceiling? Why would someone place a mirror on the floor? I furrowed my brow and stared at my surroundings, scrunching my nose to focus on the carpeted ceiling.

Something shifted on my stomach above the blanket.

I lifted my achy arm, its weight heavier than usual.

A body-temperature, fluffy creature laden with soft curls met my fingertips.

I delved into the mass of curls and scratched.

The critter growled. Had naughty Sam Kono dropped his dog, Loki, over for some sweet Tara loving? I did enjoy hugging Sam's chocolate-coloured curly-coated retriever, but why was Loki such a heavy beast?

I pushed against the mattress in a failed attempt to roll to my side. Sam needed to put Loki on a diet. "Move, dog," I said, my throat croaky and tongue dry.

He had better not drool on me.

"Huh?"

I huffed a breath. "I need to pee. You're pressing my pee spot." Why was I explaining my predicament to a canine?

"Did you call me a dog?" a deep voice rumbled.

The weight lifted, and my urgent need to visit the bathroom disappeared.

"And why're you hanging off the side of the bed?"

Oh.

I lifted my head and rolled to my side. My vision blurred and spun. I gripped my temples, lay on the mattress, and shuttered my eyelids.

"You okay?"

Blood rushed between my ears. I sucked in several slow, even breaths. What was I doing? Right. I opened my eyes and startled at the familiar face of a more-than-cute guy with a tangle of ash-blond curls and vibrant green eyes. "You're not Loki."

His lips curved into a boyish grin. "Were you expecting a loveable Marvel villain instead of me?"

I blinked, turned, and glanced ahead. The bathroom vanity and mirror now resided in conventional positions. Glad the reno team had done their job right. "Dunno." With slow, ginger movements I surveyed the unfamiliar bedroom. "Where am I?"

"My place. Don't you remember last night?"

I rolled back toward Mr. More-Than-Cute lying on his side with his stubbled angular jaw resting on his large fist, muscled arm flexed, and elbow digging into the mattress. Wow.

Almost three-and-a-half years had passed since I ogled bronzed skin and exceptional abdominal muscles like this. *Stop, Tara!* I squinted and performed a dismal set of mental calisthenics. No brain Olympics for this foolish woman.

His eyes widened. "The Harris wedding?"

I raised my eyebrow along with the blue cotton sheet. Smooth move.

"We danced and had a whole lot of fun together."

Diana and her now-husband Jonathan's wedding had blurred as the night progressed. But why was I here? I stared into his emerald orbs. "I … I remember most of the wedding. But I think I drank too many cocktails." Freaking Keanu Everton and his scrumptious liquor concoctions!

Mr. More-Than-Cute chuckled and slid his hand across the

sheet along my leg.

The casual action ignited my skin.

"You polished off several drinks and giggled about how cute the martini glasses looked in your hand. By the time I offered to drive you home, you begged me to take you back to my place so we could talk."

"Talk?" *Oh, Lord Jesus, my long-suffering Redeemer. Please forgive this stupid baby Christian.*

"You soon decided talking was overrated, so we played a game of Strip Jack Naked."

Oh shiver-me-timbers.

His dimples burrowed into his sandpaper cheeks, and his deep laugh warmed my insides.

"M-my idea?" A gush of expletives burst in my brain, and I clenched my fingers. At least I still possessed the power to hold back uttering the swears aloud. Surely that was a positive considering my past vocabulary? This Christian life was not for the fainthearted.

"Uh huh." Mr. More-Than-Cute smirked.

Should I ask? *Yes.* "Who won?"

He leaned forward, his full lips centimetres from mine.

My pulse thundered.

"Me, of course. I may've lost the game, but I won the woman with the mesmerising blue eyes."

Great. I broke an almost three-and-a-half-year sex drought with some buddy of Jonathan's after I pretty much forced myself on the poor bloke. My stomach twisted. Diana had misplaced her hopes in me ever being a good Christian.

He brushed his warm thumb along my cheekbone. "You're beautiful."

I cleared my throat. "So we … um." I pointed between the two of us.

He leaned back. "Yes. We did." He narrowed his eyes. "Several times. At your request."

My pulse spiked.

He opened his mouth, closed it, and squinted. "You seemed aware of your surroundings." His throat bobbed. "I just assumed you're a very forward type of woman." The grooves in his forehead deepened, and his voice softened. "You don't remember anything?"

Why was I so stupid? Curse you, delightful cocktails!

"Nothing's coming to mind." I pressed my lips together and clutched the sheet nearer my chin. "This might sound dumb because it's still a bit crazy to me, but I, ah, made a promise to God about a week ago that I wouldn't do"—I waved my arm over the bed—"this sort of thing anymore."

All traces of mirth vanished from his handsome features.

My stomach dropped. The poor guy. "Did we at least have, uh, fun, though?"

"I thought so, but now? If I'd known—"

"It's okay, ah … what's your name?"

"Isaac."

"Isaac. Sorry. Knowing how I can get when I'm buzzed, I expect you read all the signs correctly." I pulled the sheet and myself into a seated position, but my head rebelled, and I almost keeled over.

Isaac caught me around the waist and pulled me against his chest.

I needed a replacement brain, ASAP. *Could you arrange a lobotomy for me, God? Replace my broken brain with something similar to Diana's virtuous mind?* "Thanks. S-sorry for being a terrible person."

His chest vibrated against my back. "You're not a terrible person. Stuff happens. I'm"—he cleared his throat—"glad you ended up with me and not some other guy." He kissed the side of my head. "You're pretty remarkable, and I'm not just talking about the naked section of the night."

"Th-thanks." Heat rushed to my cheeks. Good grief, what was going on? I had not blushed at a man's compliment since I was fifteen.

Isaac nodded toward the ensuite bathroom. "Why don't you have a shower, and I'll make breakfast."

"Okay."

He gifted me with another soft kiss to my temple, slid from behind me, and crossed the room. The gorgeous view of his unclad, muscled back taunted me.

I bit my bottom lip. *Tara! Act like a Christian!* I fisted the sheets and shifted my gaze to the off-white wall despite my eyeballs pulling to see the rest of my bed mate.

Isaac ambled into an alcove adjacent to the bathroom.

I flopped against the pillow, and a scream built in my chest. Diana said all things were possible with Jesus on my side, but was this true? How could I declare celibacy one week and wake up with a hot, naked guy the next? Was I the only imbecilic Christian to rack up a monumental failure so soon on her faith journey? What should I do now?

Isaac sauntered back into the bedroom dressed in black shorts and a fitted grey T-shirt.

Was it possible the man looked hotter dressed?

He winked, his eyes sparkling, and curled his lips into a beautiful smile.

My breath caught in my throat. These ridiculous emotions needed to die. Men were more trouble than they were worth.

Isaac disappeared through the bedroom door, closing it behind him.

I untangled myself from the sheets, levered myself upright, and rested on the edge of the bed. My head whirred for several lengthy seconds. I squeezed my eyes closed and sucked in several long breaths.

Moments later, my spinning head calmed. I stood—my eighty-nine-year-old grandmother rose from her rocking chair faster than I did the bed—and toddled to the bathroom, where the shiny white throne awaited. I flopped onto the cold plastic seat, emptied my bladder to the chorus of my bliss-filled sighs, then stepped into the shower with one palm secured against the frosted glass wall.

I closed my eyes, desperate to wash away my wrongs. Water flowed over my head and shoulders, dripping off my nose and lips. I wanted to remember last night, but in a way, ignorance was bliss. If I had no recollection, I had no information to share with Diana when she found out. Because she was bound to find out.

A conversation with Isaac at the wedding floated to my mind. How Jonathan covered his shifts when Isaac had to make emergency visits to help his sister in Melbourne.

Isaac was a good guy, and I had used him.

My stomach cramped, and my legs trembled. I slammed my other hand against the glass wall and crouched on the tiles, my head now between my knees.

I'm not a prisoner to the darkness. I'm one with the light.

I inhaled several slow breaths. "I'm sorry, God," I whispered.

"I've been a Christian for a week, and I've fallen flat on my face." My eyes stung. "I guess I still need help when it comes to stopping the fun before I drink too much." I lifted my head and slowly stood. "Think You can help me with that? 'Cause I suck at it."

My erratic heartbeat and pulse slowed, and my breaths eased. I washed my hair—thankful I had chopped my blonde locks short years ago—and enjoyed a moment under the running water before exiting the shower.

I grabbed a dry towel from the wall rack, dried myself, and searched the bedroom for my underwear. My aubergine bridesmaid dress lay crumpled along a couch at the foot of the bed, my black bra strap peeking from underneath a pair of wrinkled men's dress pants. My shoulders slumped.

Whore.

I batted the familiar voice away and whipped the bra from its hidey-hole, shifting Isaac's clothing until I located my knickers. A small victory. I snuck into Isaac's walk-in-robe, tugged a denim-blue linen shirt off the hanger, slipped it on, and buttoned it up in front of the bathroom mirror. The oversized shirt covered two-thirds of my thigh. I scrunched my nose at my reflection. The shirt was cute but baggy. A thought entered my marshmallowy mind, and I grinned and pivoted. I slipped the thin, elegant belt off my dress, looped it around my waist, and meandered the hallway toward the clanging of kitchen utensils.

Isaac stood at the stove with his muscled back to me.

I cleared my throat and pressed my hands to my sides.

He glanced over his shoulder and grinned. "Wow, that looks better on you than me."

I fidgeted with the belt buckle. "Hope you don't mind I borrowed your shirt?"

"Not at all." Isaac appraised me then focused on my face. "Keep it." He turned back to the stove.

I padded across the cold kitchen tiles and peered at the stovetop. "Whatcha making?"

He flipped a pan of little pancakes. Another small pan rested nearby covered with a metal lid. "Pikelets, bacon, tomatoes, and mushrooms."

My saliva glands threw an after party. Perfect hangover breakfast.

Isaac piled pikelets onto a dinner plate. "Here, want to put these at the table? Maybe butter them while they're hot."

I carried the mini pancakes to the table and rested them near a bottle of maple syrup. My nostrils ushered in the sweet flavours of my favourite breakfast meal. I grinned, tossed several hot pikelets onto two dining plates, and winced. My poor burned fingertips. I lowered onto a seat, buttered the fluffy carb cushions, and somehow held back my drool.

Isaac placed an oven dish on the table housing crispy bacon and a mound of baked cherry tomatoes still on their truss. He returned to the stove and retrieved the small pot of sautéed mushrooms.

I leered at the breakfast spread. "This looks amazing."

"Thanks."

Everything tasted delicious. Isaac could cook! We conversed about mundane topics—amazing considering the circumstances— and I was surprised how much fun I had chatting and joking, even with a headache. Maybe this was not the huge mistake I imagined it to be. Apart from the whole unintended drunk sex stuff.

Isaac bagged my dress, and we exchanged mobile numbers, although why we swapped digits was a mystery. What purpose would it serve when I lived in Melbourne?

I strapped on my comfortable black high heels, collected my handbag, and slung the dress over my arm. "Thanks for your help. I'll, ah, maybe see you around?"

He scratched the side of his perfect face. "Do you need a lift somewhere?"

"Is Benanu's close?"

"About a block away. Turn left at the end of my street, walk to the next road, cross it, and you'll see it about one hundred metres on your left."

"Cool. I'm meant to see a friend there." And blast Keanu for creating alcoholic joy. The rascal had promised me a meal and gab session. Two months had passed since we caught up last at his bar, when he had tested some of the delicious cocktails on me which he had clearly perfected last night.

Isaac leaned in, bent low, and brushed his lips across my cheek. "Don't be a stranger."

I gazed up into his sea-green eyes and shrugged. "Not sure I'm good company after my behaviour last night, but okay."

He brushed a finger across my cheek. "I feel a bit bad about that." He straightened and ran his fingers up the back of his neck, tangling his curls. "I'm not on great terms with God, but I know how upsetting it is to disappoint someone." He stared into my eyes.

I sucked in a breath.

"Forgive yourself."

I stifled a sigh, air shuddering in my chest. Who was this guy? Mr. Swoony in the flesh? Was Diana correct in her postulations that Mr. Right did exist? Too bad for me I had a knack for finding Mr. Wrong.

I stepped through the front door and into the early November sunshine. "B-bye, Isaac. Thanks for breakfast."

"Goodbye, Tara. Thanks for everything."

I blinked and turned. Everything. Whatever that meant.

"I'm officially the worst Christian in the history of the planet." I stuffed the last potato wedge in my mouth, pushed away the crumb-covered plate, and wilted on the bar stool at Benanu's.

Keanu chuckled and wiped the inside of a glass tumbler with a tea towel. His mop of dark hair flopped near his eyes, and he tilted his head. "Yeah, nah. Pretty sure those people in the Crusades were worse."

I leaned my elbows against the mahogany bar and rested my chin on my palm. "But I slept with him. I haven't slept with anyone since … since—"

"I know." His dark brown eyes lost all signs of usual mischief and burned with unexpected fire. "Give yerself a break and think of this as a positive sign."

"What?" How could this be anywhere near the vicinity of positive? I scrunched my forehead. "How could my stupidity be spun into something positive?"

Keanu placed the tumbler on the bar and tossed the tea towel across his bulging shoulder. He zeroed onto my face, his eyes potent. "Did y'have a panic attack?"

I dug my teeth into my bottom lip. "No."

"Any bad dreams overnight?"

I lowered my arms and straightened. "No. I didn't."

Keanu dropped ice into the glass tumbler. "Then the first sexual experience since"—he waved his hand in the air—"didn't trigger any memories or send ya spiralling. In my book, that's a win."

I dropped my gaze, rolled my lips together, and snorted through my nose. "True. But it shouldn't have happened to begin with. And"—I tapped my fingers against the shiny bar top—"I don't know if this was a one-off fluke or if it'll be an issue when I'm conscious while being … intimate. Wh-when I eventually do that again." Next time I hoped I held out for the man who gave me a shiny wedding ring. Not that any sane man would want to marry me and my baggage.

He stilled my fingers with his enormous hand.

I lifted my gaze to his.

"You'll cross that bridge when ya eventually reach it, Tar. Don't make such a big deal outta this. Learn from it." His fingers slid across my knuckles and reached for the tumbler now filled with cola and ice. "Diana says God forgives, yeah?"

I nodded.

He handed me the cold beverage. "So take the forgiveness and start again."

'Thanks." I indulged in several cooling sips. "He seems like a really great guy."

"Who?" Keanu raised a brow.

"Officer Swoony. Isaac."

"Smitty?"

What? "Who?"

Keanu snickered. "Officer Swoony. Wow. You ladies and yer police officers." His smile disappeared. "Detective Smith's a remarkable guy despite all the challenges life's handed him."

Challenges? I wondered what demons Isaac had to overcome.

Keanu tilted his head toward me. "Reminds me of someone else I know."

My face heated. What was with my recent blushing?

Keanu and I had hit it off the moment we were introduced at Diana's engagement party four months ago, and I had camped out in his spare room several times. But since making Jesus a priority in my life, I chose to stay at the newlyweds' place while they honeymooned. Diana—fresh-off-the-press Mrs. Harris, who had probably been bench-pressed by her new husband overnight—had returned to her hometown, Tellarine, after we completed our journalism degrees last year, while I floated between my boring office job in Melbourne, Mum's place in Swan Hill, and Tellarine. Life in this gorgeous little town called to me.

I leaned forward. "Do you have any job vacancies?"

Keanu's eyes widened, and he furrowed his brow. "Thinking of moving here?"

"I'm sick of working for a pig, answering his phone, and making coffee for his nasty self." I sipped on my cola and enjoyed the fizz of bubbles tickling my throat. "I could do with less gross men breathing down my neck when they've an errand for me."

The irony of working in a male-dominated workplace was not lost on me. A shudder rippled through my body, threatening to unleash deeper, darker memories. I shook my head and focused on the hulking man in front of me. "Unless you proposition your staff?"

Keanu boomed with laughter, highlighting his attractive, boyish-despite-his-beard features. "You think Diana'd work for me if I propositioned the staff? She'd kick me in the nuts and drag my butt to the police station before demanding my arrest."

I chuckled at the image of Diana belting Keanu into submission. "The question still stands. Any wait staff positions? Dishwasher girl in the kitchen? A cleaner? Another personal slave, ah, assistant for yourself?"

Keanu rubbed his large hand across his neatly-trimmed dark beard and nodded. "One of the servers gave notice yesterday afternoon. Any experience waiting tables?"

My eyes enlarged. "Not really. And maybe I should table this conversation until I'm back from the U.S. after my cousin's wedding next month."

"Oh, yeah. Right." Keanu replaced an empty bottle of liqueur on the shelf behind him and turned to face me. "You decided how long yer staying yet?"

"Not really, but I need to decide soon because I gave my landlord notice two weeks ago that I'm vacating, so I've two weeks of paid accommodation before I'm homeless."

Keanu shook his head. "Nice to see you're as impulsive as ever."

I whacked his massive bicep.

"When's the last day of work? Don't make sense keeping a

hated job. Then y'can stay in the U.S. longer and live on paid-out annual leave and rental bond, or put it aside for a place up here."

I slapped the wooden bar, my fingers stinging with the connection. "I forgot about the bond! It was three grand."

Keanu coughed and grasped the bar top. "A three grand bond on that tiny city apartment?"

"Note the words 'city apartment,' hence the high bond for a footprint of space rivalling a genie's lamp."

Keanu grunted.

"What?" I quirked an eyebrow.

"Where would ya live, locally, I mean?"

A Cheshire cat smile played on my lips. "Not with you, although I'd love you as a roommate. Diana's already said it's probably not a good idea to room with a guy, and after last night, I see her point."

His gaze pinned me to the bar stool. "Think we'd end up sleeping together?"

I huffed out a laugh. "There's no thinking to it. We would, and I promised myself, Diana, and God, I wouldn't do it." I widened my eyes. "Again."

Keanu stared at me, his gaze sombre. "You think I'd do that to you?"

My eyes widened. "You don't think I'm attractive?"

His expression flickered an array of unreadable emotions. "You're a siren to my soul."

My heartbeat accelerated.

He blew out a loud breath, hunched over the bar on his elbows, and leaned close. "Thoughts of doing … things have crossed my mind."

The breath in my lungs evaporated, and my head spun. "I'd no idea," I whispered.

"Now ya do."

I swallowed a lump in my throat.

Keanu's gaze shifted from my face to Benanu's front door.

"I'll, ah, hand in my resignation on Monday and e-mail my cousin. See if Jaelle needs extra help before the wedding now I've racked up oodles of experience helping with Diana's."

"Good idea." Keanu nodded to a passer-by wearing a shirt with the Benanu's logo embroidered on his front pocket, then turned back to me. "Sticking around the rest of the weekend? I've got a meeting with the kitchen manager."

"More Saturday afternoon fun for you. No worries. I'm thinking of heading home tomorrow afternoon." Once I showed my face at Diana's church and promised God I would do better.

"Stop by for a coffee before the long drive to Melbourne, okay?" His dark eyes seemed to plead with me.

Did he care that much?

"Sure."

"Okay, see ya tomorrow. Thanks for hanging out."

"Thanks for the free food and drink. Look after yourself."

His focus lingered on my face before his gaze dropped to my lips.

A frisson of tingles sparked down my spine.

Freaky Friday. What alternate universe had I stepped in today? My heart slammed against my ribcage.

Keanu's throat bobbed before he nodded, slipped from behind the bar, and disappeared around the corner.

Another male staff member stepped in his place. "I hear the Harris wedding was a rager." The barman lifted a light eyebrow.

I nodded and smiled. "Yeah, was a great night." I drained the last of my cola. "Have a great weekend." I slipped off the bar stool, grabbed my bagged dress and handbag, and wandered into the late spring warmth.

The three-block walk to my car parked out the front of Tellarine Christian Church helped clear my head from all things Keanu back to what mattered.

My never-to-be-repeated stupidity.

CHAPTER TWO
Paying Penance

"I'm not a prisoner to the darkness. I'm one with the light," I murmured and stared at the orange brick veneer building through my windscreen. Tellarine Christian Church might be a relic from the seventies, but the ancient building held a key to free my anxious soul this morning.

I exited my car and crossed the asphalt, pressing a hand to my gurgling stomach, and willed my overactive imagination and swirling insides to take a break and have a figurative KitKat for the next few hours.

"Sweetheart." Diana's stepmum, Victoria Jacobsen, smiled from the church entryway. She pulled me against her surprisingly strong frame, her medium-brown wavy ponytail clipping my cheek, and wrapped me in her arms.

"Victoria." I breathed in her floral perfume, a tiny chunk of anxiety calming in the wake of her comforting scent and warm touch.

She pulled back, her blue-green eyes bright. "How're you doing? Get much rest after Friday night?"

"The spare bed at Di's is pretty comfy." Not that I would admit to my absence from said bed on Friday night.

"Nicholas is still coming to terms with her being a married woman." Victoria pressed away a smile.

"He still recovering from the shock?" I bit back a smirk. Diana's dad was protective of his children. What would I give for a father to care for me like that?

"I think it might take longer than a day for him to get over the idea of his baby girl shacked up in a Queensland hotel suite wearing nothing but a wedding ring." Victoria chuckled, her middling height silhouetting my below-average size.

I snorted a laugh. Diana's parents were a hoot.

"Just a moment." Victoria stepped toward an elderly gentleman greeting churchgoers on the other side of the church entry, whispered something—to which he smiled and nodded— and returned. "Doug says he's happy to continue greeting without me. Let's go in."

I clutched my oversized tote bag against my side and followed her into the auditorium, ignoring the unsettling buzz refuelling low in my gut. God would forgive me after my screw-up—that much I knew from reading the few New Testament books I had consumed so far—but what if everyone here found out about my unintended promiscuity? Would they expel me from the congregation before I had a chance to become an official part of the community?

"Looks like Nicholas saved some seats with Bee and Matt." Victoria pointed across the large room to her family and friends.

I glanced in the direction she gestured, and my breath caught. I flexed my jaw. When would I stop reacting to Diana's dad like this? No matter what I tried, I struggled to shake my response to the similarity Nicholas Jacobsen shared with another man.

The man I had lost my virginity to when I was sixteen. My first boyfriend's father.

Memories surfaced, and my chest tightened. Mr. Ormond's dark eyes and angular chin dotted with stubble. Broad shoulders and defined abs glistening with sweat, pumping and flexing, as he mowed the lawn shirtless in the sweltering Swan Hill heat.

What sort of girl had I been to seduce a thirty-eight-year-old single man, using his son to get access to him? And what kind of father was Mr. Ormond to not push me away when I had slipped into his bed in the middle of the night?

"Tah-Wah!" Victoria and Nicholas's almost two-and-a-half-year-old son slammed into my legs.

I gasped and clenched my toes, desperate to remain upright.

"Careful, Elijah!" Nicholas lunged for his son, who slipped from his grasp.

Victoria braced my shoulder, saving me from faceplanting on the well-trodden beige carpet.

Served me right for indulging in my sordid memories.

Nicholas stood to his intimidating six-foot-three height and squatted in front of his son. He captured Elijah's attention and touched the boy's arm. "No running indoors, remember?"

"Sowwy, Daddy." Elijah's bottom lip jutted out.

"I forgive you, buddy, but you could've hurt Tara." Nicholas nodded toward me. "Apologise to her, please."

Elijah wrapped his small arms around my legs and blinked up at me, his brown eyes now large, resembling a puppy dog's. "Sowwy, Tah-Wah."

Nicholas stood and draped an arm across Victoria's shoulder.

"It's okay." I scooped my favourite little man into my arms and grinned at his gorgeous face. "How's it going, big guy?"

He huffed and glared at his older sister, Jasmine, who now stood beside Victoria. "Jazzy says Di-Di luffs Jon-than mo' an me now."

I glanced at Victoria and Nicholas before eying their dark-haired son. "That's not true. Di-Di loves you just as much as she always has."

Elijah's shoulders drooped. "Y'sure?"

"Positive."

Four-and-a-half-year-old Jasmine crossed her arms and pouted. "But they's be sleeping in the same bed now."

Choking noises and stifled laughter echoed from the nearby pew.

"They are, not they's," Victoria said, her lips firming in a thin line. "And what does this have to do with how much Diana loves Elijah?"

Jasmine eyed her mother and father, glanced at the nearby pew where Victoria's best friend, Belinda Briggs, and her husband, Matt, watched on, then turned to me. "*They are* sleeping in the same bed like Mum an' Dad, and everyone knows Mum an' Dad loves each other more than anyone else."

"Even Jesus?" Elijah widened his eyes and rounded his mouth.

"No, silly. But more than us." Jasmine shrugged.

One of the Briggses coughed and spluttered.

I pressed my lips together, hiding the smile tugging at them.

Victoria rested her hands on her children's shoulders and flitted her gaze between them. "Your theory is sound, Jasmine, but Diana still loves you and your brother just as much as she did last week." She cleared her throat. "Being married to Jonathan won't change that."

"*Sleeping* with Jonathan," Jasmine said.

Nicholas growled low in his throat.

I gritted my molars together in the hopes of squashing my grin.

"Regardless of sleeping arrangements, your sister loves us all just as much as she usually does. Now, come sit. Church is about to start." Victoria released her children, shooing Jasmine toward her seat, and grabbed Nicholas's hand.

"Guess we'd better sit too," I whispered to Elijah, carrying him back to his parents.

"Uh huh." Elijah slid onto Nicholas's lap.

I slipped along the row, hugging my bag to my chest.

"Morning, Tara." Belinda smiled and flicked her blonde hair over her shoulder.

"Hey." I plonked on the pew beside her.

Matt leaned forward on the other side of Belinda, chuckling. "It's always a blast sitting with the Jacobsens."

"Out of the mouths of babes." Belinda's eyes clouded. She sighed, grasped Matt's hand, and turned toward the front of the auditorium.

I furrowed my brow. What was that about? I shook my head, popped my bag on the floor near my feet, and focused on the stage. Right. Church. I clasped my hands in my lap. This was the first time I had attended church in Tellarine without Diana. Weird.

I expelled a long breath and closed my eyes. *I'm here now, God, so let me prove to you I can do better.*

"Welcome to church!"

I opened my eyes and caught sight of movement on the stage.

A bright-eyed woman in midnight blue jeans and a long magenta cardigan held a microphone, a wide smile pasted to her face. "Let's all stand and spend some time praising God."

I stood with the rest of the congregation.

The song leader bopped and clapped in time to the music, her wavy brunette locks bouncing across her shoulders, and her cardigan sleeves dancing with each vigorous clap.

I studied the words on the projector screen above the stage and fortified myself with the peaceful atmosphere, an anchor to steady me before my tedious drive home to Melbourne.

CHAPTER THREE
Holding Pattern

"How's the packing going, love?" Mum's soft voice filtered over the phone line the following afternoon.

"Getting there." I stretched my back muscles, my petite body unprepared for the work of moving house. Not that anyone dared call this tiny, dumpy city apartment a house. More like an oversized bedroom with a two-seater couch beside the toilet, which came in handy as another seat when friends visited.

"I wish you'd let me help." Mum sighed.

"I've got it handled. Stop stressing."

"I always stress when it comes to my baby."

Sweat trickled down my back—oozing into my neon pink T-shirt—from a mere thirty minutes of physical work. So much for getting things done after a day in the office from hell. At least there had been one positive to celebrate when I handed my terrible boss my letter of resignation prior to leaving work.

I kicked a box aside, adjusted the angle of the almost-pointless upright fan, and flopped on my bed.

Bright late-afternoon sunlight streamed through the murky ninth-storey apartment window, shining across the bare floorboards and brown cardboard boxes. My therapist said light was a necessity after the darkness I had endured. Maybe that was why I had been attracted to the light inside Diana. Despite the traumas we had endured at the hands of different men, Diana never appeared to have lived on a knife's edge. Unlike me, where suicidal thoughts had once been my comforting friends.

"Have you decided where you'll store your things? I've cleared the garage." Mum's voice wavered.

Not this again. "Still working it all out." I ran my palm over my face.

"You need to be more organised. You'll be in Chicago soon and can't leave loose ends while you're away."

"I know, Mum."

She sighed again. "Will I see you before you fly off?"

"Hopefully. I'll see how everything falls on the calendar." If I accepted Keanu's generous offer to store my scant things at his place, then I could make the hour-and-a-quarter detour to Mum's. "I still need to confirm things with Jaelle."

"It's the seventh of November! Aren't you cutting it close to still be unconfirmed?"

The seventh! How had I forgotten to message Jonathan for his birthday?

Mum blew out a loud breath. "I'll leave you to it then. Love you."

"Love you too. Bye." I disconnected the call and pulled up the message app.

Me: Happy birthday, Jonno-Banono! Hope the defloration ceremony went well. ;-) Have a great time mooning your honey. Love, Tar xx

I grinned at the screen and opened the string of messages between Diana and me. Now she was several days into her honeymoon, I could send a brief update and hope she left her phone in her suitcase.

Me: Mrs. Harris! How's married life? (Don't answer that.) Just wanted to give a quick update. I quit my job, have given notice to the landlord, and am hoping to head to Chicago before the end of the month. Fun times! Sorry I'll miss seeing you (unless you visit the city on your return) but I'll be back in late Feb. Love you. xx

I dropped my mobile on my pillow and gathered several textbooks into a box.

My phone vibrated.

Jon: Thanks for the birthday love. Ceremony was worth the wait, made the deadline too. ;-)

I snorted. Jonathan had embarrassed his fiancée at their engagement party when he announced he wanted to get married the first weekend of November so he could say he had sex in his twenties. Another moment when I realised not all Christians were stuffy people. They spoke about sex like the rest of us. Well, maybe not *like* the rest of us. But topics I figured were prohibited for church folk to discuss were part and parcel of conversation I shared with Diana and her family. I smiled. I was no longer "the rest of us" but one of "them" now.

My mobile shrilled in my hand, and I jolted.

Diana's gorgeous brunette features filled the screen. Diana?

I answered the call. "Why the heck are you calling me on your honeymoon?"

"You quit your job and apartment?" Diana's voice echoed along the phone line.

"I can't talk to you now! Hang up and be a blushing bride."

"Tara. What's going on? I knew about the trip to the States, but everything else is so … unexpected."

I sighed. Seemed the woman was determined to get her answer. "I've decided to move closer to you."

"Yes!" Her laughter set off a chain-reaction smile on my lips.

"Why're you calling me? Is your private beach and naked husband not enough of a drawcard for you?" I lay back against my bed.

"Funny." She huffed a laugh. "Seriously, what's happening?"

I slid my fingers along the bare wooden bedside table ledge. "I figured it wouldn't make sense to head overseas for a few months and return to the same life, especially now you're permanently in Tellarine. I'm still unsure as to where I'm moving but will probably take Keanu up on his offer to store my things, then look for a rental either in Tellarine or Swan Hill while I'm in Chicago."

"I'm glad you've quit your job. Your boss always gave off serial killer vibes."

I chuckled. "Yeah, he's creepy. But he paid my wage like clockwork."

Diana squeaked and hissed.

I stilled. Had she just whispered, "Not now"?

"I'm glad you have … a, ah, p-plannn-ah." She squeaked again. "Jonathan, s-stop it."

I pressed my lips together to stifle my cackle. "I really think you should hang up and give the birthday boy another present."

"I agree," Jonathan said, his voice muffled. A growl thundered on the other side of the connection.

Diana giggled. "Sorry, Tar."

"Don't apologise. I'd do the same thing." Not that any decent Christian guy would want to marry me. A double virgin honeymoon filled with innocent touches was never on my cards. I had experienced many romps in the hay with a plethora of different guys before … then.

"Keep me updated with flight info. Say hi to Jae." Diana gasped.

"Okay. Go boink your husband without an audience. Bye!" I hung up, my insides twisting. I sucked in even breaths and remembered the mantra the therapist had helped me word years ago.

I'm not a prisoner to the darkness. I'm one with the light.

I closed my eyes. Warmth spread through my chest. Jesus was the light in my life now. A soft smile slipped to my lips, and I glanced at my laptop balanced on a pile of boxes. Now was as good a time as any to email my cousin.

I grabbed my device.

To: Jaelle - Work
From: tartarbinks98@gmail.com
Subject: Yo, cuz!

Jelly!

How's the Chicago snow? Turned up yet? I'm loving the November Melbourne heatwave.

So! I've finally quit my job! My last day is Friday next week, the day my apartment lease ends. Hence the e-mail address change … and my crazy life of cleaning, chucking stuff, and packing boxes. Life's a thrill.

I've attached a few photos from the Harris wedding (Diana says hi!). It was sensational as expected. So much fun! Diana looked gorgeous and so relaxed. I hope you're going to be as laid-back a bride as her.

Oh! Can you believe Diana called me to see what's going on after I messaged her about my job etc.? Called me on her honeymoon! She's probably lounging on a private beach in Queensland wearing nothing and somehow decides my life's more important than the naked husband lying next to her. I spent the first thirty seconds squealing at her to hang up, then decided to spill the info the next thirty seconds because *she* started squeaking. Argh. Honeymooners.

I also did something really stupid over the weekend. Will tell you about it when I see you. Which could be a few days after I leave my job if you want me? I need time to apply for my ESTA Visa waiver thingy, so the sooner you let me know, the better. I could stay a month or two if you want? Maybe close to three? I'd love to help use all my newfound wedding prep skills.

Okay, email me ASAP.

Love you,

TarTar

PS: I also have news to tell about Keanu (the handsome, gigantic mass of bone and muscle you met at his family's restaurant in Tellarine when you visited in September).

I pressed away a smile and pushed Send. Jaelle's response would be fun.

Something glittered in the window, and I turned. Blessed sunlight. I shoved aside the darkness which lurked on the edges of my mind, shadowy thoughts inching across enemy territory. Why had my brain conspired against me since I slept with Isaac?

I whispered a prayer Diana had encouraged me to pray, and clicked on a saved tab in my internet browser. My U.S. Visa waiver request would have to wait for another day. I clicked on the airline website and trolled through dates and flights, re-checking the ones I had thought my best options last week. So many choices and so much money. I jotted down new flights which suited my timetable and budget best, drank some water, and returned to packing.

Hours later, I snuggled against my fluffed bed pillows and checked my email—the lamp near the TV beaming light at this late hour—and was greeted by my cousin's email.

To: tartarbinks98@gmail.com
From: Jaelle - Work
Subject: RE: Yo, cuz!

You still have this email address? Hahahahaha! Absolutely fabulous!

Um, what!?!?! You've quit Pigsville at last? *Performs a happy dance* I'm so glad!! Your boss is a creep. Cah-reep! He ogled me lewdly when I met you at work. Lewdly. Gross. Paul would've punched his face in if he'd travelled to Oz with me. Lucky for your ex-boss.

Um, what's this about staying two bleeping whole months?! Are you being serious? You're not messing with me? Because if you're messing with me, I'mma gonna fly to Melbourne and sock you in the face before you finish work so I still know where you live, ha ha. What are you doing?! No job, no home? Where are you going after your stint in Chicago? Back to Swan Hill? Tellarine? You can always live with me! That would be awesome. Our new place is palatial compared to the hovel I lived in.

Oh, and puhleeze stop with the naked Jonathan thoughts. That guy is off tap (don't tell Paul I said that). Cop hotness, ooh la la.

Okay, Tar, I'm gonna be honest with you. Five minutes ago I practised my breathing exercises (and my kegels because there's never a better time to do them!) and imagined your serene face so I could calm myself. Why, you might be asking? Well, beloved cousin of mine, you need a smack on the head for your "I also did something really stupid" comment without divulging anything. Tara Marie Roberts! Have I not taught you a thing over the last two decades? Sharing is caring! And sharing via email suffices when the time difference between you and your fave cousin sucks, or your cuz never accepts Zoom or Skype invites (get with the times and video chat with me!). I'm not going to see you for at least two weeks, so you'd better load up your suitcase with Haighs or Koko Black chocolates as an apology. I'm serious. Regardless, please bring it anyway because I miss that chocolate like crack. If I ever was stupid enough to try crack, I guess. Ha ha.

Get your stuff in order, send me your flight itinerary, and come on down! Or up (which way is it?). Arrive whenever, just make sure you stay until after the wedding (19 Feb in case you forgot, Head Bridesmaid, ha) so you can get over your hangover.

Love you more, miss you so much, gorgeous.

JellyBelly

PS: Stop with the stringing-me-along stuff!! What about Keanu? Does he want you to be his personal slave (because that'd be a great improvement in employment)? Offered you a free bartending course so you can shake your booty while you shake that martini for James Bond? Declared his undying love and wants you to have his baby (your baby would grow up to be the hottest person on earth, so maybe not)? Tell me!!!

I chuckled at the craziness which was my cousin. Diana once stated I was her craziest friend, but compared to the pre-Paul Jaelle, I was a virtuous angel. Although my beloved cousin let loose around me, she had her own hang-ups. A people pleaser who had been taken advantage of more than once. I whispered another prayer of thanks to God for my cousin and for saving her from a life of promiscuity. Paul was a great guy and her perfect match. Now, if they would both embrace Jesus, life would be perfect.

I clicked back to the flight-booking website, plugged in the details—grinding my teeth at the expense—and arranged for my U.S. Visa waiver.

To: Jaelle - Work
From: tartarbinks98@gmail.com
Subject: RE: Yo cuz!

You do know you're hilarious, yeah? I love you and miss you. I can't believe we've been living on different continents for 7 years now.

Yeah, I quit Pigsville. Oink oink! It's been rough since because Mr. Lewd called his niece to fill my role temporarily, but Aimee has no idea how to do anything. *Any*thing. I actually feel sorry for her. I mean, it's enough that she has *him* as an uncle. She tries, but she just finished secondary school and wants to party, not work. Oh, to be young.

Mr. Lewd's given up the borderline sexual harassment and is just grumpy. So very grumpy he could star in that terrible movie Mum loved to watch when we were kids with those two old codgers. He demands I stay late to fix all of Aimee's mistakes, asks for coffee five times more than usual, and is making me organise the office Christmas party before I leave … although I'm not invited to go. Not that I'd be here, but it's the principle of the matter.

I can understand why you think my life's a bit of a mess, but I haven't felt this free since … well, before "then." I think I made a good decision putting a chance on God. I know you think I'm crazy, but you've seen how amazing Diana's family is. She's been through stuff too, as has her stepmum, but they were able to deal much better than I did. Yeah, they weren't abducted and raped for three days, but still. They had stuff to deal with. And while I'm openly discussing the past and not suffering a mental breakdown or rocking on my bed, I can't believe it's been almost 3 1/2 years since it happened. I know I've said it before, but thank you for your extended visit, endless phone conversations, and emails while I recovered. But please, enough with the kegels! There's only so many a woman should do.

Haighs will be loaded in my suitcase. My apartment looks like a warehouse with boxes lined up the walls. When I saw Keanu and collected a coffee for my drive home on Sunday, he insisted I have everything transported to his spare room. We kinda awkwardly parted ways the previous day (I had no idea he found me attractive!), so I think he's trying to touch base before I disappear to Chicago? I'm not sure. I feel safe around him, but he's just not into God, and I don't know if that will become an issue. Not that I see myself with any man for the time being.

I'll forward you the emails with my flight itinerary. I'm having a white Christmas this year! Mum's fine with it. I'll leave 23 Feb (and, no, I didn't forget the date of the wedding!) so it's looking closer to three months with you. Woot!

I'm so excited!

Love you, JellyBelly. Tell Paul to pick his nicest (and cutest!) single buddy so we can double date. Not that it'll be an actual date on my part. I'll feel less like a third wheel with someone else to talk to when you're both snogging in the corner booth at a restaurant.

TT xx

I glimpsed the time on my laptop—almost one A.M.—and turned toward the corner lamp, its constant light a comfort. I could have a fresh start moving back to the country. A life with friends, a church filled with kind people. A tingling lightness filled my torso, and I grinned at the mess of boxes surrounding my bed. Maybe I could take the plunge.

I slipped into a set of skimpy summer-weight pyjamas and brushed my teeth at the tiny kitchen sink. The thought of brushing my teeth in a proper bathroom in a few days' time excited me. I rinsed and spat, lay out my work clothes, and set my phone alarm for six hours' time.

My laptop alerted me to an incoming email.

To: tartarbinks98@gmail.com
From: Jaelle - Work
Subject: RE: Yo, cuz!

So excited! Just had to say it.

I'm glad you were able to move past things. It broke me seeing you how you were, and if you think God's helping you make more progress, then I'm supportive of your choice. I've got nothing against Jesus. In fact, Paul's got a new co-worker who's a volunteer youth pastor at his church. Louis is single, so maybe I can keep you here after all!

Don't pack too many clothes because I need to shop for my honeymoon, so we might as well go on a spree. Dad's given me a special gift of money for you and me to spend, so it should be a pretty cheap trip for you! Yay!

Safe travels, don't talk to strange men (unless they're hot), and I'll see you in the frigid land of the U.S. of A in a few days!

JellyB xx

I beamed at Jaelle's email then placed my laptop on my bedside table, slipped under the sheet, and closed my eyes.

Tomorrow brought me a day closer to my new life.

CHAPTER FOUR
Adventures in the Windy City

Blasted aircraft overhead luggage compartments! I stretched on my tiptoes and bit back a growl when my fingers failed to grasp my oversized handbag slash holder-of-all-things-weird-and-wonderful. Why was airplane storage located so far above my head? Was this a not-so-subtle snooty lift of the nose to my height insufficiency? Did the airline industry snigger at petite passengers like me needing a boost like a child at the kitchen stove?

"Excuse me, ma'am, can I retrieve your overhead luggage?"

Ma'am? I pivoted in the squishy aisle toward a reedy middle-aged man with a twangy accent wearing a faded baseball cap.

He nodded toward my bag.

I smiled. "That'd be great, thanks. The black bag with the red-and-yellow ribbons on the handle." I wrapped ribbons around all my luggage like a craft-enthusiastic two-year-old. One could never be too careful when travelling.

The man removed my bag—which bumped the brim of his cap on its descent—and rested it in my outstretched arms.

"Thank you."

"Ma'am." He tipped his hat, smiled, and joined the throng of slow-moving passengers toward the exit doors. Had we flown back to the nineteen-fifties?

I returned to my aisle seat. When the departing mass of travellers trickled to a handful of people, I stood, slipped into my long woollen overcoat, and toted my bag down the aisle.

A tall, slim, pretty brunette in a still-crisp hostess uniform smiled beside the aircraft door. "Welcome to Chicago. Thank you for flying with Qantas. Have a great day."

"Thanks." I followed the other passengers along the carpeted airbridge toward the baggage claim area. My shoulders and neck ached with each footfall. Almost twenty-four hours had passed since I left Australian soil.

Why had I thought flying Melbourne to Los Angeles direct, then catching a flight to Chicago five hours later a good idea? At least I had already processed through Customs. I cringed. A similar, reversed, long-haul flight in February still awaited me. Yay.

I trekked the familiar marathon distance to the baggage carousel flashing my flight number and waited. A few stray bags chugged the loop three times before fresh luggage appeared.

Someone stood close, subtle cologne wafting to my nostrils. "What am I looking for?"

I turned and yelped at my cousin's fiancé. "Paul!"

Familiar grey eyes sparkled at me.

I launched at his solid chest.

He wrapped his arms around me for a quick hug.

"What're you doing here? Why aren't you at work?" I glanced back to the luggage carousel.

"Your flight info's on the fridge and I don't have any important meetings until late morning, so I thought it'd be fun to surprise you. Jae stayed up late doing I've-no-idea-what, so we can surprise her too."

I grinned and nudged him. "I appreciate it. I mean, it's not the end of the world doing the usual taxi thing, but this's nice."

He nodded toward the carousel.

I yipped. "That's mine! The dark blue bag with red-and-yellow ribbons."

"Just one bag?"

"Yep."

He launched forward, clutched the heavy suitcase, and planted it at my feet.

I extended the handle and slipped my oversized handbag straps over my checked-in bag handle.

Paul seized my luggage. "Ready?"

"Let's go."

Forty minutes later, Paul parked outside a new apartment duplex opposite Wicker Park.

My eyes widened. "I didn't Google-Maps-stalk this place. It's massive! How many bedrooms?"

"Three."

I eyed the brick-and-concrete facade before glancing at Paul. "Well done, you. Nice location."

He unbuckled and gazed at the building. "It's worth every penny, although we might be renting for the rest of our lives with the small fortune this place costs."

I smirked, unbuckled, and assisted Paul with the luggage. "So long as you're both happy."

We entered the building, and I breathed in the new house scent. Paul unlocked his apartment door, rested my bags below a nearby wall mirror, and pointed to the lounge room. "I'll see if Sleeping Beauty's awake." He disappeared down the walkway.

I flopped onto the comfy grey couch.

Someone shook my shoulder. "Wakey-wakey."

I blinked and stared at my beaming cousin. Had I fallen asleep?

Laugh lines deepened around Jaelle's hazel eyes. "Up-up. I made breakfast. Paul popped your things in your room before he headed to work."

I rubbed my palm across my eyes. "How long was I out?"

She scrunched her nose. "Forty minutes?"

"Huh." I stretched my limbs and thrust a hand at my gorgeous, frizzy-haired cousin. "Help?"

She grabbed my fingers and pulled me upright into her embrace. "It's so good to have you here, Tar."

"It's great being here." I yawned. "Apart from the lack of sleep, I'm great."

Jaelle released me from her arms. "First breakfast, then I'll give you the grand tour."

I followed her to the spacious kitchen, where we dined on a healthy tasting egg-white omelette thing. I admired the white marble countertops, two-toned timber cabinetry, and hardwood floors.

"I'm back at work tomorrow for the rest of the week, then I'm off over Christmas and New Year's. Have you decided what you'll do with yourself while Paul and I work?"

"Haven't thought about it yet." I shovelled another mouthful of food-like matter into my mouth. If only I had packed Keanu in my luggage, then I would have had a decent cocktail with this boring breakfast. Not that I should indulge in those glasses of temptation. Were cocktails allowed at breakfast time? Another random question to ask Diana.

"Well, feel free to stay here, where it's warm. Otherwise, venture out whenever you like." My cousin deposited her dishes into the dishwasher.

"Thanks." I added my dishes to the dishwasher rack. "Is there anything you need me to do wedding-wise? I had a decent practise run with Diana's wedding."

Jaelle sprayed the bench top and wiped crumbs into the sink. "We'll get to that." She rested the cloth on the sink edge and crossed her arms. "First, house tour, then you're going to give me my Haighs, and we're gonna stuff our faces with chocolate while you tell me every little minute detail related to Keanu and whatever other stupid thing you alluded to in your emails."

I withheld my burning desire to pull a childish face. "You're so bossy."

Jaelle elbowed my side and directed me through the kitchen archway for my grand tour.

♥ ♥ ♥ ♥ ♥ ♥ ♥

"This is perfect!" Jaelle's uncontrollable laughter filled the spacious upmarket apparel change room.

I wrinkled my nose at the grotesque light-mustard chiffon dress with off-white craggy patterns splotched along the bodice and sleeves. "I look like a baby barfed all over me."

My cousin collapsed to her knees onto the carpeted floor, her face a mottled puce. Tears streamed her cheeks. "Baby … b-barf …"

I pressed my lips together, but my cheeks puffed with a smile. Cheeky. I dug around in my handbag for an unused tissue and threw it at my cousin's head. "You're drooling."

She hiccupped and wiped her face. "Am not."

"No. You weren't." I chuckled. "Can I get out of this monstrosity now you've had your fun?"

Jaelle snorted a fresh round of laughter. "The best five minutes of the week."

"You sure you're not bored with Paul?"

Her eyes widened. "Hey!"

I snickered and turned. "Unzip me, please."

Jaelle helped unsheathe me from the horrendous garment—her breaths short and laughter barely under control—and I donned the next outfit.

The silky sea-blue A-line dress hugged my petite frame, accentuating my mild curves.

Jaelle's eyes twinkled. "That's really lovely on you. Compliments your eyes." She retrieved her phone from her jacket pocket. "Lemme send this to Paul." She snapped a pic.

I scrutinised my figure in the mirrors.

"Have you thought more about where you'll go and what you'll do when you head home in Feb?"

I glanced at my cousin before returning to my reflection. "Tellarine's been like a second home to me the last few months. I've found a few job possibilities in Robinvale, but even if I worked there, I think I'd like to live closer to Diana."

Jaelle's phone beeped. She glimpsed the screen and cackled.

"What?"

"Paul said he showed his buddy Louis the pic, and the poor guy fell off his ergonomic chair." Jaelle waggled her brows.

"Men." Smoothing a hand down my side, I inspected the dress. "Will this hue work with the rest of your wedding colours?"

"Definitely." She stepped closer and adjusted the hem. "It could be a tad shorter so your legs don't look so stumpy."

I dropped my gaze to my legs and cringed. "I agree. Most dresses are long on me."

"Tends to happen when you're tinier than the average bear."

I poked out my tongue. "What about the other bridesmaids? Won't they want to have some say in what they get to wear?"

Jaelle's countenance sobered and seemed to pale.

"What's the matter?"

She fidgeted with her phone. "It's just … I haven't given you the full story about the others."

"Okay?" I changed back into my comfy jeans, fluorescent yellow T-shirt, and jacket.

Jaelle toed the carpet.

I touched her shoulder. "What's going on?"

She sighed. "I did something I really regret."

I raised an eyebrow.

She shuffled her feet. "Zoe, my college friend, has assumed the role of bridesmaid without my permission."

"What?" I scrunched my brow.

Jaelle widened her eyes. "You know she can be a little overbearing and aggressive."

"So you're having her in your bridal party?" I gaped. How could Jaelle give in to her so-called friend so easily?

She shrugged. "I don't want to have to deal with a big fight on top of everything else."

"That's insane! You can't let her push you around like that." My hands vibrated. I pressed them against my sides.

"It is what it is. So now it's you, Camilla, Peggy, and Zoe as my bridesmaids. Paul said he'd just ask another work mate to join the wedding party."

I disliked how Zoe manipulated my cousin. From the moment I met her years ago, I had never liked her. I sighed. "Where to now?"

Jaelle opened the change room door, her arms laden with rejected dresses, and nodded toward my bridesmaid gown. "We'll pay for that, then do a little lingerie and swimsuit shopping, followed by cake tasting at the cake maker's boutique nearer to home."

"Yum." I clutched the sea-blue dress and followed her to the fitting room exit.

Jaelle approached the raven-haired assistant. "Would you prefer I return these to the racks?"

She shook her head and reached for the outfits. "I'll put them away for you."

"Thanks," Jaelle said with a smile.

We stepped into the main shopping area and ambled toward the nearest payment register.

"Oh, we're also having dinner with Louis tonight."

"What?" I stumbled and extended my arms to stop my fall. My lungs wheezed for oxygen. I blinked at my hands, now planted on the buttocks of a bikini-clad mannequin. The blue bridesmaid dress hanger had somehow hooked to the back of the mannequin's skimpy bikini top. I stabilised my feet, retrieved the dress, and turned to my cousin.

Jaelle covered her mouth with her palm and puffed a strangled laugh.

I straightened the low-rise bikini bottoms. "Sorry for the inappropriate grab, but thanks for breaking my fall, Beach Babe."

A nearby customer narrowed her eyes at me, huffed, and disappeared between the clothes racks.

Jaelle burst into loud giggles.

I shrugged, deposited the dress on the counter, and waited for my cousin to gather her wits and pay.

We moseyed back to Beach Babe and trawled through the swimsuit collection.

I extracted a pair of bright-blue boyshorts with miniature yellow stars and a matching tankini top. "Why're we having dinner with Paul's work colleague?"

Jaelle stared at a crimson low-cut one-piece. "You said you didn't like being the third wheel."

I scrunched my nose. "I was joking. I'm fine with you two making out while you wait for your coffee to brew each morning."

"Don't you want to meet a nice guy?" She raised a brow.

Did nice guys willing to accept my baggage even exist? Unlikely. A dim image of *his* face flitted to my mind before his voice echoed in my head.

You're my whore now.

I gritted my teeth, whispered a prayer, and grabbed a mint-and-silver one-piece. "Nice guy or not, I'm going home in February."

"You can never have too many friends, right?"

"I s'pose."

Jaelle selected a classic triangular-shaped yellow bikini. "And I figured you might like to attend church while you're here."

I met my cousin's serious expression. "You did?"

"I know your faith's important to you, and even if I don't understand it, Paul and I have both seen a lighter, more open, softer side to you which is new."

Warmth spread through my chest. Jaelle had always been the perceptive one of the two of us, even if she was crazier. To hear her say these things was all the encouragement I needed to keep focused on God and His love for me. A love I still struggled to comprehend.

Jaelle glanced at the swimsuits she held. "And maybe if you had friends here, you'd think seriously about my suggestion to move to Chicago."

Huh? I furrowed my brow. Had Jaelle been serious about her

hints all these years? I had assumed her remarks said in jest were inconsequential. I loved my cousin more than most people, but relocating halfway across the world was a daunting prospect. I bit the inside of my cheek.

She raised her head and met my gaze. "When Dad accepted the job here, I was devastated to move. But as the years passed and I met Paul, many of the voids inside were replaced, one by one. But my designated 'Tara place' can only ever be filled by you." Her eyes misted, and she blinked. "When Aunt Alannah called after you were abducted, I caught the next available flight to Melbourne even before I knew they'd found you. And since then, I've wanted to keep you close."

I tucked my arm around Jaelle's waist and rested my head against her shoulder.

"I love you, Tar. And I miss your gorgeous face whenever we're apart."

My chest tightened in tandem with my throat. "I love and miss you too, but I'm doing so much better than I was back then."

She sniffed. "I know."

An idea floated to my mind. "I could compromise …"

Jaelle shifted against my arm and captured my gaze. "How?"

I wrinkled my nose. "I could video cha—"

"Yes!" She shimmied. "Done. We're booking weekly video chats in the calendar tonight."

Argh. "Fine." I huffed a breath and refrained from giving her a deserved eyeroll.

She grinned, grabbed a handful of swimsuits off the rack, and dragged me back to the change rooms for another round of dress up.

CHAPTER FIVE
Single Christian Men

"Knock knock."

I turned from the guest bedroom ensuite mirror and smiled.

Jaelle flopped against the bathroom doorframe in her cute rubber-ducky-print flannelette pyjamas, her chaotic head of bed hair bunched at her shoulders. Faint white flecks crusted at the corners of her eyes, a matching dried white smear stretching from her mouth to the side of her cheek.

I pressed away a smirk and dabbed my fingertip in my tiny tub of pinkish lip gloss.

My cousin yawned, long and loud.

I glanced back to the mirror and swiped the rosy lip gloss across my mouth.

"Still can't get over how little make-up you wear these days."

All because of him. I pressed my hand against the side of my neck.

"Sorry," she whispered.

He can no longer hurt me.

Jaelle covered my hand with her palm. "I hate how I trigger you like that."

God, how I hate the power he still wields. Help me be free from him.

"Louis is waiting downstairs, but you don't have to go. Church will still be there next Sunday morning."

"No, it's okay." I met my cousin's gaze. "I'm okay."

"If you're sure." She lowered her hand and scrunched her brow.

"I've been looking forward to it." Last week's dinner with Louis Kenyatta had piqued my interest. In the church, not the guy, despite his handsomeness.

Jaelle stepped from the doorway and flopped on the edge of my bed. "Have enough American dollars in case you go out afterwards?"

"Yup." I slipped on my woollen coat, dropped my Bible inside my large tote bag, and kissed Jaelle's forehead. "Go back to bed."

She yawned and covered her mouth with her palm. "Think I might."

I descended the stairs and snatched an apple from the kitchen fruit bowl.

Louis emerged from the lounge room, an overcoat stuffed under his arm, and focused his dark-brown eyes on me. "Ready?" He slipped a knitted beanie over his short, wiry pitch-black hair.

"You're not fussy about people eating in your car, are you?" If Louis was anything like Jonathan's buddy Sam, I might have to hang my head out the passenger window to eat my breakfast.

"No."

"Cool." I gulped a glass of water and extracted the spare key from the mug near the coffee machine. "Did you say it takes about twenty minutes to get to your church?"

He nodded and gestured toward the front of the house.

I munched on my apple, locked the front door, and trailed Louis through the overnight snowfall whitening the footpath to his black sporty-looking car farther down the street. Chicago had turned on its White Christmas weather. Perfect for this Aussie gal wanting a new experience. Although freezing my little butt off was starting to get a bit old. How could Jaelle have stolen my summertime just to have her long-dreamed magical winter wedding? I hoped my gorgeous cousin appreciated the sacrifices I made for her.

Louis opened the passenger door and flashed a small smile, exposing contrasting white teeth to his umber complexion.

"Thanks." I buckled and tracked his quick, huddled movements to the driver's seat. "What can I expect at today's service?"

He rubbed his gloved hands together. "Lots of people who love God?"

Lots of people?

Louis drove down the quiet road, where it seemed many of the local residents preferred to stay indoors at eight-fifteen on a Sunday morning.

"Is it a big church?" I had forgotten the church name, so had no way of looking it up before today.

"Pretty large. The congregation's predominately black too, so your blonde hair might stand out."

"Might?"

He slowed at a set of traffic lights. "Some of the women dye their hair, but there's more black than blonde on any given Sunday."

I smiled. Now I would stand out for being uber short *and* Caucasian.

"That won't be a problem for you?" Louis's voice buzzed with unexpected intensity.

"God knows I've slept with my fair share of black men."

Louis spluttered and gripped the steering wheel.

I widened my eyes. "I mean, I *used to*. I gave that up a while ago." Apart from my post-wedding fail. *Sorry, Lord.*

"Right." Louis's voice sounded strained.

"Probably more than you wanted to know about me." I chuckled and glanced at the man behind the wheel. "But isn't it a bit late to ask me whether I'm a card-carrying KKK member? Shouldn't you have vetted me before today?"

Louis emitted a strangled laugh. He glanced at me before focusing on the road. "From what Paul's said in the past, and then observing you at dinner last week, you didn't seem …"

"Racially exclusive? Xenophobic? A bigoted apartheid lover?"

Louis coughed and cleared his throat, tightening his grip on the wheel. "Something like that."

Oh boy. The guy needed to relax.

Or maybe you need to tone it down.

I wrapped my hands around my half-eaten apple and slowed my breaths. "In answer to your original question, no, it won't be a problem. I enjoy meeting new people regardless of race and gender."

I turned to the windscreen and admired the scenery ahead. An eclectic mix of brick and stone buildings—crumbling, neglected structures beside the bright and new—filled my view, blanketed with a thin sprinkling of snow. Paul said the early snows were picturesque when fresh and white, but come January, the roads and walkways would be grey and less Winter Wonderland-looking.

Louis fiddled with the heating vents. "That okay?"

"Fine. Thank you." I nibbled the remainder of my apple,

wrapped the core in a tissue, and dropped the small bundle in my tote bag.

Louis merged onto the four-lane expressway.

I snuck a furtive glance at Paul's friend. Having only attended church with Diana a handful of times, I lacked the experience of understanding single Christian men and their quirks. Was Louis a typical specimen with his awkward, almost uptight way of speaking to me? Or was Jonathan and Nicholas's relaxed, kind manner the norm? Although, they were married men. Perhaps Christian men relaxed after finding their life partner?

Another thought crossed my mind. Maybe I induced this awkward response because of who I was? I shook my head. No, Diana's Uncle Steve had always been casual and approachable when Diana and I lived with his family while at university.

But he too was happily married.

I glanced at Louis again. Perhaps single Christian men were highly strung because they lived without sex? And if they abstained until marriage, what would they think about an over-experienced girl like me who could train them in every avenue related to the topic?

"Are girls like me a turn-off to single Christian guys?" Had I said that aloud?

Louis swerved closer to the sludgy expressway edge.

"Sorry. Didn't mean to blurt that out."

Louis cleared his throat. "What do you mean?"

I shrugged. "Yanno, girls who used to sleep around before they found Jesus. Is that a turn-off? Or do single Christian men have sex?"

He blew out a prolonged breath. "I can't speak for all single Christian guys, but I know plenty who do." He turned and briefly caught my gaze. "I'm not one of those men."

"So you're a virgin?"

"Yes." His voice sounded strained again.

"Not that there's anything wrong with that." I clasped my hands together. "M-my best friend recently married, and she and her husband were virgins. She's the one who introduced me to Jesus."

"She sounds like a wise woman." Louis tapped his thumbs against the steering wheel.

I smiled. "Yeah, she is."

"It's more intimidating than a turn-off." His voice croaked.

"Huh?" I furrowed my brow and allowed his words to penetrate my mind. "Oh. You mean, it affects a guy's ego or something when he knows the girl has a heap of experience and he has none?"

"Precisely."

"But it's not *her* fault she didn't meet Christ until after she was sexually active." I huffed a breath and crossed my arms.

"Of course. But it's still intimidating."

"Maybe *single Christian men* should rethink the situation and not see the experienced girl as an intimidation but as a blessing." I snorted a laugh. "I mean, how many guys can say they've had amazing sex from their first time? Not many."

"I never thought of it from that perspective." Louis glanced at me and smiled.

We travelled the remainder of the journey in not-quite-companionable but not-awkward silence. Louis slowed his vehicle at a shopping centre, drove past several shops and parking spaces, and entered an expansive bitumen car park.

"This is your church?" I gaped at the jam-packed parking facility outside the huge glass-and-tan-bricked building. I had imagined a church in similar size to the one Diana had attended in Melbourne. Not one with over five-hundred parking bays.

"Been coming here since I was a kid."

I whipped my head around to stare at Louis. "Does your family attend?"

He unbuckled and grabbed his phone, Bible, and notepad. "My parents and aunt attend the earlier service, so we should miss them."

"There's an earlier service?" Were people in Chicago off their trees?

"Seven o'clock for the early birds."

I blew out a slow breath, grabbed my bag, and opened the passenger door. Meeting the family of a man I barely knew seemed like more than I could do so early in the morning.

We weaved around parked cars, stationary vehicles waiting to exit or searching for parking, and entered the church building.

A heavy-set middle-aged man with deep bronze skin and luminous dark eyes stood inside the entry doorway. His tailored brown suit hugged his large body. A wide, infectious grin spread across his weathered face. "Mornin', Louis. Ma'am."

"Kevin." Louis shook the man's hand and gestured to me. "This is Tara. She's visiting from Australia."

"The Great Southland of the Holy Spirit. Welcome to Chicago, Tara."

"Thank you." I accepted his extended hand and smiled. "You have a lovely city, even if I'm missing out on summer at home."

Kevin chortled. "Are you stayin' for Christmas?"

"I'll be here until late February."

"Wowee." Kevin gushed with more laughter and clapped. "Will we be seein' more of you here then?"

"Probably." I grinned and turned to Louis, who nodded and stepped away from the door.

We trod the blue-and-tan-patterned carpet through the foyer to the main sanctuary.

I widened my eyes. The room bustled with hundreds of people, young and old. A rectangular raised platform hosted a long set of metal stage risers, and to its right a large boxed-off area where several musicians milled about their instruments. Hundreds of navy-coloured chairs lined the royal-blue floor in neat rows, and four banks of grey tiered seating filled the back section of the room.

Louis nudged me toward the middle seating section on the floor.

"How many people can fit in here?"

"I don't know the exact number, but I know it holds over fifteen-hundred seats."

Whoa. Big.

He nodded to several young men nearby and pointed to two empty seats. "Those okay?"

"Sure." I slipped past several seated folk, plonked in the chair beside Louis, and placed my tote near my seat leg. "Thanks for inviting me."

"Happy to help you get to church while on vacation." Louis gifted me another soft smile.

I reciprocated with a grin and faced the front.

A choir in matching garb trailed the platform and ascended onto the risers. Several women and a few men stood at the front of the stage holding microphones. The musicians in the pit-like cordoned space settled with their instruments.

"Good morning!" A suited man bounced on his toes in the middle of the stage.

"You ready?" Louis whispered in my ear.

"You ready to hear a strangled cat?"

He bent closer. "Pardon?"

"I can't sing in tune, so I hope you're ready."

"We can sing badly together." Louis grinned, the sight extraordinary to the subpar smiles he had previously unleashed.

I turned to the front and clapped in time to the music, thankful to have found a place where I could worship God and show Him that He still mattered to me, even when on holiday.

CHAPTER SIX
Black and Blonde

I lay ensconced in thick blankets on the queen-sized bed in Jaelle and Paul's spare room, staring at the latest text message from Diana.

Di-Di: HAVE YOU DECIDED WHAT YOU'RE DOING WHEN YOU COME HOME? K-MAN ASKED A LOT OF QUESTIONS AT THE NEW YEAR'S PARTY AT MY PARENTS. IS SOMETHING GOING ON BETWEEN YOU TWO?

Di-Di: FYI JONATHAN'S HAPPY TO HAVE YOU STAY IN OUR SPARE ROOM INDEFINITELY! I DIDN'T EVEN NEED TO TWIST HIS ARM OR SEDUCE HIM INTO GIVING THE CORRECT ANSWER. ;-)

Di-Di: PS I MISS YOU XX

What *was* I going to do? The first week of January was almost over, and with the hectic schedule I maintained with helping Jaelle arrange her wedding plans, my brain had set some time-sensitive alarms, hastening me to decide.

I sighed, glanced at the time in Melbourne, and tapped my reply.

Me: I'M LEANING TOWARD TELLARINE WITH POTENTIAL JOB LEADS IN ROBINVALE, BUT I'M NOT KEEN ON CRASHING YOUR NEWLYWED WORLD. YOU'VE ALREADY TOLD ME JONATHAN WALKS AROUND SHIRTLESS MOST OF THE TIME. TOO MUCH FOR THESE MORTAL EYES. ;-) AS FOR KEANU, WE'RE GREAT FRIENDS, NOTHING TO WORRY ABOUT. HE PROBABLY WANTS TO KNOW WHEN HE'LL GET RID OF ALL MY JUNK HE'S STORING! OH, AND PLEASE DON'T INVOLVE ME WITH YOUR SHADY SCHEMES OF MANIPULATION AGAINST YOUR HUSBAND. ;-) MISS YOU LOTS TOO.

My phone vibrated in my hands, and I squeaked. No way Diana was awake this early in her day. I checked my message app.

JellyBelly: I FOUND IT! ABSOLUTELY GORGEOUS LITTLE PLACE RIGHT IN THE CENTRE OF TELLARINE NOT FAR FROM KEANU'S RESTAURANT. CHECK OUT THE LINK.

Tellarine on my mind. Again. Was God trying to get my attention? I shifted in my blanket cocoon and clicked the link.

A cute whitewashed self-contained bungalow filled my phone screen, and I pursed my lips. Not bad from the outside. I skimmed through the few photos—one highlighting a lime-and-white striped retro three-seater lounge suite and large pine sideboard, another showing a neat kitchenette with a funky retro all-in-one oven, grill and stove, and the last photo depicting an average-sized bedroom with what looked to be a queen-sized bed—and flipped back to the all-important cost and features.

"This must be wrong," I whispered, staring at the lower-than-market rental price blazing off the screen. The bungalow seemed small but larger than the city apartment I had vacated. Not tiny enough to warrant such inexpensive rent. How could it be so cheap? What was wrong with the place? Had someone died on the premises? I narrowed my eyes and scrutinised the photos, wishing the landlord had provided more pictures, and reread the advertisement. Everything seemed above board. But would the place still be available when I returned to Australia?

I switched over to my message app and replied to my cousin.

Me: LOOKS GREAT (PERFECT, REALLY) BUT WHO KNOWS IF IT'LL STILL BE AVAILABLE WHEN I'M BACK.

My chest squeezed. Maybe it would still be waiting in February.

JellyBelly: TRUE. CAN YOU EMAIL THE PROPERTY OWNERS?

I glanced back at the property listing and noted a phone number for a Mrs. Arby. No email. Hmm.

Me: ONLY A NAME AND PHONE NUMBER.

JellyBelly: UGH, SO OLD-SCHOOL. MAYBE THEY'RE NOT TECH-SAVVY? COULD BE OLD PEOPLE? OR SOMEONE WHO REALLY NEEDS THE INCOME?

Me: PROBABLY HAS A TECH-SAVVY GRANDSON ADVERTISE ONLINE FOR THEM, LIKE PAUL DOES FOR HIS GAMMY? WHATEVER THE CASE, IF IT'S STILL AVAILABLE IN SIX WEEKS THEN I'LL CALL AND CHECK IT OUT. THANKS FOR THE FIND.

JellyBelly: ANYTIME. XX

JellyBelly: BTW, WILL BE HOME LATE TONIGHT. BOSS HAS ASKED

ME TO ORDER DINNER FOR THE TEAM. PAUL'S OUT TONIGHT TOO, SO FEEL FREE TO RAID THE FRIDGE OR FREEZER.

I flopped against the cushions behind me and closed my eyes. Although I loved my cousin, I could see how meshing my life with theirs on a permanent basis would get old sooner rather than later. I grabbed my phone.

Me: NO WORRIES. I'M PLANNING ON SLUMMING IT THE REST OF THE DAY, SO HAVE FUN. SEE YOU LATER.

The doorbell rang, and I groaned. Which of Jaelle's neighbours needed a cup of sugar this time?

I slid off the bed, pocketed my phone, and traipsed downstairs, fingering my messy hair. Too bad if I looked like I lay around the house all day. I rotated my shoulders, sucked in a deep breath, brandished an amiable smile, and opened the front door.

Louis stood on the landing, dark-brown eyes larger than usual. We had hung out together a few times with Paul and Jaelle and with some people from church he had introduced me to over the last few weekends. Louis oozed a genuine love for God, although he still seemed awkward around me.

Keep it casual and help the guy relax. I leaned my hip against the door's edge and grinned. "Hey, Louis. What's up?"

He stuffed his hands into the pockets of his drab, oversized winter coat. The cool, jewel undertones of his smooth umber complexion appeared brighter under the building's fluorescent entryway light.

Huh.

"Is Paul around?"

I furrowed my brow. "Jaelle said he's out tonight."

His shoulders slumped, and he expelled a long breath. "I must've gotten my wires crossed. I thought we were meeting here."

"That's Paul for ya. I'm totally out of the loop, sorry, but you're welcome to come in." I stepped away from the door and gestured to the lounge room. "It's warmer in here, anyway, so maybe call him from here?"

Louis ran his palm across his wiry hair. "Thanks." He stepped inside, shut the door, and moved closer, his pace tentative.

I brightened my smile. "Want a drink to warm you up? Coffee? Tea?"

He retrieved his phone from his back pocket, his gaze focused on a spot over my shoulder. "I don't want to make extra work for you."

"No trouble at all. I feel like having a cup of something." Now I had been forced from the warmth of my bed. I nodded toward his phone. "When you're finished with your call, come sit in the kitchen."

The creases along his dark brow retreated. "Thanks."

I nodded, swivelled, and traipsed to the kitchen, my brain working overtime on ways to loosen up my guest. An old conversation with Diana sprang to mind, and I snorted a laugh. Throwing myself at a guy and kissing him worked back at university, but I suspected this would have the opposite effect in this situation. I was like a virgin when it came to interacting with the opposite sex in the Christian community.

I filled and switched on the kettle, grabbed two oversized mugs, and raided Jaelle's well-stocked pantry for drink options.

Louis's footsteps echoed against the hardwood floors.

I glanced up from sorting through three different types of marshmallows. Americans had some weird marshmallow options. Not to mention that frightening bucket of fluff stuff I had seen a friend of Jaelle's scoop straight into her mouth. Ew. What happened to Pascall's pink or white soft pillows of sweetness we had back home?

I caught Louis's gaze. "How'd you go?"

He eyed the assortment of items strewn across the bench top. "I was right. He had to stop somewhere on the way home, so told me to entertain myself until he arrived."

"Allow me the honour of entertaining you." I shimmied on the spot and ended my routine with a flounce of jazz hands.

A deep, resonate laugh burst from my guest.

I held back a satisfied smirk.

"Not sure Paul meant that kind of entertainment."

"Your loss. So, waddaya want to drink? You expecting a long night of partying hard?" I rearranged the items closest to me then tapped the instant coffee jar lid. "'Cause we have instant and espresso."

Louis cleared his throat. "Just a quiet night out with some of the guys from work."

"Your group isn't big on partying?" I raised an eyebrow.

He shook his head.

"No prowling for women?"

His head shake intensified.

"Oh. Must be a different workplace to where I recently quit my job."

He blinked and wrinkled his forehead. "How so?"

"The guys went out religiously every Friday night to a strip club."

"What?" Louis's eyes widened, and his Adam's apple bobbed.

"Yeah. Classy, I know." I huffed a breath. "The first year I worked there, I was invited every single Friday."

He flinched. "That's … that's—"

"Life." I spread my arms and pointed to my face. "Not to seem full of myself, but I know I'm pretty all right to look at, so it comes with the territory."

His nostrils flared. Something unreadable flashed across his eyes. "You shouldn't have to put up with that."

"Such is life." Rape victim or not. I snatched the hot chocolate powder and spooned two heapfuls into my mug. "Decided on your drink?"

He leaned forward and his jacket brushed the bench edge, rustling when he touched the instant coffee. "Let me help."

"It's okay." I opened the coffee jar and added a teaspoonful to the other mug. "How'd you like it?"

"Black. Nothing added."

I lifted my gaze and bit back a smile.

"I'm pretty boring. Everything's black with me." His eyes sparkled.

I snorted and covered my mouth. My cheeks bloomed with unexpected heat.

His deep chuckle warmed the space between us.

"I can't believe you said that." I wiped the damp corner of my eye with my index finger.

He grinned, baring brilliant white teeth against his dark-brown skin. "If I can't say it, who can?"

"Fair enough."

He leaned closer. "And you can't tell me the thought didn't cross your mind."

The heat in my cheeks intensified. The thought *had* crossed my mind, but only in the most complimentary way. But as a blonde with blue eyes, society deemed my particular observation unacceptable. Yet the same society deemed me a ditzy blonde. The irony.

Louis nudged my shoulder with his arm. "It's fine, Tara. I'm black, you're white. We'd be the perfect chess pieces."

I nudged him in return. "I'd be the queen, but which piece are you?" I grinned, made our drinks, and offered his mug.

He thanked me and sipped. "I've always wanted to be a knight in shining armour."

"You have plenty of kingly qualities." The pastor at church had preached last weekend that we were kings *and* priests in God's kingdom, and I had peeked at Louis and imagined a crown on his head.

Louis chuckled. "Not sure how I'm meant to take that since you're the queen …"

Oh sugar. "Not in the way it sounds! I, ah—"

"I'm just playing."

I narrowed my eyes. "I thought you were the shy, awkward type. What happened between now and your phone call with Paul?" I blew against the surface of my hot chocolate.

"I suppose you bring out the boldness in me."

I leaned my hip against the kitchen cupboard beside the dishwasher. "You don't talk much with women, do you?"

"I'm more comfortable with technology and computers than living, breathing beings." Louis rubbed his smooth jaw.

I sipped my delicious beverage. "You're a nice guy. You gotta get out there and talk to women."

"Isn't that what I'm doing right now?"

"But I don't count." I planted a hand on my hip.

"I beg to differ."

"I'm leaving in a few weeks."

"So?"

I huffed a breath. "I'm good practise, but I'm not moving to Chicago anytime soon."

He drained his mug and placed it in the sink. "Thanks for the drink."

"You're welcome."

Louis stuffed his hands in his pockets and rolled back on his heels. "For what it's worth, Jaelle and Paul would love if you moved here.”

“I know.” I sighed. “I just don’t see it happening at the moment.”

The front door creaked. “Hey, man, you still here?” Paul’s voice boomed through the entryway.

Louis caught my gaze and held it for several seconds before a soft smile laced his lips. He stepped toward the lounge room. “Yep, still here.”

I slurped the dregs of my drink, tidied the bench, and pushed away my cousins’ pleas to stay, which still echoed inside my head.

Hours later, someone knocked on my bedroom door.

I paused the episode of *New Girl* on my laptop and shifted on my bed. “Come in.”

Jaelle slipped into the room and collapsed beside me on the bed. Her eyes were puffy and red-rimmed.

“What happened?” I slipped my computer off my lap, reached out, and pulled her into a hug.

She dropped a colourful swear bomb.

I grimaced.

“Zoe’s a hag.”

I squeezed Jaelle tighter. “What did she do now?”

“You know those gorgeous shoes we found for my wedding dress?” My cousin sniffled.

“Yes?”

Jaelle huffed. “She bought the same pair.”

I leaned back and straightened. “But they’re your special shoes!”

She yanked a tissue from the tissue box on my bedside table. “I guess she thinks she’s as special as the bride.” Jaelle blew her nose. “And she threw a tantrum over the dress colour.”

“I hope you put your foot down.” The muscles in my back tightened. I loved my dress. Not many dresses had helped me feel feminine and beautiful since …

She nodded. “I said we’d bought three of the four dresses and it was too late. If she couldn’t be bothered to do the dress shopping over the weekend, then she’d wear what everyone voted on. Camilla and Peggy love the sea-blue material and look gorgeous in their chosen dress styles.” She huffed a breath. “Why can’t Zoe be happy for once?"

I shrugged and squeezed her hand. "I'm sorry you're dealing with this. If you need me to tell her where to go, as Head Bridesmaid, I'd be happy to do the job."

Jaelle sighed, her face drawn. "It'll be fine. I just needed to vent, and Paul's still out."

"If you're sure." I pursed my lips. "At least you've still got a month to go, so maybe these hiccups will vanish into the ether of your excitement."

She chuckled. "You're weird sometimes."

"Comes with the territory of writing."

"How come you haven't pursued journalism since graduating?" Jaelle whispered.

I glanced at my laptop screen. "I guess I lost the drive when I lost myself." I turned to face my cousin. "Diana never lost her passion to write even when she questioned her studies. But it's like … my words were locked away after that storm happened, despite what I said to anyone who asked." My pulse thrummed. "And … having lived through the legal trial of those m-men, I can't seem to see myself out there chasing stories. Not like a journalist should."

"What about writing for fun? You used to write the best stories growing up."

"Call it what you like—permanent writing block or whatever— but I've struggled when it comes to my imagination." My breathing quickened, and heat spread across my chest and under my arms. "I'm a little afraid of what I might find if I allow myself to imagine."

Despite my newfound faith in God, the "off" switch to my fears was nowhere to be found. Diana and Victoria had said I needed to renew my mind with Scripture and trust Jesus to help me overcome the darker parts of my past.

"Do you still dream about him?" Jaelle wrapped her long arm around my back.

"No." I ground my molars. I knew exactly whom she meant. "But since I slept with Isaac, his voice and face sometimes wash over my mind."

She pressed me closer. "He's behind bars for a long time. He can't touch you."

"I know." I pointed to my laptop. "Wanna watch the rest of this episode?"

She glanced at the paused screen. "Is this one of the episodes with Jess's sister? Hawkeye's wife?"

"Yeah. The one Winston freaks out about his LAPD entrance exam."

My cousin bumped my shoulder.

I scooted across and made more space for her on the bed.

"Thanks for being here."

I leaned against Jaelle's shoulder. "Thanks for letting me stay."

She smiled at me. "Anytime and always."

CHAPTER SEVEN
Taking Out the Trash

"Tara, we have a problem." Aunt Daphne poked her head through the gap in the doorway where Jaelle, myself, and the other bridesmaids readied for the ceremony.

What? My stomach fluttered an odd beat. I turned from the mirror, where I stood behind a seated Jaelle, and faced the door, stilling my fingers at the top of my cousin's head where I pinned her hair.

"We sure do!" Zoe aimed her squinty eyes in my direction. "I don't even know how to walk down the aisle!" She wrinkled her nose and glared at Jaelle. "You need to show me the steps and timing."

Jaelle's shoulders stiffened.

"Maybe you should've turned up to yesterday's rehearsal." I pressed my palm against the bride's tense shoulder.

"I already told you, the timing didn't suit." Zoe sighed like the weight of the modern world was crushing her shoulders.

I plunged a hairpin into Jaelle's updo and turned back toward my aunt. "What happened?"

Aunt Daphne narrowed her eyes at the rogue bridesmaid, blew a kiss to her daughter, and refocused on me. "Paul's cravat is missing, and Louis's shirt is the wrong size."

Of course. Nothing like some wedding day mayhem. I smiled at Jaelle in the mirror. "I'll get it sorted, okay?" I glanced at Zoe fussing with her dress. "All of it."

Jaelle's lips pressed into a firm line. She nodded, inhaled a slow breath, and smiled. "Okay. Can you stay and help then, Mum?"

"Of course, darling." Aunt Daphne wiped the corner of her eye.

"See you soon." I marched down the hallway, a hand on my fluttering tummy. Enough with the internal weirdness! Today was going to be enough of a challenge without nerves and a gassy stomach.

I knocked once on the groom's preparation room door and barged inside. "Hope you're all decent."

Paul paced in the corner near a full-length mirror. "My cravat's missing. I've searched everywhere. Didn't I pack it in the suit bag last night? I thought I had."

"Stand still and breathe." I approached him and pressed my hands to his shoulders.

He stilled, closed his eyes, sucked in several noisy breaths, and lifted his eyelids.

"Okay." I smiled at the flustered groom. "Have you checked all the pockets in your bag?"

"Four times now."

"And what about your suit pockets?"

"Huh?" He wrinkled his brow.

"Your pants pocket? Jacket pocket? Shirt pocket?" I glanced around the room at the groomsmen in varying stages of undress and widened my eyes at Louis's unbuttoned too-small shirt. "What happened to you?"

Louis quirked an eyebrow and crossed his arms, the open shirt almost skin-tight on his biceps. "They gave me the wrong shirt."

"Obviously." I stepped closer, pushed his arms away from his chest, and attempted to pull the two sides of the shirt together. No luck. "Can you swap with one of the other guys?"

"Found it!" Paul brandished a crumpled cravat. The lines which had marred his forehead vanished.

"Excellent." I gestured to Louis. "Now to find him a suitable shirt, unless you want a shirtless groomsman?"

The men chuckled, their deep laughter bouncing off the papered hotel walls.

"Would you complain with that particular arrangement?" Paul tied the material around his neck.

My skin warmed, and I caught Louis's gaze for a fraction of a second. "I don't think Jaelle'd appreciate it." I eyed the five men in the room and pursed my lips. "Can you all remove your jackets please?"

The men shuffled out of their navy woollen suit jackets without a fuss.

I inspected their outfits. The shirt worn by Paul's red-headed friend—whose name escaped me—was looser than necessary, and with a leaner body shape to Louis, he seemed the perfect candidate for a swapsies.

I pointed at the redhead. "Take off your shirt, please."

"Really?" He smirked.

I narrowed my eyes. "Off."

He shrugged and unbuttoned.

I turned to Louis. "Take yours off too."

The men removed their shirts, and I failed in my good Christian duties to avert my gaze.

Man oh man, Louis won the competition by a kilometre. Not the most chiselled man I had ever seen, but decent enough. Sharp lines and detectable grooves separated his considerable-sized muscles. A soft spattering of dark hair dusted his umber torso.

I swallowed hard. "Swap shirts, and we'll see if that's workable."

The men exchanged shirts and re-dressed. I cheered in my head when both men were able to button their entire shirt, albeit snugger fits. I nodded toward Paul. "Acceptable?"

"Guys?" Paul raised a brow.

Louis rotated his arms and lifted them in different positions. "Still tight but at least this one closes."

I held his wrist, stopping his motion. "Think you'll pop a button? Or will this do?"

He crossed his arms, swivelled his shoulders, and relaxed his arms back by his sides. "This should work."

"Great." I turned to the redhead. "You all good?"

"This'll do."

"Wonderful." I glanced at each man. "Any other disasters to avert before the ceremony?"

Kane—a groomsman whose name had stuck when we were introduced—chuckled. "This calls for a celebration." He dragged a chair from the small dining table at the other end of the room.

Paul raised his hand. "C'mon, man, not today."

Two groomsmen chanted, "Jump, jump, jump!"

I wrinkled my brow. What was going on?

The redhead stood in the middle of the room and held the back of the dining chair.

Kane removed his suit jacket and stepped onto the chair facing the seat back.

"What're you doing?" My voice sounded shrill to my own ears.

Paul sighed. "It's never a dull moment with Kane around." He nodded to his mate. "Go on, get it out of your system so we can get going."

Kane straightened and rotated his shoulders. He stepped backward until he balanced on the edge of the seat.

My stomach dropped. Was he about to backflip off the chair?

He swung his arms back and launched into the air, legs bent.

My pulse thudded in my neck.

Kane landed on the floor. His foot buckled underneath him and he fell against the plush carpet with a loud groan.

The guys fired off a round of expletives—apart from Louis— and crowded around their insane friend.

I covered my mouth with my hand, eyes wide, thankful I had swallowed the foul language my body had wanted to spew. Baby steps.

Kane burst out laughing and clutched his left leg.

"You okay?" Paul grasped his friend's shoulder.

Kane shook his head, chuckling. "Think I screwed it up that time."

"You think?" Paul's brows buckled. "Can you stand?"

I stepped closer and stared, my mind frozen with my limbs.

Kane grunted. "This hurts worse than my dirt bike incident."

Paul straightened and paced. "Jae's going to kill me"—he levelled a dark stare at his injured friend—"and then you." He glanced at his watch. "We're meant to be getting married in fifty minutes!" He ran his fingers through his styled hair.

Kane closed his eyes. His breaths laboured for several seconds before he gritted his teeth, grunted again, and met Paul's gaze. "Sorry, man." He sucked in a haggard breath and flashed a smile. "Can we get a paramedic?"

Oh, shoelaces! I snapped to attention. "Louis, can you call it in?"

"Sure." He stuffed his hand in his right pocket, extracted his mobile, and stepped to the corner of the room.

I pressed my palm to Paul's arm. "Okay, let's stay calm. We need to make a plan so Jaelle's not stressed by this"—I glanced at the man lying on the carpet—"unfortunate situation."

He laughed, the tight chuckle almost convincing. "We're down a man. The wedding party photos are going to be mismatched, not to mention uneven numbers during the ceremony."

"An ambulance is on its way," Louis said from across the room.

"Thanks, man." Paul ran a hand down his face. "We need to get rid of a bridesmaid."

The redhead raised his hand. "I vote for Zoe. She missed both rehearsals."

Why had I not thought of that? "Works for me." I pressed away a grin.

The sparkle in Paul's eyes returned. "Perfect." He turned to Kane. "Scratch what I said earlier. Jae's going to love you for sacrificing your leg. Now Tara can tell Zoe to take a hike."

My heart stilled. "M-me?"

"Uh huh." He pointed to his chest. "I'm the groom, remember? Can't see the bride until she walks down the aisle."

"Right." I sucked in a stabilising breath and nodded to the guys. "Don't do anything else that'll cause me to strangle you." I leaned down and touched Kane's arm. "Look after yourself."

"I'll be backflipping in no time."

The guys groaned, and Kane chuckled.

I exited the room and marched back to the ladies.

Zoe stormed toward me. "Where've you been? I need to know my cue for walking down the aisle."

I gritted my teeth and stepped closer to Jaelle. "Where's Aunt Daphne?"

"Dad called her to the ballroom." My cousin crinkled her forehead. "Is everything okay?"

"Everything's under control."

The high-pitched whine of an ambulance pierced the air.

Jaelle's eyes widened. She stood and clutched my arm. "What happened?"

"Kane had a little … accident. He—"

"He didn't." Jaelle's mouth slackened.

I tilted my head and shrugged. "He might've broken his leg."

The blushing bride cursed like a drunken sailor at a pub after a year away at sea.

I turned to Zoe. "Unfortunately, with Kane out of action, we have one too many bridesmaids."

Zoe's eyes flashed. "I'm not going." She straightened and pointed at Camilla and Peggy. "Pick one of them."

Jaelle sagged against her chair, her eyes trained to the floor.

Heat suffused my chest. How dare Zoe act like a bridezilla when she was barely a bridesmaid?

I called on my inner intimidating-tall Diana and stretched to my shorter-than-average height, then levelled my scariest glare toward the now ex-bridesmaid. "No. Camilla and Peggy have attended all the pre-wedding events and even helped us set things up for the reception." I narrowed my eyes. "You couldn't be bothered to turn up to the rehearsals and then put the pressure on Jaelle—the bride, in case you forgot—to fix your problem." I pointed to the door. "Problem fixed. You don't need to walk down the aisle."

Zoe's face reddened, and her chest heaved. She turned to Jaelle and stabbed her finger in my general direction. "You can't be serious!"

Jaelle rose from the chair and met Zoe's gaze. "I think it's best if you step away from this responsibility."

My insides warmed and fluttered again. I touched Jaelle's arm, my focus zeroed in on the daggers I imagined flying from Zoe's eyeballs and not the gas bubbles threatening to escape my derrière.

Zoe screwed up her face. "You suck." She strode to the corner, collected her bag, and huffed back to the open doorway. "You can all go to hell."

"Too late for Tara," said Jaelle. "She's tight with Jesus."

I stifled a laugh.

Zoe clenched her fist and departed, removing her squally temperament from the room.

Jaelle's shoulders eased.

I wrapped my fingers around her wrist. "Sit, take in a few deep breaths, and you'll be ready to walk down the aisle to the love of your life."

She nodded, rested on the seat, and closed her eyes.

"Is it mean of me to say, 'Good riddance'?" Peggy whispered.

A soft smile slipped to Jaelle's perfect lips. "She told us to go to hell, so 'good riddance' seems almost amiable."

Camilla and I snorted with laughter.

"What a beautiful ceremony." Aunt Daphne dabbed her long nose with a frilled handkerchief.

I held back a smirk. My aunt had been old-school for as long as I could remember. "It was." I clutched my tall glass of lemonade and smiled at passers-by mingling after the dinner portion of the reception.

"I wish Alannah had been able to come." My aunt sighed and tucked her hanky under her bra strap near her collarbone, a trick she had learned from my grandmother.

"Mum wanted to be here, but it's a pretty exxy trip." I sipped my drink.

"I know, dear. We chatted last night. Apparently, Alannah's excited to see you when you're home next week. Are you going to stay with her in Swan Hill?"

I met my aunt's gaze. "I'm planning to settle in Tellarine, so it's not far from Mum in the scheme of things." Less than an hour and a half by car.

Aunt Daphne's hazel eyes sparkled. "I haven't been to Tellarine in over a decade. Your mother and I ended up at some atrocious restaurant-like pub where they overcooked and over-fried everything." She shifted her gaze to me. "Is that delightful place still there?"

I chuckled. "Doesn't sound remotely delightful. The only restaurant with bar facilities is Benanu's, and it's pretty decent, even by Melbourne standards." Keanu's image invaded my thoughts, and I blinked the picture away. "My friend's family owns it. I think they've only been there for seven, eight years, maybe? But from what Diana told me, it was a dump when the previous owner managed the place."

"Could be the same establishment." Aunt Daphne fluttered one of her hands at her throat. "When Charles and I visit your mother next, we'll be sure to stop by and see what Tellarine looks like now."

A loud voice rumbled over the speakers.

I turned toward the front of the large ballroom where the dance area was surrounded by elegant floral decorations in contrasting

Jaelle-approved colours.

Paul's cousin stood in the centre of the dance floor, microphone clutched a little too close to his face. "While our gracious hosts prepare for the cutting of the wedding cake, Paul and Jaelle will have their first dance." A cheer resounded across the room. "Come on down, Mr. and Mrs. Anders!"

Paul and Jaelle glided onto the dance floor, pressed against each other, and swayed to the love ballad.

Someone snuffled beside me.

I turned.

Aunt Daphne wept into her hanky.

I slipped an arm around her. Where was Uncle Charles when I needed him?

The final beats of the song sounded, and the guests clapped and cheered.

"Time for the bride's and groom's parents and the wedding party to join the lovebirds on stage."

I escorted Aunt Daphne to Paul's father and searched for my partner. Where was Louis? My hands shook, and I fisted my fingers.

Louis stepped forward and planted his right hand on my waist. Heat seeped through the light layers of my dress, and my breaths laboured.

Wow, straight shooter. Nothing like allowing a girl a second to acclimatise to a guy's closeness.

He met my gaze, offered his signature soft smile, and slipped his left hand over my right, lifting our arms into position.

I inhaled a long breath, forcing my sluggish lungs to work— how could my body not remember I was in charge?—and lifted my clammy left hand to his shoulder. His firm, broad shoulder. *I can do this.* Just a simple dance with an attractive man. I had slept with the equivalent number of men found in the Royal Australian Army Ordnance Corps back in the day. What was the big deal with a single dance?

The music tempo remained slow, but my heartbeat increased.

Louis lowered his head, levelling the gap between our height differences. "Have you enjoyed the day?"

"It's been a beautiful wedding." I leaned a margin closer.

His eyes sparkled. "Even with the costume malfunctions and Kane's performance earlier?"

The image of bare-chested Louis blazed my memory, and I pressed my lips together. *Focus, Tara.* I dropped my gaze to the buttons on his shirt. "Haven't popped a button yet?"

He chuckled, the vibration of his deep laughter travelling the length of my arm. "Not that I'm aware of. But feel free to double check."

I raised my head. "You're not what I expected you'd be."

"What were you expecting?" Louis guided me on our small portion of dance floor.

I pursed my lips. "I'm not sure. But knowing I had every intention of returning home, I guess I didn't think about my expectations."

His warm breath puffed close to my ear. "So, have you changed your mind? About leaving?"

"Afraid not. I need to go home."

He nodded, his gaze sombre yet tender. "Well, don't forget us. You've plenty of friends here who'd welcome you in a heartbeat."

A smile slipped past my guard. "Thanks. And don't worry, I won't forget anyone." In particular this delightful gentleman and his umber-gold chest.

CHAPTER EIGHT
Falling Apart

JellyBelly: You sure Dad can't take you to the airport tomorrow? Or I'm sure Louis would be happy to assist? ;-)

I stared at the message for longer than necessary. Why was my cousin messaging me while on her honeymoon? What was with brides these days! I huffed a laugh.

Me: Would you stop worrying about me? You're on honeymoon! Go bask on the beach in that barely-there bikini you bought, and stop fussing about me.

I emptied my suitcase of its contents, a habit Mum had instilled in me from my first school camp in grade five. The contents of one's suitcase failed to return to its original precise packed state without re-packing everything. I removed unused socks stuffed in the side pocket and slid my fingers along the inner grooves of the firm canvas walls.

My phone vibrated on the bedside table.

JellyBelly: I've already sunbathed for hours today. Paul's in the shower so I thought I might as well check up on you. I can't persuade you to have someone take you to the airport?

Me: I'll Uber it just fine, cuz, and lock up here as we discussed. It'll be fine. I'll be fine. Go ogle your hubby. xx

I tossed my phone on the bed and emptied the final suitcase pocket. My favourite yellow T-shirt! "That's where you've been hiding!" I unrolled the T-shirt, and my trusty menstrual cup—secured in its travel bag—slipped free of its cotton confines, dropping to the carpet.

Huh? I gazed at the small zipped bag at my feet and retrieved it. I furrowed my brow. How had this been hidden for three months? My mind buzzed. I closed my eyes, sucked in several calming breaths, and refocused on the object in my clammy palm. This had been wrapped up the entire trip …? No. *No!* My insides plummeted, and I clutched my stomach. This could not be happening.

Not again.

I lowered to the mattress on hollow legs and clutched the bed edge with shaky hands. *Breathe, Tara.* Jumping to conclusions without proper evidence was ridiculous, and false alarms happened often. I rubbed the back of my neck, focused on slowing my breaths, and prayed the rock in the pit of my stomach would dissolve.

After several minutes of listening to blood pumping between my ears, I glanced through the window at the park across the street littered with white. No fresh snow this week, but the murky clouds offered little comfort. I stood, slipped on my knitted red-and-white striped scarf and matching beanie, slid into my warm woollen overcoat, and removed my black gloves from the jacket pockets. Where was my wallet? I searched under my unpacked items on the bed and pocketed my wallet, phone, and keys.

I locked the apartment, descended the external building steps, and embarked on the five-minute walk to the closest pharmacy. *Please let this be a false alarm, God.*

After staring for what seemed like an hour at the large, confusing selection of pregnancy tests available—did women truly test six days *before* their period was due?—I purchased one without all the bells and whistles and headed back home.

Memories of another pregnancy test at a difficult time in my life careened to the forefront of my thoughts. I choked back the lump in my throat, discarded my winter overgarments, and locked myself in the guest ensuite. My latest purchase stared up at me from the bathroom vanity, the existence of the shiny box shooting pangs through my veins.

I sucked in a tremulous breath. My heart hammered against my ribcage, and I rested an unsteady hand on the vanity edge. So what if three months had passed? My cycle had erred from its usual course a few times in my life. This could be another path diversion. Clever scientific people with degrees, knowledge, and know-how had proven time and time again how stress affected the female reproductive cycle. Today would be more proof.

I counted to five and ripped open the box. The white plastic stick taunted me from its cardboard enclosure. *Please be negative.*

I palmed the device, stepped to the toilet, and prepared for the second-most nerve-racking pee of my life.

My mobile phone buzzed from the adjacent room, snapping me from my daze. The oxygen-less void of my existence.

I heaved a breath and palmed my damp cheeks. What was I meant to do now? I glanced at the positive pregnancy test clutched in my right hand, and my lungs compressed. I wheezed a breath and lifted my chin. My red-rimmed eyes greeted me in the ensuite mirror. I shook my head. What a mess.

After several deep breaths, I trudged to the bedroom, dropped the double-line stick on the bedside table, and retrieved my phone.

Di-Di: I WOKE EARLY AND HAD A SUDDEN URGE TO PRAY FOR YOU. I HOPE EVERYTHING IS OKAY. HAVE A SAFE FLIGHT TOMORROW. I LOVE YOU, MISS YOU, AND LOOK FORWARD TO SEEING YOU NEXT. REMEMBER, YOU'RE WELCOME TO STAY WITH US FOR HOWEVER LONG YOU LIKE. ALL YOU NEED TO DO IS KNOCK ON THE FRONT DOOR. XX

Tears trickled down my cheeks. How could I face Diana with this life-altering, shame-filled news?

Pregnant. From a cocktail-fuelled one-night stand with a complete stranger.

Fresh sobs vibrated against my chest, and I flopped onto the pile of unpacked items covering the bed.

Pregnant.

Pregnant! When had my world spun out of my control and completely off the court? What was I meant to do this time? After conversations with Diana and some church friends, I knew life as a Christian was different to how I used to live. Moral choices mattered, even when old voices and memories breathed their poison within me.

I grabbed a tissue, dabbed my face, and blew my nose. What to do? Diana would forgive me—I hoped—but could she look past the things I had hidden from her all these years? The truth I had buried deep in my soul, now clawing its way to the surface.

I glanced at the pregnancy test. So similar to the test three-plus years ago.

Heaviness pressed against my shoulders and chest. I blinked back fresh tears. The familiar darkness which had wrapped its tentacles around my heart and infected my thoughts, demanding my sacrifice during the months after my abduction, had reappeared. The same suffocating weight which had locked me in a darker place after I had aborted my baby. My rape baby.

How was this fair, God? I had barely come away with my mental faculties intact after that procedure. Why must I face this again? Was I doomed to a life of brokenness?

I crushed the white plastic stick inside my palm. How could I have a baby now? Memories flooded my mind. Mum's soft smile, her whispered words, and reassuring grip covering my hand in the recovery room. The awful pangs in my chest, physical and otherwise. The tug of war in my head, unsure if I had done the right thing yet relieved the baby was gone.

His baby.

And the guilt. The stifling, constant press in my brain and body.

No one at the clinic ever mentioned the mental impact. They talked about seeking help if I struggled with my mental health. But the discussion lacked any element of reality, simply words rattled off down the long list of requirements they had to meet. Maybe there were compassionate staff out there, but once the people at the clinic knew I was a rape victim? Keeping the baby seemed like the worst choice for me. Or maybe that was how I interpreted the discussion because Mum wanted the baby gone.

"Why would you want a daily reminder of your ordeal?" Mum had said at the small kitchen table in her little apartment, her hand clutching my shoulder. "I can't imagine looking at my only grandchild and not seeing the monster he or she spawned from. How could you possibly put yourself through that, day after day?"

I had understood her logic. I still did. Yet something fragile inside me had tugged in the opposing direction. Something I had pushed aside. Ignored.

I scraped my palm down my face, smearing tears and snot. Ew. After cleaning my face with an unused tissue, I slipped the pregnancy test and its packaging into my oversized handbag—no way would I leave that thing in the bathroom bin!—and re-packed my suitcase before readying for bed.

Tonight would be another sleepless night.

I gasped for air and clutched the blankets closer. My heart hammered. *Please, stop.* Sweat beaded along my brow, dampened my back, and soaked my armpits. My arms trembled and my chest squeezed. *Breathe, Tara.* I focused on the nightlight shining through the open ensuite doorway.

Heat burned the backs of my eyes, and I blinked away tears. I was safe at Jaelle's. Safe. I counted my breaths, as my therapist had taught me years ago, and focused my mind on my current surroundings. Each breath a moment closer to calm. Peace. An end to the latest flashback.

After several minutes, I slipped out of bed and padded to the toilet. The pressure on my lungs eased a fraction, and I thanked God for small mercies. But the memories vibrated in my mind, their nearness far from comforting.

His oval, dark-hazel eyes. The crooked nose I had wanted to bite off his face. The twitch in his jaw—the sole hint of what was to happen next—before he hit me.

My thigh ached, and I groaned. I stepped closer to the nightlight and inspected my leg. Was my body producing sympathy pains again? Not a bruise in sight yet the familiar resonating ache brought his manhandling to my mind.

My hands quaked. I leaned against the side of the vanity and closed my eyes. Pressure built against my shoulders and chest. I thought I had moved past this unnerving fear? Would I ever reconcile what happened to me?

Beautiful yet weak. His voice echoed through me, the words he had spoken when he entered my small prison and laid his large, rough hands on me.

I heaved a sob and opened my eyes. Tears trickled off my chin and dripped onto my sweat-stained pyjama top. I swiped my palm along my jaw and stared at my reflection. Familiar puffy features and wide, fear-filled eyes.

Maybe he was right.

I gathered my waning strength and returned to the bedroom, tumbling against the cooled sheets.

His face blurred into the back of my memories.

I heaved a sigh.

Another room filled his wake and sprang to mind. White and sterile. Cold.

I shivered and burrowed under the blankets, squeezing my eyelids closed. Mum's relieved features. My aching insides. A little life I regretted, gone.

I palmed my fluttery stomach, my hand cold against my warm skin. Another baby, yet not *his* baby. My tight chest eased by an increment. *What am I to do, God?*

Diana's face materialised.

I cringed. Would she understand why I never told her about my baby all this time? Or would my omission break our friendship? I rubbed the soft skin of my belly, my one connection between my lost and current child.

Diana would advocate for keeping this baby. A small slither of my soul agreed. Yet, how could I parent a human? After what I had endured and the decisions I had made? Was there any point contemplating keeping this child?

I pulled the covers close to my neck, turned on my side, and closed my eyes, praying a dreamless sleep would take me from the conscious world.

CHAPTER NINE
Contrasts

"Excuse me." A tall, stocky man with a deep voice brushed past me, his arm skimming my right shoulder.

My lungs froze. I surveyed the congested airport lounge overflowing with men in business attire.

Too many men, like the cursed sandwich shop Diana and I had entered long ago.

Light-headedness buzzed inside my brain. My vision tapered, and I gasped for oxygen.

Too many men.

Another bustling person bumped my left side, jolting me. "Sorry, ma'am."

The room tipped. I lunged forward and grasped the back of a nearby seat.

Help me, Jesus.

A light-haired man in a crisp suit and tie stood from the chair I clutched and swivelled toward me. "You okay, miss?"

My throat tightened, strangling any words I attempted to speak.

His brows buckled, and he touched my elbow. "Miss?"

My breathing intensified along with the rush of blood between my ears. White spots dotted my eyesight.

The man lowered me to the chair he had abandoned.

I collapsed against the firm cushioning and blinked away the chalky specks and mounting moisture. My breaths remained shallow.

"You look pale. Let me get you some water." The man trotted away.

I stared straight ahead, unmoving, in the bustling waiting area while old images from a previous time of unimagined stress swarmed my mind. Passers-by blended with the slideshow of my past.

A water bottle was thrust into my line of sight.

My head reared back.

"Here, miss."

I focused on the plastic bottle. "Th-thanks." My voice rasped like the wrinkled old lady on the cigarette commercial I recalled from my childhood. I lifted my fingers and clasped the bottle. My hands trembled.

"Let me help." The suited man kneeled, unscrewed the plastic cap, and lifted the bottle to my lips.

I fought to suppress the eerie memories of a similar moment with my captor. Tears threatened to unleash. I drank despite my agitated tummy and tightened my grip. *Get it together, Tara.*

"More water?"

I latched onto this man's differences. The absence of an icy edge or constant low rumble in his voice. His comforting American accent and how the word "water" sounded like "wah-dur." His pleasant cologne instead of the acrid smell of cigarettes, beer, and body odour. The lack of sharp rings on his fingers.

"More?"

I nodded, sipped twice, and leaned back against the chair. I might have even smiled. I hoped my lips had formed a smile for the kind man.

Not all men were monsters.

The man closed the water bottle and placed it on the seat near my knee.

"Thanks," I whispered, meeting his gaze. Not a familiar feature on his face. I relaxed against the backrest.

"Happy to help." He furrowed his brow, his slate-blue eyes focused on me. "Do you need anything else?"

I shook my head.

He studied me for several more beats, nodded, and relocated to a nearby seat.

I stared at the water bottle, my limbs numb, and gritted my teeth. I hated this. Recalling the mind games and the tools he used. The scent of fear. The darkness.

How could I move past ... everything? Mind over matter had

failed me. A tear slipped past my barrier, and I swiped it away with shaky fingers. *Help me, God. Please.*

I counted my breaths until my pulse slowed.

A sweet little girl—two or three years old at a guess—with blonde waves tied high in pigtails, and a frothy light-pink skirt, giggled and skipped across the aisle to her mother.

My baby would have been her age.

Heaviness weighed across my shoulders, and my chest constricted. Did I have a son or daughter waiting for me in heaven? Was my child blonde? Or darker like—*no.* I swallowed the lump in my throat, severed the current train of thought, and glanced at the cabin crew and airline staff moving outside the gate where my flight waited.

An announcement echoed over the sound system, and my flight number was called. A neat queue formed across the gate lounge, a long line of men in suits.

I sucked in several timed breaths. Why were there so many men on my flight? I pressed my damp hands together in my lap, staunching the quiver in my fingers. I could do this. I *had* to do this.

I waited until the final call for my flight before gathering my carry-on and water bottle and slowly stood. A handful of white spots filled my vision. I leaned against the chair, then joined the queue.

"Good afternoon. Ticket, please." A pretty brown-haired air hostess smiled.

I retrieved my phone for scanning.

"Enjoy your flight."

"Thanks." I plodded along the airbridge, sharp awareness of my fellow passengers tingling my limbs. Now to reach my seat without interacting with anyone.

A different hostess smiled and pointed me toward my allocated seat.

I slipped along the skinny aisle. My breath hitched with each brush past someone, my throat tightening with each step. Men everywhere. My breaths laboured, and my arms trembled. I struggled more than usual to stuff my luggage in the overhead locker.

"Let me help." Another hostess palmed my bag higher into the storage space.

"A-appreciate it." I shuffled to my seat. My seat located

between two broad-shouldered, wide-thighed men in suits.

No. My stomach fluttered and churned. Freaking men everywhere.

The man in the aisle seat moved his legs, creating a passageway. Maybe they would exit the aircraft when we arrived in Los Angeles? The thought infused a frisson of hope in my tumultuous brain.

I slipped past the long-legged man, plopped onto the vacant chair, and buckled the cumbersome seatbelt with shaky fingers. My back and upper arm muscles tightened, and I hugged the water bottle to my chest.

The man in the window seat shuffled his legs, angling his feet in my direction.

I lowered my chin and closed my eyes. Out of sight, out of mind. I remained fixed and rigid—my shoulders painfully tight and curved inwards—the entire four-and-a-half-hour flight to Los Angeles, my mind refusing to rest and, instead, intent on buzzing with images of babies and men.

CHAPTER TEN
Hideaway

"**Welcome to Melbourne.** Thank you for choosing Qantas." The captain's voice rumbled over the aircraft speakers.

Thank God, I made it home. I glanced at my hand resting over my unsettled stomach. *We* made it home.

I completed my Customs declaration form, popped my pen in my jacket pocket, and waited for the nearby passengers to clear the aircraft. I had fared better than expected with one serious panic attack during the fourteen-plus-hour flight from Los Angeles. Mabel, the elderly lady seated beside me, had handed me an empty vomit bag, rubbed my back, and whispered soothing words as I breathed into the paper bag. God bless Mabel.

"You sure you'll be fine, dear?" Mabel patted my hand which clenched our shared armrest.

"I'll be fine. I promise."

She pursed her crinkled orangey-red lips. "'Cause I can share an Uber?"

Uber? What did a woman with snow-white hair and papery-thin, wrinkled skin know about an Uber? I smiled. "I'm feeling much better now. Thanks."

"Can you help a little old lady retrieve her bag then, please?"

"I hope so." I stood and prayed my vertically challenged frame reached our belongings in the overhead locker.

"Sorry, dear, didn't realise you're pint-sized like me." Mabel chuckled.

I cocked a hip, stretched my arm, and recovered both our bags. I pulled out Mabel's handle. "Here you go, young lady."

Her cheeks pinked. "Oh, pish posh." She clutched her bag.

"Take care of yourself, dear."

"You too."

She toddled down the aisle with a friendly wave.

I gathered my things and followed at a distance to the baggage carousel.

Three teenagers flanked Mabel before engulfing her in hugs and kisses. So much for a shared Uber.

My chest ached. I focused on the empty carousel spinning a similar pace to my thoughts.

Thirty minutes later I rode the air-conditioned airport courtesy bus to the long-term car park, dragged my bags along the warm asphalt, and located my car. Perspiration beaded across my brow. Nothing like leaving the snowy depths of wintry Chicago only to be hit with Melbourne in all its summer glory. I offloaded my bags and settled behind the steering wheel.

Where to now? I gazed out the windscreen at the mostly white, grey, and black sea of stationary vehicles and rested my palm over my stomach. Should I go to Swan Hill and fulfil my daughterly obligations?

Mum would lose it if she discovered I was pregnant again. She had been patient—and persistent—the last time because of the trauma I had endured. But now that I had fallen pregnant in circumstances akin to how I came about in the world? No. My pulse spiked. Not a conversation I wanted to deal with today. Or any other day. And although I was still unsure as to what I should do about this growing human inside me, Mum would pressure me to abort if I stayed with her. I was certain.

I sighed and rubbed my temples. Was there a safe place I could go without dealing with this disaster for a few days?

The cheerful image of the bungalow in Tellarine crowded my mind, and I dug inside my bag for my phone. I refreshed the internet tab I had saved weeks ago. The listing was still untenanted. A teeny spark of hope lit my insides. I checked the time—ten minutes to nine in the morning—and dialled the phone number.

"Hallo?" A spright-sounding man greeted me.

I cleared my throat. "Uh, hello. Mr. Arby?"

"'Tis me."

A smile slipped to my lips. "My name's Tara an—"

"Pleased to meet you, Tara. How can I help you?"

I stifled a chuckle. "Is your bungalow still available for rent?"

A shuffling sound crackled over the phone. "Lemme find out for you." More crackling sounds. "Yes, it's still free. Are you interested?"

My lungs expanded, and I leaned against the seat back. "Very. How soon could I inspect it?"

"My good wife says any time during civil hours."

I snickered. "I could be there this afternoon."

"Sounds good. When do you think you'd want to move in if you like the place?"

I rubbed my forehead. "Straight away, if possible."

"That can be arranged."

I farewelled my future landlord, ended the call, and caught my reflection in the rear-view mirror. Black under-eye rings and glassy blue orbs. I yawned. Sleep had eluded me on the flights home. My stomach tightened. Truthfully, sleep had eluded me longer than the last twenty-four hours. And a bone-weary fatigue had weighed my limbs for weeks now. I rested my palm over my tummy, certain this stowaway was the reason. *Precious cargo.*

I set an alarm on my phone, adjusted my chair, and leaned back, determined to catch an hour of shuteye. Hopefully without any accompanying nightmares.

I slowed at the front of an aged weatherboard house in Tellarine and switched off the car engine. Afternoon sun and heat beat through the windows. I stretched my arms and gyrated my shoulders. The stiffness in my back eased. I retrieved my oversized handbag, exited the car, and stood at the foot of the driveway.

The long gravel trail snaked past a banged-up metal garage and the grey weatherboard home, ending at a single-vehicle carport at the rear of the block. The bungalow must be situated behind the house, hidden from view. Perfect.

I approached the Arby residence and knocked on the front door.

An old woman opened the door. "You the girl we're expecting to look at the bungalow?"

"Yes. I'm Tara."

She harrumphed, grabbed a set of keys from a key rack beside the door, and gestured toward the carport.

I followed her brisk steps to the back of the property.

"It's not big, but it's got all the essentials. Our last few tenants chose to use the furniture provided." She glanced at me and charged past the carport, up the few front steps, and unlocked the cute bungalow.

I stepped inside the quaint space and closed the door behind me. "I have a small couch and a queen-sized bed in storage." And little else.

Mrs. Arby pointed toward the tidy kitchenette. "Would you want to keep the washing machine, table, and chairs?"

I surveyed the room. "Yes, please." I pointed to the large sideboard and tall pine bookshelf near the front door slash lounge space. "Can I keep those too?" I stepped closer to the retro three-seater couch and glided my fingers over the lime-and-white calico.

"Of course."

"This couch and armchair look in great condition."

Mrs. Arby harrumphed again. Delightful woman.

"Could I keep all this furniture, please? My couch is small and might not work well here."

She stepped toward a doorway opposite the kitchenette. "Makes it easier leaving it here. What about the bed? The last tenant left their mattress behind on our bed base"—she brandished her weathered hands toward the bedroom doorway—"which looks to be usable, but I could get young Nicholas to remove it."

Young Nicholas? Did she mean Diana's dad? I sucked in a few ragged breaths. My hideout would be exposed.

I shook my head. "No need. I won't be able to get my things for a while, so can we leave everything as is?"

Mrs. Arby nodded. "So, you want it?

I soaked in the views of my new, little home. "Please."

She handed me the key and nodded toward the front door. "Can you come down to the house and sign paperwork now? Mr. Arby and I are going out shortly."

I smiled. "Now works."

We returned to the Arby house, where I filled out my relevant information, still shocked at the little cost of monthly rent, and shifted my car off the street under the carport.

I toted my luggage indoors, followed by a few pantry staples, a loaf of bread, and essentials—basic crockery and cutlery, a queen-sized sheet set, blanket, and pillow—I had bought in a neighbouring town. Despite my waning stamina, I unpacked everything. I wanted to start my day fresh tomorrow without regret.

I yawned and glanced at the time on my phone. Almost six o'clock. The last forty-eight hours had drained me of my usual vitality, and who knew what energy the tiny life inside me consumed. I rubbed my hands over my face, ate a Vegemite sandwich, and gave in to my exhaustion, curling up on the bed.

My boxes at Keanu's could wait a few more days.

A sandy, pebbled beach spanned the vista ahead and flooded my peripheral vision. Aquamarine waters ebbed along the shoreline, its slim white frothy edge sliding over the compacted sand. Warmth from the sunny sky soaked into my bare skin, ensconcing me with delicious heat. A faint musty scent, tinged with salt, swirled around me, and the subtle breeze grazed my arms and legs.

I inhaled lungfuls of seaside air and trod the cool, damp sand, my chest aflutter, excited to experience my childhood holiday as an adult.

Something slithered inside my brain, stirring. Needling my thoughts.

I stared at the ocean and spotted a watercraft slicing through the waves. What or who was out there? I pressed my hands to my sides and squinted.

A bright red jet ski controlled by a large man, steered in my direction.

My skin prickled, sparking goosebumps. The air chilled, and I shivered.

The engine whirr increased, the sound wrapping around me. The gravelly noise morphed into the familiar echo of footsteps against wooden floorboards.

I palmed my ears and sucked in a breath. My wrists and ankles burned.

The sunlight dimmed, and the seashore scene dematerialised.

I cried out but my voice was mute.

The man stepped toward me, dark-hazel eyes ablaze. Creases

lined the bridge of his crooked nose, and his lips upturned in a snarl.

My chest convulsed, and I struggled to lift my feet and run. *Move, Tara! Get away from him!*

He coiled his large fingers around my neck.

I pinched my eyes shut.

His hot fingers squeezed my throat, reducing my airflow. He laughed.

I gasped for oxygen, my churning stomach hot and fiery.

"Open your eyes, my beautiful whore."

I opened to the familiar darkness.

No.

The click of the oil heater.

The stench of cigarettes.

My pulse skyrocketed, beating fast in my neck.

Make it stop.

He slackened his grip and leaned close, his breaths heating my face.

I slowed my breaths to avoid inhaling the sickening smell. Bile crept up my throat.

"Why did you kill our baby?"

I awoke and shot up in bed, breathing hard. My back was drenched with sweat. I searched the room, the little lamp in the corner of my bedroom lighting the darkness, and I collapsed against the pillows.

"I'm safe. I'm safe," I whispered, soaking in the comfort of my true surrounds.

My head ached, and I pushed away the latest theatrical experience my subconscious created for me. A mishmash of reality and fantasy.

He would never have asked about the baby.

I shuddered, closed my eyes, and counted my breaths. I turned my head and my cheek slid across dampness. I flipped the tear-stained pillow, settled back in bed, and grabbed my phone. Six-forty in the morning. Would my body allow me a few more hours of sleep? Or should I be thankful for the five hours I slept before the nightmare?

My phone chimed. I grabbed it and eyed my message alerts. An email from Jaelle which had arrived while I slept, and Diana had texted moments ago.

To: tartarbinks98@gmail.com
From: Jaelle - Home
Subject: Naughty, cuz!

Dearest Needs-to-be-Disciplined Cousin,

You ignored my video call invite! Naughty! You promised me weekly chats. Just because I'm on honeymoon doesn't negate your responsibility. ;-)

Paul says hi (don't worry, he's fully dressed. About to go golfing with a new friend from the hotel. His wife and I are having a spa afternoon. Talk about luxury!). We'll be home next week, so no skipping our next chat date.

Love you,

JellyBelly

Jaelle needed to know about the baby. I sighed. Could it wait until my head cleared a little, once she returned home? Would she forgive me for waiting for our next video call? I squeezed my eyes closed and imagined the reprimand my cousin would hand me for not telling her straight away. Jaelle had been by my side after the abortion, a constant support through all of my struggles. Would she stick by me if I chose to keep this child?

I wiped away the final residue of tears from my cheek, rubbed my fingers across my lips, and read Diana's message.

Di-Di: HOPE I DIDN'T WAKE YOU, BUT WAS THINKING OF YOU. IT'S BEEN OVER A WEEK SINCE YOU LANDED IN MELBOURNE SO I CAN ONLY ASSUME YOU'RE AT YOUR MUM'S. CAN JONATHAN AND I VISIT YOU NEXT WEEKEND? HE'S NOT WORKING ON SATURDAY, AND I'VE MISSED YOU SO MUCH. CALL ME OR TEXT. I LOVE YOU XX

I collapsed back against my pillow. Was I ready for this conversation? I sure was ready to get out of the house, though. Eight days hiding and not venturing anywhere was wearing on my nerves.

I rose from the warmth of my bed and gathered my splintered courage, pulled clothing from my cupboards, and padded to the shower. A walk before breakfast would do me some good.

CHAPTER ELEVEN
Hot Off the Press

"Cra-zy … pppreggo." I slowed my pace, heaving mouthfuls of oxygen, and diverted from the concrete footpath to the nature strip near a spindly eucalyptus several minutes from home. Morning sunshine filtered through the foliage.

What had possessed me to attempt jogging in my current state of mind, soul, and body?

I shook my head and trod on the spot, my palms bracing my hips, and glanced down the side street. Of course.

Benanu's.

I pressed my hand against my flitting torso. My breaths quickened, faster than the heavy puffs from my earlier exertion. Was my stomach revolting over the idea of talking to my friends, or were these baby movements?

My heart tripped. The website with the pregnancy calculator I had used yesterday also shared the stages of foetal growth. If I was actually close to the nineteen-week mark the online due date calculator had suggested—after entering the same data six times— movement was possible. Butterfly-like flutters or sensations similar to gas bubbles. A light tickle or flicking. Proof of life.

I leaned forward and clasped my knees. How had I not realised I was pregnant? Why had I not noticed missing periods? Was I so out of touch with my own body and cycles? My legs and calves trembled. I breathed through my nose and blew air out my mouth. *Calm your farm. Beating yourself up won't change a thing.*

I pushed away the self-incriminations, muttered a prayer, and straightened. Steps I needed to take filtered through my thoughts like a hazy mist. Not the physical steps down this path to Benanu's—

conversing and reconnecting with Keanu seemed like child's play despite my fears—but telling Diana … everything.

I shimmied my fingers through my hair and grabbed my phone. The GPS app suggested the road ahead a suitable shortcut home. Might as well familiarise myself with my new home base. I turned down the oddly familiar street and trudged the uneven concreted footpath, my gaze glued to the gorgeous scene above. Beautiful large and wide deep-green leaves spanned the tops of thick-trunked trees. I wandered the path and halted beside the biggest tree on the street. What humungous leaves! I raised my arm and spread my fingers, my hand span almost the same size as the low-hanging canopy.

A battering of feathery wings and bird squawks above my head interrupted my peace-filled moment.

I startled and squeaked, stepping away from whatever battle ensued nearby.

"You okay, miss?"

I turned and blinked at a smooth-faced police officer approaching from across the road, his shaved head gleaming in the sunlight. Why was his voice so familiar?

He removed a pair of sunglasses from the bridge of his nose, revealing vibrant green eyes, and grinned. "Tara."

My lungs seized, and I covered my flat stomach with my hand. "Isaac." Of all the roads to wander down.

Tell him.

I gritted my teeth and surveyed my surroundings, sucking in slow breaths. No wonder the street seemed familiar. I stared at Isaac's head. His bald head. "What did you do to your beautiful curls?"

He chuckled and ran his palm over the top of his head. "Had a meeting with the big boss last week and thought it'd be best to toe the line."

How could he massacre those wonderful curls? Would our baby have curls like him? I punched the thought away and squinted. "Toe the line?"

He crossed his tanned arms over his chest, biceps rippling with the movement. He looked remarkable in uniform.

I bit my bottom lip. *You made a baby with that hot man.* My insides fizzled.

"I'd just returned from an undercover stint before Harris's

wedding, so my hair was longer than usual. As a detective, I can get away with longer hair"—he chuckled again—"but not that long. I trimmed it before my first shift back."

I scrunched my face and pointed toward the fine mist of hair sprinkling his scalp. "That's way more than a trim."

His eyes sparkled. "With my meeting with the higher-ups, I figured I'd err on the side of caution. Plus it was time for a change."

"Okay." Mission accomplished. Without the scruff on his face and, well, *any* hair on his head, Isaac was almost unrecognisable. "It's safe to assume anyone you worked with undercover wouldn't know it was you."

He tilted his head. "What gave me away?"

I narrowed my eyes and surveyed the scrummy cop. "Your familiar voice, then your eyes."

"Good to know." He nodded toward his house on the other side of the street. "Want some breakfast?"

Memories of the most delicious breakfast he had served me filtered through my mind. Along with other less appropriate memories. I closed my eyes. *God, please help me scrub my mind of how nice this man looks without clothing.*

"Tara?"

I opened my eyes. "Sorry."

He raised a brow. "Have breakfast with me? It's been a long night and spending an hour with you before I crash sounds like the best end to my day."

I glanced at his eyes again and noticed the fine lines and signs of fatigue. "I dunno." He needed rest, not a chat with his one-night stand.

He widened his eyes and steepled his palms together. "Please?"

Tell him about the baby. His baby. I shook my head. "I was walking home—"

"You live nearby?"

I wrapped my arms around my belly. "I moved into a rental last week."

Isaac grinned and displayed his boyish dimples. "That's fabulous!" He slipped his bronzed arm through mine and tugged me across the street. "Celebratory breakfast on me, neighbour."

Do not think about having breakfast on him, Tara!

"Do you have work nearby?" He slowed his pace so I could

keep up with his long steps. "Or maybe a boyfriend?"

Was his fishing for information?

Isaac opened the front door and ushered me into the kitchen. "Give me a moment to get out of my uniform." He disappeared down the hallway.

I slumped onto a nearby dining chair, crossed my arms against the table top, and rested my head on my arms. What was I meant to do now? Defending myself against the onslaught of tempting thoughts drained me. And what about the baby? How could I tell him and blow up his life? Isaac deserved better. *Jesus, please help me here!*

I closed my eyes and gave in to the draining exhaustion. Maybe embarking on a walk was not the best idea while this pregnancy drained me of energy, and broken sleep and nightmares sucked out the rest of my vigour.

"Tara." Isaac's firm hand rubbed my shoulder.

I blinked and lifted my head. "Think I fell asleep."

He squatted beside me. "Not sleeping well?"

I met his gaze. "No."

"Something on your mind?" His eyes displayed a fathomless depth.

Tell him.

"I'm pregnant." The words tumbled from my lips before my consciousness realised. My heart stopped.

His eyes widened, and his lips curled into a delicious grin. "Really?"

What have I done?

He laughed, kneeled, twisted me in the seat so I faced him, and wrapped his arms around my waist. "That's phenomenal. Congratulations!"

"I ... I haven't told anyone else."

He pulled back and met my gaze. "Not even Diana? From what I gathered from Harris, aren't you two best friends?"

Pinpricks needled my skin. "I'm ... nervous ... to tell her." But I need to tell her, regardless of her judgement.

"You think she'll give you a hard time because you're a Christian?"

Why did Isaac remember so much about me? Had all the guys I slept with years ago recalled as much after one night with me?

"I've hung out with Harris and Diana a few times since being back." He raised my chin with his thumb. "I don't think you'll have an issue with her. But either way, I think you should confide in someone."

I nodded. "Trying to work up the courage to tell the people who need to know."

He smiled at me, deepening his dimple. "Who's the lucky guy?"

Was he for real? How was he happy for me? Did he not comprehend what was happening? Not that I understood any of what had transpired in the last two minutes.

His eyes widened further, and his smile near split his face. "Are *we* having a baby?" His body seemed to vibrate, and he resembled Jaelle when she was ecstatic.

Tears pooled in my eyes. "Why're you excited by the idea of having a baby? I'm terrified." I squeezed the seat beside my left thigh, my fingertips tingling with the pressure.

"Are you telling me you're pregnant with my baby?"

I nodded, and tears slipped from my eyes.

"That's …" Isaac's voice broke, and he cleared his throat. "That's the best news I've heard in a long time."

What?

He lifted my chin with his warm fingers and met my gaze. "We're having a baby."

Something warm settled in my chest. Yes, we were having this baby, no matter what Mum said.

Isaac beamed. "I know we don't know each other well, but I want in on parenting this child." His voice wavered. "I'm thirty-three. I thought I lost my chance at being a dad when I lost my son several years ago."

My throat tightened. "Y-you had a son?"

He glanced down before meeting my eyes again. "I lost my wife. She was pregnant when she died."

My chest cramped. I reached across and pressed my right palm against his firm chest, his steady heartbeat a comforting force like the rest of this unexpected man. "I'm sorry for your loss."

"Thank you." He leaned close and brushed his lips against my cheek.

Heat unfurled inside my abdomen. How had this moment become so intimate?

"I'm all for co-parenting, but"—his breath feathered my cheek before he leaned back—"maybe we'd make a good team?" His emerald eyes pierced me with intensity. "No pressure. I just want you to know I'll support you in this pregnancy and be whomever you need."

I stared at the handsome, tired man kneeling before me. How had I gone from not knowing what to do about the baby to knowing without a shadow of a doubt I wanted to keep my child and befriend his or her father? Was this what the Scriptures meant in Romans eight about God working all things for our good? I smiled at the sweet man kneeling in front of me and blinked back tears. "How about we make you some breakfast so you can rest?" Keeping busy would distract me while I thought how best to fess up to my bestie.

He turned and stroked the back of my left hand still clasping my seat.

CHAPTER TWELVE
Confessions

"It's going to be okay." I stared at the quaint weatherboard home through the windscreen, gripped the steering wheel, bowed my head, and whispered another prayer. Somewhere between my quick phone call to Diana while I walked home—despite Isaac insisting he drive—and getting into my car for the short trip to Diana's place, my courage had waned.

What would I do if my best friend flipped out and turned her back on me? Diana's love and support had been the sole lifeline which kept me from overdosing on meds a month after my abduction. Although she was unaware at the time, the only text messages I read were hers. The afternoon I contemplated swallowing ten times the dosage of my prescribed anti-depressants, I listened over and over to a voicemail message Diana had left me a few days after our ordeal.

I'm thinking of you and praying for you. Love you.

I closed my eyes as her sweet, tortured voice filtered through my mind. Somehow, knowing she had called upon a Higher Being just for me had steeled my mind for the split second another part of me begged to end it all. And Diana never gave up on me, sending me links to uplifting songs with meaningful lyrics, encouraging sayings, and kiss-face emojis at random times of the day and night. I stopped counting the times her text messages coincided with my weakest moments.

I opened my eyes and lifted my head. Would today be the final straw to end our imbalanced alliance? Because I was extremely aware Diana was often the "give" and I was the "take" in our friendship.

Everyone had their limits.

I unbuckled and exited the car. Unlatching the small metal gate, I lumbered to Diana's childhood home in which she now lived with Jonathan. My footsteps echoed along the concreted path and up the wooden stairs connected to the front verandah. The weatherboard seemed brighter than the last time I had visited.

"Like the new paint job?"

I turned toward the front door and stepped closer.

Diana leaned against the doorframe, her brunette plait draped over her shoulder, brown eyes gleaming in tandem with her brilliant smile.

"You finally got around to it?" I nodded at the house.

"Once we returned from Queensland and Jonathan was back into his work routine, I tackled it." She grinned and opened her arms to me.

I stepped into her embrace, my anxiety melting away with the force of Diana's hug.

"I missed you so much, Tar."

"Ditto." I leaned up and kissed her cheek.

She pulled me indoors, and we walked side by side to the kitchen.

I glanced around the room which appeared larger. "You repainted in here too?"

"Yep." She pointed to a mirror on the wall opposite the window. "I found it at the Salvo's and refurbished the dated edging. It brightens and enlarges the space while being functional." Diana grabbed a blue whiteboard marker from a nearby shelf and scribbled "DH 4 JH 4eva" under several Scripture verses.

I grabbed a red marker and enclosed her words in a large love heart. "Better."

Diana chuckled. "That *is* better."

We returned the markers and flopped on the kitchen bar stools. "Want a cuppa?"

"Sure." Anything to delay the inevitable.

Diana stood, filled the kettle, then leaned back against the kitchen cupboard near the kettle, opposite me. "Did you enjoy your time with Jae?"

I rested my elbows on the island bench top. "Yeah, was great spending so much time with her, using my newfound bridesmaid skills.”

Diana laughed and shook her head. “I still can’t get over that mess with her nasty friend.”

I groaned.

“Or Paul’s crazy friend breaking his leg.”

I snorted a laugh, memories of Kane’s disastrous backflip filling my mind. “Apparently Kane’s hanging out to get the plaster off in a few weeks so he can get back into practising his backflips.”

Diana’s eyes widened. “He’s insane.”

“Something like that.”

The kettle boiled, and Diana prepared two cups of peppermint tea.

I had read once that peppermint was good for digestion. With the way my stomach flipped, a herbal aid seemed like a smart idea.

“Want to sit in the lounge? Our new lounge suite arrived yesterday afternoon, so I’m still in the ‘work out which is my favourite spot’ mode.”

I chuckled and followed Diana, my hot mug of tea warming my hand.

“Here she is. What do you think?” Diana smiled at the plush-looking black leather modular big enough to seat a family of ten large people.

I raised my brow. “You planning to pop out a gazillion babies anytime soon?”

Diana’s cheeks tinted. “We figured bigger was better, especially when family and friends visit.”

“Fair enough.” I eyed the new furniture mixed with the old. Diana’s dad had stored some of his furniture which he once shared with Diana’s mum, and Diana and I had trawled through it a week before her wedding, choosing pieces which would suit her and Jonathan’s needs. “The coffee table suits this space better with a modular than the three-seater and armchairs. What happened to them?”

“We gave them back to Sam.”

I scrunched my brow. “Were they Sam’s?”

Diana removed two coasters from a drawer in the coffee table. “They were Jonathan’s, but he’d used them in their house. Made sense to return them since Sam doesn’t seem interested in getting another housemate.” She lowered herself to the middle of the couch and sagged.

I balanced my mug on a coaster and lolled on the cushion beside her. "It's comfy." I turned and stretched my legs along my side of the couch. "I could totally sleep here and still leave space for others to sleep."

She chuckled. "You're welcome to crash on my couch anytime."

"Thanks." I twisted around and rested against the seat back, crossing my legs, and bumped Diana's side.

"Speaking of which, do you need a place to stay overnight? Or are you heading back to your mum's later?"

Heat stung my cheeks. I grasped my knees and inspected the swirled woodgrain pattern in the coffee table leg. "About that …"

Diana touched my flexing fingers. "What's up?"

I turned and met her gaze. "I haven't been at Mum's." And, boy, Mum had let me know it with the ramping-up of her text messages. Soon she would start calling, then I would know I was in trouble.

"Where've you been?" A wrinkle marred her forehead. "It can't be Keanu's because we had dinner with him last night and he asked about you."

Keanu had asked about me? He probably wanted his spare room cleared of all my junk.

She widened her eyes. "It's not Sam, is it? 'Cause he's good at keeping his friends in the dark when he's holding someone else's secret."

I shook my head. "I haven't been staying with any of your men."

Diana scrunched her nose. "They're not my men."

"I beg to differ. Keanu and Sam are wrapped around your pinky. Sometimes I wonder if they're wrapped tighter than Jon." I smirked. "Mind you, Jon's the one wrapped around all the other parts of you these days."

She laughed, and her cheeks coloured.

"It's great, isn't it?"

"What's great?" Diana asked.

"Sex." A million years seemed to have passed since I actively participated in such illicit pleasure. Well, apart from Isaac. I still struggled to recall our night together—a blessing in disguise for this ex-sexaholic—so he did not count.

Diana's face and neck mottled with redness, and her eyes softened to an almost dreamy expression. "Yeah. It is."

"Did my, ah, little hints and tips come in handy?" What else was I to do with all my firsthand knowledge other than to equip my virginal friend for a positive first experience?

"I can't thank you enough for all your info." She grabbed my arm. "Seriously. It not only meant I was prepared for all the possibilities, but also equipped me with the courage to step a little out of my comfort zone and take charge a few times." Somehow, Diana's blush darkened. "When I confessed that you had answered several of my questions and gave me a few tips, Jonathan said he appreciated my insider trading."

I burst out in laughter. Lightness filled my chest.

"Then he admitted to some insider trading of his own."

I choked on my laugh. "Lemme guess. Sam."

Diana's grin engulfed her face. "And Keanu. The night they played pool and insisted it was a no-girl zone."

"Ah." I wiped the wetness from my eyes and slowed my harried breaths.

She sipped her tea. "So, where've you been staying?"

My insides tightened, and I eyed my mug. To drink or not to drink.

"Tara?"

I reached for my mug and sipped. "Do you know the Arbys?"

"Dad's done work for them for decades now."

I deposited my mug on the coaster and leaned against the cushioned seat back. "I'm renting their bungalow."

Diana's eyes widened. "Are you serious?"

I nodded.

She squealed, dumped her mug on the coffee table, and wrapped her arms around me. "That's so exciting! You live a three-minute walk from me."

"It's a cute place."

"Victoria lived there before she married Dad." Diana released her hold.

I stared at her beaming smile. "Really?"

She nodded. "And Dad's installed and fixed a bunch of things there."

So I had been correct. "Young Nicholas" was Diana's dad.

"Guess I know who to call when there's trouble."

Diana laughed. "Hopefully there's less trouble in your life now you've quit that awful job and moved here."

If only she knew.

"Oh! You could help me with research at the newspaper now you're permanently local. Just like we did at uni!"

I pressed a hand to my churning stomach, closed my eyes, and swallowed the sudden lump in my throat. Not facing that particular fear today. The baby news would be enough.

Diana touched my shoulder. "What's wrong?"

I counted five breaths, opened my eyes, and met her gaze. "I've some hard things to tell you, and I'm not sure where to start."

"May I pray for you?" She slid her hand from my shoulder to my fisted fingers.

Tears stung the backs of my eyes, and I nodded.

Diana clasped my fingers between hers and prayed.

Warmth blanketed me, encompassing my entire body, and eased my taut back. *You can do it, Tara.*

She squeezed my fingers. "Take your time."

I repositioned on the couch, cross-legged, and wriggled my toes. "I …" I cleared my tight throat and glanced at my friend. "You know how my cycle is regular?"

Diana nodded and pressed her lips together.

"A few weeks after Mum brought me home to Swan Hill—"

"Following our—"

"Yeah. Then. I realised I hadn't had my period since …"

Diana grasped my hand and squeezed my fingers.

"Part of my hospital treatment after the police found me was to take the morning-after pill. The nurse warned me it wasn't a guarantee."

Diana rubbed her thumb over the back of my hand. "And it didn't work for you?"

"Ah huh. I was hyperaware of every change in my body afterwards, so I picked up on the possible pregnancy straight away." Heat stung my eyes. "I had an abortion two weeks after my positive pregnancy tests."

"Oh, Tara." Diana's eyes glistened. She wrapped her arms around me and pulled me against her side. "I'm sorry you had to go through that."

"So am I," I whispered.

Diana pressed closer. "I always wondered if you'd avoided a pregnancy or whether you …"

Killed your baby.

I squeezed my eyes closed, thankful my friend had chosen to leave those words unsaid.

"I'm glad you feel brave enough to tell me now."

A heavy weight thudded in my stomach, and I leaned away. "I'm not sure how to say this next part."

"You can tell me anything." Diana touched my shoulder, her fingers gentle against my vibrating skin.

I peeked at her kind, dark eyes, dropped my gaze, and stared at my lap. "You'll be disappointed."

"I'll still stand beside you despite how I might feel." She huffed. "At least give me the benefit of doubt to have your back."

"I'm pregnant." Again.

Diana's body stiffened, and she hissed a sharp breath.

Ice spread through my tight chest. What would I do without Diana? Could I navigate life alone? Without her championing for me? I counted my shallow breaths, praying the silence would pass before I passed out.

Diana pulled me closer.

My tense upper body flopped against her.

"When did this happen? While you were in the U.S.?" Diana's sweet voice penetrated the quiet room. Not an ounce of judgment echoed in her words.

I closed my damp eyes. "I overindulged in Keanu's cocktails at your wedding and somehow ended up in bed with one of Jon's work friends."

Diana's breath hitched. "Which friend?"

"Isaac."

"Smitty?"

"I'm keeping Detective Smith's bun in my oven."

Diana snorted a laugh. "He's a great guy. At least Drunk Tara has decent instincts."

"Just not decent enough to not fall into bed with a wedding guest."

She tightened her grip around me. "What's done is done. Have you told him?"

I nodded, leaned forward, and swiped my mug from the coffee table. "We unintentionally crossed paths this morning." The almost tepid tea glided down my parched throat.

"Unintentionally?" Diana dropped her arm and grabbed her mug.

I imbibed the final drops of tea and returned the mug to its coaster. "I'd been cooped in the bungalow since I landed and needed to stretch my legs. I went for a walk and followed Google Maps down his street, which I forgot was his street, on my way home. Isaac's on overnights and just arrived home. He spotted me."

Diana's eyes widened, her lips slightly curved up. "Small world."

I settled back against the couch, my mind and stomach calmer than it had been in over a week. "Do you think this is what Mum calls providence?"

"Maybe?" Diana rubbed her forehead. "I see your bumping into Isaac as God's favour leading you, a sign of His love for you." She grasped my hands. "He wants the best for you and this new life you're growing. Perhaps that means reconnecting with Isaac so you have a larger support network as I assume he was fine with the baby news?" She cocked her head.

I nodded.

"Figured as much. So now you have a built-in system with me and Jonathan, Sam, Isaac, Dad and Victoria, Keanu and—"

"You can't assume they'll all be supportive."

Diana met my gaze. "I can. My family cares about you. And the guys will protect you, Keanu especially."

Was she right? Would my friends and adopted Tellarine family have my back?

"Speaking of Keanu, do you have employment lined up? Because he told me one of the waitresses quit." Diana squeezed my hand. "You should call him. Ask for a job."

"I don't want to tell anyone about the baby for now."

A deep line creased Diana's brow. "Are you thinking of … aborting?"

"No." Air gushed from my lungs, and I breathed in with ease. I covered my belly with my palm. "Not this time. But I'm still trying to get my head sorted out. I still need to tell Mum …"

"You don't think she'll be happy if you kept the baby?"

"I think she'll push for another abortion."

Diana widened her eyes. "Why? You're almost twenty-four. It's not like you're sixteen."

"She was the driving force for my last one." I ran my fingers along the soft fabric of my T-shirt covering my abdomen.

"Really?" Diana bit her lower lip.

I shrugged. "I think she found being a single mum to be a huge burden." Parenting me was a huge burden.

Diana shook her head. "She'll come around once you make it clear you're not aborting."

I could hope.

"You'll get through this. Despite the mistakes we make in life, God has a knack for enveloping us in His arms in the middle of life's storms." She nudged my shoulder. "We'll get through this. Together."

I sighed, my thoughts clearer, my heart buoyed with hope. Hope in Jesus and my ability to make better choices in future.

CHAPTER THIRTEEN
Bunions and Whooping

I peeked at the local doctor's waiting room wall clock for what seemed like the fifth time in as many minutes. I thought GPs ran late only in the city? I scrunched my brow and recalled the few recent appointments I had attended with Mum's doctor in Swan Hill. Lateness had never been an issue for ancient Dr. Bruin.

I slouched against the hard seat back and stared at the white ceiling.

"I need to see the doc-tah! Me bunions ache like heck."

I repositioned and eyed an elderly man stooped against a wooden cane near the reception desk.

"Do you have an appointment, Mr. Lake?" The twenty-something receptionist offered the man a bright smile.

Mr. Lake grunted. "Me bunions ache, so shouldn't I get seen as priority?"

"I'm afraid you'll need an appointment." The young woman gestured to the waiting room. "Dr. Fallow has several patients waitin—"

"What about the pretty Asian doc?"

"Dr. Yeoh isn't in today." The receptionist's tone sounded strained. "How about you come back after lunch an—"

"I can't walk all the way home with these aching bunions!" The grumpy man eyed the waiting patients. His gaze landed on me. "She looks healthy 'nuff. Make her wait."

Was the rude elderly man speaking about me? What did he know about my state of being?

"Please, Mr. Lake, lower your voice." The receptionist's cheeks reddened.

I straightened, clasped my hands in my lap, and smiled at the red-headed woman sitting across the room who had pulled a face.

"Unless it's an actual emergency, you'll need to make an appointment for this afternoon." The young woman tapped at her computer keyboard and sighed.

Poor thing.

"Does two-twenty work for you, sir?"

"Oy! Blondie!"

"Mr. Lake!" The receptionist's tone sharpened.

Blondie. How original. I relaxed my jaw and brushed non-existent lint from my jeans.

"You, over there. Pretty, healthy thing. Take pity on an old man and gimme your appointment."

I glanced at the old codger and fluttered my eyelashes. Two could play this childish game. "Are you speaking to me?"

He nodded and stepped closer. "What's wrong? You look strong enough to wait a few hours. Can't be that important an appointment. Not like me bunions."

Him and his blasted bunions. I pinched my knees together.

The red-headed woman across the room shook her head and muttered under her breath.

"What's wrong with young people these days? Don't stand up on the bus for the elderly to sit. Don't show respect for elders. Don't sacrifice a measly appointment for an elderly gentleman." Mr. Lake harumphed.

Gentleman, my foot.

The receptionist stood and stepped around her desk. "That's quite enough. I'll have to ask you to leave if you don't calm down."

"Ungrateful young people," Mr. Lake said, his tone containing more gravel than the Arby's driveway.

I leaned forward, sucked in a huge breath, and coughed. Loud and sharp seal-like noises filled the waiting area. I had perfected a hacking, whooping cough during my Year Ten drama performance. Who knew it would come in handy again?

"You okay?" The redhead furrowed her brow.

I nodded and coughed, my throat now tingling with well-earned discomfort. The suffering one must make for her art.

The receptionist pointed a slack-mouthed Mr. Lake to an empty chair before rushing around the corner.

My cheeks heated—I was certain my face now resembled the hue of a delicious red capsicum—and head buzzed, but I sustained the cough, wheezing air between barks.

The young receptionist returned, carrying a disposable cup of water. "Catch your breath, then have a sip."

I eased my wheezing breaths and coughed at intermittent intervals until I stopped my accolade-worthy performance.

The reception desk telephone rang.

"There you are." The receptionist handed me the cup, patted my shoulder, and dashed to her desk, glaring at Mr. Lake.

I sipped and sighed as the soothing, cool water slid down my sore throat.

"Miss Roberts?" An average-height man in his mid-to-late forties glanced at a folder in his hand.

I swigged the final drops of water, grabbed my bag, and stood.

"I'm Dr. Fallow. Come this way."

I followed the doctor down a short hallway to a medium-sized consultation room housing a long examination table with a privacy screen and large bendable lamp, a tidy sink area, an oversized leather chair on wheels behind a wooden desk, and two comfy-looking chairs near the door.

Dr. Fallow pointed to the chairs beside the desk. "Have a seat." He lowered to his desk chair and shook the computer mouse.

I sank to the chair and dropped my bag to the floor.

"Your cheeks are pink. Was it you coughing in the waiting room?"

I bit back a grin. "You did hear me coughing, but it was more for Mr. Lake's benefit than anyone else."

"Mr. Lake?" He furrowed his brow.

"His bunions ache, apparently, so he saw fit to single my healthy-looking self out and demand I give up my appointment." I smoothed my palms along my thighs. "I gave him a persuasive performance."

Dr. Fallow chuckled, his green-hazel eyes shining. He ran his fingers through his short-cropped salt-and-pepper hair. "If you're not here for a cough, what can I help with today?"

I met his gaze and held it. "From what the online calculator suggested, I'd like confirmation I am indeed close to nineteen weeks pregnant."

His eyes flared a brief moment before he nodded and glanced at my torso. "What makes you believe you're nineteen weeks pregnant?"

"I haven't had a period since the twenty-second of October, I had sex for the first time in years in early November, I've taken several positive pregnancy tests, and my waistband's getting tight."

"Once we confirm the pregnancy, we can discuss your options." He leaned back and extracted something from a nearby cupboard, spun in his chair, and grabbed a small specimen container from underneath the sink. "How about you take a urine sample for me? Have you performed one of these before?"

"Several times. Does it matter when in the stream I catch a sample?" I recalled Dr. Bruin had required me to pee a little, then catch my sample. Not the easiest task to perform while hunkered over a small toilet bowl.

"A mid-stream collection would be ideal. Before screwing the lid on the sample container, dip this tester strip in your urine for a few seconds, toss the stick in the front of the plastic sleeve and the sealed container in the back pocket."

"Will do."

Dr. Fallow stood and opened the door.

I grabbed the fun items from the doctor's outstretched hand.

He pointed down the hallway. "Bathroom's to the right."

"Thanks, doc." I trod the firm, thin carpet, locked the bathroom cubicle, and readied myself for the glamourous task of pee catching.

Several minutes later I returned to the consultation room, warm sample in hand, and closed the door.

"All done?" Dr. Fallow turned from his computer monitor and reached for my bag of sample goodies.

I nodded, handed him my bodily fluid, and reclaimed the seat near his desk.

He scrutinised the test stick. "Your deductions are accurate." He raised his head and met my gaze. "Is this a planned pregnancy?"

"No." I pursed my lips.

The sparkle in his eyes dimmed, and his facial features tightened. "In that case, I need to disclose that termination of the pregnancy is available up until twenty-four wee—"

"No termination." I shook my head. "I'm not aborting." Not again.

Dr. Fallow relaxed in his chair, and his expression lightened.

Was he relieved by my response?

He opened a page on his computer. "When did you say the first day of your last period was?"

"October twenty-second."

"And how long is your monthly cycle usually? The average twenty-eight days?"

"Thereabouts. Maybe twenty-nine days?" My cycle had taken a beating after my ordeal but seemed to have normalised in the past year.

He clicked the computer mouse several times. "That gives a twenty-ninth of July due date."

"That's what I worked out too." I shifted in my seat.

"How about you tell me a little about yourself?" He glanced at his computer. "Are you new to the area?"

"Yeah, I just rented a small place around the corner. My bestie, Diana Jacobs—er Harris, lives here."

"Nicholas's kid?"

I snorted a laugh. "Is Di's dad royalty or something? Everyone in town seems to know him."

Dr. Fallow chuckled. "He's the only decent electrician in the area, so he's well-known."

"Ah."

"But we also went to high school together. A group of our mates who still live locally try to catch up monthly at Benanu's."

"So you'd know my friend Keanu too?" I had forgotten what a small world it was living in a country town.

"I've known him since before he was born." He chuckled. "I delivered him in this very room twenty-something years ago."

"No way!" I glanced around the small space and wrinkled my brow.

"His arrival was unexpected. Mrs. Everton was experiencing what she thought were strong Braxton Hicks contractions and wanted my predecessor to double check everything was okay. I had only graduated from university months before, so was shadowing my soon-to-be-retired great-uncle before taking over his practice."

I pressed back a smirk. "Sounds like you were thrown in the deep end. At least I'll be in safe hands should I go into unexpected labour."

Dr. Fallow crossed his legs. "These days, government and medical bodies prefer pregnancy care be handled by hospitals. I'll give you a referral to the team in Robinvale, but I'm happy to take you on as a patient for your general healthcare."

"Thanks."

"Or if you'd prefer a female doctor, Dr. Yeoh works at the clinic four days a week." He gestured to the examination table. "Would you mind if I had a feel of your abdomen?"

"Sure." I climbed on to the paper-covered bed.

Dr. Fallow warmed his hands under the hand dryer near the sink and stepped closer. "Can you lift your top a little?"

I pulled the hem of my hoodie and T-shirt until it rested below my bra.

He pressed his warm hands against my skin and palpitated my stomach. "Do you mind unbuttoning your jeans? I just need to get a little closer to your pubic bone."

I nodded and unbuttoned.

Dr. Fallow pressed lower and wrinkled his brow. "You're hiding this baby away well, aren't you?"

"I guess so?"

"No wonder you only recently realised you were pregnant." He stepped back. "You can redress and sit over here."

I buttoned my jeans and straightened my top half.

"Do you need assistance sitting up? Now would be the best time to get in the habit of rolling to your side before sitting up."

"I'm fine." I rolled and lifted myself with my palms pressed to the examination table. I had started rolling on my side before sitting up in bed a few days ago. Who knew this was the correct way of sitting up when pregnant?

Dr. Fallow lowered to his seat. "It might only be days until your uterus expands to the point where you can no longer hide the belly swell."

I descended and plopped on the chair. "Days?" Was I ready for the rest of the world to know about this baby?

"It might be days, or it might be a few weeks. Each woman's body is different." He turned and typed on his computer keyboard. "Let me sort out the referral for the hospital and for a twenty-week ultrasound."

"Are there many 'do's' and 'don'ts' I should stick to?"

He clicked the mouse button, and the printer whirred to life. "Avoid lifting heavy objects, if possible, don't push yourself physically further than you usually would. I'll print out a pamphlet about foods to avoid."

"Great." I pressed my hand over my fluttering tummy. "Is it possible to feel movement yet?"

"It certainly is, especially with your slight frame. Women with a lower body fat percentage usually feel movements sooner." He handed me several printouts. "Book your ultrasound as soon as possible. Most women get their mid-pregnancy scan about now."

"Okay."

Dr. Fallow pursed his lips. "You said earlier this pregnancy was unexpected. Do you have a support network? Is the father on the scene?"

I folded the papers and tucked them inside my tote bag. "I have some people on my team, and the father responded positively when I shared the news. But I … have a difficult history when it comes to … this area of my life."

He glanced at his watch and met my gaze. "Would you feel comfortable sharing a little more? I understand if you need to go."

How was this man so good at setting me at ease? Was it a Tellarine thing? I nodded, looped my bag over my shoulder, and leaned back. "This isn't my first pregnancy."

His green-hazel eyes darkened.

"Do you recall the Black Dagger trial?" Local and national newspapers had reported on the trial, not to mention the numerous Asian countries embroiled in the illegal activity.

"The international human-trafficking ring Victoria Police dismantled?" A deep V indented his forehead.

I nodded. "I was one of the final abducted women."

His eyes widened.

"Thankfully D—someone shared vital information, saving me from being trafficked. B-but I was raped many times while held captive." I sucked in a breath. "I aborted a child."

"I'm sorry you suffered such an ordeal. Would you like me to refer you to a local therapist?" He tilted his head. "Pregnancy has a way of affecting women differently. You might like a listening ear and someone to walk with you as you journey motherhood."

Maybe.

"You know whom to chat with if you'd like a referral."

"Thanks."

Dr. Fallow stood and opened the door. "Please book an appointment any time you need to speak to someone."

I nodded and rose from the chair.

"We bulk bill many of our patients, especially low-income earners, so please rest assured Dr. Yeoh or myself will always be accessible to you."

I smiled up at the doctor. "Thank you. I appreciate it."

"Look after yourself."

"Will do." I walked the short hallway back to reception, signed the Medicare bulk bill document awaiting me, and wandered the short distance home.

CHAPTER FOURTEEN
Table Thirty-Two

I paced the tiny space between the couch and kitchen table in my bungalow, my hands jittery. My fingers struggled to hold my mobile phone, my fingertips damp with perspiration. *Calm down!*

I dropped onto the couch and reread the text message I had sent to Keanu ten minutes ago.

Me: HEY. I'M IN TELLARINE AND HEAR YOU MIGHT HAVE A WAITRESS JOB OPENING UP? ALSO THOUGHT YOU MIGHT LIKE TO CLEAR OUT YOUR SPARE ROOM. MESSAGE ME WHEN YOU'RE FREE.

Despite the casual tone, I needed this job. I had spent two more fruitless days of job searching and disliked the idea of someone else getting the position at Benanu's while I tried to find work elsewhere.

My phone vibrated in my hands. I sucked in a breath and opened the message app.

Keanu: YOU STAYING WITH DI?

I stretched and fisted my fingers until the vibrations eased.

Me: I'M RENTING A LITTLE SPACE OF MY OWN.

Keanu: IT'S OFFICIAL? UR STAYING?

Me: YES. CAN YOU LIVE WITH THAT?

Keanu: SURE CAN. COME DOWN IN TWENTY AND WE CAN DISCUSS THE JOB.

Shivers tingled along my skin, igniting my nerves. I could do this.

Me: SEE YOU SOON.

I launched off the couch and paced a path from the front door to the kitchenette. I glared at my hands. Why were my fingers trembling? How could I be a freaking waitress with the shakes? I needed to get it together.

But what about the baby?

I gritted my teeth. What about the baby? Dr. Fallow had assured me yesterday I could do whatever I liked. And I still had time to announce my news. Although being in my fifth month of pregnancy meant I might balloon at any moment. Ugh.

I ignored the creeping niggles in my mind. A little more time was doable. Then I could share about the baby with everyone who needed to know. People like Mum. And my boss. Once I had a boss. But not before I secured a job. I needed to make myself indispensable wherever I ended up working—I hoped Benanu's— so I still retained my role *after* I shared about my impending motherhood. I had lived and worked long enough to know some bosses were horrid to mothers and pregnant women, as though our worth to their company diminished with the creation of human life. Keanu seemed like an understanding guy, but who knew how he might respond to my news?

I checked the time, then gathered my phone, keys, and purse. My arms seemed incapable of remaining still, so I locked the front door and walked past the car. The last thing I needed was to cause an accident.

A soft afternoon breeze blew through the surrounding trees. I breathed in the cleansing scent of eucalyptus with traces of honey and crunched along the Arbys' driveway. Leaves jingled above my head, dancing in the sunshine which heated my back.

I turned onto and surveyed the country street, eying every movement. An elderly man weeded a nearby garden, his aged body bent over a bed of small, bright flowers. A dog yapped behind a neighbouring fence. Two primary-aged children zigzagged on bicycles up and down the tarred road.

My heart skittered when a large man lifted his head from underneath the hood of a parked ute and eyed me. I increased my pace and focused on the path ahead while my ears zeroed in on the man now two houses behind me. Two and a half. Three. Three and a half. I strained to hear every pinprick of sound. No other footsteps echoed behind me.

I released a breath and crossed the road, Benanu's large structure now in sight. Scanning the area around me, I navigated into the car park and through the entry without an issue.

I approached the crowded bar with balled fists and caught

Keanu's attention. Loud voices, obnoxious laughter, and wafting beer infiltrated my senses. A typical Saturday afternoon crowd.

My legs stiffened and froze. How could I work here, serving so many men?

"Y'okay?" Keanu stepped close, shielding me from the rabble of customers behind his wall of body.

I blinked up at him.

He turned and communicated something to the barman, pressed his enormous hand on my lower back, and ushered me to the quiet of his office. "Sit."

I wilted onto the proffered chair and piled my hands in my lap.

Keanu opened a bottle of water and handed it to me. "Drink."

I sipped. A sudden desperate need to drink overcame me, and I guzzled water, breathing hard.

"Better?" Keanu's dark eyes sparkled at the half-filled bottle squeezed between my fingers.

"Thanks."

He watched me with an unreadable expression on his face.

Did he somehow know I was pregnant? My chest compressed.

"Did something happen overseas?"

"What?" My breaths quickened.

Keanu leaned back in his large black leather swivel chair and crossed his arms. His eyes narrowed a smidgeon. "I haven't seen ya react to a crowded bar like that." He stared at me. "But I've seen Di do it."

Why was he so observant? This did not bode well for my plans to hide the baby for another few weeks.

I cleared my throat. "I've experienced a few … triggers … over the last few weeks, and it seems I've had some setbacks."

He furrowed his brow. "Will y'be able to serve tables?"

I straightened and lifted my head. "Yes."

He rubbed his bearded jaw. "One of my morning weekday staff resigned, so the shifts would be at times where people don't usually congregate unless they're after coffee."

I released a long breath. "That sounds perfect."

He harrumphed. "Can ya commit to three mornings a week?"

"I can do that." I hoped.

"Six AM start on Monday morning?"

"Um … sure." The last time I had waitressed was prior to my

abduction. I suspected I might need to brush up on my skills.

"Isabelle's happy to run through a few things once she finishes her shift in half an hour, or y'could come back tomorrow after the Sunday lunch rush and I'll go through some training."

An image of the restaurant swathed in an overabundance of men shot shivers down my spine. "Tomorrow might be better."

Keanu narrowed his eyes again. "You might be right. Come by after two when things slow a bit."

"I will." I smiled at my new boss. "Thank you for taking a chance on me."

He grinned. "Anytime."

I pursed my lips. "Do you need me to take everything stored at your place? Or can I collect a few things?"

"Yeah, sure, whatever works. I've got the space if ya don't."

I relaxed against the seat back. "Thanks. I'm staying in a really small place that's furnished, so I'm not sure what to do about my queen-sized bed and couch." Not that my small couch was the best specimen. Nor my bed, to be honest. I had purchased both second-hand from a middle-aged fellow whose home had smelled like smoky cheese. It had taken months of vacuuming powdery vanilla-scented carpet cleaner in the fabric couch to remove the odd smell.

Keanu tapped his fingers along the desk edge. "Happy to keep it as long as ya need. Not planning to fill my spare room with a family just yet." He chuckled.

Because people our age were typically not ready for parenthood. I withheld a cringe. "Th-thanks."

He tilted his head and scrutinised my face. "I'm working a half day on Wednesday and'll finish at a similar time to you. Why don't we grab a bite to eat here, then go back to my place to sort through your things? Maybe we can set the room up for use with yer bed and couch, and Mum'll get off my back about my 'unwelcoming bachelor pad' at last."

I pressed my lips together and hid a grin. "Want my frilly pink bed set to add to the ambiance?"

Keanu scrunched his face. "Let's not go that far. Mum might think it's a green light to set me up with someone."

I laughed and shook my head. "We can't have that happen."

The sparkle returned to his eyes. "No, we can't."

Do not drop it! Sweat beaded across my brow as I balanced two large dinner plates and a bowl filled with piping-hot food from Benanu's kitchen to the small table with a young couple and their toddler.

The mother—a tired, sweet-smiling brunette with dishevelled hair—moved her son's blocks from the table top while the father bounced said toddler on his lap.

I placed the food in front of the trio with quivering hands, relieved not to have dropped anything. "Do you need anything else?"

"No, thank you," the man said while strapping the little boy into a high chair.

I smiled. "Enjoy your meal."

The mother offered a small smile, her eyes bright despite her drooping shoulders.

I pivoted and glanced at the bar.

Keanu watched me. He nodded and returned to pulling beer from the tap.

Five minutes until our shifts ended. Tiny fizzles bubbled in my chest cavity, my nerves screaming for attention. *Play it cool, Tara.* Shifting boxes and reorganising Keanu's spare bedroom would not expose my slight baby belly to my new boss.

I sucked in a slow breath and moseyed to table twenty, where a middle-aged lady jotted notes while she sipped her second cup of tea. She had arrived for breakfast an hour into my shift.

I stepped near her table.

She lifted her head and smiled.

"My shift's about to end. Would you like anything else before I go?"

The lady's smile stretched farther across her face. "Aren't you a sweetheart for thinking of me." She glanced at her now empty cup and gathered her things. "But I'm off to meet a friend for lunch." She chuckled. "Early retirement has its perks."

"Something to look forward to." I smiled and gathered her used crockery. "I'll bring you the bill."

"Thank you, dear."

I carried the dirty dishes to the collection station while running through the steps in my head on how to print a tax invoice and successfully printed said invoice faster than the previous six times I had completed the same task today. Not bad for my second day at work.

I returned to table twenty, bill in hand, and presented it to the waiting customer. "Here you go."

"Thank you." The lady extracted cash from her wallet. She placed two notes on top of the invoice and handed one to me, a fresh grin splitting her face. "For you."

I gawped at the hundred-dollar note resting in my palm. "That's too much! Your entire bill was less."

"You earned it, dear. You've been attentive and polite and gone above and beyond when I wanted some off-menu items for morning tea. I deem this quite adequate for your services."

I blinked. "Ah … th-thank you." Who was this woman?

She stood. "I look forward to my next visit to Tellarine."

Same. "Have a safe trip."

She nodded and strode from the building.

I pocketed the cash, collected the invoice and payment, and deposited the latter into the till.

"Something up?" Keanu's voice rumbled behind me.

I plunged my hand into my pocket and showed him the money. "She gave me a hungie as a tip."

He whistled low. "Whatever yer doing, keep it up. Ms. Traders informed me on her way out on Monday that 'the new girl's an asset in more ways than her pretty face.'"

My skin warmed.

Keanu chuckled. "You clocking out now?"

"Yeah." I walked toward the staff lounge with Keanu.

"Doing okay?"

I shrugged. "Uh huh."

He stuffed his hands into his pockets. "Ya seemed a little uncomfortable with table thirty-two earlier."

Ugh, table thirty-two. The pinstripe-suited man with roving eyes and twitchy fingers which gravitated to my thigh whenever I delivered and retrieved anything from his table. I had practised breathing techniques after each encounter but suspected the final press to my thigh had drawn more attention to me as I had fumbled and caught his dirty plate and glass before they crashed to the carpet.

I stepped to my locker and grabbed my things. "I had it under control."

"We've had issues with him before." Keanu touched my shoulder and turned me around. His eyes were fiery. "Did he touch you?"

Air escaped my lungs, drying my throat. I struggled to find my voice.

"This is meant to be a safe place for our employees. Dad and I don't tolerate inappropriate behaviour from customers."

"Okay," I whisper-squeaked.

Keanu narrowed his eyes. "Y'haven't answered the question."

What would happen if I admitted the truth? Would there be retaliation from Mr. Touchy-Feely because of my honesty? Was it worth the potential issues to myself or Keanu's family business? Or could I pretend everything was fine and move on?

"Tara."

"Sorry." I slipped my handbag over my shoulder. "Everything was fine. No issues with table thirty-two." *Liar.*

Keanu pursed his lips. "Tell me if you ever have problems, okay?"

"Will do." Maybe.

We exited the staff lounge and headed toward Keanu's office, my three small steps making up for one of his casual strides. How was it Keanu towered over me with his enormous, attractive body, yet I never experienced a trickle of fear with him? Not once had fear been in the equation. When we first met, I had been filled with intrigue and interest. Anticipation.

Keanu held his office door open. "Want to grab food to go or eat here?"

I glanced around the room, surprised how safe this space seemed to me. "As in, eat here?" I pointed at his desk. "Or restaurant space 'here'?"

"Not fazed either way." He quirked his brow and studied his desk. "If we eat here or at my place, there'll be less chance of distraction." He dropped his chin and met my gaze. "But if you feel more comfortable eating in the restaurant or staff kitchen now that I'm your boss, I totally understand. We're not *just* friends anymore. Dad'll probably prefer we either eat with the staff or leave the premises."

"Hadn't thought of that." The last thing I wanted was to look like I was kissing up to the boss.

Keanu grumbled. "Not that any of the staff here would care. Just Dad protecting our business."

"As I should." A low, deep voice sounded behind me.

I turned and stared up at Mr. Everton, his striking image similar to his son yet different. His eyes were almost black, and his complexion several shades darker than Keanu's. A handsome, imposing man with distinct islander heritage.

Mr. Everton narrowed his eyes. "What am I protecting our business from?"

Keanu straightened. "Nothing, Dad." His features were sharper than his father's.

"What's going on, love?" A beautiful, lithe blonde with delicate peaches-and-cream skin padded down the hallway and sidled up to Mr. Everton. She raised an eyebrow and stared between the father-and-son duo, turned to Keanu, and pressed an elegant hand to his chest. "Keenie, love?"

Keenie? I pressed my lips together.

"It's nothing, Mum." Keanu leaned down and kissed his mother's cheek. He turned to his father. "Tara and I were just discussing how our friendship might get curbed during office hours."

Mrs. Everton twisted toward me and beamed. "You're Tara? Oh, it's a pleasure to meet you. I've heard so many good things about you."

She had? I blinked up at Keanu, who now avoided my eyes. Hmm.

Mr. Everton nodded and clapped a hand on Keanu's back. "Glad you're taking this seriously."

Keanu's jaw flickered. "I always take the business seriously."

"Akamu." Mrs. Everton tsked.

Mr. Everton pulled his wife against his side and eyed Keanu. "You off for the day?"

"Yes."

"Are you enjoying working here?" Mrs. Everton smiled at me.

For a woman whom I had never met, she seemed to know a lot about the comings and goings of the business. "I am. I've appreciated this opportunity." I glanced at all three Evertons.

"Thank you for taking a chance on me."

Mr. Everton nodded. "Keanu's doing a decent job managing the staff. His last few hires have been acceptable."

What a warm and fuzzy recommendation. Something chilled in the pit of my stomach, and I stepped closer to my friend.

Keanu nodded toward the kitchen. "We were just going to grab some food and head off."

I met Mr. Everton's heavy gaze. "I intend to pay for my mea—"

"Nonsense. We look after our staff." He nodded to Keanu and grabbed his wife's small hand in his oversized mitt.

"Enjoy your afternoon," Mrs. Everton said before she was whisked down the corridor by her husband's long strides.

I turned to Keanu.

His pulse thudded in his neck.

"You okay?"

He nodded and pulled his office door closed.

"Things always that tense with your dad?" I walked down the hallway beside him.

He harrumphed.

"He's an interesting person. Frightening, but interesting."

Keanu stopped and touched my shoulder. "Yer safe here, Tar. Dad'd never harm a woman."

I widened my eyes. "I didn't mean to insinuate he would. He's scary in a father-figure way. Like I expect a father would react when he discovered you scratched his car or snuck out after curfew." Stuff I imagined a father might do, not that I had any personal experience in this regard.

Keanu's shoulders relaxed. He ran his fingers through his floppy, dark hair. "Yeah, he's particularly scary in that scratched-car scenario."

I giggled and covered my mouth with my hand. "Sorry."

We walked into the restaurant kitchen and stopped near the serving station.

"Waddaya want? Hot or cold?" Keanu asked.

"I'm happy with anything quick and easy so long as there're hot chips involved." I had craved hot chips all week. Today seemed the best day to indulge.

Keanu stepped toward the friers, nodded to the head chef, and glanced into its oily depths. He met my gaze. "Will wedges do?"

"So long as you pack sour cream and sweet chilli sauce." Hot potato in any chip-like form would work.

"Can do." Keanu navigated the kitchen, chatting with staff while he prepared two takeaway boxes. He exuded a quiet confidence—a stranger could assume who was in charge by how Keanu interacted with his colleagues—without a sliver of his father's taciturn demeanour. Mr. Everton had been polite and professional during our rare, brief interactions but seemed to run his business like an impassive captain commanding a ship. He shared little rapport with his subordinates, while Keanu held it in spades.

Isabelle slipped by me with a smile and grasped two dinner plates on the nearby warmer. "You settling in?"

I offered her a soft smile. "Yes. Thanks for asking."

She leaned closer. "I'm happy to have you on the team." She glanced over my shoulder. "Bossman likes you too."

I peeked behind me and met Keanu's gaze. Warmth heated my cheeks, and I turned back to Isabelle. "He's a good friend."

She waggled her eyebrows and dashed from the kitchen.

"Ready?" Keanu approached me with two heavy-duty brown paper bags.

"Yep." I followed him to the staff car park, where his mud-slicked old clunker awaited. "This rust bucket still runs?"

He opened the ute passenger door and gestured for me to sit. "She may be old but she's not rusty."

"Just dirty." I buckled and extracted the bags from Keanu's meaty hands.

He rounded the front of the vehicle, his long legs swallowing up time and space.

Isaac's frame resembled a muscled cyclist while Keanu shared the build of a huge rugby player often used as a human wall. Although I had never seen Keanu with his shirt off like I had Isaac—and then some, yikes!—I imagined he hid a lovely set of firm abdominals underneath his layers of casual business attire. The glimpses of his forearms I had peeked when Keanu had rolled his shirt sleeves back on Sunday afternoon gave the impression my friend was packing some serious muscle on his sizable bod.

"Enjoy your stare?" Keanu smirked at me from the driver's seat.

I blinked and turned to the windscreen ahead. "You wish."

He started the engine without a struggle and drove the short distance to his two-bedroom unit several streets away.

We trundled into his quaint kitchen and consumed the delicious food. Hot, tasty crumbed chicken fingers with a scrumptious honey-and-mustard dipping sauce, and fat potato wedges with sweet chilli and sour cream.

I wiped my forefinger along the inside of the tiny, cylindrical condiment container, popped my finger in my mouth, and devoured the final dregs of honey mustard sauce. "So good."

Keanu's eyes darkened, and his Adam's apple bobbed.

I dropped my gaze, wiped my hands and lips with a napkin, and gathered our rubbish from the small kitchen table, identical to the table and chairs in the restaurant. I lifted my brow. "Is this a spare setting from Benanu's?"

He pointed underneath the table. "Some idiots got into a tussle last month and damaged the base, so I fixed it. Dad replaced the entire set and said I could keep it."

"That's nice of him." I stood and shoved the rubbish in the kitchen bin.

Keanu grunted. "Wanna sort through yer stuff?"

I nodded and trailed my big-footed friend down the hallway into the spare room. Everything seemed untouched from my last visit. "I really do appreciate you having stored all my stuff for so long. I'm still happy to pay a storage fee."

Keanu raised a thick, dark brow. "I don't think so."

"Wouldn't it help with rent?" I bit my lower lip.

"I own the joint."

"Oh." Was I the only person our age with life in a shambles? I stooped and gathered a light cardboard box near the doorway.

Keanu flopped on the end of the exposed mattress beside an overflowing washing basket of clothing. "What're ya wanting to collect?"

I dropped the box on the bed beside him and rifled through its contents. "Clothes. Maybe a sheet set, some useful kitchen utensils, and pans. Books." I spotted a DVD set and grinned. "And a few old-school DVDs." I spun, opened the wardrobe, and extracted my ancient DVD player.

He chuckled low. "With streaming services available, you still opt for that?"

I shrugged. "A lot of the shows available online are garbage. And heaps have sexual content I've curbed since …" I gritted my teeth and dumped the DVD player in Keanu's lap. No one had mentioned to me how sex scenes might trigger my panic attacks. My therapist had encouraged me early on to avoid watching such content, and Diana had suggested a few shows which were better for my mental health.

"Is that an issue for you?" Keanu's features softened.

I nodded. "It's not as bad as it was. I can cope with on-screen physical affection nowadays. M-rated sex scenes with limited skin exposure are okay if they're tame and brief, but anything more has sent me spiralling." My chest tightened and hands vibrated. "And if any scene hints at a non-consenting encounter, I need to shut it off." Before my brain sends me back to a time I wished I could forget.

Keanu shifted the DVD player to the bed, met my gaze, and clasped my hand. His dark eyes searched mine for several heartbeats.

Was he seeking my permission? I stepped a few centimetres closer.

He gently pulled me onto his lap—my back to his firm front—wrapped his warm arms around my waist, and rested his chin on my shoulder.

I relaxed against him, closed my eyes, and inhaled deep breaths tinged with his scent.

"I wish I'd been there to stop everything that happened. You an' Di didn't deserve it." His tight, gravelly voice burrowed inside my chest.

A sea of unwelcome faces swam into view, and I scrunched my nose and forehead to chase away their images. "Some of them were bigger than you," I whispered.

"Doesn't matter." He heaved a breath, his arms pressing me closer. "I would've protected y'both or died trying."

Tears stung my eyes. Diana had talked about her big, burly teddy bear friend since we met at uni. Although Keanu and I were introduced years after my abduction, I knew he spoke the truth.

He leaned back and released my waist, his hands running gently along my sides in the process of unlocking me from the confines of his arms.

I stifled a gasp and launched off Keanu's lap. The baby! My pulse thundered. I turned and searched his eyes. Had he discovered the physical changes I had noticed? The marginal thickness around my torso. A slight swelling of hip and belly. Why had I indulged in his comforting embrace?

He stared, molasses eyes intent on me.

Did he know?

I wrapped my arms around my stomach.

He tilted his head and narrowed his eyes a fraction.

Should I tell him? My breaths seemed to evaporate in my lungs. What was my reason for stalling with this news? I glanced at the cream-coloured walls behind his head.

Mum. I had to tell her about the baby before I shared my news with anyone else. *God, please help me get through that particular conversation.*

"Back to work, slacker." Keanu's words broke me from my thoughts.

I whacked his arm and pointed to the heavy box in the corner. "Use your brawn and pop that box and everything on the bed at the front door while I find my least feminine-looking bedspread and sheet set for your new spare bed."

He grinned and saluted. "Yes, ma'am.

CHAPTER FIFTEEN
Catching A Glimpse

The familiar crunch of gravel echoed outside my little home followed by the slam of a car door.

I gathered my bag and keys, slung my lightweight cardigan over my shoulder, and opened the front door.

Isaac startled, fist poised to knock on the now wide-open door. "I heard your car."

He lowered his arm, stepped back, and smiled. "Great hearing."

Three life-changing days had sharpened my hearing. I sucked in a breath, turned toward the bungalow, and locked the door. After a quiet prayer I pivoted and nodded toward Isaac's car.

"Ready for the next part of this adventure?" His gaze dropped to my stomach, and his grin widened.

No. "Definitely." Warmth pooled in my chest at the reality of today's ultrasound appointment. My first chance to set eyes on our baby.

My baby.

Isaac clasped my elbow and directed me to the passenger side of his car. He opened the door.

"Do you know where we're going? I haven't looked the address up yet." I slipped into the seat.

"Sure do." He closed the door and slid into the driver's seat. "Haven't been to the radiology clinic in Robinvale before, but I've sent patrols past it numerous times. You'd be surprised the crazy things some people do to get their hands on expensive equipment."

I glanced at Isaac and marvelled how Diana coped with Jonathan's job. The precarious situations Isaac and Jonathan found themselves in on a daily basis were beyond me.

Isaac tilted his head in my direction, met my gaze, and turned his attention toward the road. "Thanks for inviting me."

"No problem." How could I have denied him this right to connect with his flesh and blood? When I had booked my ultrasound appointment earlier in the week, a sudden urge to see if Isaac wanted to be involved had burned bright inside my chest. Plus, his company helped staunch my overzealous nerves, the jumpy blighters still out of my control. Would the storm inside my mind soon calm? *Help me, Jesus, to think on good things and focus on You, not my problems.*

I peeked at Isaac's profile and grasped the comfort of his presence. With so few people knowing about my pregnancy, I relished his support.

Things will change. I sucked in another breath. Jaelle's image flashed across my mind, her kind eyes staring through the computer screen. She had taken the baby news much better than I anticipated. She had—no surprise—also growled at me for not telling her sooner. Last night she had helped me select a deadline for when I would tell Mum. Thursday next week after my shift.

"Is there anything you need me to do in regards to the baby?" Isaac's deep voice drew my attention from the "Congrats! You're a granny!" conversation always on pause in my brain.

I cleared my head and shrugged. "In what way?"

"Any way. Every way." He glanced at me. "Bubs will need furniture, clothing. Maybe a bigger place to live."

I stared at him and furrowed my brow. "Not sure I'm comfortable with you subsidising my rent so I can afford a bigger place."

"Why not?" He caught my gaze once more and raised an eyebrow. "You don't have space to fit a cot and change table in your bungalow, let alone toys and clothes. I've no problem giving you a few hundred dollars a week so—"

"That's way too much." My chest compressed.

"Not in my book." Isaac slowed behind a dawdling hatchback on the main road to Robinvale. "Our baby is all I have in this world. I'm stepping up to the plate and hitting a home run, Tara."

I swallowed to release the lump in my throat. "It's just that—"

"Please." His voice croaked. "Let me do this for you."

My lungs squeezed, and I pressed my hands together in my lap.

"Okay."

His shoulders relaxed. "Thank you."

I penned "find a new house and move" to the lengthening mental to-do list. Baby was due in less than five months. Could I add more burdens to my fragile shoulders? *Please help me rely more on You, God.*

We reached the outskirts of Robinvale ten minutes later and entered the clinic with five minutes to spare. The clinical ambiance rattled my nerves.

I stepped to the front counter, filled out the patient paperwork, and lowered to the empty chair beside Isaac. A passing comment Mum said years ago bounced to the forefront of my brain. Something to do with her placenta being near her cervix during her pregnancy with me and the associated complications. Was my placenta in the wrong spot too? I pressed my palm against my swirling tummy.

Isaac leaned close. "Ever had an ultrasound?"

I shook my head.

"Heidi was nervous the first time too, but the moment she saw our tiny baby on the screen, she relaxed." Warmth oozed from Isaac's voice. "And the first time you hear that whooshing heartbeat"—he lifted his gaze and beamed—"you'll be a goner."

A tangle of ice and heat fought for first place in my stomach. Isaac had never said his wife's name before. "Thanks." I searched his green eyes. "You still love her."

"I'll always love her and will forever regret how she died." He closed his eyes.

I touched his shoulder. "Do you mind me asking what happened?" How had he lost his entire family?

A tortured expression crossed Isaac's face.

I cringed. How could I be so insensitive? "You don't have to tell me," I whispered.

He lifted his eyelids, and a sheen of moisture veiled his eyes. He blinked. "We lived in Melbourne. Heidi was a social worker. She became involved in a challenging family dispute which had gone to court."

My stomach soured.

"The dispute dragged on, and her team became aware of links to a particular underworld figure. After the spate of Melbourne gangland killings in the nineties and noughties, their team was on high alert."

I pressed my lips together and grasped the fabric chair on either side of my thighs, my nails digging into the firm seat. I had grown up hearing names like Moran and Mokbel in nightly news snippets related to murder and drug importation trials and knew Heidi's story would be unpleasant.

"A week into the custody court proceedings, Heidi disappeared."

I bit my lower lip. My vision blurred.

"Her body was found three weeks later, burned beyond recognition in a car fire." Isaac cleared his throat and blinked.

Three weeks. I had barely survived three days of torturous mistreatment. What horrors had his wife suffered at the hands of her captors? And their baby? A tear scuttled down my cheek, and I swiped it away. "I'm so sorry." My voice rasped.

"Tara Roberts?" A plump woman with a pixie haircut, sharp nose, and piercing dull-blue eyes surveyed the waiting room.

I waved and stood.

The brown-haired woman smiled and nodded toward a hallway. "This way."

I followed her the short distance into a small room, conscious of Isaac behind me.

She closed the door and gestured to a seat against the wall near a long examination bench decked out with a white pillow and a paper-thin blue bed cover. "Dad can sit there, and Mum can lie down for me." She settled at a large desk with a heap of weird-looking equipment.

I peeked up at Isaac, shrugged, and lay on the table.

Isaac settled beside me and held my hand.

"Please shift across a little closer."

I elbowed the flimsy bed cover in place and slid a few centimetres closer to the desk.

The sonographer clicked away at a computer keyboard before sanitising the curved end of a small handheld instrument which slotted into a rack on the side of the desk. "Please lift your top and unbutton your pants."

Uh, okay? I lifted my T-shirt until it just covered my bra and unbuttoned my jeans. "Do you need me to unzip too?"

She glanced at my exposed skin and narrowed her eyes. "Please."

I pressed my lips together and unzipped, avoiding Isaac altogether.

She tucked and folded a thin towel over the top of my jeans and under, her fingers shoving my underwear down farther.

Okay then.

"The gel will be cold and sticky, so I'll do my best not to get it on your clothes."

"Thanks."

She grabbed a nearby white squeeze bottle and squirted a generous amount of cold, clear goo on my belly.

Fruit loops! "You weren't wrong. It's cold."

Isaac chuckled.

I snuck a furtive glance at his grin and relaxed against the table.

The sonographer picked up the sanitised tool and rubbed it against my skin. The pressure was firm, almost uncomfortable when it pressed nearer my pelvis. "Just the right amount of fluid in your bladder. Good."

I stared at the screen above me, my attention fixed on the images flashing onscreen, no longer caring about my discomfort. "What's that?"

"Your cervix." She clicked something and lines appeared and disappeared on the screen. "Now to check for placenta positioning."

Please, God, no issues for me.

"Placenta placement is good."

I closed my eyes for a brief moment and breathed.

"Is that …" Isaac's voice filled the quiet space.

"A foot."

Isaac squeezed my hand.

I blinked away tears. Our baby's foot.

The sonographer clicked and tapped at the keyboard with her right hand before twisting the instrument with her left hand to a new location. "And this looks like the head." A line appeared on the monitor, followed by measurements.

I smiled at the limb now on display, a bone measurement.

"Abdomen." More movement and measurements. "Your baby's very accommodating." She clicked the computer and a whooshing beat filled the air.

Was that …?

"A healthy heartbeat."

I melted against the pillow and revelled in the sound.

"Checking the heart chambers and blood flow." Colours pulsated on the screen.

I grinned at the marvel of technology, showing me intimate detailing of my tiny, half-baked baby.

"Looks to be the right size for twenty weeks' gestation."

"And everything looks fine?" Isaac asked.

"Seems within normal range, but the report to your GP will contain all necessary findings." She moved the instrument into several new positions, twisting and turning, clicking and recording data. "Do you want to know the sex?"

I turned to Isaac.

He shrugged. "Totally up to you."

I furrowed my brow. Diana had seemed to enjoy the guessing game of not knowing the gender of her siblings. And apart from the initial shock related to this pregnancy, deep down I liked surprises. Good surprises.

"Tara?" Isaac raised his brow.

I turned to the sonographer. "I'd prefer not to know."

She nodded. "I'll do my best to navigate this next section and hopefully not reveal anything. If you're familiar with ultrasound, it might be best to look away. Just in case."

I huffed a small laugh. "First time for me, so I hope this means I'll be clueless."

"Unless it's obvious." Isaac chuckled. "Heidi's ultrasound was very obvious."

I glanced at him and wrinkled my brow. "How?"

"My son was easy to pick. Took after his old man." He winked.

The sonographer snorted a laugh.

My cheeks warmed, and I pushed aside thoughts of Isaac's implied maleness.

Several minutes later, the sonographer downed her tools and wiped my stomach. "The gel will wash off in case there's residue on your clothes. I'll give you a moment. Once you're dressed, head back out to Reception." She stood and exited the room.

Isaac ran his fingers through his short hair. "Do you need help or …?

"I've got this." I removed the thin towel and wiped my skin, buttoned my pants, and rolled to my side. Despite the small being inside my uterus, his or her collective weight added up. What would it be like to carry this child several more months? No wonder Diana's stepmom had waddled in her final weeks of pregnancy with her son, Elijah.

Isaac reached out his hand. "Help up?"

"Okay." I clasped his fingers and held tight.

He pulled me upright on the examination bench, his frame now close to mine. He touched my cheek. "You did great."

My mouth dried. "Th-thanks."

Isaac's eyes darkened. He glanced at my lips.

What was happening?

He cleared his throat and stepped back. "I suppose we should discuss baby names sometime."

Oh man, another thing to add to my mental list.

"C'mon, let's hit the road."

I eyed my baby's father, slid off the bench, and followed him through the doorway.

I closed my work locker, lowered to a nearby chair at the long staff lounge table, and peeked at my phone for the latest email from Jaelle.

To: tartarbinks98@gmail.com
From: Jaelle - Work
Subject: Baby Baby...

How's things in Tellarine? Swell like your expanding tum? Send me the latest photo because this week-by-week growth change video thing we're creating is going to be awesome! It's given me lots of ideas for when Paul impregnates me in a billion years' time (sorry, not riding the baby train for a while yet, cuz, but happy to be honorary auntie!).

Just a quick message to remind you that you're loved and you're brave and able to tell Aunt Alannah about her soon-to-be-grandchild. Have a little faith in your mum. Your last pregnancy was during a very difficult time for you both. Sure, she might be disappointed a hot cop knocked you up, but it's not like she can throw it back in your face. I mean, c'mon, she was a single mother after a fling with some guy we still don't know. At least you can give your baby access to his or her father. Your baby won't agonise like you did over not knowing.

I love you. Stand tall, be proud, and share your happiness with her.

JellyBelly

I blinked away tears and smiled. *Thank You, Lord, for Jaelle.* After a quiet prayer and several deep breaths, I exited the room and smiled at the Benanu's staff members I passed in the back corridor. Hitching my handbag over my shoulder, I palmed open the large door leading into the restaurant area, relieved the final shift of my second week here was complete. I wiped my clammy hands over my thighs and smoothed the wrinkles in my black work pants. My stomach swirled knowing this afternoon's impending conversation. I had put Mum off long enough.

"Another successful week." Keanu stepped from behind Benanu's bar.

I stopped at the side of the bar. "Yeah."

He furrowed his brows. "Something wrong?"

I shook my head. "I've been avoiding my mum and promised myself I'd call her after work." Now I wished I had somehow talked myself out of it. Why had I discussed this with Jaelle and decided today was the deadline? Now she would hold me accountable to my plan. Ugh.

Keanu pulled a face. "Know the feeling. Mum's been in twice this week, and I can hardly kick her outta my office."

I chuckled. "Nice to know I'm not alone in my mum troubles."

"Never." He nodded toward the hostess desk, and his smile disappeared. "Almost forgot. Detective Smith called about half an hour ago."

I scrunched my brow. "For me?" Why would Isaac call me at work when he had my mobile number? I fumbled for my phone in my handbag and saw two missed calls and a "CALL ME WHEN YOU CAN" message from him. How had I not noticed them when I checked Jaelle's email? Was a one-track memory or lack of attention to detail some weird pregnancy quirk? I hoped not.

"I didn't know you were seeing him."

"I …" The swirling in my stomach eddied into tumultuous territory. What could I say until I told Keanu about the baby? I pressed down on my toes and straightened. "Could I speak with you after my shift on Monday? I need to … update you on some things."

Keanu nodded, his gaze glued to my face. "I'll check my calendar and message you."

"Thanks."

He ran his fingers through his hair. "Have a great weekend."

"You too." I scurried from the restaurant, my mind clanging with conversations I wanted to avoid. First Mum, then Keanu. But what about Isaac? Had I imagined the way he had looked at me after the ultrasound last week? We had texted a few nights ago without any resolution on how to navigate our new world of parenting.

I crossed the road and headed in the direction of home, weaving around a fresh doggy deposit on the footpath. What happened to rules about cleaning up after your dogs? Gross. I glanced across the road and caught sight of Isaac's street. Should I message him back or brave a face-to-face conversation?

My back pocket buzzed twice. I stopped under a huge tree and yanked my phone out.

Di-Di: THINKING OF YOU. XX

Di-Di: WANT TO BE PART OF SAM'S MARVEL MOVIE MARATHON ON SATURDAY? I THINK HE'S WATCHING A FEW OF THE MORE RECENT MOVIES BEFORE HE SEES THE LATEST AT THE CINEMA.

An evening with friends seemed just what I needed. A reward of sorts. Once I spoke with Mum, I suspected I would need a lot of love from my bestie.

Me: SOUNDS FUN. I UNEARTHED THE CROCHETED INFINITY GAUNTLET I BOUGHT ON ETSY LAST YEAR.

I stared at the street sign, bit my lip, and opened my text thread with Isaac.

Me: YOU RANG/MESSAGED/CALLED/WANTED ME?

My phone vibrated in my hand.

Di-Di: WHAT???

I snorted a laugh.

Me: I DIDN'T TELL YOU ABOUT THAT? I SAW IT ON ETSY AND THOUGHT OF SAM. WAS GOING TO GIVE IT TO HIM WHEN I SAW HIM NEXT, BUT THEN ALL THE STUFF BLEW UP BEFORE I HEADED OVERSEAS

AND FORGOT ABOUT IT UNTIL I FOUND IT LAST WEEK AFTER COLLECTING MY STUFF FROM KEANU'S.

My phone buzzed in my palm, and I startled. The ringtone blared, shattering my quiet surrounds.

Isaac.

"Hi." I leaned my shoulder against the tree trunk.

"Hey. You finished your shift?"

"Yes, walking home. What's up?"

He cleared his throat. "Want to come over? I, ah, wanted to chat about something."

What was with me needing to have serious conversations today? I stepped away from the tree and crossed the road. "I'm just around the corner. See you soon."

"Okay."

I disconnected the call and checked my messages, my eyes glancing at the path ahead. After the comments my mum, aunts, and their friends had made about my generation and our obsession with walking and using our phones, I liked to play into the stereotype in case an older person wanted to "tsk" at me. Tsk away, grumpy old men and women.

Di-Di: THAT'S HILARIOUS AND AWESOME. SAM WILL PRETEND TO HATE IT, BUT HE'LL SECRETLY LOVE IT.

I chuckled. I expected nothing less from Mr. Kono.

"Don't trip."

I glanced up and caught Isaac's smile. "Messaging my bestie."

He gestured me through his front gate and up the front steps. "How's Diana? Has Harris knocked her up so you can have babies together?"

I choked on a laugh, my heavy shoulders easing with each breath.

"Too soon for jokes like that?" Isaac's eyes widened to match his grin.

I flopped onto Isaac's three-seater couch and lay along the comfortable furniture, eyes closed. "Since you did the knocking up, I think you have the right to joke."

"Long day?"

"Yeah."

The other end of the couch sank, and Isaac grasped my ankles with his warm hands.

I stiffened, opened my eyes, and sucked in a sharp breath.

"This okay?" Isaac furrowed his brow and glanced between my face and feet.

When would I move past my initial reaction to touch? How could I contemplate having a relationship with a guy—any guy—if I flinched when he touched me?

But when Keanu hugged you, you were fine.

I scrunched my brow. Was it because Keanu had sought unspoken permission from me before he pulled me to his lap? Did we share a special connection because he knew my story? Or had Keanu proven himself trustworthy from months of friendship with me and years of protecting Diana? While Isaac and I knew little about each other and—

"Tara?"

I swallowed the lump which had formed in my throat. *Make a choice. Will you trust Isaac?* I lifted my chin and studied Isaac's eyes, ignoring the questions swirling in their emerald depths, and nodded.

He tilted his head and considered me for several pulse-increasing seconds.

What could he see? Had his police officer instincts sniffed the scent of my past? Or triggered an alarm in his mind?

Isaac lifted my legs, swished along the seat, and lowered my feet to his lap.

I tracked his nimble fingers as he removed my shoes and socks, each movement slow and deliberate, like a trainer with a skittish horse.

"Breathe. I just want to help you unwind." He held my feet between his large hands.

I could do this.

He massaged my aching feet, each tactual press loosening the knots and twists inside my chest.

I closed my eyes and groaned. "So … good."

He chuckled. "Now I have you off your guard—"

"What?" I snapped my eyes open, my back and legs rigid.

"Relax." His clear eyes shone. "Stress isn't good for our baby."

My cheeks warmed. Would the embarrassment of inadvertently creating a baby with this man ever wear off?

His dexterous hands worked along my toes, under my tense

arches, and up to my shins.

I melted against the couch.

"Would you consider going on a date with me?"

What? My breaths quickened.

"Hear me out." His warm fingers slid along my bare feet, soothing my nerves. "Our baby's going to be a permanent part of our lives going forward. And if I'm not mistaken, we get along well."

I shifted my head against the couch arm and met his gaze. "We do."

"Why not give us a go? We could surprise ourselves." His gaze dropped to my lips.

My heart scuttled. So my imagination had not created an illusion last week.

He licked his lips and captured my gaze again. "My intentions are honourable. I like you a lot, Tara. I know we don't know much about each other, but we have time to see where this goes." His fingers kneaded my shins. "You don't seem the type to jump in without thinking this through, so I need you to know I'm serious." His gaze flickered to my lips again.

My dry throat tightened. Could this work? I scrutinised his handsome face, different from Keanu's dark features. *Not now.* I inhaled and exhaled, blowing away all thoughts of my boss-friend.

Isaac focused on my face, his gaze burning my skin.

Should I make this work for the sake of our child?

He leaned closer, slipped an arm under my back, and gently lifted me to sit beside him, leaving my legs stretched across his thighs.

"What about my faith in God?" My voice squeaked.

He caressed my cheek with his warm fingers. "I've no problem with God."

I creased my brow. "Would you be willing to visit church with me?"

He nodded. "I've attended a few of the men's meetings Harris invited me to recently."

He had?

"I'm willing to see what a Sunday service is all about." He leaned closer, his minty breath ghosting the side of my face. "Will you take a chance on us?"

I stared at his lips. His soft, delicious-looking lips. Blame it on pregnancy hormones, but I wanted to tether my mouth to his and extract all the sweetness he had to offer. "Kiss me."

His eyes darkened to a deep sage, and he lowered his head to mine.

I pressed my lips against his, warm softness melting the last of my nerves. Heat threaded through my heavy limbs and settled low in my belly, stirring memories and long-forgotten want. Desire. Not fear. *Thank You, God.*

Isaac pulled me onto his lap.

My breath hitched. I pulled back until our lips separated a fraction and breathed in cool mint. No cigarettes.

"You okay?"

"Mmm-hmm." I relaxed my shoulders and wrapped my arms around his neck, pressing closer, lips colliding. Flaring intensity engulfed my torso, and I deepened our hot kiss. The familiar tempest of need swirled and eddied inside me. My breaths shortened, my lungs burning for oxygen.

Isaac detached his mouth from mine with harried breaths, chest heaving. "Is sex still off the table?"

I nodded, my head hazy. Had I really kissed a man by choice?

"Then we'd better stop before I strip you naked."

I slipped my arms across his shoulders and sucked in mouthfuls of air.

He glided his hands down my sides and smirked. "You're going to look magnificent carrying my baby. It's a shame I can't enjoy you completely."

Heat stung my cheeks.

He swatted my backside and chuckled. "Hop off. Let me drive you home."

I stood with Isaac's help and gathered my belongings. "I think a walk home will do me good." A walk detouring through the neighbours' garden sprinkler would be even better.

He smirked. "Okay. Message me when you get home." He walked me to the front door and pulled me against his chest. "We're going to have a lot of fun, sexy mumma."

"Not too much fun." Had I chosen a path overloaded with temptation?

His eyes twinkled. He leaned down and kissed my lips. Another

perfect kiss. "Message me."
I nodded. "See you soon."

CHAPTER SIXTEEN
Taken By Surprise

I paced the scant space between my bed and the small wall heater, my gaze glued to my phone clutched in my shaking hands. "You can do this," I whispered. I pulled up Mum's contact information, pressed the green Call button, switched on the speakerphone, and tossed the handset face-up on the bed.

"How are you, love?" Mum's sweet voice echoed through my modest bedroom.

"Great." I slowed my steps. "Kept busy since we messaged last?"

"You know I have. It's a good life here in Swan Hill. You sure you don't want to move in here for a while?"

I sighed. "I found a rental, remember?"

She huffed a breath. "Which you could easily offer your notice and get out of the agreement."

"I like it here." Tellarine was … safe.

My bedside clock clicked over another minute.

"When're you visiting next? I haven't seen you since you returned."

My breath hitched. What kind of daughter was I to not have visited my mum in almost a month after having been away for three months?

"It's been such a long time since I hugged you, Tara." Mum's tone dropped.

I cringed. Daughter fail alert. "I've been busy with my new job." I flopped onto the bed and rested my head closer to the handset. "But I might be able to visit next Friday. Or the following Friday." *If you stay calm after I tell you this news.*

"That would be great, love. But can we switch to video call now that I'll have to wait at least another week to see your beautiful face?"

I plunged my fingers through my hair. What was with everyone wanting to video call?

"I'll call you back." A dial tone replaced Mum's voice.

I rolled to my side and righted myself, switched the overhead bedroom light on, and lowered to the bed, propping myself against the pillows.

My phone buzzed with the still unfamiliar tones of a video call request.

I sighed and accepted the call.

"That's better." Mum's cute blonde bob filled the edges of my smartphone. She scrunched her button nose, which was a little too close to the screen. "Where are you?"

"On my bed."

"You've put on a little weight." She leaned back and pointed to her cheeks and chin.

I squinted at my tiny image reflected in the corner of my phone screen and stretched my neck.

"You look great, love. Healthy. Almost … glowing. America and Jaelle must've done wonders for you."

I suspected I glowed for a very different reason.

"How long will you stay?"

"Stay?"

Mum raised her brow. "During next week's visit?"

"Oh." *Tell her.* I sucked in a breath. "It depends how you deal with what I'm about to tell you."

Mum inhaled a quick intake of air. Her image jiggled on the screen before straightening. "What's going on?"

Guide my steps and words, please, God.

Her blue eyes widened. "Tara? Did something happen?" A high-pitched edge coloured Mum's voice.

Jaelle said not to beat around the bush.

"Tara?"

"I'm pregnant." I bit my lower lip.

"What?" Her mouth slackened.

I rubbed my temples where an ache bloomed.

"You're pregnant?" Mum blinked and shook her head.

"Yes." I transferred the phone from my right hand to my left, ready for whatever Mum dished out to me.

"Oh, love." Brokenness seeped into each syllable. "How did this happen?"

I stared at her face on the screen. "How do you think it happened?"

"Don't get smart with me." Mum's tone sharpened.

"Sorry." I scrunched my face. "I drank too much at Diana's wedding and—"

"That was months ago!" Mum vanished from the screen before reappearing. "How far along are you?"

I glanced at the off-white ceiling. "Almost twenty-one weeks."

"Over halfway!" Mum swore under her breath. "Why didn't you tell me sooner?"

"I only found out the day before I flew back—"

"You've known that long? And not consulted me?" Mum's nostrils flared.

Consulted her? I furrowed my brow. "Mum, this baby's mine, and the decision to keep him or her is also mine."

"But—"

"I wasn't raped this time."

She blustered a breath and narrowed her eyes. "Do you know the sacrifices you'll have to make to keep another human alive and healthy all on your own?"

I could hazard a guess.

"Do you even know the father?" Her voice ratcheted with each word.

"He works with Jon. He's a detective."

A hideous, difficult-to-read expression flitted across her features before she wrinkled her nose.

Disgust?

"Just what you need. A man working a dangerous job. One day he pays child support, the next he's dead in a ditch."

"Mum!" I gritted my teeth.

"It's one thing for your friend to choose the path of an officer's wife, but you don't have to be forced into any of it." She huffed a breath.

"I know." My words sounded like a growl through my tight jaw.

"You can still safely abort."

"No!" I sprang off the bed, dropping the phone with its screen against the doona, and recommenced my earlier pacing. "I'm keeping my baby, *and* I'm going to see whether a relationship with the father is feasible."

Who knew Pregnant Tara would be so decisive all of a sudden?

"Don't be ridiculous!" Mum's muffled words detonated in the room.

I leaned over, flipped the phone face-up, and marched the length of the bed.

"It's enough you're throwing away your life for a baby. Don't complicate it by entangling yourself with the sperm donor."

I stopped in my tracks and watched Mum on the screen. "Is that what you did? Threw away your life?"

"That's not what I meant."

I rubbed my aching jaw.

"And would you please pick up your phone and talk to me like an adult? This talking to the ceiling thing is ridiculous."

"I thought keeping my baby and pursuing a relationship was ridiculous." I dropped to the bed, clutched the phone, and glared at the screen.

"C'mon, Tara. See reason. You talk about wanting a better life, doing your church thing"—she wrinkled her nose as though she whiffed a bad smell—"but you know who'll judge you for your recklessness? Those church folk you love so much. They'll judge you for drinking alcohol to the point of sleeping with a random guy. Then they'll judge you for being a single mother. They'll pity you." Mum stared at me and lifted her chin. "You want their pity?"

"It won't be like that," I whispered. Diana and Jonathan would never judge or pity me. Nor would Diana's family.

Something tapped in the background, and Mum glanced off-screen. "You'll know soon enough."

I shook my head.

"Call me when you see reason." The video call disconnected.

I tossed my phone on the bed beside me and flopped against my pillows. Had Mum shared wisdom gained from years of experience? I would never abort again, but should I heed her advice and be cautious of getting too close to Isaac? Was I setting myself up for heartache and a lifetime of awkwardness if our relationship failed?

I wiped my palms along my wet cheeks.

♥ ♥ ♥ ♥ ♥ ♥ ♥

I blinked away tears and tore around the corner. The back left wheel impacted the kerb and juddered. I yelped and squeezed the steering wheel.

Please, God, not again.

Voices echoed through my skull, smothering road and vehicle noise. Mum's angry comments scrambled with the vicious retorts of my inner demons. And *his* words.

The inferno in my chest short-circuited my ability to breathe. I hurtled along Sam's street, my quaking arms impairing my grip. My head pounded, and my arid throat constricted with each desperate pull for oxygen. I settled my pinpricked gaze on the familiar shrubbery and forced my leaden foot to brake.

The tyres screeched and the seat belt punched my torso.

I hissed a breath, deactivated the engine, and slumped forward. The hard steering wheel cooled my clammy forehead.

I clutched my shaking hands in my lap and counted my breaths in an effort to squelch another panic attack. Why had I pushed myself again?

"God. Please." My voice rasped in my tight throat.

Ask for help.

The words echoed in my head, distracting me from the tension in my chest. Maybe I should have taken Diana up on her offer for a ride to Sam's.

I lifted my head and stared at Sam's weatherboard rental. Exhaustion flooded my body, and I closed my eyes. Would a five-minute drive deplete my physical and mental capacities for the rest of my life? The rest of this pregnancy? Or was this a passing phase I would overcome soon?

"Jesus, please help me overcome this debilitating anxiety. I don't want to live like this anymore, but …" I opened my eyes and leaned my temple against the cold driver's door window. "I'm afraid. Help me through this."

A vehicle rumbled down the street, its brakes squeaking at the T-intersection several houses away.

I straightened, shook my arms loose, and grabbed my tote bag from the passenger seat. My shins twinged like they did after a long run. I exited my car and dragged along Sam's front verandah. After several slow exhales, I rotated my shoulders, plastered a smile to my face, and opened the front door. "Hey, hey, party people."

Loki barked and bounded toward me.

A genuine grin slipped to my lips. I slammed the door behind me seconds before Sam's curly ball of love propelled me against the cold wood and pinned me to the door with his paws. My tote bag slipped down to my elbow.

"Loki! Down!" Sam called from the lounge room.

I laughed and rubbed Loki's neck, his soft curls caressing my fingers. "It's okay!" I leaned closer to the dog, thankful his paws crushed my thighs and not my belly. "Now shove off, you."

Loki yipped, dropped to the carpet, and nudged my leg with his perfect doggy head.

I shouldered my bag, scratched around his ears, and entered the lounge room.

Sam stepped toward me, his jet-black hair styled to perfection above his expressive deep coffee eyes.

"You survived another welcome?" Jonathan grinned from where he and Diana perched—aka glued to each other—on the couch.

"Sure did." I brushed my fingers through Loki's chocolate-coloured coat, surveyed the room, and eyed Sam. "You enjoying having furniture in your lounge room again?"

Sam's boyish features morphed into a delighted grin. "Beats those horrid blow-up chairs a mate gave me." He shuddered.

Diana and I laughed.

"I told you they'd be a pain in the butt." Jonathan smirked.

"A pain in *your* butt when you popped the waste-of-space chair." Sam chuckled.

I stared at Jonathan, wide-eyed. "When'd this happen?"

"While you were gallivanting overseas. He had a sweet-looking bruise for over a week on his perfectly delicious rear end." Diana waggled her brows.

"Please stop." Sam scrunched up his face and rubbed his temple. "You're bringing on another 'my best friend gets laid more often than me' headache."

Jonathan's bronzed face tinged a darker hue, highlighting the faint scar near his right temple.

"It probably has more to do with the cocktails you've been downing the last half hour." Diana narrowed her eyes at Sam.

Cocktails.

Sam nodded toward the kitchen. His lips moved, but the sudden thudding between my ears blocked out his words.

How could one word set me off? *God, am I destined to be broken forever?* It seemed I was fated to screw up and live with the shame of every single decision and consequence for the rest of my days.

"Tara?"

I squinted at Sam.

Loki pressed against my leg and whined.

"What's your poison tonight?" Sam lifted a half-filled glass in his hand. When had he grabbed that?

"I ... ah." I rubbed Loki's soft fur and turned to Diana, widening my eyes. *Please help me out of this.*

Diana extricated herself from Jonathan's arms and leaned forward on the couch. "Weren't you doing a cleanse? Eating and drinking clean?"

Brilliant. "Yes, only juice or water at the moment." I *had* told Diana I would watch what I ate. A cleanse of sorts.

Sam snorted. "C'mon, you can't turn this down. Free quality alcohol from the Mixmaster himself. One small drink won't ruin your cleanse."

My mind clouded, my thoughts muddled in a hazy mix of whooshing blood and light-headedness.

Sam touched my arm and directed me toward the kitchen.

"I can't." My voice cracked.

"Don't be silly. You need to relax more." He tugged on my elbow.

"No." Not if I wanted to ease my overbearing daily-life-choices guilt.

Sam furrowed his brow and studied my face.

Something warm and wet stroked the back of my hand.

My chest seemed trapped in a vice. I gasped for oxygen.

"Leave it be," Jonathan said, his deep voice echoing around my fuzzy head.

My lungs burned. Not again. Where had the air gone?

"Just share some of your precious orange juice." Diana sounded like she stood in a tunnel with an oncoming train.

I pressed my hands to my temples and squeezed my eyes closed.

Someone pressed a warm hand on my shoulder.

The noise inside my brain crescendoed, and words tumbled from my mouth. "I'm pregnant!"

Something crashed onto the kitchen tiles.

The cacophony silenced, and oxygen filled my lungs. I sucked in mouthfuls of air, counted several breaths, and opened my eyes.

Keanu's unreadable gaze collided with mine.

No.

He fisted his hands at his sides, his hulking frame barely contained under the kitchen archway.

My stomach plummeted.

Loki whined again and rubbed his head against my thigh.

Sam hovered in my periphery, released my shoulder, and grabbed his dog by the collar. "I'm sorry I pushed you." He glanced behind me. "Did you both know?"

"Yes." Diana's voiced seemed unsteady.

I raised my chin and focused on the man in front of me. "I'd planned to tell you after work on Monday." *I'm sorry.*

Keanu's chest heaved.

What would I do once he fired me? My mouth dried.

"That why Smitty's been keeping tabs and calling?" Keanu's tone tremored. Was he angry?

"It's Smitty's baby?" Sam whispered.

I searched Keanu's face.

Unreadable eyes lacking their usual mischief. The tight line in his jaw.

My parched tongue velcroed to the roof of my mouth. *Please, help me, God.*

Ugh, I was getting sick of hearing my own desperate prayers.

Diana wrapped her arm around my shoulders and pressed to my right side, Jonathan appearing beside her.

"Isaac and …" I glanced at the Harrises before returning my gaze to Keanu. "We're going to make a go of it."

"You're dating Smitty?" Sam's voice sounded weird.

Keanu's eyes flashed, something in their depths fighting to break through. Hurt? Betrayal?

Diana's arm stiffened against my back.

I was screwing this up! Heat burned the backs of my eyes.

"Tar?" Sam touched my left shoulder.

I turned to him. "Yes. For the sake of the baby." Had I made the right decision? Or had I missed it? *Did I screw up, Jesus?*

Sam snuck a furtive glance at Keanu, nodded, and dropped his hand. "I hope it works out."

So do I. I turned back to Keanu.

He stepped closer, his palms unfurled and shoulders looser. "Y'okay?"

You still my friend? My boss? I nodded.

He rubbed his bearded chin and narrowed his eyes. "Might have to look into a new role at Benanu's when you're too pregnant to serve tables."

"I still have a job?" My vision blurred.

Keanu harrumphed. "Course."

"Thank you," I whispered.

"Nothing to thank me for. Any decent boss'd do the same."

Any decent boss. Not friend.

Diana shifted at my side. "Maybe we can start training Tar with the tasks I mentioned last week."

Keanu nodded. "Perfect solution."

Training me? "What's going on?"

"The local paper wants me to write a feature article focused on local business the alternating week to my fortnightly column." Diana beamed. "I'll be employed full-time and publish once a week, but the feature articles will take most of my time with research, et cetera."

I slid my arm around Diana's slim waist and hugged her. "That's awesome."

"I know! Now there's no excuse for you not to come into the office and help me plan and research."

Not this again.

"But for now, it seems you might need to learn and fill my cushy work-from-home gig with Keanu." Diana glanced at our boss.

I lowered my arms and stepped from Diana's embrace.

"Think yer qualified for the position?" Keanu's dark eyes searched my face before he cocked his head at Diana. "Although I suspect Dad'll want less work-from-home and more work-in-the-office time. Circumstances were unique while y'lived in Melbourne, and Dad's talked about expanding the role to a full-time position."

A full-time position?

"Really?" Diana's eyes widened.

"After you told me about needing to transition out over the next few months, he decided to share thoughts he's had about your role since day one." Keanu shrugged.

"Like what?" What was with me and words tumbling from my lips without my permission?

Keanu's eyes lightened. "More one-on-one time with me."

"Oh."

A soft smile slipped to his lips. Too small to accentuate the dimple in his chin. "Less accounts management now all the bugs are fixed and more hands-on work assisting me."

Hands-on work with Keanu. Oh boy.

Sam emitted an odd snorting-choking sound. What was his deal?

"Did you tell your mum yet?" Diana touched my shoulder.

Ugh. Boom-crash to reality. "As expected, it didn't go well."

Diana cringed. "She'll come around."

"Maybe." Hopefully before pigs flew.

"How about we prep some mocktails?" Sam eyed Keanu. "You said you had plenty of practise creating them?"

"Made my fair share while Ms. Burke—"

Diana snorted.

"Who?" I pulled a face.

"Mrs. J." Keanu growled. "How many years has she been married, and I'm still kicking the habit."

Diana chuckled. "I suspect Victoria secretly loves that you still see her as your favourite teacher."

"Did you have a crush on her?" I smirked.

Keanu eyes widened. "Wasn't like that. She … cared. Helped me when I struggled. Between her and Di, I made it to graduation."

"Wish I had teachers who cared as much at my school." I glanced at my friends and shrugged. "So … mocktails?"

"Any cravings?" Sam rubbed his hands together.

"Not yet."

"How about we let the boys sort it out." Diana gripped my hand and pulled me toward the couch.

Sam, Jonathan, and Keanu disappeared under the kitchen archway.

I flopped onto the nearest armchair. "Then we can perform the Infinity Gauntlet ceremony."

Diana lowered to the couch, snorting with laughter.

"Wake up, sleepyhead." Warmth engulfed my shoulder, eliciting tingles along my arm.

I blinked and stared up at Keanu—who leaned over me with his ginormous hand on my shoulder—from where I lay on Sam's comfortable couch. When had the movie ended?

"Sleep well?" He squatted in front of the couch, dropping his hand from my arm. His eyes regained some of the sparkle which had disappeared after my unfortunate baby reveal.

"What's the time?" My voice croaked.

"Early Sunday morning."

I glanced past him and spotted Jonathan scooping a sleeping Diana into his arms. "Did I miss much?"

"Last half of Spider-Man. Not sure how ya both slept through all that."

I pressed my palm over my mouth and yawned.

"Yer catching a ride with me." Keanu stood and clicked his neck from side to side.

Yes! No driving for me. I smiled at the perfect turn of events. Well, almost perfect. "But my car …"

"Need it in the morning?" He extended his hand to me.

I grasped his warm fingers and rose. "Nope." Thank God my little slice of life was within walking distance of all the important places.

"Sam and I'll drop it around sometime tomorrow afternoon." Keanu snatched my bag from the floor.

I nodded toward Jonathan and Sam, misstepped, and fell against Keanu. "Oops."

Keanu grunted, steadying me with his meaty fingers. His dark gaze connected with my eyes, their depths swirling with … something I struggled to read.

My heart jolted.

His eyes narrowed a margin before he slid his hands around and swept me into his strong, warm arms.

I sucked in a frantic breath and wrapped my arms around his neck.

Keanu turned to Sam and Jonathan. "See ya later."

Sam thrust the crocheted Infinity Gauntlet toward me. "Always a blast, Tara."

I yawned a chuckle.

Keanu strode toward the front door, accompanied by whispered farewells from our non-slumbering friends, and exited the house.

I shivered in the cool evening air. Autumn would be here soon.

"Cold?" He tucked his chin lower, his bristled beard brushing my arm.

"A little." I pressed closer to his expansive chest.

"My mighty white steed's just down the street." He motored along the footpath in the opposite direction to my car.

I smiled, conscious of the frisson of fresh goosebumps prickling my arms. The sooner this rider found his horse, the better.

Keanu stopped at his old ute several houses away, unlocked his clunker, and deposited me on the passenger seat.

I buckled and burrowed against the seat back, missing his warmth. Not that I should crave Keanu's warmth. Isaac should be the one carrying me and driving me home.

Keanu slipped into the driver's seat, handed me my tote bag, and removed his jacket. "Wanna give me yer car keys?"

Oh. Yes. "Sure." I rummaged through my bag and separated my car key from the other keys—some of which I had no idea what they unlocked. "Where'd you want it?"

He opened the small loose change drawer in the dashboard beside the cigarette lighter.

I dropped the key inside the drawer and slid it closed. "Thanks."

"No, thank you." The thought of driving my car again spun my insides in loops. I pushed the unpleasantness away and slouched in the seat.

Keanu covered me with his picnic-rug-sized jacket, his scent and body heat cocooning me.

"You don't need to do that." I breathed in lungfuls of deliciousness.

He rubbed his hands along his thick thighs, turned the ignition, and silenced the radio.

I stifled a yawn, my limbs heavy.

Keanu drove down the street, the rocky, bouncy movements lulling my eyelids shut.

"Tara."

I opened my eyes and spotted my bungalow. How had we arrived so soon?

Keanu chuckled, leaned forward to collect my pile of keys from the floor, and dropped them in my tote.

"Thanks." When had I dropped them?

"Gonna be home in the afternoon?"

"I think so, unless someone invites me out for lunch after church."

He grunted. "I'll slide y'key under the front door if need be."

I unbuckled, shifted toward the door, and lay his folded jacket on the edge of my seat near the gear stick. "Thank you for the lift home." *And thank You, God, for working this car thing out in my favour.*

"Anytime."

Anytime? I met his inscrutable gaze.

"I mean it."

I bit my lower lip. "I'm sorry I didn't get to tell you my news in the way I wanted."

"S'okay."

Was it really okay though?

Keanu rested his hand on his jacket. "Anytime you need anything, let me know. Okay?"

I pressed my lips together, sensing the importance of my response. "Okay."

The lines on Keanu's forehead disappeared.

I opened and closed the vehicle door with my bag clutched to my side, extracted my keys, and rushed into my little home.

CHAPTER SEVENTEEN
Appointments and Plans

"Enjoy the rest of your day." I stood near Benanu's point-of-sale computer—feet throbbing—and smiled at the delightful elderly couple who had tipped me twenty dollars. Not a bad little bonus for serving them less than an hour.

They waved, turned, and wandered through the main doors, hand in hand.

I glanced at the remaining patrons. Any chance the squabbling couple at table fifteen would tip me too? I huffed a breath. Probably not.

"Ready to take your break?" Isabelle stepped beside me and pointed to the time on the computer monitor.

"Didn't realise it was already mid-morning." I rubbed the back of my neck and wriggled my toes. How would I cope working on my feet in a month or two when I was already struggling? Diana blamed my tiredness on my petite frame carrying a growing child fathered by a taller-than-average man. But I knew better. Something had shifted after the horrific car ride to Sam's last weekend.

Isabelle touched my arm. "I'm sorry I didn't get you off your feet sooner, but Mr. Everton had a bunch of questions about certain procedures we do out here, and it seemed I was designated answerer to all things."

"It's okay. Really." I offered a weak smile, desperate to put my feet up for my fifteen-minute break.

"Hey! Excuse me!" The man at table fifteen waved his arms in the air, redness blotting his cheeks.

Oh boy.

Isabelle exhaled a loud breath, winked at me, and turned to our impatient customer.

I stepped toward the staff-only exit, my legs aching with each step.

Someone called my name.

I halted, sighed, and turned.

Isaac beamed at me near the entry in his hot cop uniform, arms raised. He jogged toward me and wrapped me in a quick hug. "Hey, sexy mumma," he whispered.

"Hey."

"Did I miss your break?" He eyed Isabelle working near my usual tables.

"Just started."

"Good." He grinned and grabbed my hand. "Let me order some takeaway coffees and sit with you while they make them."

We walked to an empty couch near the bar, and I lowered to the semi-comfortable seat, rubbing my back on my descent.

Isaac released my hand and strode to the bar. He chatted with the new guy—I should do the right thing and remember his name—chuckled, and tapped his credit card.

How could a man with a serious job and tragic past be so … cheerful?

He pocketed his wallet and stepped toward me with his usual happy demeanour.

I smiled up at him. "Exciting shift so far?"

"Don't ask." Isaac lowered beside me and wrapped his arm around my shoulder. "You look tired."

"I *am* tired." Worn out.

"Have you got the dates for those hospital midwife appointments you mentioned?" Isaac rubbed my shoulder and crept his fingers closer to my neck.

I slumped closer. "Yeah."

He brushed several hairs behind my ear, leaning nearer.

"Are you allowed to be affectionate in public?" I pursed my lips. "Aren't there rules about what an officer can and can't do in uniform?"

He waggled his eyebrows. "If we were making out on the couch like some X-rated movie, then, sure. It could be an issue. But, no, Victoria Police aren't strict like other branches of law enforcement." He brushed his lips across mine in a feathery kiss. "My pregnant girlfriend needs a little TLC, and who best to give it to her than the man of her dreams?"

Someone nearby cleared his throat.

I glanced up at Keanu, his hands deep in his pockets.

He furrowed his brow.

"She's on break, K-Man." Isaac chuckled, stood, and slapped Keanu's back. "Keeping busy?"

Keanu nodded and rubbed his beard. "Plenty to do around here."

Why did his voice sound tight?

"You looking after my girl?" Isaac winked at me.

Heat bloomed along my cheeks.

"Always." An uncharacteristic gravelly tone scraped Keanu's words.

I narrowed my eyes at my boss. What was wrong?

"Officer Smith!" The barista's voice travelled through the room.

Isaac bent, kissed my lips, and straightened. "Message me with the dates, and I'll see if I can make your appointments. Can't promise you I'll be at all, or any, really, but I'll do my best."

"Okay."

Isaac strode to the bar, collected the tray of coffees, and disappeared out the door.

"Everything okay?" Keanu's voice had lost its hardness.

"Was going to ask you the same thing." I stood and glanced at the clock. Eight minutes left.

"I'm fine." He thumbed in the direction of the staff-access doorway. "You going in?"

"Yep."

We followed the corridor to the empty staff kitchen. I sank onto one of the chairs at the table and lifted my feet onto another.

Keanu pushed the chair under my feet closer. "Better?"

"Thanks."

He grabbed a bottle of water from the fridge, opened the lid, and handed the drink to me. "I noticed you don't drive to work."

I sucked down half the bottle. Refreshing. "Never have."

He straddled a nearby chair and rested his arms on the seat back. His potent gaze searched mine. "I'd prefer it when the weather cools and the mornings get darker."

My pulse stuttered. No thank you. "I-I'll be fine."

"But I won't."

What did he mean?

"I'd feel better knowing yer safe in a car."

I huffed a laugh. "You wouldn't think that if …" I pressed my lips together.

"What?" He rubbed his chin. His eyes glowed with intensity.

"Nothing I can get into with a few minutes until my break is over." I closed my eyes and lowered my head against the firm seat back. Should I tell him? I needed to tell someone, and Keanu deserved to know what a messed-up employee I was.

"Tell me."

I lifted my eyelids and met his gaze. "I can't drive," I whispered.

"Can't?" He tilted his head.

I leaned forward. Heat burned in my lungs. "My head won't let me."

He studied me with pursed lips. "Anxiety again?"

Why did he remember everything Diana and I had told him?

"When the weather cools, I'll pick y'up."

"You don't need to—"

"It'll give me peace of mind."

I stared up at him, wondering why he cared so much, and nodded.

"What was this about appointments Smitty mentioned?"

"Baby check-ups at the hospital in Robinvale. And an antenatal class." I massaged my shins and gritted my teeth. I could work another few hours.

"Need a chauffeur?"

I scrunched my face. "You can't possibly be offering to be my beck-and-call boy."

"Why not?" Keanu's eyes twinkled. "Don't think my knightly steed can handle it?"

"You're extremely busy and needed here. I can't possibly expect you to add to your load to ease mine." I lowered my legs and stood with a soft groan.

He leaned back from the chair he straddled and crossed his arms. "I offered."

"But—"

"Nah uh. I told ya last weekend to ask for help. This's me offering when ya should've asked."

"I … just …" I tugged at the end of my short ponytail. Was this an answer to my prayers?

"Lemme help." His eyes softened like deep pools of chocolate fondue. "Please."

I stepped closer. "I'll forward you the dates after my shift." *Thank You, God, for being on my side and looking after me and the baby.*

"Don't forget." He pierced me with his penetrating gaze.

My stomach thrummed. Nothing about this moment seemed forgettable.

CHAPTER EIGHTEEN
Focus on the Family

"See you next time." I waved to the midwife, my arms laden with pamphlets and pregnancy information, and closed the hospital room door. Manoeuvring my phone from my back pocket, I switched it on and grinned when my phone beeped several times.

Keenie: HOW ABOUT BORIS? OR ENGELBERT?

Keenie: VLADIMIR? ARISTOTLE?

Keenie: GIRLS NAMES … DRUSILLA? AMORETTE?

Keanu had kept himself busy while I attended my appointment.

I snorted a laugh and ambled my six-months-pregnant self down the corridor. Sometime in the last month we had fallen into a funny routine of texting each other weird baby names.

Keanu sprang from the seat he occupied in the hospital waiting area and grabbed my papers. "How'd it go?"

I groaned. "That glucose tolerance test sucked."

He stacked the papers on top of his pile of files. "But you passed?"

"Yeah. No gestational diabetes for me." *Thank You, God!*

"Need to pee before we leave?" Keanu nodded toward the nearby ladies' bathroom.

"Might be better to be safe than sorry after drinking that gross drink." Frequent urination was not fun.

"I'll wait here."

I met his gaze. "I didn't expect you to stay the entire time with the extended appointment. You really didn't need to."

"I know." He gestured toward the bathroom.

I smiled and pushed past the heavy door, emptied my wussy bladder, and returned to my chauffeur. We headed to the hospital exit. "The midwife thinks everything's progressing well. I'm measuring a centimetre bigger than expected—"

"Twenty-nine centimetres?"

I halted and stared wide-eyed at him. "You really have been listening to me waffle about tummy measurements aligning with pregnancy weeks?"

"Course." He shrugged. "Helps me understand better and keep track."

Wow.

"And now it's the third trimester, appointments will happen more often?"

I squinted at Keanu. Who was this guy?

He stared at me several heartbeats before raising an eyebrow. "Yes."

We descended a flight of stairs—Keanu's warm hand pressed to my lower back with each step—and dodged a group of people in the corridor.

"Do y'have a decent moisturiser for the stretching skin?"

I glanced at my friend with wide eyes.

He stared ahead, keeping to his usual slower pace when he walked with me. "The pregnancy app says—"

"No way." I snorted a laugh. "You downloaded an app?" Not even Isaac had done anything this outrageous.

Keanu pushed open the door to the car park. "Apparently the stretched skin could get itchy. A moisturiser might help."

I nudged Keanu's side with my shoulder. "You're sweet, you know that?"

He grunted.

"But you're right. Victoria suggested a particular brand which she thinks helped reduce her stretch marks." I lowered my voice. "Not that it can stop the tiger claw lines already on my butt." Stupid stretch marks.

Keanu cleared his throat and ran his hand across his bearded chin. "We can get some on the way back if y'like?"

"Ow!" I stumbled against Keanu, yelped, and pressed my hand near my hip. Tiny kicks pummelled my insides.

He steadied my shoulder. "What happened?"

"Baby dearest is at it again." I grabbed Keanu's free hand and slipped it under my cardigan.

Keanu's fingers tensed under my touch before relaxing against my T-shirt over the spot where my little person practised drop punting my protruding stomach. A real little footballer in the making.

I held still, my heart thumping. "Sometimes the movements repeat and other times …"

Another kick thudded my stomach.

"Hah!" I grinned, my fingers tingling from the contact with Keanu's skin.

Keanu's breath hitched, his expressive eyes awash with wonder. "That's strong."

I pulled a face and huffed a breath. "The midwife says this is nothing compared to the coming months."

He opened his mouth and stared at me. What thoughts circled inside his head? Thoughts about me?

Stop it. I squeezed his big fingers and slipped my hand from atop his. "Isaac's still waiting to feel movement."

Keanu's throat bobbed. Once. Twice. "He hasn't felt this?" He removed his warm touch from my belly.

I shrugged and stepped toward the ute. "Once baby's bigger, movement will be easier to catch. Or so I've been told."

He unlocked and opened the passenger door.

I slipped into the cabin and checked the figurative lock on the rattling door of my heart. *Focus on your baby. Your family.*

We drove to Tellarine in relative silence, an unfortunate situation while my untrustworthy heart screamed for attention.

My phone chimed in my bag.

Mum's face surfaced in my mind, and my heart jolted. Had she replied to my "HAVE YOU FORGIVEN ME YET?" text I sent yesterday? Over a month without so much as a single emoji communicated.

I retrieved my phone with trembling hands, opened the message app, and sagged against the seat back. Not Mum.

Hot Cop: HOW WAS YOUR APPOINTMENT? JUST FINISHED MY SHIFT. FEEL LIKE GOING OUT? OR STAYING IN?

How thoughtful. I slid my fingertip over Isaac's message. A kind man set to be a wonderful father. The last month and a half with him had eased my anxiety. Our growing friendship—with kissing benefits—had settled me, and the frequency of my nightmares had decreased.

I gripped the phone tighter. Mum was wrong about Isaac. Despite not having told him about my past. But I would share my dark history soon because he was trustworthy. I had made the right choice taking a chance on sharing a future with him.

"Still want me to drop ya home?" Keanu's voice snapped me away from my thoughts.

I focused on my phone screen and pursed my lips. Go out? Stay in? Or go home? I reread Isaac's message. "Actually, could you drop me at Isaac's? Please?"

"No problem." He clicked his neck.

Had I imagined tautness in his voice?

"Thanks." I swiped a reply to Isaac.

Me: I'LL BE THERE IN ABOUT 10–15. CAN WE STAY IN? MAYBE WATCH A MOVIE? I'M A LITTLE TIRED AFTER TODAY'S TEST.

I shifted my legs and observed the familiar countryside outside the passenger window, the late-afternoon early-May sunshine dancing over passing shrubs. Mini me kicked near my bladder, and I suppressed a snort. Cheeky peanut.

Keanu switched on the radio to some awful local station with cringe-inducing hosts prattling about their lives instead of playing music. So much talking!

Music filled the cabin—finally!—and I closed my eyes. Keanu hummed off-key, the sound soothing in its normality. This was what people did every day without a second thought. Travelled in vehicles and listened to music. Thought about what to eat for dinner and what activity to do over the weekend. Not dwelling on the direction one's heartstrings were tugged or the whispers of their past trauma.

Normal people did normal things. And so did I.

I opened my eyes and straightened in the seat. Almost there. "Thanks again for today."

"Happy to help." Keanu slowed at the main T-intersection into town, and several minutes later, parked in Isaac's driveway. "Hope you have a good night."

"You too." I grabbed my bag.

"Don't forget the papers." He nodded to his pile of stuff at my feet.

"Oh yeah. Thanks." I extracted my paperwork, stuffed it into my bag, and opened the door.

"I'll pick ya up bright and early tomorrow for more training."

He tapped the steering wheel with his large palm.

"Thank you. Bye." My chest warmed. I padded along the driveway and knocked on Isaac's front door. How indebted was I to Keanu for ferrying me to and from work, training me in the office, and taking time out of his hectic schedule to support my pregnancy-related appointments? Was his selflessness without bounds?

Isaac opened the door, waved to Keanu, and pulled me inside.

I slammed against his chest and gasped.

He wrapped his arms around my waist and steadied me. "Aren't you a sight for sore eyes."

A sight for sore eyes? We had spent the afternoon and evening together only four days ago.

Isaac's gaze dropped to my lips and travelled farther south.

The image of Keanu tapping his large, capable hands on the wheel of his beloved rust bucket brightened inside my mind, pinning itself to the top of my memories.

Isaac lowered his head, puffing hot breaths against my skin.

How could I extract Keanu's handsome face from my mind?

My boyfriend suctioned his warm mouth to the side of my neck.

My boyfriend. *Get it together!* "Uh … Isaac?"

He slid his lips up my neck and nibbled my earlobe. "Hmm?"

I tilted my head away, wriggled from his grip, and pressed my palms against his firm chest. "It's been a tiring afternoon. Think we can just … take it easy on the couch and watch a movie or something?"

"Sorry. I wasn't thinking of anything but your gorgeous face." He glanced at my feet before grabbing my hand and escorting me to the couch piled high with what looked akin to a pillow fort. "Get comfy while I finish preparing dinner."

I slipped off my shoes and flopped onto the couch, repositioning cushions to support my back and my pulsating feet.

"Want a drink?" Isaac rearranged a cushion behind my head.

"That's better, thanks. No drink for now. I feel like I've consumed enough liquid for the next few days."

He chuckled and loosely tucked my feet under a blanket. "But the test went okay?"

"Yeah. No problems."

"Great." He grabbed the TV remote from an armchair and placed it on my thigh. "There're a few movies on Amazon Prime I added to the list a few days ago, plus our growing Netflix list. If nothing piques your interest, pick whatever you feel like."

"No worries."

Isaac bent and kissed my forehead. "We should also make a time to start a name list. Won't be long before junior's here needing it."

Baby names? I grimaced. Was I up to the task of naming a living, breathing creation made in God's image?

Isaac smirked and disappeared through the archway.

I grasped the remote and enabled the TV, determined to make this life with Isaac work.

CHAPTER NINETEEN
Unexpected Offers

A week later, Diana tugged me through the chiming doorway of The Tella Tribune's ancient glass-fronted premises the local newspaper had occupied for decades. "Come on, you won't regret it."

"I already regret it," I mumbled and jerked my hand from her grasp, eyeing the smaller-than-expected office space. Five mismatched, chipped woodgrain-and-metal desks filled the open-plan space beside a glass-walled cubicle. Three people typed at their laptops, lifting their heads to nod at Diana and stare at me.

My friend waved at her colleagues, caught my gaze, and pointed toward the empty desk. "I'll find another chair for you, but first"—she gestured to the fish-bowl-like office—"I want to introduce you to Roger."

"It's really not necessary."

She linked her arm with mine and knocked on the closed office door.

"C'min!" A deep voice resounded through the closed wooden door.

Diana dragged me into the office and shut the door behind her.

"Di." A crotchety-looking middle-aged man in a wrinkled white shirt and loosened tie scrunched his bushy grey eyebrows together and aimed his piercing brown eyes at me.

"Roger, this is Tara Roberts." Diana nudged me closer to his mammoth oak desk strewn with documents, overflowing filing trays, a computer monitor, and a laptop plonked atop more papers.

"Nice to meet you at last, Tara." Roger stood and extended his arm, his shirt cuffs rolled to his elbows.

"Hi." I reached over the mound of murdered trees and shook his hand. "It's nice to finally see this place."

Roger rumbled a laugh and clicked his mouse—or what I assumed was a computer mouse from the sound behind the wall of paper—while glancing at a third monitor I had missed altogether. How could one desk house so much stuff?

Diana snuck glances between me and her boss.

Roger huffed a breath, clicked a dozen times, and slipped out from behind his desk. "Let's go out for coffee before I throttle Mackenzie."

I raised a brow at my friend. Was she in the habit of going out for coffee with her boss?

Diana widened her eyes and shrugged. "Uh, sure."

Maybe not.

"Good." Roger fossicked through the pile on the corner of his desk, pocketed his phone and keys, and charged out of his office.

Diana startled and strode from the room.

I ambled behind her.

"I'll be back in an hour. Spencer, submit your ideas before I return. And ignore all calls from Mackenzie. If he steps through that door"—he stabbed a finger toward the entry—"tell him to leave before I return, or I'll rip his throat out."

I suppressed a laugh.

A chorus of "yes, sir" filtered through the cramped space.

Roger grunted. "Harris. Roberts. On your bike." He stormed from the building.

A lanky skinhead with a beard eyed Diana. "My commiserations. You better get going."

She pulled my arm and yanked me out the door.

"Where're we going?" I searched the empty footpath and nearby cars. Where had Roger disappeared to?

"Either the bakery with subpar coffee or Benanu's." Diana retrieved her phone from her back pocket. "I'll call hi—"

"You coming?" Roger's gruff voice echoed from the edge of the building along the pavement, keys tinkling between his fingers.

"Bakery or Benanu's?" Diana approached her boss.

I trailed behind and noticed a four-wheel-drive vehicle parked in the alleyway.

He wrinkled his ungroomed brows. "What'll make me want to

kill Mackenzie less?"

"Benanu's," Diana and I said.

Roger rounded the vehicle. "Need a lift?"

Diana shook her head. "My car's just around the corner."

I nodded to Roger, hurried with Diana to her car, and travelled to work. "And on my day off too."

Diana parked and unbuckled. "Roger's a bit … volatile at times. So I try to stay in the good books, and if that means having coffee …?" She shrugged.

"Then let's have coffee." I laughed and wandered indoors with my friend.

The restaurant was a little noisy but to be expected for a Friday afternoon. We examined the available tables.

Roger approached us from the entryway. "Found a table?"

"Let me sort it out." I stepped around the bustling dining area and squinted at the back end nearer the pool tables.

"Looking for something?" Isabelle bumped my shoulder.

I grinned. "Got a quiet spot for three?"

She searched the room and pointed to table forty-seven. "That's your best shot."

"Thanks." I gestured for Diana and slipped into the chair, thankful to be off my feet again.

Diana seized the seat beside me, and her boss lowered to the chair opposite.

"My shout." Roger grabbed the menu and cracked it open.

I turned and widened my eyes at my friend.

"So, ah, Roger." Diana clasped her hands together. "Was there anything … in particular … you wanted to chat to us about?"

Isabelle ambled close and flashed a bright smile. "Afternoon. Can I help you with anything?"

"I skipped lunch." Roger tilted his head and glanced at our server. "Got something light to recommend?"

"Light like a salad?"

He wrinkled his nose.

"A quiche or—"

"The crumbed chicken tenders and wedges will do." Roger tucked the menu away.

I suppressed a smirk. Light indeed.

"Anything else?" Isabelle asked.

"A double shot espresso." Roger turned to Diana and me. "Ladies?"

"Hot chocolate, Diana?" Isabelle raised an eyebrow.

"You know me too well." Diana shifted on her seat, smiling.

Isabelle turned to me. "And peppermint tea? With a biscuit?"

"Ooh, could I have a biscuit too please?" Diana raised her hand.

"Done." Isabelle strode away.

Roger leaned back in his seat, loosened his tie further, and crossed his arms. He scrutinised my face. "Di's told me a lot about you and sent me some of the articles you wrote at RMIT."

I whipped my gaze to my friend. She had?

"You've a clear, relatable voice."

I blinked. "Ah. Th-thank you."

"There's room for improvement, but that can be said for any journalist, author, copy editor"—he gesticulated with a swipe of his hand—"screenwriter, poet, or lyricist at every stage of our careers."

"I agree." My voice squeaked.

Diana snuffled beside me.

"I think you'd be an asset on the Tribune team."

Was he offering me a job? I glanced at my expanding stomach.

Roger leaned forward. "When's the bundle due?"

"End of July." I rested a hand on the table. "I appreciate the offer, but I'm not sure how easily I could fit another role in my life at the moment."

"No rush. We'd start you off small like Di and go from there." He rubbed his jaw. "A bigger opportunity might present itself if I murder Mackenzie," he muttered.

Isabelle swooped in and lowered a tray with two bowls of fried food, a small plate with a selection of biscuits and cookies, and three mugs of steaming beverages.

Moments later, I nibbled a shortbread with orange zest and sipped my hot tea.

"Have at it." Roger stuffed a wedge in his mouth and chewed.

"When would you need an answer from Tara?" Diana grabbed a chicken tender and dipped it in honey mustard sauce.

Oh yeah, the job offer. I flicked biscuit crumbs from my fingers and eyed Diana's boss.

"It's"—he glanced at his watch—"May fifth. How about you let me know by the end of the month. Mid-June at the latest."

"And what exactly are you envisioning I'd do?" I sipped another mouthful of perfectly brewed peppermint.

"What do you believe you could offer the team?" He sculled his espresso in one long swig.

The man must have an asbestos-lined throat.

"What do you see as your strengths?" Roger's intense eyes focused on my face.

I clutched my mug between my hands and rested my wrists against the table edge. "I discovered the joy of research in my final eighteen months of uni." When I had struggled despite lying to Diana that I had no second thoughts and had encouraged her to stick with it.

Yes, I had lied to my friend.

"Diana said as much." Roger chomped on a chicken tender.

"I enjoy my current job, and with the baby making a grand entrance in under three months, I don't want to overcommit."

"The pay's garbage, but the experience will keep your options open." Roger brushed his chin and shrugged. "Motherhood isn't the end of the world. You're young and should keep your career options open."

Mum had to believe otherwise, or she would be talking to me again.

Diana lowered her almost empty mug. "I can go over some things I've worked on to give Tara a better idea of what to expect."

"Good idea." He shovelled another wedge in his face and checked his watch again. "I need to stop by the Bottle-O, so I'm shoving off."

I smirked at Diana.

"You planning to work at the office?" Roger stood and stuffed in a final carb-loaded mouthful.

Diana gestured to a passing server, what's-his-name. "I can go back—"

"Don't bother." Roger waved his hand in the air. "It's Friday afternoon. Take the rest of the afternoon off."

What's-his-name approached our table. "How can I help you, Diana?"

"Dominic, would you please be so kind as to assist Mr. Fulton with the bill?"

Dominic!

"Of course." Dominic stepped back and motioned toward the point-of-sale kiosk. "Follow me."

"Ladies." Roger nodded and followed Dominic away from our table.

"So?" Diana bumped my shoulder with her own. "What do you think? Tell me what's going through that brain of yours."

I pointed to the last chicken tender. "Want it?"

Diana shook her head.

I bit into the cooled protein, my mind whirring with jumbled thoughts. Could I keep my foot in the door and work with the Tribune team? Was I brave enough to try? My baby required me to think about job security, and peanuts for pay was far from secure. But the connections within the industry would be priceless ... *if* I wanted to embark down this road.

"Well?" Diana stacked the empty bowls together.

"Honestly? I'm not sure. This offer's come as a surprise."

"I'm sure it has."

"I'll have to think about it." And pray.

She turned to face me. "*I* know you have a wonderful work ethic and skillset perfect for the paper ... but do *you* believe it?"

I shrugged.

Diana touched my arm. "I'll be praying for you."

"Thanks."

"Where to now?" She slid her phone from her pocket. "Jonathan won't be home for another hour. What about Isaac?"

"I'm a little foggy on his timetable." Awful-girlfriend alert. I located my phone and checked my text messages.

Keenie: DORCAS? RADDIX?

I pressed away a smile.

Hot Cop: CALL ME WHEN YOU CAN.

"I can drive you home if you like?"

I flashed my phone screen. "Isaac wants me to call."

"Want me to leave?"

"Nah." I dialled Isaac's number.

"Hey, sexy. Where're you at?" Shuffling sounds muffled Isaac's end of the line.

"Benanu's with Diana."

"Perfect. I'll be there in a few." The line disconnected.

I stared at my phone screen.

"That was quick." Diana pocketed her phone.

"He'll be here soon, so …" I shrugged.

"Is everything okay?" Diana tilted her head and creased her brow.

Apart from the unexpected pregnancy, an upset mother, the potential life-changing job offer, and the pull between two doting men, things were peachy.

"You know you can talk to me, right?" The grooves in Diana's forehead deepened.

"I know." I huffed a long breath. "It's just … sometimes I wonder if I've made the right decisions. I mean"—I brandished my hand over my belly—"clearly I've screwed up some things, but … am I screwing up more? Will I continue to mess things up?"

Diana rested her hand over mine. "Lean on Jesus to help you make the right decisions. Don't choose a particular path out of obligation or because it seems right to your logic. Good choices are fine, but God choices are better."

I rubbed my domed stomach and nodded.

"Afternoon, ladies." Isaac flopped on the seat opposite us in his police uniform.

"Smitty. I was just heading off." Diana squeezed my hand and stood. "Are you going to the men's night at church with Jonathan next week?"

Isaac scrubbed a hand through his short-cropped hair. "Hoping to."

A tiny shard chipped off the burden weighing against my chest.

"That's great to hear. Maybe we'll see you at church on Sunday?" Diana winked at me.

"Maybe." Isaac chuckled.

Diana waved and disappeared.

Isaac leaned across the table and clasped my hand.

"Just finished your shift?"

"Yeah. Want to get out of here? I have enough leftover lasagne for the both of us."

Mmm, lasagne. My mouth watered.

Isaac smirked. "You dreaming about lasagne now?"

"It's possible."

He barked a relaxed laugh.

"Okay, you talked me into it." I tugged my hand from

underneath his and grabbed my bag.

♥ ♥ ♥ ♥ ♥ ♥ ♥

I groaned beside Isaac on his couch. "Now my food and human babies are duelling for prime real estate."

Isaac laughed and shook his head. "You're so much fun." He pulled me against his side, kissed my temple, and snuggled close.

I relaxed into his warmth.

"Do you think about the future?"

I huffed a laugh. "Pretty sure that's all I do every day … think about my future."

"I know it must be getting crowded in your mind, what with the baby, all the new things you're learning at work, and now today's job opportunity." He swirled his thumb across my knuckles. "But what about us? Have you thought of things becoming more… permanent?"

I stilled. "How so?"

He grazed his fingers along the back of my hand. Slow, calming strokes. "Marriage?"

Marriage?

"Not the casual Friday night conversation you were expecting, hey?"

"Not really." I cracked a small smile.

Isaac shifted and turned me to face him. "But you see the merit of marriage, can't you? Stability for you and the baby, a united partnership as parents."

Stability and unity, two of my "hot buttons." If we married, Isaac's job could sustain all of our financial needs and allow me leeway to pursue journalism. Or any career path I wanted. And a united front? Having lived my entire life in a single-parent household, the idea of blessing my child—and future children, God willing—with two parents sent giddy shivers across my chest. But marriage seemed so … adult. Grown up. Was I ready for such a monumental decision?

"And let's not forget a lifetime of wild, satiating sex." Isaac waggled his eyebrows.

Talk about incentivising my decision! Oh, Lord, have mercy on my weak soul. I dropped my gaze, desperate to hide the blush heating my face. *Chill your beans, woman.*

The therapist had been right, and my sex drive had reignited. I craved the freedom to express myself within a safe, satisfying sexual relationship. But what about my promise to myself and God to marry a man who held the same values as me? A relationship with a Christian guy—or *any* guy—had seemed unreachable back when I declared my intent. A pipe dream of sorts. But was it possible now? With Isaac? I needed to know where he was, if at all, on his walk with Christ, although I hated to come across as pressuring him.

No one entered heaven on someone else's hope.

Isaac lifted my chin and met my gaze. "What's concerning you?

I stared into his green eyes.

"Is this about church? And God?" He brushed his thumb along my jaw.

I nodded.

"Thought so." He dropped his hand and sighed. "I get that Christianity's a big part of who you are now, and I'm all for raising our kid with Christian values, but I also don't want to pretend I'm crazy for Jesus when I'm not."

I widened my eyes. "I don't want you to fake it either. I just want to partner with a man willing to be open to the Gospel and the amazing love of God."

Isaac relaxed his shoulders. "I'm glad. I appreciate your authentic faith, even with life's ups and downs, and the genuineness of the people at your church."

I clasped his fingers between mine.

"Just give me time to acclimatise. Okay?"

"Of course. I want Jesus to be real for you like He is for me." Isaac's life would be revolutionised if he allowed Jesus in his life and heart. I just knew it.

"Cool." Isaac focused his green eyes—now flickering a deeper shade—on me. "Then does this change how you feel about marriage?"

If I knew Isaac was serious about making an effort to allow God into his life, would I be willing to choose him as my life-long husband?

Dark, mischievous eyes shining underneath a mop of black-brown hair infiltrated my mind. *No. Isaac is the man on offer.* I flexed my fingers. My heart was a terrible instrument to gauge. An untrustworthy organ, with a history of lusting after unsuitable or unobtainable men. I closed my eyes and squeezed Keanu's image away.

"You don't need to answer me straight away."

I opened my eyes and met Isaac's tender gaze.

"Just think about it. Okay?"

I nodded.

He smiled, reached across me, and grabbed the TV remote. "A movie or an episode before I drive you home?"

"Either." I leaned back and settled against his chest.

"Hey, isn't it your birthday at the end of the month? May twenty-ninth?" He navigated the Netflix menu.

"Di tell you?"

Isaac chuckled. "So I'm right?"

I huffed a breath. "Yeah. Haven't really thought about it, what with everything going on."

He selected an M-rated heist comedy film. "This okay?"

I scanned the screen details and eyed the actor list. "Looks good. Several A-grade actors." And little potential for on-screen sex, unless sleeping with someone as a distraction was part of the plot. Unlikely.

"Awesome. I watched it when it came out a decade ago, but I've forgotten most of it. Unlike your birthday." Isaac's warm breath fluttered across my ear.

Tingles danced along my skin and down my neck.

"I'm taking you out somewhere nice." He gathered my hair, brushing his fingers along my heated skin, and skated his hot lips along the nape of my neck.

My heartbeat thundered, and my breaths laboured.

"Maybe we'll celebrate our engagement too?" His gravelly voice and open-mouthed kisses elicited another layer of goosebumps.

I stifled a moan. "Maybe," I whispered.

"Maybe gives a man hope." He planted a final kiss behind my ear, reclaimed the TV remote, and pressed Play.

I shuddered a breath. *God help me.*

CHAPTER TWENTY
S.O.S.

"What about Gertrude? Or Murgatroyd?" I fiddled with my phone in my lap and shifted against Keanu's passenger seat. Anything to keep my mind off what I had to do.

Keanu parked his ute and pulled the hand brake. "Y'wanna be screaming one of those names down the road when playtime's over?"

"Not really."

He reached across the cabin and engulfed my jittery hands—still holding my phone—with his huge, warm paw. "Y'sure about this?" His dark eyes mirrored the dubious thoughts flitting about my brain.

"Certain." Almost.

He glanced through the windscreen at the large parkland abutting Tellarine Cemetery and pulled his hand away. "I'm still not comfortable dropping—"

"Keenie." I crooned his nickname, just like his mother. Finally, an appropriate moment to use it!

"Don't." His tone dropped low. Dangerous.

I repressed a grin.

"Show me yer phone." Keanu reached out, palm up.

What? "Why?"

He narrowed his eyes, glanced between his hand and my phone, and crooked his fingers. "Now."

"Ugh, don't chuck a wobbly." I slammed my phone against his palm.

Keanu lit up my phone's home screen. "Eighty percent battery remaining. I s'pose—"

"I'm not going bushwalking. Just a small walk to"—I indicated a deserted wooden bench two hundred metres away—"the seat so I have fresh air and privacy for this conversation."

"I can wait."

I shook my head. "It's a ten-minute walk home. I'll be fine."

He leaned closer to his car door and squinted, eyes surveying the partly-cloudy mid-May sky. "Call me if it rains."

I huffed. "Okay, I promise. Can I go now?"

He straightened, turned to me, and grunted.

I grinned, pecked his cheek, and escaped the rust bucket. "Thanks for the lift!"

"Anytime."

I shoved the creaky passenger door closed, pulled my parka around my swelling belly, and ambled across the dewy grass on springy legs. A soft prayer trailed from my lips, my foamy insides spiralling into turbulent territory.

Would Mum answer my phone call?

I grafted myself onto the bench seat—my back to the car park in case Keanu broke his word and waited—whispered another prayer, and dialled her number.

The phone seemed to ring for minutes.

"Tara." Mum's tone was polite but cool.

"Hey. Mum. Long time, no see." Could I sound more awkward? I cleared my throat and wiggled on the hard surface. My butt would pay penance later this afternoon.

"How's—"

"How're you doing?" I snorted a laugh. "Sorry, didn't mean to talk over you."

"That's okay, love." A smile edged her voice. "So, how're you doing? How's, ah, the baby? You're … how many weeks now?"

"Thirty weeks tomorrow."

"Thirty. Wow."

"Yeah."

The sun disappeared behind a cloud and cooled the air. A sudden breeze disturbed nearby shrubbery and eucalyptus trees and chilled my ankles and neck. I shivered. Stupid ankle socks! I fumbled with the handset and pulled up my parka collar, Elvis style.

Help me say the right words, God.

"I was hoping to chat to you about something." My insides

spasmed, and I pressed a palm to my torso mound. I had survived telling her about the baby, so I could endure this conversation.

"Oh?" Trepidation vibrated Mum's words.

"Isaac and I had dinner a few nights ago. And he … well. He brought up the topic of … marriage."

Air blustered on the other end of the phone line.

"I've been thinking about it. Praying too. And it seems like it might work."

The leaves rustled in the trees, swaying in time to the thudding between my ears.

"Wh-what do you think?" Would Mum support my decision?

"You're seeking my opinion?" Mum's voice tightened. "Or are you just placating an old woman?"

"I'd hardly call forty-three old. But, no, this is a genuine request. I'd like to know what you think."

"I'm not sure you do, love."

"Of course, I do."

She sighed. "Can I be honest?"

"Please." I studied a willie wagtail darting across the grass, foraging and whipping its long, feathered tail.

"The first thought to cross my mind was that abortion's still possible after twenty-four weeks, but more complex to qualify for the right."

I sucked in a breath and clutched my phone tighter. *Pretend Mum never spoke.*

"I know you didn't want to hear that, but—"

"You're right, I didn't." I clenched my teeth and slowed my breaths.

"I wanted to be honest." Mum sniffed.

I relaxed my jaw and fingers.

"If you insist on having the baby, why not consider adoption?" Adoption?

"It's an honourable alternative, what with increased infertility these days. Your child would be given a happy life with a family desperate to parent them."

"Don't you think I'm capable of raising a child?" I gripped the aged wooden seat with my free hand, stinging my fingernails.

Another sigh. "I think you'd be a great mother."

"Then why're you so against this?" Pain lanced my temples.

"I just don't want to see you struggle like I did. One day, when you're older and found the right man, you could start a fam—"

"But I've found a man, Mum. A man willing to marry me." A wonderful, sweet man.

"Do you love him?"

No. "Does that matter? Many happy marriages have started with less affection than Isaac and I share."

"But why add more pressure to yourself? Why're you so determined to keep this baby *and* the man?" Mum's tone increased with each word.

"What's wrong with wanting to raise my child with his or her father?" My young, innocent, fatherless heart had once yearned for a similar upbringing.

"Plenty of people successfully raise their children in separate homes! Be reasonable, Tara. Parenting's serious business." Mum's matter-of-fact words sliced my heart.

I launched from the bench seat, pressed my toes against my shoe soles, and paced the nearby grass.

"You need to be level-headed, not sentimental."

"Like you? Parent alone without an ounce of sentiment? Teach my child that men are unnecessary sectors of society best left alone?" I kicked against the soft, grassy earth.

"I think you're exaggerating a little, love."

"You moulded me into that dysfunctional girl who secretly craved the attention of men because they fascinated me." No way would I do the same to my child.

"You can't be serious!" Mum laughed, her caustic tone grating on my ears. "You had a good childhood."

"I did. But I also wanted a father." Or a man who would love me.

"Men aren't worth the heartache they leave behind."

I stilled. "What happened with my father?" Would I get an answer at long last?

Mum growled.

Uh oh.

"He was an insignificant, ill-thought, one-night stand."

"Ill-thought?" My throat croaked. "Because you ended up stuck with me?"

"I was nineteen. Think how you'd have responded in my shoes.

A humble country girl, pregnant and unattached. I was young and didn't know how to access any available services other than to birth the baby, but if I'd known how to access an abortion, I might've done it."

An explosion of fire and ice fragmented my insides, and I gasped. Did she understand how devastating—how humiliating!—this was for me, her unwanted baby?

"Do you remember Joe? He lived with us for a few months when you were five or six."

My legs trembled. I clutched the phone and lowered to the wooden bench. *Focus on Mum's words, not your own heartbreak.* "Uh. I—"

"I thought myself in love with him." She chuckled bitterly. "And for the three months he lived with us, I was happy. Content."

I turned and peered in the direction of the cemetery. Muttering a prayer, I furrowed my brow and strained to remember the last man in Mum's life. I recalled a young guy with kind blue eyes and sandy hair who had stayed with us. Images of my old tree house trickled to memory. "Did he build me the tree house?"

"Yeah." Something rustled on Mum's end of the phone call. "And then he left without a trace."

What?

"He was just after what little money I had."

"I'm sorry to hear," I whispered.

"I thought I was wiser, but I was still a fool. He encouraged me to get a new car—the car loan in my name—and several other big-ticket items. He'd give me cash for small down payments, but when purchase or loan time came, I was the idiot at the store signing my life away."

I glanced at the car park, slouched forward, and wrapped my free arm around my waist. I wished Keanu had defied me and stayed. *Not that you should rely on him when contemplating marriage to another man.*

"Then one afternoon I came home from work before collecting you from the after-school sitter, and the fridge, washing machine, and dryer were gone. So was my new queen-sized bed and matching bedroom furniture. All that remained in my bedroom was a heap of clothing he'd emptied from the missing drawers."

My throat constricted. "Mum," I whispered.

"I'd extended the sitter because I wanted to come home and surprise Joe with my news."

"What news?" I closed my eyes. Could Mum's story get any worse?

"I was pregnant."

I had a sibling? Oxygen escaped me, setting my lungs on fire. I straightened and focused on breathing.

"The good-for-nothing scumbag had also emptied my bank account, leaving me in a horrible financial mess for years. What hope did I have working a low-paying admin job with a kid, no savings, a new car loan I couldn't afford, and payments on whitegoods I no longer possessed?" Mum cursed. "And a pregnancy on top of it all."

My head spun. "I-I don't understand. Wh-what happened? I don't remember anything."

"I shielded you as best as I could. That's when I started sleeping with you in your single bed. Remember our extended winter sleepover?"

That was the reason for her unusual affection? A robbery? I had loved snuggling with Mum during the cold, wintry nights.

"A work friend helped me sell the new car and move to a smaller rental."

I scrunched my brow. "Wonder why he didn't take the car?"

"Too easy to track."

Oh. "Was that the granny flat we lived in for a few years?"

"Yeah."

"And the baby?" I choked down the lump in my throat. Did she abort my sibling like I did my eldest child?

Mum huffed a long breath. "A lady at the pub where I had picked up weekend work shifts passed along some information for a sympathetic doctor. The abortion laws were stringent back then, but with my mental, emotional, and financial stress, she figured I'd qualify."

I thumbed away wetness from my cheeks. "So you got rid of your unwanted, inconvenient child." Just like she would have done to me.

"I was sorry to abort that pregnancy because you would've been a great big sister. But to keep Joe's baby would've twisted the knife in my chest every day for the rest of my life. If I lived much longer.

I was losing my mind, and the doctor believed an abortion was necessary to preserve my wellbeing. Mental health was just starting to become recognised back then. In order to mother you, I had to get rid of it."

"Him or her," I whispered.

Mum cleared her throat. "That's why I want you to seriously consider your options. You're better off as a single parent, but the child might enjoy a higher quality of life with another family. Adoption's a good option."

I tapped my feet against the hard ground. "I can offer a good family home with Isaac."

"You think you can, but do you know him well enough? I thought I could with Joe, but look what happened."

"I know it'd be better for my baby to have his or her father and mother involved in their life." That much I *did* know.

"Think what you like, but that wasn't the case for you as a child. You'd have had more issues if any of the men I dated back then had stuck around."

"Or maybe you just needed to prioritise my need for a father figure and find nicer, more trustworthy country boys to date." How many years had I longed to talk or complain about my dad like the other girls at school?

"You've no idea what you needed." Steel threaded Mum's voice.

"'Cause you're always right, hey, Mum?" I ground my molars.

"When it comes to you, yes. I'm your mother."

"And I'm this child's mother." I exhaled a breath and stood, my thighs tense. "So I'll make the decisions for baby and me."

"Fine," Mum whispered. "Then I don't see the point of this conversation."

"You don't. You've missed it completely. That a girl sometimes wants her mum to care for her and not try to decide everything for her." I swiped my hand across my face, focusing on the calming outdoor sounds. "I love you, Mum. Call me when you're ready to meet Isaac."

The frequent rustle of tree leaves was my sole companion.

I whispered my farewell and ended the call. Not how I had imagined our conversation would go. Next time I had a serious decision to make, I would call someone inclined to build me up and support me.

I opened my message app and selected my conversation thread with Diana.

Me: Are you home tonight?

Despite knowing my friend disagreed with abortion and thought it best to date Christians, she still supported me. Prayed with me. Loved me.

Di-Di: Yeah, hubby dearest was called in for a shift. Pick you up for dinner and a sleepover?

Me: Perfect.

A small, cold raindrop kissed my cheek. I wrapped my parka around my unsteady frame, pocketed my phone, and waddled home.

"Sure you don't mind? I just need to collect my USB stick and drop something off quickly for Roger." Diana glanced between her side and rear-view mirrors and reversed onto the road outside the Arbys'.

"I don't mind stopping. Really." So long as no one at the Tribune asked for my decision yet. I needed to nut out my life before I lost control. Was this how Mum had felt when her world had imploded?

"Thanks." Diana drove the short distance to her favourite parking space near her workplace and pulled the hand brake.

I located my phone from my tote bag.

She unbuckled, grabbed her laptop bag, and waited. "You coming?"

I held my seat belt buckle. "If you want?"

"Yes, come in!" Diana exited the car and opened my door. "Need help, preggoes?"

"I'm not elephant-sized yet." I looped my bag over my shoulder.

"You won't get that big." Diana extended her arm and grasped my fingers.

I stood with her help. "Isaac's not a huge guy."

"Even if you had"—she looped her arm through mine—"a baby with Keanu's genes, for instance, you'd still be fine. I mean, look at Victoria. She's a little bigger than you and has popped out two huge

Jacobsen babies!"

I forced a laugh and travelled the footpath with Diana while constraining my mind from dwelling on babies with her dad's DNA. Fictitious babies resembling Mr. Ormond. Would I ever tell Diana that her dad was a trigger for me?

Probably not.

We entered the premises and the overhead bell jangled. I guessed news people disliked surprises.

I followed Diana to her desk where she rummaged inside a drawer.

"There you are!" She clutched the flash drive like a medal winner at the Logies. "Want to wait here?"

I flopped onto her too-firm swivel desk chair.

Diana dumped her laptop bag and gathered a few papers from her almost-bare desk, a stark contrast to her boss. "Be right back. Amuse yourself." She strode across the small room, knocked on Roger's office door, and disappeared inside his fish bowl office.

I clutched my bag to my chest, rotated in the chair, and surveyed the quiet room. So this was what a local newspaper looked like at five o'clock on a Wednesday.

A blond guy I recognised from my brief visit last week—I guessed not the infamous Mackenzie—typed at his laptop, gaze glued to the screen. The other desks were unoccupied, but the closest table held a laptop with its screen illuminated.

I peeped around the room, lowered my tote to Diana's desk, and rolled closer to the luminous laptop. A freeing, almost-giddy shot of bubbles burst inside my chest. Oh boy, I needed to get out more.

I leaned nearer and squinted at the screen. Huh? I stumbled across several words before eying a semi-familiar face. Was that—

"Spencer!" Roger boomed through his glass cage.

I startled and steadied myself against the chair.

A heavy-set, dark-haired guy wearing a chequered shirt and jeans barrelled around the corner and opened Roger's door. "Boss?"

Roger's deep tone reverberated, but his words were too soft for me to hear.

Spencer clutched the door handle, nodding. "I'm working on it but was copying the—"

"We've a connection you've not utilised! Standing right here!" Roger's voice rang clear and loud.

I winced.

The guy at the other desk grimaced and hissed through his teeth.

"Can we chat tomorrow morning, Di?" Spencer leaned farther into the room.

I strained to hear her response. What was this all about?

"Done. Now go away," said Roger.

Spencer closed the door and turned.

I leaned away from what I assumed was his desk and smiled. "Tough gig."

Spencer widened his eyes and occupied his seat. "It's a huge break for me, though. I had no idea Di was connected." He turned toward the other man. "Did you?"

The blond guy raised a brow. "Black Dagger?"

Black Dagger?

My lungs seized, and I clawed the edge of Diana's desk for support.

Spencer nodded. "Not sure of her connection, but I'd be interested in her thoughts about the guy up for parole."

What guy was up for parole? Was it … *him*? My chest burned, desperate for oxygen. I gripped the desk tighter and whispered a prayer.

I'll never forget you, my beautiful whore.

Days after the verdict Mum had said he would serve a seventeen-and-a-half-year non-parole period. I squeezed my eyes shut. Had she miscalculated? Or had I heard her wrong? My head thumped, and my fingers numbed.

Please, God, not him. Let it be someone else up for parole. I beg you. Please. My insides crawled. Bile seared my throat, and I shuddered.

"Tara? What's wrong?" Diana's hand clasped my shoulder.

I opened my eyes and stared into her widened rich-brown eyes. What if he came after both of us?

Her eyes enlarged further. "What happened?" She released my shoulder and squatted in front of me.

Wooziness clouded my head, and my heavy tongue refused to cooperate.

"Is something wrong with bubs? Do you need to see the doctor?"

A sudden whoosh of nausea and heat flooded my body. My head

spun, my thoughts tossed and jumbled amongst old memories. Moments best buried and forgotten. If only I could extract and erase every trace of *his* existence.

"Tar?" Diana stared at my mouth. "Your lips are white."

Darkness leaked into my vision, and I swayed on the seat. My limbs weighed a ton. So did my eyelids. I closed my eyes and surrendered to the debilitating fatigue. My shoulder and arm slammed against something firm.

"Spencer! Fabian! Help!" Diana's voice muffled within my cotton-filled head.

Sound, light, and sensation vanished. Was I conscious? Floating? What was happening? Time seemed to stand still. Or maybe speed up? I could hardly breathe let alone think in this inky space.

Frantic-sounding voices hummed in and out. Jolting movements tickled my skin.

Was this the tunnel leading to heaven? *Not yet, Lord. I want to birth this baby.*

The intense heat burning my insides subsided.

"The ambos are on their way," a low voice whispered above.

Beads of moisture erupted along my brow and the nape of my neck. Sweat soaked my armpits and lower back. I moaned.

"Thanks," someone whispered.

Ice circulated through my blood, and my skin pimpled with goosebumps. I shivered and blinked at a sea of brown. The Tribune carpets? I opened my eyes and spotted someone's knees on the floor near my head. I shifted against whatever warm and soft item lay under my head and met Diana's gaze.

"Easy." Her features were drawn, her brow riddled with creases.

"She still looks grey." Spencer's voice echoed beside me.

Diana gently squeezed my ankles where my elevated feet rested in her lap.

My teeth chattered.

"Use my jacket." Roger's gruff voice sounded nearby.

"Thanks." Diana lay the heavy blazer over my torso, enveloping me with an earthen, woody scent and coveted warmth.

I nuzzled into the supplied heat, desperate to still the quakes pulsing my entire frame. My eyelids shuttered in the bliss of warmth.

"How far along is she?" Roger's tone had lowered.

"Around thirty weeks?" Diana whispered.

"They'll probably want to keep her overnight for observation." Spencer's voice held a note of concern.

What a sweet guy. Too bad he chased horrible news stories about men unfit for release back into society.

"I'll grab some water." Roger's footsteps disappeared.

"Need to contact her partner?" Spencer's voice lowered. "Or is she single?"

Was Spencer judging me like the rest of the world? I clamped my jaw tight and hoped to still my sore teeth.

"She's spoken for." Was Diana smirking?

"It's not what you think." Spencer's words were a bare whisper.

"Really? Looks to me it is." Diana chuckled softly. "She's wonderful, so I don't blame you."

"Is she awake?" Roger's voice loomed. "Have her sip this."

"Sounds like the ambos." The other guy called from the front door.

Maybe working here with these thoughtful people would be okay after all. If I could get my blasted body into submission and stop these stupid fainting panic spells. I thought I had moved past these types of reactions?

Someone stroked my cheek twice.

I opened my heavy eyelids.

Diana shifted underneath my feet.

"Can you sit up and sip this?" Diana pointed to the cup Roger held.

"Think so." I turned to my side and slowly lifted onto my shaky elbow. My heavy head whizzed. Whoa.

Diana grabbed the cup and rested the rim against my lips.

The cool water quenched my parched throat. I lay back and closed my eyes. Was it sleep time yet?

The front door chimed, and footsteps approached. Shuffling, a few clunks, and soft whispers permeated the space around me.

"Ms. Roberts?"

I opened my eyes and stared at a gloved brunette paramedic kneeling with a reassuring smile, her tall, lanky partner standing behind her. The Tribune staff had moved back.

"How're you and bubs doing?" The brunette scrutinised my face and checked my pulse while the lanky man opened a box of equipment.

"Okay." My voice rasped.

"Any pain?" She scanned my forehead with a thermometer gun.

"My head hurts." My mind and heart too.

The tall, lanky paramedic removed Roger's warm jacket and velcroed a blood pressure cuff to my upper arm.

"A headache? Or did you fall and bump it?" The brunette pressed a stethoscope against my chest and listened to my heart.

"A headache." I breathed long, slow breaths. In and out.

"She passed out on a chair, and I caught her," Diana said from somewhere behind me.

The female paramedic turned. "Was she unconscious for long?"

"About a minute?"

The brunette accepted a small torch from her lanky partner and flashed the light in my eyes. "Were you lightheaded?"

"Yeah." I squinted against the pain in my head and now my eyeballs. "I … think my fainting was set off by a panic attack."

The puffy cuff compressed my arm in a string of firm squeezes, adding to my collection of discomfort.

The two paramedics whispered between each other before Mr. Lanky disappeared.

"Do you faint or have panic attacks often?"

"Not as much as I used to." I met the female paramedic's gaze and glanced around the room.

Diana had shifted closer. Her lips moved like she might be praying.

I hoped so.

"Have you eaten much today?" The brunette smiled and held my wrist again.

"I …" I furrowed my brow. I had nibbled a bite of toast for breakfast and stewed over my decision to call Mum, then consumed a cup of tea and a biscuit at lunchtime while I waited for Keanu to pick me up. I had not eaten anything since.

"Your heartrate's slightly elevated, so we want to have one of the doctors in Robinvale check you out. Make sure everything is fine with you and the baby after your blackout."

The door jangled, and Mr. Lanky assembled a stretcher bed on wheels.

"Can you stand?" The female paramedic tilted her head and assessed me.

"Think so."

"Let's roll you on your side." She helped me stand and supported my shoulders for the few steps to the awaiting stretcher.

"Do you have a bag?" Mr. Lanky tucked a blanket over me and secured me to the bed.

"Here." Diana deposited my bag beside me. "I'll follow the ambulance, okay?"

"Okay." I closed my eyes and ignored the questioning looks from Diana's co-workers.

The trolley wheels squeaked as I was trundled from the Tribune offices, the bumps and jolts rocking me to sleep.

CHAPTER TWENTY-ONE
Face from the Past

Something squeezed my left arm, and I flittered my heavy eyelids. Ow, bright light and arm compression. Where was I? I lay still, eyes closed, and counted my breaths. Something pulsed and beeped nearby. Wheels squeaked and voices whispered. Disinfectant filled my nostrils with each inhale. The hospital? I flexed my right hand and crinkled thin, coarse cottony fabric.

Someone's warm hand brushed against my flexed fingers.

I turned my head right and opened my eyes.

"You're awake." Diana's shoulders relaxed. "How're you feeling?"

"Calmer." I glanced around the small, curtained hospital space I occupied. An automatic blood pressure cuff wrapped my left arm, and a baby monitor was attached to my abdomen.

"You scared me for a moment." Her voice cracked.

My throat tightened, and tears pricked the backs of my eyes. "Sorry."

"Not your fault." Diana squeezed my hand and offered a wan smile. "What happened? You said something about a panic attack to the ambos."

"Your colleagues mentioned 'black dagger' and 'parole' and …"

"It's not him." Diana locked her gaze with mine. "He has many years left behind bars before parole's an option. And if he screws up inside—which I secretly hope he does—then he'll be there indefinitely. You heard the judge at sentencing. He's lucky to have only been given twenty-five years."

Although I had avoided anything to do with the Black Dagger

trial when it occurred—which had been a challenge to avoid when plastered all over the media—I had succumbed to Mum and Diana's urgings and listened to a recorded snippet of the judge's verdict. Diana was right, that man would be locked away for many more years.

"I informed Roger about my abduction at my job interview—just so he was aware of potential triggers when asking me to chase a story—and he believes my perspective would be invaluable. I'm not sure what light I can shed on the situation since I don't recognise the guy now up for parole." Diana retrieved her phone from her pocket. "Maybe you recognise him?"

If I recognised the guy, he would have played a minor role in my captivity—maybe the man who stood guard during my few bathroom visits? My mind had blanked out the faces of the men who had gang raped me. Twice. I recalled their rough handling, their overwhelming masculine scents, and their satisfied grunts. But not their features. Only *him*. That evil man had dragged a wooden chair into the room, lounged back with crossed arms, and watched his men violate me. I knew every contour of his wretched face, every twitch of his jaw when they abused me. The heat in his eyes.

I shivered. Sicko.

"You don't have to loo—"

"It's fine." I motioned for Diana's phone.

She creased her brow, swiped her phone screen, and handed over the handset.

I gasped at the face of a familiar Greek god doppelgänger with curly blond hair. "Zeus," I whispered.

"That's him?" Diana seized her phone and stared at the screen. "The guy who recommended Sammy's Sandwich Bar to you?"

Freaking Zeus, my last sexual encounter before my abduction. If only I had ignored his over-the-top urge to "taste Melbourne's greatest sandwiches for less than a latte," Diana and I would never have been captured. I shivered again. "That's him."

"Mustn't've been his first rodeo. Check out Spencer's message." Diana turned her phone screen toward me.

Spencer: DONOVAN ARCHIBALD RICHARDSON III. PLED GUILTY TO STATUTORY COMPLICITY (ASSISTING, ENCOURAGING OR DIRECTING WITH RECKLESSNESS) BECAUSE OF FAVOURABLE SENTENCING INDICATION. HE'S COMPLIED WHILST IMPRISONED, AND

WITH NO PRIORS, PAROLE WILL LIKELY BE GRANTED. UNSURE WHETHER HE'LL BE ADDED TO THE VICTORIAN SEX OFFENDER REGISTER.

Donovan Archibald Richardson III? What a pretentious name! My stomach curdled. How many other women had slept with him and were lost to the devastating world of sex trafficking? I choked back bile.

Diana's phone chimed. She retracted her hand and stared at her phone. "Keanu's checking in on you. I talked him down from leaving a crazy-busy Benanu's to be here."

Oh, Keanu. Why did he have to be so caring and thoughtful? I sometimes wished he were standoffish so it would be easier to ignore the way he accelerated my heart.

"Can I snap a pic of you?" Diana raised her phone toward me. "Sure."

"And maybe smile so he doesn't stress out." Diana chuckled.

I smirked. "This better?"

Diana snapped a picture, grinned, and typed on her phone.

"Oh, can you please ask him to cover my shift for tomorrow morning?" That would give me enough time to recover for Monday's shift.

"Already done. He might call and make sure you're okay to work next week."

I needed the money, so I would be fine come Monday.

"He also asked me to tell you 'Darth, Apollo, Nimrod, Binx.' What the heck do you two talk about...?"

I wheezed a laugh. "Baby names."

"You're both insane." Diana smirked, swiped her phone screen, and screwed up her face. "I still can't believe you slept with that guy."

"What guy?" Isaac widened the opening in the curtain at the foot of my bed—looking glorious in his Victoria Police uniform— and peered between my best friend and me.

My chest tightened.

"That why you haven't accepted my marriage proposal yet? You getting action with other guys before giving me exclusive rights to your body?"

Oh shoot. I glanced at Diana.

Her eyes widened.

"I'm joking. I know you're not sleeping around." Isaac bent and kissed my forehead. "You and baby okay? You had me worried for a bit, but you're looking pretty good."

"I-I'm better than before." I darted a glance in Diana's direction. Had she contacted him?

Diana's expression now reflected complete neutrality. Was she upset I had withheld from her the past few days?

Isaac stroked his thumb across my cheek. "I can't stay long as I'm mid shift, but wanted to see for myself that you're okay."

I offered him a bright faux smile. "I understand."

He leaned and brushed his warm lips against mine. "Take it easy. You need to look after yourself and our precious cargo."

"I will. Promise." I smiled and accepted another soft kiss.

"Message me when you're home." Isaac stepped toward the curtain.

"Bye, Smitty." Diana grinned at him.

"Oh. Bye, Di. Thanks for messaging me." He rubbed a hand behind his neck and disappeared from the cordoned space.

Diana raised her eyebrows and widened her eyes. "What was that about?" She lowered her voice. "Marriage?"

"That was one of the many things I'd intended to talk to you about tonight."

She stretched her long legs and leaned back in her seat. "When did he propose?"

"A few nights ago. I … told Mum about it this afternoon."

Diana gaped at me. "You didn't."

I winced.

She shook her head. "It didn't go well, did it?"

"No." At least I knew about the sibling I had lost. Something heavy and not baby related weighed inside my stomach. "Mum doesn't want me to follow in her footsteps but fails to realise every time she says something horrible like, 'If I had the opportunity, I'd have aborted you,' it makes me feel terrible."

"She didn't!" Diana leaned forward and gathered my right hand between hers. "Did she?"

"As God is my witness." I sighed and smiled at my friend.

"I'm sorry," she whispered. "I can't even imagine …"

"She aborted a baby when I was five or six."

"No." Diana's hands squeezed my fingers.

I inhaled slow breaths and turned toward the machinery lining the curtain wall. "I don't want to be a single mother like her, so I think I should marry Isaac."

A middle-aged nurse bustled through the curtain. "How're you doing, Tara? You're looking better." She checked the monitors and clicked several buttons. "Baby seems fine, and your blood pressure is within normal range."

"When can she go home?" Diana asked.

"Bloods came back without any obvious issues, so once the doctor signs off, she'll be free to go." The nurse scribbled on the chart at the end of the bed.

Diana touched my shoulder. "Jonathan and I think you should stay with us for a few days."

"That sounds like a grand idea," the nurse said. "The doctor will give you further instructions, but rest and a low-stress environment will aide with your healing."

"Okay."

"I'll let the doctor know to come see you when he's available." The nurse smiled and departed.

Diana rotated her neck and straightened. "We should talk more once we're home."

More about Isaac and marriage, I assumed. "Yeah." Maybe by the time we chatted, I might have decided about Isaac, my potential role at the Tribune, and have a semblance of an idea for ways to discourage my Keanu-struck heart.

Hot Cop: ARE YOU HOME YET OR STILL AT THE HARRISES? WAS HOPING I COULD POP BY AND SEE YOU AFTER SHIFT END AT 1700 AND TAKE YOU OUT FOR DINNER.

I relaxed against Diana's comfy couch and contemplated my next move. How would I tell Isaac I was all in with him?

"That Keanu?" Diana glanced up from the romance book she read.

"Isaac. He wants to take me out for dinner tonight."

"Oh." She scrutinised my face. "You're going to give him an answer, aren't you?"

"Yeah."

Diana lowered her paperback to her lap. "May I offer one piece of advice?"

Here we go. I pursed my lips and nodded.

"Please make sure you're at absolute peace before you accept his marriage proposal."

I suppressed a bitter laugh. Absolute peace? Did such a thing exist? Not with my experience—even with Jesus cheering me on—and defunct heart sensors. Surely God saw the wisdom in my marrying Isaac?

"And I also think it's very important to disclose what happened to you." Diana slid her fingers over her smooth book cover. "You need complete openness in marriage, and in order for your relationship to flourish and grow, he needs to know how to navigate that minefield."

I sagged against the couch cushions. She was right, as usual. I knew I needed to tell Isaac about my trauma, but what if things changed between us?

Keanu's mischievous eyes flashed across my mind. He had accepted me from the moment we met, even knowing my history. Would Isaac do the same?

I rubbed my growing belly. "You're right. I'll tell him tonight and see if he's still interested."

My phone vibrated.

"He will be." Diana's smile seemed off. Was she sad? Apprehensive?

I shook my head—enough analysing!—and woke my phone. "I might suggest he picks up some food. I'd prefer not to talk about my experiences within earshot of strangers."

"Good idea." Diana nodded toward the kitchen. "Want another cuppa?"

"Yes, please."

Diana stood, gathered our empty mugs, and strode away.

I glanced at my phone, and my breath whooshed away.

Keenie: Doing ok? Want a visitor?

I closed my eyes and rotated my tight shoulder muscles. *Let it go, fallible heart.* I needed to flick the kill switch on these feelings.

The kettle whistled in the kitchen.

I opened my eyes and typed a message to Isaac.

Me: Dinner sounds great, but could you pick up

SOMETHING SO WE CAN EAT AT YOUR PLACE OR MINE? I HAVE SOME STUFF I'D LIKE TO TALK ABOUT. XX

My phone buzzed a few minutes later.

Hot Cop: AM I IN TROUBLE? ;-) OF COURSE. IF YOU HAVE A FOOD CRAVING, LET ME KNOW. ARE YOU HOME?

Me: SORRY, I'M AT DIANA'S. I'M DOING MUCH BETTER AND THINK ONE NIGHT HERE IS ENOUGH, SO WOULD LIKE TO SLEEP IN MY OWN BED TONIGHT. DIANA COULD DROP ME HOME IF YOU WANT TO COME OVER? OR IF YOU PREFER YOUR PLACE, SHE COULD DROP ME THERE?

Hot Cop: HOW ABOUT I SWING BY AND COLLECT YOU AFTER I GRAB SOME FOOD?

Me: SURE. I'LL BE READY. LOOKING FORWARD TO SEEING YOU.

Hot Cop: DITTO. I NEED THAT HOT MOUTH OF YOURS ON MINE.

Heat snaked through my torso, and my skin tingled. Isaac knew how to get my attention. *Would Keanu be as forthright?* I fisted my hands and forced his dark eyes from my mind.

I switched to my texts with Keanu.

Me: I'M MUCH BETTER, THANK YOU. THANKS FOR THE OFFER, BUT AM GOING OUT WITH ISAAC SOON. SEE YOU AT WORK ON MONDAY!

I stared at my sent message and rubbed against the heartburn stinging my chest.

Keenie: GLAD UR OK. SEE YOU MON.

Diana carried two steaming mugs into the lounge room. "All sorted?"

I nodded and accepted my hot drink. As sorted as my shambled life would be for now.

She lowered beside me, mug in hand. "You know Jonathan and I are always here for you, right? We've always got your back, same with Keanu, Sam, and my parents."

"I know." I blew the surface of my tea and sipped.

Diana searched my eyes. "I know you want to avoid single motherhood, but you have a network here to support you if you were a single mum. From the stories you've told me, and my brief conversations with your mum, she didn't have that. Or she felt like she was alone and acted alone. But it's different for you."

But was it? I dropped my gaze and watched occasional vapours wafting from my mug.

"You're brave and strong. You can overcome your adversity, and with the Holy Spirit inside your heart, you can accomplish anything." Diana sipped and rested her mug on a coffee table coaster.

"Thanks." Could I parent alone? The responsibility of single motherhood seemed astronomical. Mum gave up so much to parent me. She missed out on the many joys of life without a partner by her side, supporting her. Would I become embittered like her if I embarked on this journey alone?

I drank my cooling tea. Isaac would be around the corner to perform his fatherly duties—when he was available—but with his crazy schedule, living with him seemed … smarter. His house could become my home, his bed and body a comfort.

I smiled. The therapist had been right all along. Sex with Isaac equalled comfort in my messy brain. What a hopeful sign after all I had endured.

CHAPTER TWENTY-TWO
Divulging Information

"Your place is cosy." Isaac lowered to my lime-and-white striped couch beside me, ripped open the hot butcher's paper packages filled with succulent battered fish and well-seasoned chips, and piled my plate with food.

I squeezed lemon juice over our fish. "It's private, although too quiet at times."

"Won't be long, and you'll have a tiny screaming bundle to liven up the place." He chuckled. "Want to pray?"

"Yeah." Warmth spread through my chest at his request. I prayed a quick prayer and dived into my meal. My third-trimester pregnancy-induced appetite was no joke.

We ate in silence, my brain spinning over all the things I needed to say. Was Diana right? Would Isaac take me, mess and all? Because his rejection would hurt more than I wanted to admit.

I groaned and shovelled the last of my chips into my face. When had humble fish and chips become such a gastronomic experience?

"Good?" Isaac smirked his oil-slicked lips.

"It's like pregnancy switched my food-enjoyment dial to maximum." I brushed my salty fingers together, ripped off a section of butcher's paper, and blotted my greasy mouth.

Something dimmed in his eyes. "Heidi was so sick the first four months of her pregnancy and was excited when her appetite returned at about five months."

And then she disappeared.

"Sorry." Isaac stood and gathered our dirty dishes.

"It's fine. Really." I wrapped the scant leftovers into a small parcel. "You can talk about her anytime you want. I … I like hearing about her."

He carried the leftovers and dishes to the kitchen. "Want me to pop this in the fridge?"

"Please."

Isaac returned to the couch and draped his arm across my shoulder.

I lifted my chin and pressed my lips to his. *Please love me.*

He hauled me onto his lap, his hungry mouth fully engaged in tasting mine, and settled his hands on my lower back.

I leaned as close as my baby bump allowed and indulged in the tingling heat engulfing my body. Maybe my past was immaterial to our palpable attraction.

Isaac pulled back, gaze focused on my mouth. "Tell me that's an inviting kiss from my soon-to-be-wife."

I rested my palm, fingers spread, over my belly. "I need to tell you something first."

He furrowed his brow.

I blustered a breath and stared at his shoulder.

"You can tell me anything." He lifted my chin and forced my gaze to his.

I clenched and unclenched my jaw. "I have … a lot of baggage."

"I figured as much." He brushed my cheek with his thumb, his other hand pressing my waist. "But so do I."

The oxygen around me thickened, and I forced myself to speak before I choked.

"I was abducted and almost trafficked when I was twenty."

His hand at my waist tightened.

I drew in a desperate breath. "I was held captive for three days."

Isaac's eyes darkened. His Adam's apple bobbed, and he flexed his jaw.

"Diana and I were both abducted, but she was taken by a guy who had gathered intel about the operation. Intel wh-which led to my discovery and release." I forced my words past the knot in my throat. "He shot himself at a police station in Melbourne."

Isaac's thighs stiffened underneath my backside. "The Black Dagger file?"

Did everyone on earth know about it? I nodded.

Isaac swore under his breath. "Sorry."

"Don't apologise." Sometimes I wanted to swear too. *Sorry,*

Lord.

"One of my detective buddies handled the investigation. We were in the same training class. Did you ever speak with a Detective Calhoun?"

Memories of the detective's deep, comforting voice reverberated in my head. "He was the first senior officer I met the evening they found me."

Isaac slid both of his arms around my waist and engulfed me in a hug. "I'm sorry you went through that."

I rested my ear against his firm shoulder.

"Calhoun shared bare minimum details with me over beers when I visited Melbourne a few weeks after they charged those involved." He whispered several more expletives. "I forgot how much he struggled with hatred toward one particular smug sonofa … gun."

Dread pooled in my stomach.

"Apparently this dirtbag managed the trafficking side of the Melbourne operation and conditioned what he called "the cream of the crop" targets. Women he believed would excel in their newfound craft." His last two words were spat in a low growl.

My insides tossed. Was it *him*?

"Really clever lowlife. Ruthless. Ended up with the maximum sentence because the sleazebag let his guard down and bragged about his last protégé to a cellmate a week before the trial. Calhoun said the damning evidence was filthy as sin. The cellmate had somehow recorded the conversation and cashed in for a reduced sentence."

Oh, God. He had bragged about me? I clutched my tempestuous belly.

Isaac sucked in a sharp breath and dropped a swear bomb Jaelle would be proud to claim. "That was you … wasn't it?"

I closed my eyes and pressed the tears away.

He growled. "I wanna rip his depraved head from his shoulders and shove it up his—"

"Isaac." I straightened and met his fierce gaze. "He's not worth festering in hatred."

His chest rose and fell in ragged breaths.

I pressed my palm over his accelerated heart. "Trust me. He's not worth it."

Isaac slowed his breathing and relaxed his shoulders. "You're amazing."

"I wouldn't go that far—"

"I would." Isaac cupped my face and brushed his lips against mine. "You've been to hell and back and can still smile and plan your future. Amazing."

My heart softened, and I smiled. *Thank you, God, that rejection was off the table.*

Isaac ran his hands over my shoulders and down my arms. "Was there anything else you wanted to share?"

"I …" I brushed non-existent lint from his shoulder. "Other than our time together in November which I still don't really recall, I haven't had sex since"—my throat clamped—"then. A-and I'm not sure whether I'll struggle with intima—"

"Hey." Isaac raised my chin with warm fingers. "I might talk about sex and wanting you all the time—I mean, I'm addicted to adrenaline—but I'll never pressure you. I won't be expecting you to drop to your knees the moment we say 'I do.'"

My cheeks heated. I huffed a breath. "Surely you have expectations. You've already tasted the goods, and"—I forced back a grin—"now you know I'm the cream of the crop—"

Isaac's eyes widened, and he barked in laughter.

My heart lightened. "I just … I need you to know what you're committing to."

He pressed several kisses to my mouth. "I cherish your vulnerability and will stand by you."

"Okay." I drew in a deep breath. "Then I'll be your Mrs. Smith."

"My Mrs. Smith." Isaac wrapped his thick arms behind me and pulled me against his chest. "You know, it's getting more difficult to hold you close with that bump hogging space."

I grinned and slid my hands around his neck. "I'll be much bigger by the time bubs arrives in two-and-a-bit months."

He licked his lips and stared at mine. "Think we can arrange a shotgun wedding? I hear pregnancy sex is the best."

I smirked and kissed his jaw. "I hear married sex is better."

"Married pregnancy sex must be off tap then." His fingers dug into my hips.

"We'd better get everything organised so we don't miss out." I pulled away with harried breaths and pointed to my phone.

He blinked with dazed eyes. "You mean right now?"

"Uh huh. My cousin used an awesome online wedding planner app which I think you'll enjoy. We could jot down venue ideas and whatever you'd like for our big day." I stood with Isaac's help and smoothed my maternity pants. "Plus I need to cool down from your scorching kisses."

"Glad to know I'm heating you up." He winked and rubbed his bare chin in a similar way to Keanu.

My appetite for more kisses fizzled. I stepped to the kettle and prayed I was doing the right thing.

"It's gorgeous." Isabelle edged forward on her seat in the staff lounge and admired my shiny new diamond solitaire engagement ring. "Did you choose it?"

I nodded and shifted against the hardbacked chair. "We picked it out yesterday afternoon." It still seemed weird to be an engaged woman. And engaged to an upstanding police officer! How adult-sounding and responsible was that?

Isabelle glanced at the open doorway. "Does Keanu know?" she whispered.

"Not yet." Mrs. Everton had picked me up this morning because Keanu had an early off-site appointment with his dad.

"I saw him and Mr. Everton return ten minutes ago."

Of course, he arrived when I was in the bathroom. I shrugged. "I've only a few minutes left on my break, so I'll pop into his office after my shift."

"I could cover for you? If you needed extra time to … chat?"

"That's very sweet of you, but I don't think it's—"

"Ladies." Keanu strode into the room and aimed his mischievous grin at me.

My pulse spiked, and I hid my adorned ring finger under my right palm.

Isabelle stood. "Bossman. Much on for the rest of the day?"

"Hoping it'll be slower." He rubbed his bearded chin and turned to me. "Break almost over?"

"Yeah."

Isabelle widened her eyes at me.

I squeezed my hands against my lap.

She nodded in Keanu's direction.

I stood, braced my hand on my stomach, and faced my boss. "Actually, could I, ah, talk with you for a moment?"

"Everything okay?" Keanu's voice softened.

"Yeah. Can we chat in your office?" I flicked my gaze to Isabelle's.

She nodded and exited the room.

"Course," Keanu said.

I followed him to his office, closed the door, and wilted on the chair in front of his desk.

He lowered to his seat and creased his brow. "Did something happen this morning? Mum say something?"

"No, nothing like that." I sucked in a breath and fought against the pull of Keanu's dark eyes. "I … have some news."

He stilled. "Is it the baby?"

"Nothing like that. I …" Why was it so difficult to tell my boss I was engaged? He was my boss. My friend. Nothing more.

"Tar?"

I cleared my throat. "Isaac and I are getting married." There.

Keanu's eyes widened for a millisecond. "I see." His voice sounded cooler than normal.

Was I imagining it?

"Congratulations." He clicked his neck from side to side, then smiled without mirth. "When'd this happen?"

I cringed. "Thursday night." Soon after I had rejected his offer to hang out.

"Right." He straightened in his chair and clasped his hands together on the desk edge. "When's the big day?"

"W-we're still working on that but likely to be late June."

"That soon?" His jaw tightened.

"Yeah," I whispered.

"Okay." Keanu's tone sounded like our conversation was over. He shuffled a few papers on his desk. "I'd better get back to it."

I stood and opened the door, my stomach somersaulting. "Are you still okay t-to drive me to work tomorrow?"

He grunted. "Why wouldn't I be?"

My cheeks warmed. "Right. Thank you."

"Unless yer fiancé objects." A tense vibration coloured his

words.

I touched the door frame and inadvertently caught the light on my new ring.

Keanu stared at my hand before meeting my gaze.

"I don't think he will. He's pretty busy with work."

An unreadable emotion filled his eyes. He nodded and focused on his computer.

Had I detonated the peace in our friendship by deciding to marry Isaac? I sighed and returned to the restaurant for the remainder of my shift.

Three hours later, I farewelled the regular patrons in the dining area and snuck into the kitchen for a bite to eat before walking home. A mixture of delicious smells wafted to my nostrils. Charcoaled meat. Something fresh and herby. The creamy sauce Isabelle and I had overdosed on last week over leftover rice. I closed my eyes and breathed in the aromas.

"Lunchtime?"

I startled and wrenched my eyes open.

Mr. Everton loomed nearby and grabbed a plate from the warmer.

"Y-yes. If-ff that's okay." Why did he trigger my anxiety? Was it knowing he paid my wage and held the power to break me if I screwed up at work? Or was it his mammoth build I could never fight back against? But Keanu was almost as big, and I never feared him … just hurt him.

"You know it is." His mouth curved up ever-so-slightly—the biggest smile I had witnessed on his face—before his lips flattened. "Planning to eat here or takeaway?"

Did he have a problem with me eating onsite after my shift?

He pocketed some cutlery wrapped in a napkin. "I ask because you often eat with my son, and …"

I furrowed my brow.

Mr. Everton pursed his lips. "Don't know why, but he's become a bear since we returned from our meeting."

My throat dried.

"Not sure what's bugging him, but I suggest you steer clear today."

I rubbed my engagement ring. "Thanks," I whispered.

His gaze dropped to my hands, and his eyes widened. "Is that …?"

I nodded.

"You're marrying that officer?"

"Detective Isaac Smith."

"Smitty. Right." Mr. Everton rubbed his bearded jaw like his son. "You tell Kea—"

"Earlier today." I shifted on my feet and glanced at the food nearby. What could I grab and run?

"All makes sense now." He cleared his throat. "Enjoy your lunch, Tara."

"You too, sir." I turned, boxed a chicken and avocado focaccia, and collected my things from the staff room.

After double checking the hallway and not seeing Keanu or his parents, I hustled from the premises as fast as my petite, somewhat swollen legs and broadened belly allowed.

Mr. Everton's words looped and spiralled in my head with each step I trod. *He's become a bear. All makes sense now.*

I clenched my tote bag strap against my shoulder blade and stomped along the footpath. Was Keanu so upset by my news? Why?

A high-pitched squeal pierced my musings. A little boy in a fenced yard tossed autumn leaves above his head.

I dropped my gaze to the path ahead and focused on my echoing footfalls. The surrounding houses evaporated from view as Keanu's image engulfed my attention. Was there more to this situation? I inhaled a sharp breath and picked up my pace. Did he possess feelings for me? I knew he was physically attracted to me, but was there more on his side?

Was there more on mine?

My lungs squeezed, and I quickened my steps.

Grass, shrubs, and concrete flitted through my vision. My footsteps echoed along the path, their frequency increasing. Colours splashed and mixed before my eyes. *Stay calm and focus.*

I heaved and struggled to count my breaths. *Count and breathe.* My chest strained, and my stomach ached.

A car horn blared.

I yelped and halted less than a metre from a dirty metal ute grille, breathless. When had I stepped onto the road?

"Watch it, crazy woman!" A male driver cursed through the

opened driver's window.

I scuttled off the road and searched the unfamiliar street. Where was I?

The driver saluted me with his middle finger, revved his engine, and screeched around the corner.

My legs faltered. I gripped a nearby tree trunk and closed my eyes, wheezing in and out. In. Out. My heartrate slowed, and I whispered a prayer of thanks.

Something below flashed and sparkled in the light beaming through the clouds, and I stared at my hand.

Isaac. I committed to be Isaac's wife. No one else could be on my mind. I pressed my lips together and pushed my shoulders back. This afternoon would be consumed with setting up my bridal registry and booking a time with Diana to check out wedding dresses.

I set my jaw, retrieved my phone, and opened my maps app. After plotting my modified route, I ventured home on unsteady legs and pushed aside thoughts of Keanu.

CHAPTER TWENTY-THREE
Hidden Gem

"**I'm so excited!**" Jaelle beamed on my laptop screen, her eyes twinkling. "We're both going to be old married women soon."

I chuckled and repositioned my achy hip where I lay on my side, my belly flopped along my bed. A lengthy day of wedding venue inspections and florist scouting with Isaac had worn me out.

"I'll help as best as I can from here, but …" Her smile disappeared. "I'm not sure I'll be able to get enough time off work to be there. My boss didn't appreciate my 'longer than average' honeymoon, so—"

"It's okay." I smiled and rested my chin on my palm. "I wasn't expecting you to—"

"But I want to be there on your big day. For you." She pouted.

"I know." I shrugged. "Maybe we can work out a live stream thing?"

Jaelle's eyes widened. "I never imagined the words 'live stream' would ever exit your lips, what with your tech aversion."

I poked out my tongue. "Just because I don't generally enjoy using it doesn't mean I've an aversion. I know more than you might think."

"I know." Her tone hinted at a deeper meaning. "And how's your handsome boss? What's his take on your news?"

My insides plummeted. Keanu had been polite but reserved when he picked me up for work yesterday. It stung.

She scrunched her nose. "Went well, huh?"

I stared at my image reflected in the corner of my screen and sighed. My pained expression gave me away. "I'm … he can do what he likes. I've decided to marry Isaac, and I plan to stick to my decision." No matter my grief over the fragile state of my friendship with Keanu. He was no longer an acceptable discussion topic. *Now listen to my edict, heart, and move forward with Isaac.*

"What an amazing declaration of love." Jaelle curved a brow.

I stared at the screen and ignored her comment.

Jaelle's expression softened. "So, when do I officially meet my future cousin?"

"Isaac generally works when you're awake."

"Well, I'm not meeting him for the first time on your wedding day!"

"Of course not." I glanced at the brochure I had collected from a venue in Robinvale. Something about marrying at church while pregnant squirmed my insides. "I'll check with Isaac and email you potential times."

"Good." Jaelle covered her mouth and yawned. "Okay, I've gotta shower and ready for work."

I stifled a yawn. "And I should sleep."

She furrowed her brow. "I've been thinking …"

"Hmm?" I rested against my pillow and shifted my laptop.

"I'm happy to get up at six A.M. for these catch ups, but maybe we should switch it to my evening instead of yours … so you can get more sleep."

I glanced at the clock. Seven minutes past ten and I struggled to keep my eyes open. Had I become an old grandma already?

"What time do you finish your work shifts?"

"Two in the afternoon." I checked the time converter on my mobile phone. "That'd be too late for you."

Jaelle pursed her lips. "What about a day you're not working? Nine A.M. Melbourne is—"

"Six P.M. Chicago. That would work." I suppressed another yawn. "Or eight-thirty? So your dinner isn't interrupted."

She tilted her head. "Now you're fussing like a mum."

"Funny."

She chuckled. "Let's switch to nine A.M. on your Tuesdays. Gives me something to look forward to on Monday nights. I might vent depending on the day."

"I don't mind." My jaw vibrated, and I succumbed to an extended yawn.

"Excellent. Gotta go before I'm late for work." She blew me a kiss. "See you Monday night!"

I snatched her kiss in my palm. "Love you!"

"And don't forget to tell me what you want for your birthday next week!"

Oh yeah. Another "thing" to think about. "Will do."

The call disconnected. I closed my laptop and shoved it to the other side of the bed, climbed under the covers, and drifted off to sleep.

Diana and Victoria escorted me along the footpath to a "hidden gem" wedding dress shop an hour from home.

"How did you hear about this place?" I glanced at the small boutique shopfront and unlinked my arm from Diana's.

"Nicholas, actually." Victoria opened the heavy door and gestured me indoors.

I shuffled through the doorway and pressed close to a rack of silky dresses separating the entry from the rest of the shop.

"Dad's done some electrical work here over the years." Diana sidled close and allowed Victoria to slip by.

A rotund middle-aged woman with a speckled brown-and-grey bob approached. She grinned at Victoria. "Welcome. You must be Victoria. I've been anticipating meeting Nicholas's lovely wife."

Victoria shook the boutique owner's hand. "You're too kind. It's a pleasure to finally meet you, Bonita."

Bonita glanced up at Diana. "And you must be his gorgeous girl. You have his eyes and his height."

"Pleased to meet you." Diana touched my arm. "And this is my best friend, Tara, the bride-to-be."

"Aren't you a petite darling." She eyed me from head to toe. "How far along are you?"

"Almost at the end of my sixth month. Thirty-one weeks."

She furrowed her brow. "And you were hoping to wed before bubs arrives?"

I nodded.

"I have a few ready-made options which might work for you. But with the rapid growth of the final trimester, I find my clients need regular dress fittings plus a final check a day before the wedding." Bonita pursed her lips. "Would that schedule suit?"

I pursed my lips. "I'm … not driving at the moment, so transportation might be an issue."

The boutique owner waved her hand. "We'll work it out"—she glanced at Victoria—"won't we?"

"Of course." Victoria smiled at me.

Bonita clapped. "Right. This way."

I followed her to a mirrored lounge area with an antique sofa and armchair.

"Take a seat, and I'll grab some dresses which I think may suit." Bonita disappeared around the corner.

Victoria lowered to the armchair, her gaze glued to the surrounding racks of flowing white, cream, beige, and ivory gowns. "I wish Nicholas had told me about this gem before we married."

"Me too." Diana pulled me onto the couch beside her. "I would've enjoyed a girls-afternoon-out dress shopping here."

I smirked. "I'd say, 'maybe next time,' but that's not the done thing when it comes to marriage."

Victoria chuckled. "There's always later in life if you wanted to renew your vows."

Diana scrunched up her nose. "I've never understood why people do that. Isn't marriage a binding covenant between you, your spouse, and God? So how could one of the aforementioned forget and need to renew their vows?"

Victoria chuckled. "For some, it's a way of expressing that their commitment to their spouse is still important to them."

"Wouldn't standing by your loved one for twenty-odd years be a clear sign of said commitment?" Diana shook her head.

"You've got a point, Di." I slipped off my shoes and wiggled my toes. "Each to their own."

Bonita wheeled a rack of dresses into the nearest change room, returned to us, and eyed me. "Will you need help getting dressed?"

I stood and smiled. "I should be fine."

The next half hour flew by in a flurry of silk and stretchy lace, zippers, and pearl buttons. Three of the gowns looked okay but were stretchier than I anticipated or required, one simple creamy-bone dress gave the illusion of height I lacked, and one outfit was so ghastly Victoria had snorted pink, bubbly mocktail out of her nose.

I pulled a face at my unappealing reflection in the change room.

If dowdy matron was my aim, I had struck gold.

"You coming out?" Diana's voice echoed over the partition.

I opened the door and plodded toward the waiting women.

Victoria wrinkled her nose and Bonita creased her brow.

I turned toward Diana and stared at her wide, blinking eyes. "It's frumpsville."

All three ladies burst into laughter.

"It's not very becoming, is it, dear?" Bonita circled me and tutted. "Nothing redeemable about this garment. I'm sorry my judgement slipped."

I smiled. "It's fine. I'll go to the next one."

A ringtone blared in the quiet room, and Diana yelped and stood. She extracted her phone from her back pocket and glanced at the screen. Her eyes bulged, and she met my gaze. "Do you mind?"

"No problem." I waved a hand at her, smiled, and returned to the change room.

Diana's voice floated over the three-quarter height wall. "Everything okay? … no, no, of course it's fine…" A moment passed, and she laughed.

I sighed. It had to be Jonathan. *God, will my relationship with Isaac ever be easygoing and overflowing with love like the Harrises? Or the Jacobsens?* Isaac was a great guy, and we shared plenty of laughs, but the way Nicholas and Victoria, and Jonathan and Diana, anticipated their partner's responses, desires, and preferences appeared … deeper. Stronger. Each couple knitted together, spirit, soul, and body.

I rubbed my aching sternum and stripped the drab dress from my body.

Diana's laughter filled the quiet space. "What did you need?"

I reached for the next gown, slipped into the pretty cream—almost pale yellow—satin-and-lace material, and managed to tug the stiff zipper halfway up my back. Had my hand weakened with all this zipping? I glanced at myself in the full-length mirror and smiled. Not half bad. Apart from the half-zipped back. I opened the door and stepped toward the couch.

"He wants to know if you can help tomorrow morning." Diana held her mobile phone against her chest and spoke to Victoria.

"Lovely!" Bonita clapped and fluttered around me.

"At his office?" Victoria asked.

Office? Why would Jonathan need Victoria's help at the police station?

"What do you think, Tara?" Bonita tugged at my back.

Diana raised her phone to her ear. "Victoria will stop by Benanu's after dropping Jasmine at school. That work?"

Benanu's?

"Apart from the sticky zipper." Bonita tugged again. "I should be able to fix that easily."

"Sorry I couldn't help, but you're in good hands." Diana chuckled again. "Yeah, Jonathan and I will see you Friday."

Keanu? My heart thundered.

"And we might cinch it here"—Bonita pinched fabric at my waist—"just a little."

I met Diana's gaze. "Keanu?"

She pursed her lips and nodded.

Her laughter and joy-filled conversation had been with Keanu? Ice slithered inside my gut, along with a vibrating, unsettling tension. Would I ever share another care-free conversation with him?

"Yes, that will be perfect." Bonita clasped her hands and beamed. "Your intended will be thrilled.

I squinted and turned to the boutique owner. "M-my intended?"

"Your affianced, dear. I've been reading too many historical romances." Bonita chortled and covered her throat with her hand. "Was it love at first sight? How did you meet?"

Love at first sight? If only. "We, ah, met at Diana's wedding."

"How lovely! You must be so excited to wed." The boutique owner circled me once more, humming. "You'll be a delicious bride, and your betrothed won't know what to do with himself."

I avoided Diana's intense gaze and nodded.

"What's the consensus, ladies? Is this 'the one'?" Bonita met all of our gazes and settled on me. "Or would you like to try on the final few gowns?"

My appetite for dress shopping had fizzled, and my stomach churned. "I ..."

"How about I help with the final few?" Diana approached, pressed her hand to my back, and escorted me into the change room.

"The zip's ... sticky." My throat scratched.

Diana waggled the zipper until it released.

"Thanks." I stared at my reflection, and my vision blurred.

"You don't have to do this." Diana's hushed words seeped into my soul. She touched my shoulder and met my gaze in the mirror. "I know being a single mum frightens you—"

"I have a man willing to be involved in his child's life. It makes sense," I whispered.

"But you don't love him." And might never, her words seemed to echo in my head.

Not while my heart stirred for another man. I stepped away from my friend's gentle touch and wiped wetness from my eyes with my fingers.

Diana assisted me from the dress into another.

"Too puffy." And too white.

For a whore like you.

I stripped off the dress with trembling fingers. *Get out of my head.*

"Would you consider waiting? Not rushing into marriage?" Diana hung the puffy dress on a hanger. "Jonathan and I needed time and didn't rush into marriage the moment we reunited."

"But you weren't pregnant with his baby, so you had the luxury of time." I stepped into the final dress and slid my quivering arms into the chilled sleeves. Almost as cool as my heart.

"You have the same luxury, Tara. Please. Wait until after baby is born to marry Isaac." Diana's pleading voice knifed my insides.

I shook my head, hoping to bat away her words which niggled under my skin, disturbing my thoughts and plans. "What's done is done." Not even my heart could stop me.

"What about Keanu?"

I stilled. "What about him?"

"Don't pretend you don't harbour feelings for him."

I undressed and pulled my jumper over my head. "What difference does it make? Keanu's my friend and my boss. Isaac wants me and his baby. And he's more open to God than Keanu has ever been."

Diana handed me my stretchy black pants.

"Thanks." I pulled my pants over my swelling legs and straightened. "I'm doing the right thing by my baby."

"But is it the right thing for you?" Diana's eyes resembled dark chocolate.

What did I matter in the scheme of things? "It's right my child knows his or her father."

Diana sighed.

I grabbed the pretty not-white dress and exited the room. "I'd like this one."

"Superb choice," Bonita said. "Let's arrange an alteration schedule and get you ready for your big day.

I forced a smile and nodded, wishing I could prepare for what was to come.

CHAPTER TWENTY-FOUR
Old for New

"Are you excited?" Matt Briggs stood in the church foyer after the Sunday service and flashed a brilliant smile toward me.

I met his blue-eyed gaze. "Do you mean the baby or the wedding?"

"Both." He chuckled, tightening his grip on his black leather Bible against his chest, and winked. "Isaac seems keen."

I snuck a glance at my fiancé laughing with Nicholas and Jonathan. He fit in well. "I'm looking forward to it." My stomach flipped, and I pressed my hand against my melon ball. The baby more than the wedding.

"Bee's been fussing over your cake details." Matt shook his head. "My wife's a perfectionist, but she enjoys it."

"I really appreciate Belinda stepping in to make the cake. So glad Victoria suggested her." Although Belinda's fixation on my belly while we discussed the cake on Monday evening had been unsettling. I supposed even the nicest Christians struggled not to silently judge my unmarried, pregnant self.

"And the big day's on Saturday?"

"Ah huh." My insides swirled, and I pressed harder against the nausea. Dr. Fallow said my illness was normal, and some women became nauseous during their final trimester.

I knew better.

No matter how much I threw myself into the wedding and baby plans, my suffocating heart cried out, echoing Diana's words. *Please. Wait until after baby is born to marry Isaac.* But how could I wait? My baby needed a father, and I needed someone I could rely on. Single motherhood was not an option.

Keanu is reliable and available.

Enough! I fisted my hands at my side.

"Bee was suitably impressed to hear the Evertons had insisted on catering at no cost. They're a great family to support an employee so generously."

"It's j-just finger foods." Heat effused my body at the memory of last week's catering offer. Mr. Everton's eyes had been firm, but something else lurked in their depths. Probably pity. Who knew why he pushed for me to accept his crazy offer, especially with Keanu behaving so … professional and staid.

"I wish you and Isaac the best in the future." Matt glanced behind me.

"Thank you." I shuffled my tired feet and tried to catch Isaac's attention.

Belinda approached and leaned against her husband. "You well, Tara?"

Matt clasped Belinda's elbow and brushed his lips across her temple. Another wonderful example of a happy Christian marriage.

I smiled and shrugged. "Doing as well as a woman can reaching beached whale status."

Matt laughed, and his wife smiled, but the light dimmed from her eyes.

Jonathan and Diana waved on their way out the door.

I eyed my bestie, lifted my hand to my ear, and gestured a telephone handset.

Diana nodded and mouthed, "Talk tomorrow."

Isaac crossed the foyer and wrapped his arm around my shoulders. "Matt. Belinda. How're you two keeping?"

Belinda lifted her focus to Isaac, her countenance also lifting. "We're great. You ready for your big day?"

Isaac pressed closer. "A little nervous…"

"That's to be expected, mate." Matt quirked a cheeky grin. "You and me aimed far above our stations when we snatched from the cradle."

"Matt!" Belinda whacked her husband's chest.

Isaac's torso echoed with his quiet laughter.

I smiled at Belinda. "What's your age gap?"

"Eight years. But you'd think it was twenty the way this man carries on sometimes." She shook her head. "But I remind him I don't marry old men."

I laughed. "I'll have to remember that."

Matt met his wife's gaze. "Ready to go? Nick's invited us over for lunch."

Belinda nodded. She snuck several more peeks at my belly before saying farewell and disappearing out the church doors.

"Poor woman," Isaac whispered.

Poor woman?

He nodded to the exit. "Ready?"

"Please. I need to put my feet up."

He ushered me under the archway with his hand nudging my back. "We could have a quiet afternoon? Or we could tackle the nursery some more … and talk names."

Baby names. Baby rooms. Baby paraphernalia. I glanced around the semi-empty car park. "What did you mean by 'poor woman'?"

Isaac unlocked his vehicle. "Matt shared some stuff at the men's meeting on Friday."

"What stuff?" I opened the passenger door and wilted against the seat back. Could the door close itself? I sighed, leaned forward, and pulled the door. So much effort to do simple tasks these days.

He buckled and reversed from the parking bay. "Apparently they've been struggling with infertility."

Air sucked from my chest. No wonder she stared at my pregnant belly.

"There's been a few miscarriages over the years. And Matt knows she's quietly struggled with how easy her best friend conceived."

I widened my eyes. "Victoria?"

Isaac glanced at me. "She best friends with Belinda?"

"Yeah."

He shrugged and turned the corner. "Must be her."

My chest constricted. What was it like for a woman in Belinda's shoes? Her best friend conceiving without much effort and my flaunting my growing belly, carrying an unwanted child.

No! Unexpected, not unwanted. I rested my right hand on my tummy and thrummed my thumb. *No matter what happens, sweet little one, know that I'll never tell you you're unwanted or best aborted.*

"Hmm." Isaac slowed at the front of his house.

Why were we parked on the street? I glanced over my left shoulder and noticed an unfamiliar red car in his driveway. "Who's that?"

He furrowed his brow and switched off the engine. "I don't know."

I gathered my bag and double checked my phone and keys were in their designated pocket. Good. With the phenomenon of "baby brain" I had succumbed to in recent weeks, I re-checked where I stored important things. One evening of waddling down to the Arbys' for a bailout was enough of a prompt to initiate the new rule.

I opened the passenger door and struggled onto my fat feet. *How much longer, God?* With seven weeks until my nameless child's due date, I had far too much to deal with. Whose smart idea was it to add a wedding into the already crazy mix of my life?

A strangled cry filled the air.

I twisted toward the sound.

Isaac kneeled on the damp grass with his arms wrapped around a young boy. A boy with a tangle of ash-blonde curls.

I stilled, my lungs denying all oxygen.

A lithe woman in jeans, a white-and-grey woollen jumper, and a grey beanie stood distanced beside the red car with tears streaming her face.

All the blood seemed to drain from my body, one limb at a time, and I leaned back against Isaac's car, frozen. *Not possible.*

The boy wriggled from Isaac's hold and gestured for his mother. The woman wept, her gaze flitting between her son and me. Maybe she was his sister from Melbourne? But he never mentioned a nephew.

Blood rushed between my ears. A pounding throb ricocheted under my skin, invading my veins. I splayed my arms on the cold metal shell and gripped the door handle. *Slow your roll, Tara.*

The woman creased her brow, her eyes trained on me.

Was my heart as cold as this vehicle? No. Pain jackhammered my chest. This blasted organ experienced every needling tear.

Isaac stood, the boy clutched at his side, and turned toward me. Flaring nostrils, wide eyes. He recalled my existence at last.

My vision blurred. I closed my eyes and counted my breaths in an effort to slow my mind, my heart, and my bouncing thoughts. But my fuzzy head refused to clear.

"Tara?"

Why did this have to happen to me?

Sudden heat overwhelmed me, and nausea tumbled my guts. I opened my eyes but dimness crowded my vision.

"Tara!"

My legs faltered and darkness engulfed me.

I opened my gritty eyes and blinked in the bright surroundings. Machines beeped and voices whispered. A torturous rhythm rattled my left shoulder, and I moaned. Who ran over my arm?

"She's awake." Diana's face hovered in my vision, her eyes wet and bright.

Jonathan and Sam crowded either side of my best friend.

Not Isaac.

Or Keanu.

I coughed and gritted my teeth. Had someone ripped strips from my throat when they trampled my shoulder?

Diana touched my cheek. "Please stop scaring me like this."

"Water," I rasped.

Sam scuttled to the end of the bed, grabbed a cup with a straw, and handed the drink to Diana.

She lowered the plastic straw to my lips.

The cool water soothed my scratchy throat, and I sucked that baby down like a greedy toddler scarfing apple juice.

"More?" Diana asked.

I shook my head and grimaced. My neck ached too.

Where was Isaac?

Sam held his phone and snuck furtive glances at me while he typed.

"No sudden movements, okay?" Diana's heavy gaze pinned me to the bed.

"Wh-what happened?" I squinted, desperate to recall how I landed back in hospital. Did I have another panic attack? But why did my shoulder hurt like the dickens?

Jonathan rubbed Diana's arm, straightened, and set his jaw to "policeman face" mode. "Do you recall anything that happened after church this afternoon?"

I closed my eyes and focused. Church. Church. "Um …"

"You were chatting with the Briggses when we left," Diana said.

Oh, yes. Poor Belinda. I opened my eyes. "Did you know they have infertility issues?"

Diana scrunched her face. "Who?"

"Matt and Belinda."

She nodded, her expression grim.

"Isaac told me on the way home. I … felt guilty."

Sam looked up from his screen. "Why?"

"Because they've been desperate for a child and lost pregnancies while I'm pregnant with an unexpected baby." *Not unwanted.*

An image of a curly-haired boy embracing Isaac punched between my eyes, and I gasped. "It's … he's …" Tears welled in my eyes.

"He's what, Tara?" Jonathan's steady voice pulled me from the crashing waves.

"He's not his nephew." My throat constricted. "Heidi's alive, isn't she?"

Several tears trailed down Diana's cheeks. She gripped my fingers. "I'm sorry."

"I've spoken with Detective Smith and his"—Jonathan cleared his throat—"wife. It seems the authorities faked her death, but no one realised the precarious situation she'd been involved in would drag on longer than a year."

Isaac was still married. Married with a son.

You'll never be a decent single mother.

Wetness pooled at my ears. I turned my neck and groaned.

Diana squeezed my hand. "Don't move. Your shoulder was dislocated."

Dislocated? I glanced to Jonathan. "When?"

"You collapsed outside Isaac's residence." He pursed his lips. "No one moved fast enough to catch you."

"I fell?" I closed my eyes and grasped for my last memories. Darkness, then flashes of concrete guttering and lush grass. Someone yelling my name. Warm, steady hands. A siren. Whispered prayers. This room.

Jonathan nodded.

"I had a panic attack," I whispered. "I … can I see Isaac?"

Diana bit her lower lip.

Jonathan's dark eyes oozed softness. "We can arrange a visit after you're discharged from the hospital. And I insist you stay with us."

"Okay."

Sam stilled. "You're surrendering without a fight?"

"What's the point?" I was adrift, my world disintegrated. Again.

My eyelids drooped, and I begged sleep to take me. But no matter how still I lay on the hospital bed, my riotous mind turned its wheels, rotating cogs and dislodging my thoughts.

What would I do now? If the authorities—whoever they were— had faked Heidi's death, they must have had a plan to 'bring her back to life' to reunite with Isaac. So where did that leave me? Was Isaac still legally married to Heidi? Or had she been "dead" so long their marriage dissolved and he was now free to marry whomever he chose?

I recalled the emotion swimming in Isaac's eyes as he embraced his son and stared at his resurrected wife. *No way would he choose me.* Pain bludgeoned my chest, and I forced even breaths.

Low conversation accompanied the noise of hospital equipment. Sam's and Jonathan's voices rebounded with the occasional word from Diana.

Would Isaac split time between his returned family and me? Or would his time be monopolised with reuniting with Heidi? Isaac had said he loved her and always would.

But what about me? Was I destined to follow in Mum's footsteps?

You can't even keep a man, let alone a baby.

My heavy eyes and sore shoulder weighed me but not enough to induce sleep. I focused on my breathing, counting like my therapist had instructed, and within minutes the whispers of my friends dimmed.

I stirred—how long had I napped?—and tuned into the sounds around me without lifting my eyelids.

"Can't believe it. I wanna congratulate and pummel the guy all in one."

Keanu?

"If he doesn't do right by her, ya better lock me up before I kill him."

My pulse tripped. Keanu, no doubt about it.

"We've got her back," Jonathan's low tone rumbled. "Reign it in."

"She's fragile. We need to support her." Diana and her kind heart.

"Y'know I'd do anything for her."

Keanu's words sucked the breath from my lungs. Who was he talking about? Me? *No way.* My eyes and chest burned. A cough built inside my ribs, and I expelled it.

Someone squeezed my hand.

I opened my eyes and stared into Diana's sweet face.

"Sleep well?" Diana swirled her thumb across the back of my hand.

"Yeah." I croaked and peeked past her side. Jonathan, Sam, and Keanu stood nearer the door.

Keanu stared, dark eyes vibrating with intensity.

I struggled to breathe under the weight of his heavy gaze. What were his eyes trying to communicate that his lips never spoke? Had the reserved veneer shattered? Were we friends again? *Heart, be still and shut up.*

Keanu cleared his throat and stepped closer.

God, please return my friend to me.

Diana released my hand with a squeeze and sidled up to Jonathan.

Keanu rubbed his large hand over his beard. "Feeling okay?"

"Like you ran over my shoulder with your rust bucket."

His eyes glowed. "At least ya think my rust bucket's capable of the job."

I laughed and wheezed with pain. "Oy, don't make me laugh."

"Sorry." He eyed my strapped shoulder. "You're on admin duties when you return to work."

"What?" Since my engagement a month ago, waitressing had filled most of my hours at Benanu's even though the timeline we had set stated otherwise. It had suited me to a T because less office work meant less interactions with this man who confused my heart.

"That's been the plan all along." Keanu harrumphed. "No more service shifts."

"But what about—"

"No. More." His gravelly voice twisted at something lodged deep in my chest.

"Yes, sir."

Keanu smirked before flattening his lips. "Message me for anything. Anything at all."

"We're friends again?" I whispered.

A pained expression crossed his features.

My throat thickened.

Keanu nodded. "Course."

But would he abandon me again if Isaac chose me?

"Rest up. You've a ton of work waiting in the office."

I flexed my jaw. Were we friends, or was I convenient since I had completed my office training?

Keanu brushed my hand with his large index finger and departed.

I muttered a prayer that God had everything worked out for my good—which was not single motherhood—like the Bible said.

CHAPTER TWENTY-FIVE
Weighing Options

I rested on Diana's couch beside her, nervous energy whizzing through my tired limbs, and reread the text message Keanu had sent me this morning. A pleasant surprise after his recent silence.

Keenie: MORNING, HAVEN'T SENT IDEAS IN A WHILE. WHAT ABOUT THESE? GEO, LAKYNN, HURRICANE, UTERAZ, VANDERSON, CARRION, ADALBERT.

I smiled at the screen, peeked out the lounge window ahead where a wintry scene sprawled, and fumbled a one-handed reply.

Me: YOU'RE IN FINE FORM. ADALBERT'S A WINNER.

Staccato tapping reverberated against Diana's front door.

I dropped my phone in my lap.

Jonathan entered the room and levelled his dark eyes toward me, nodded to his wife, and disappeared around the corner.

Diana squeezed my knee. "You sure you don't want me to stay?"

I adjusted my sling, leaned against the comfy cushions supporting my left arm, and balled my right hand on top of my protruding belly. *Please, God, let him choose us.*

Why would he choose a whore?

I shook my head, pushed away the invading thoughts, and listened for Isaac's voice.

Low rumbles sounded in the entryway before Jonathan and Isaac entered the lounge room.

"I'll be praying," Diana whispered. She caught her husband's gaze, stood, and left the room holding Jonathan's hand.

Isaac rubbed his palm over the top of his head and lowered to the armchair a metre away from me. "How's your shoulder?"

My shoulder? What about my disintegrating heart? Or his baby? I exhaled and regarded my fiancé.

Deep lines and dark splotches blemished the area around his red-rimmed, bloodshot eyes. The stubble on his cheeks had lengthened since I saw him two days ago.

"You look as good as I feel," I said.

He puffed a humourless laugh before he slumped forward, leaned his elbows against his knees, and stared at the carpet.

Would I survive this conversation?

Isaac lifted his chin and directed dull green eyes at me. "I don't know what to say."

Nor did I.

"I dreamed many times Heidi would walk through my door, but …"

I swallowed a lump which had lodged in my throat.

"I'm sorry."

My eyes burned with tears. Part of my chest seemed to crack—was this how Adam felt after God had extracted his rib?—and I whimpered.

"I can't abandon Heidi and Thomas."

But he could abandon me.

"I just can't."

What was left of my heart crumbled to dust like all those people had after the stupid glove-wielding purple dude in Sam's Marvel movies snapped his fingers.

Isaac had Thanos-ed my heart.

"I hate that you're in this position." Isaac rubbed his face and growled. He blasted a sharp, foul word in a similar way my cousin had spat at her laptop a time or two.

Jaelle's image invaded my mind, and my tears overflowed. What would she say to this next instalment of drama?

"Say something, Tara."

I swiped my right hand across my cheeks. "What's to say?" *You chose them over us.*

He shrugged. "I …"

"What happens now?" How could I parent alone?

"I need time to work that out."

I stared at my oversized belly. "Time's not on my side. I'm almost thirty-four weeks, remember?"

"I know!" He shot from the seat and paced the aged carpet. "Don't you think I know this? And I keep thinking … if they'd told me about Heidi, I'd have waited for her, and we wouldn't be in this position."

What? "You r-regret our time together?" Another lump clogged my throat.

"Yes … no." He sighed and collapsed back in the armchair. "I'm screwing this up."

At last we agreed on something.

Isaac levelled his green eyes at me. "You're a wonderful person. I'd have happily married you on Saturday, but now everything's changed, and I'm getting a second chance with Heidi."

Fresh tears fell down my cheeks. "Do you still want to be involved with our baby?" Did I want him and his happy family involved in my baby's life?

Isaac flopped his head forward. "Give me time to think about how we should co-parent."

"Truly?" I whispered.

"Maybe."

Help me, God. Please.

"Heidi's being very understanding about you and me, but"—Isaac's voice cracked—"I refuse to lose her a second time. I'm … working out my options."

"Your options?" My voice shrilled, and heat suffused my cheeks. "Wh-what about my options?"

"What do you mean?"

A hot coal burned against my ribs. How dare he think he could determine the course of my future without my input!

"Can you appreciate how difficult this situation is?" Isaac's voice hardened.

I scoffed. "If you're not one hundred percent on board to parent, then maybe you should forget us altogether."

He widened his eyes. "You don't mean that."

Did I?

"Have some patience and let me work out what I can commit to."

"No." I palmed my phone, leaned, and awkwardly rose from the couch. "If you can't commit now, then you won't later. I'll send you paperwork to sign after the baby is born." What was I doing?

"Tara—"

"Jonathan!" I padded toward the doorway.

Isaac swore and leaped from the armchair. "Would you stop and—"

"What's going on?" Jonathan filled the archway, his dark eyes tracking between me and my ex-fiancé.

"She's being unreasonable," Isaac said with a growl.

I stared up at Jonathan. "I'd like to go home."

Isaac touched my free arm.

I pulled away, my heart thundering.

"C'mon, Tara, let's table this discussion until—"

"No!" I pushed past the guys and beelined to my backpack of clothes near the front door which Diana had collected for me.

Too many men.

"Tar?" Diana approached, eyes wide, and relieved me of my bag.

"Take me home. Please." My voice wavered, my breaths erratic.

She wrapped her arm around me. "Let me stay with you?"

"I want some time alone." To think and plan.

"This is ridiculous," Isaac said.

"Home. Please." Where I could break down in private.

Diana grabbed her keys and escorted me to her car.

Should a whore raise a child?

I clenched my trembling fingers. Why was *he* back, tormenting me? *Go away!*

"You still with me?" Jaelle's damp eyes stared at me through the computer screen.

"Sorry." I blew my nose, threw the soiled tissue on the used-tissue piles covering my bedspread, and rubbed my tired eyes.

"Don't apologise." She opened and closed her mouth. "I still don't know what to say."

"Me either." What was the point of it all? Was a messed-up wreck like me capable of rearing an impressionable, tiny human?

"Do you still want to stay in Tellarine so you're close to Diana? Or would you like to …"

"What?" I lay against the pillow fort at the head of my bed.

"Come to Chicago. Stay here a few months. Or longer."

"Before the baby's born?" I shook my head. "It's probably not safe for me to travel such a distance while this pregnant." And what sane woman wanted to be on a plane with a newborn?

Jaelle pursed her lips. "Come here after baby's born. Paul's office could probably offer sponsorship, and you could work with him and Louis."

I stared wide-eyed at the screen. "Move to America?"

She shrugged. "Why not? Mum'd probably volunteer to watch bubs for you, and Louis is still keen."

Possibilities and scenarios filtered through my slushy brain. "I don't want to turn out l-like Mum though."

Jaelle's expression softened. "You won't. But …" She expelled a huge breath. "You mentioned adoption before. Maybe it's worth researching?"

Adoption? Belinda Briggs's gorgeous face meandered through my thoughts. There were many couples wanting children. Could this child be an answer to Belinda's prayer?

"What're you thinking? I can see the cogs turning." Jaelle leaned closer, her face enlarged on my laptop.

"There's a, ah, sweet couple at church who've miscarried several times."

"That's so sad." Jaelle leaned back.

I stifled a yawn. "You've given me a lot to think about. Thanks for being here for me. Again."

She smiled. "You're welcome. I'd hug you if I could."

"I know."

She glanced off-camera. "Keep me in the loop? I've got to get to work."

I nodded. "Thank you for answering my call. We'll chat soon."

"Love you." Jaelle blew me a kiss.

After reciprocated kisses and goodbyes, I closed the video chat application and stared at the screen. Despite my exhaustion, my brain buzzed with questions. I stifled another yawn, opened a fresh internet tab, and set to researching. Maybe I could offer this baby a better future.

I scoured cyberspace and stumbled headfirst into the abyss of adoption, permanent care, and fostering in Victoria. The complicated processes boggled my brain—with more answers for those wanting children than those giving them up—and the late-night information overload unsettled my nerves.

Now I had more queries than answers.

I rested my right hand over my belly and read additional jargon on a government website. My baby had to be sixteen days old before I could give my consent, so visiting Jaelle had to wait another three months. At least I would catch some sunshine this trip. My questions surrounding choosing a specific family also remained unanswered.

Could I offer up my baby to strangers? My chest prickled, and I wriggled my numbing backside. If I kept the baby, I could travel not long after the birth, but I would still be a single mother. The quandary.

I rubbed my tired eyes, opened my Notepad application, and jotted the questions flooding my brain.

My phone vibrated on my bedside table.

I peered at my clock and squeaked. Almost midnight? Where had the last hour-and-a-bit disappeared? I grabbed my phone.

Keenie: SPOKE WITH DI EARLIER. YOU'RE HOME ALREADY?

No surprise they were talking about me. Did Keanu know Isaac was reuniting with his "dead" wife? And that I had blown any future interactions between my child and his or her father out of the water? I pushed aside the niggling thoughts.

Me: I NEEDED SOME SPACE.

Keenie: WHY?

Did he truly care to know why? I dropped my phone on the bed and opened another laptop browser tab while I was on a research roll. Flights to Chicago were next on my list.

My phone beeped.

I focused on my findings. Prices had increased marginally since I last booked tickets.

Another beep.

I sighed and unlocked my phone.

Keenie: IS IT A STATE SECRET?

Keenie: WHEN DID THE DOC SAY YOU CAN WORK?

I smiled at his first message.

Me: NO SECRET, JUST NEED TO PROCESS MY CURRENT CIRCUMSTANCES. RESEARCH MY OPTIONS. I'VE A DOCTOR'S CERTIFICATE COVERING THE WEEKEND. CAN WORK ON MONDAY.

I had a few days to get my head sorted so I could survive the onslaught of questions the Benanu's crew would ask. And everyone at church on Sunday.

Keenie: OPTIONS?

Why was he so interested in my business?

Because he cares for you.

I gritted my teeth and ignored my sappy heart. I needed to hold my tongue until I knew what I wanted to do.

Me: OPTIONS. TIME TO SLEEP, SEE YOU MONDAY MORNING.

The baby jabbed near my pelvis, and I dropped the phone.

"You little scallywag." I rubbed the spot where I imagined a tiny fist protruded until the little lump disappeared again, then stretched my legs. Bedtime. I gathered my technology and dumped it on the bedside table, snuggled under the covers, and prayed my brain would hibernate long enough for me to fall asleep.

My phone buzzed.

I rolled over, flopping my heavy belly on the mattress, and grabbed the handset.

Keenie: BE THERE FIRST THING MONDAY. SLEEP WELL, MOTHER OF SEMAJ.

I smiled at Keanu's latest awful suggestion. Warmth spread through my chest and up my neck. Not everyone had deserted me. Yet.

CHAPTER TWENTY-SIX
A Serious Decision

I awoke drenched in sweat, tears soaking my pillow, and despised images strobing like flashcards in my brain. A vice clamped my lungs, and the battle for oxygen recommenced.

I'm not a prisoner to the darkness. I'm one with the light.

I counted my breaths, but the creeping, familiar heaviness encroached. How long could I sustain this life of limbo? Several days of researching, thinking, praying, planning, and running around in mental circles had taken its toll. I needed to get off this terrifying merry-go-round.

Lifting my weighted frame from bed, I showered, settled my left arm in its sling, and prepared for my next task. An S.O.S. to Diana. For several days her daily "just checking on you" text messages had been my sole connection to the outside world, and I appreciated the delicate tightrope she traversed. Since day one, Diana had had a way of making me feel cherished and unforgettable—especially through the darkest days after my captivity—without smothering me.

I plodded to my teeny lounge room and lowered to the aged couch, bone weary. *Help me be brave today, Jesus.* I gripped my phone with shaking fingers, unlocked the screen, and was sucker punched by the date.

Saturday. Today was my wedding day.

Hot tears spilled down my cheeks, my phone free-falling to the carpet. Another dream snatched away. I covered my face with my right hand and screamed at the top of my lungs. Long and loud.

After what seemed like hours of destroying my vocal cords, I clamped my lips together. My screeches repeated in my ringing ears, filling the silence of my tiny home.

You'll always be my beautiful whore.

"Enough!" I clenched my fists, controlled my breaths, and staunched my tears with a wad of tissues. Today my torment would end. All of it. I retrieved my phone and dialled Diana's number.

"Tara. You okay?" Diana's comforting voice echoed through the phone line and straight into my distressed heart.

I fought burning tears—how had they replenished so soon?—and croaked through my scratchy throat. "I …"

"Want me to come over?"

A sob ripped through my chest, and I hiccupped. "Please."

"Give me a second." Scuffs, whispers, and shuffling resonated.

I closed my eyes and rubbed my stretched, itchy torso.

"You there?"

"Yes," I whispered in a squeaky voice.

"I can be at yours in ten minutes. May I bring Victoria?"

"Yes." Maybe Victoria would have some additional wisdom or insight to share.

"Sit tight, we'll be there soon."

I dropped my phone on the coffee table, slipped off my sling, and massaged my shoulder. The physio had suggested I perform several gentle movements and exercises a few minutes each day, so what better time than the present?

I stood, squeezed my shoulder blades together, counted to six, and relaxed. Discomfort bloomed with each repeated movement. I gritted my teeth, thankful for the distraction. What would I say to my friend? How could I tell her Isaac had ghosted me since I basically told him to take a hike? If his silence the last few days was his answer to our parenting quandary, then single motherhood was a given. And could I also admit that blasted evil man still whispered his awful, unforgettable words to me? That his haunting voice afflicted me once more?

I glanced at the wall near my bedroom door where I usually performed two more exercises and shook my head. Maybe tomorrow. I plonked on the couch and relocated my discarded sling.

Someone jangled the front door handle. A key scratched in the lock, and the door squeaked.

I slipped my left arm into the sling and turned toward Diana and Victoria. "I'm sorry if I ruined your plans." So many ruined plans today.

Victoria closed the door. "Not at all. Nicholas appreciates extra Daddy time with the children."

Diana lowered to the couch on my right and wrapped me in her arms. "Dad and Jonathan were fixing something in our kitchen, but I'm pretty sure the job was finished in five minutes, so now the men can roughhouse with the kids while we hang out with you."

"Thank you." Tears welled in my eyes.

"Mind if I make some tea?" Victoria nodded toward the kitchenette.

I sniffed and nodded.

Victoria filled the kettle. "It's a little weird being here. Seeing the familiar furniture but knowing it's not my home."

"I've cried on this couch a few times"—Diana grabbed a handful of tissues from the box on the coffee table—"so what's a few more tears?"

Laughter bubbled in my chest.

"I mourned my marriage and my family in this place," Victoria said, eyes shiny and thoughtful. "And I healed here too."

Victoria had lost her children and her marriage. How did my troubles compare?

Diana whispered prayers while Victoria prepared our drinks.

I leaned my head against Diana's shoulder. *Help me, God, to say what I need to say to these wonderful faith-filled women.*

Victoria deposited three steaming mugs on the coffee table and settled beside Diana on the couch. "Do you mind if we pray, Tara?"

"Please do." I breathed in their two distinct perfumes as the warmth of my friends' hands covered my own.

Victoria's gentle words soaked into my parched, desolate heart.

Diana nudged my shoulder. "So. What's going through that gorgeous brain of yours? I know it's performing calisthenics up there."

A small smile crept to my lips. "You know me too well."

"Yeah, I do."

I sighed and glanced between Diana's brown eyes and Victoria's blue-green orbs.

"Take your time." Victoria offered a smile of encouragement.

I expelled a long breath. "Isaac's out of the picture ..."

"Completely?" Diana creased her brow.

"Yes." Accepting anything less than we had planned—marriage and partnership—pained my chest.

Victoria pursed her lips.

"And you know how I feel about being a single parent." I puffed through my nose.

Diana scrunched her face. "You can't change that at the moment."

I straightened as best as I could on the cramped couch with my aching shoulder. "I can adopt the child out."

"What?" Diana whispered.

"Tara … I"—Victoria leaned across her stepdaughter and touched my hand—"I think you should take your time to think about such a serious decision."

"I've thought about it for several days now. And read a lot."

Victoria zeroed onto my face. "But giving up your child is more than … theory."

"I know. But I don't want to end up like my mum."

"You won't. Have more faith in yourself, your God, and the people who love you." Diana's eyes lit up. "I'd help however I could. You know I love babies!"

Victoria smiled at Diana. "She's brilliant with Jasmine and Elijah."

"I can't do it alone," I whispered.

Diana tightened her jaw. "Aren't you listening? You won't be alone."

"But I will be at two o'clock in the morning feeding or changing the baby whilst exhausted, trying to gain a few hours of sleep before a work shift. I'll be the one getting up to look after a sick kid or cleaning up a toilet-training incident when all I want to do is collapse on the couch. I'll be the one running on empty, pushing myself to get food on the table, clean the dirty laundry, pay the bills."

Diana's eyes had widened incrementally while I spoke.

"While everyone is at work and carrying on with their lives, I'll still be here, mothering."

Diana shook her head. "C'mon, we can help with cleaning and food and even give you nights off."

"But I can't rely on you to bail me out for the next fifteen years. You'll have children of your own to worry about." I grabbed my tea and sipped. Tasteless and lukewarm like my soul.

Victoria cleared her throat. "What's your picture of adoption?"

I stared at the mug in my hand. "I'd love my child to live with a wonderful family … like the Briggses."

Diana squeezed my knee.

"Maybe I'd see the baby a few times a year."

"I think Bee would be blown away by such a thought." Victoria's voice wobbled. "But where would you be?"

"My cousin, Jaelle, suggest—"

"No." Diana glared at me through narrowed eyes. "Don't you dare run away to Chicago."

Victoria stilled.

"Y-you can't leave behind your child, let alone me, a-and start another life on the other side of the world!" Diana gripped my uninjured elbow and tugged until she met my gaze.

Tellarine had once been a haven, but now this place reminded me of my pain and loss. My failures.

Tears coursed Diana's cheeks. "Please. Don't leave."

Victoria slid from the couch, kneeled in front of me, and lowered her head until she met my gaze. "Move in with us. Nicholas and I will help you any way you need."

I thumbed away wetness from my cheeks. "I can't expect that of you." No way could I live under the same roof as Diana's father. Not when his face still triggered memories of another man.

Freaking men triggering me.

"I'm offering. Nicholas will be with me one hundred percent." She nodded to her handbag on the carpet. "I can call him right now if you like?"

I shook my head.

"Bee and Matt have discussed adoption, and I wouldn't want to take a child from them, but …" Victoria touched my cheek. "This is your baby, sweetheart. Not theirs. And we love you. If you want a pledge of support for the next two decades, we Jacobsens—"

"I'm a Harris now, remember?" Diana smiled.

Victoria chuckled. "The Jacobsens and Harrises will be your support network for however long you need."

What had I done to deserve such loyalty? More tears slipped along my cheeks.

"But you need to learn to rely on God first." Victoria's eyes softened. "Jeremiah one and Psalm one hundred and thirty-nine teach us that God knew us before we were born, so we know for a fact God knows and loves your baby, but He also loves you. Very much. Psalm sixty-eight says He's the father to the fatherless and a defender of widows."

"God has your back," Diana whispered.

Victoria nodded. "Trust in Him to make your paths straight."

Had I been trusting in God since I discovered my pregnancy? Not really, but maybe I could learn. My chest loosened, and I released a cleansing breath.

"You were born for such a time as this." Victoria smiled, her eyes gleaming with tears.

Diana gripped my uninjured arm. "Whatever you decide, promise me you'll pray and let peace lead you. Okay?"

"Okay."

"Now." Victoria stood with a groan and stretched her legs. "Would you like to stay with us—"

"Or us?"

Victoria smiled at Diana. "For the next few days? Take it a little easier while you contemplate the future?"

I rotated my neck. "I'm back at work on Monday, so I'll stay here. But thanks for the offer."

"What about an overnighter?" Diana swallowed the final dregs of her tea. "You can come back to my place, have dinner, then go to church with us in the morning."

Church. My chest deflated. Isaac would no longer take me to church.

"Yeah?" Diana pressed her palms together, pouted, and blinked her wide eyes. "Please?"

How could I resist? "Let me pack an overnight bag."

Diana squawked a loud "yes!" and assisted me from the couch.

Maybe I could share about *him* another day.

I stared out Diana's kitchen window, hunched atop a bar stool—as best as a rejected fatso preggoes non-bride with a sling could—and rested my right elbow on the bench. Rare afternoon sunshine filtered through the clear glass and traced lines over the aged wooden counter.

Childish laughter drifted from the backyard through the security screen door, followed by several whoops and shrieks. Diana and Jonathan's heads bobbed in and out of my window view along with Elijah and Jasmine's feet and arms.

I smiled, dropped my gaze, and woke my sleeping phone where it rested on the bench. This list would never write itself. I reread my notes and tapped my fingertip on the bench top. The first section listed everything to do with adoption, including contact information for an adoption agency I stalked online and the many questions bumbling through my brain. The next section contained potential dates and flights to Chicago, possible work ideas, and reasons whether to go with or without the baby. And the last part recorded all the pros and cons of single parenting.

So many cons.

"Nicholas! Not now." Victoria's hissed words travelled from the lounge room, where she and her husband were probably procreating.

I slumped forward, squishing my belly against the bench edge. Would I find a man who would still want to make out with me like a lustful teenager when I'm in my forties? *God, help me to make the right decision about this baby. And if Mr. Perfect-For-Me exists, can you nudge him my direction?*

The little contortionist within me pushed against the bench.

"You cheeky rapscallion." I leaned back and rubbed at the pressure point.

The distinct squeak of leather and several snickered snorts floated to my ears.

I smiled, straightened, and released the phrase which had been on the tip of my tongue. "Get a room!"

A quiet "oof" rang out. Nicholas rounded the corner clutching Victoria's hand. "With pleasure."

Victoria glanced up at her husband and shook her head. Her cheeks and neck were mottled pink. "Want a drink?"

"I'm fine." I nodded toward the backyard. "The kids are busy, so you could copulate in the spare room."

Nicholas rumbled with husky laughter.

"Don't give him ideas," Victoria said.

"Give *me* ideas?" Nicholas widened his eyes.

Victoria pressed her lips together. "We need to give Tara the impression we can control ourselves otherwise she'll think we … uh …"

"Boink each other all the time?" I smirked.

Victoria's cheeks darkened.

The back screen door slammed against the wall, and footsteps thudded against the polished pine floorboards.

A grinning Nicholas escorted Victoria back toward the lounge room.

"I'm fwee! Can't catch me, Evil Woe-bot!" Elijah ran around Diana's kitchen bench with his arms raised high.

Jonathan stomped into the house like a stiff-legged Bigfoot. "Not for long," he said in a stilted cyborg monotone.

Diana sidled indoors, Jasmine in tow.

I twisted on the bar stool and smirked at the spectacle.

Diana perched beside me on a stool and leaned close. "I love when he plays with them. Gets me every time."

"I bet it gets your ovaries calling his name too," I whispered over my shoulder.

"Tara!" Diana snorted a giggle.

"I'll save you!" Jasmine bounded into the fray, pushed Elijah behind her, and stepped in front of Jonathan.

"Ow!" Elijah elbowed Jasmine's back.

Jasmine stuck her backside out and bumped her brother.

"Daaa-deee!" Elijah crossed his arms and glowered at his sister.

Diana and I choked back laughter.

Jasmine stared up at Jonathan and narrowed her eyes. "I'll show you for being a bully."

Nicholas re-entered the kitchen. "What's going on?"

Jasmine flexed her right arm and punched her brother-in-law—hard—in the groin.

I sucked in a breath. What the heck?

Jonathan's eyes widened and watered. His caramel skin paled, and he gasped like a fish out of water.

Diana squeaked. "Jonathan!"

"Victoria!" Nicholas winced—his pained face pale—and grabbed Jasmine and Elijah by their hands.

My now neutered friend groaned and collapsed to his knees with a loud thud.

Jasmine stood rooted to the floor, her eyes wide, lip quivering.

Diana scrambled to her husband.

Victoria rushed to Nicholas's side. "What happened?"

"Jazzy punched Jon in the goolies." I held back a snort of laughter.

"What?" Victoria turned to Jasmine, aghast. "Why would you do that?"

Jasmine's eyes glistened. She sniffed and stared at the floor. "I didn't mean to. I … I missed his leg."

Wrong leg. I covered my mouth with my hand, swallowed my laughter, and watched the show unfold.

Diana whispered in her wheezing husband's ear.

Poor guy.

Nicholas squatted and cupped Jasmine's shoulders. "You've hurt Jonathan and need to apologise. And you need to promise me you won't punch anyone … *there*… unless it's a *real* bad guy like we talked about with Mummy."

Diana assisted Jonathan to his feet.

Tears trickled to Jasmine's chin. "Yes, Daddy."

Jonathan bent forward with his eyes closed and gripped his thighs.

Diana rubbed her husband's back, lifted her gaze to mine, and pressed away a smile.

I snorted.

Jasmine shuffled toward her victim and touched his arm. "I'm sorry."

Jonathan lifted his chin and smiled—which appeared more like a grimace—at the young girl. "I forgive you."

Jasmine palmed her damp cheek. "Does it still hurt?"

"A bit."

"A lot," Nicholas muttered.

Jonathan slowly straightened and gritted his teeth.

Now the show was over, I slid off the bar stool, grabbed a bag of peas from the freezer, and handed it to Diana. "Maybe this'll help."

"Thanks." She escorted Jonathan down the hallway, one arm around his back and the other securing frozen peas to the trauma site.

"How about we prepare a nice snack for Jonathan?" Victoria pulled a tray from the cupboard and busied herself in the kitchen.

"Us too?" Elijah asked.

"Of course, sweetheart."

I lowered to my seat and observed this little family in action. Nicholas filled the kettle, warmed the coffee machine, and gathered mugs while sneaking peeks at his beloved wife and children. Elijah decanted sweet biscuits from a pantry container—with Victoria's watchful help—and Jasmine arranged cheese and crackers on several plates.

The unity of family. A foreign entity in my childhood home.

I glanced at my phone notes and rubbed my tummy. Could I trust God to help me parent this baby alone? Was I strong enough to take on this lifelong role even without the promise of a husband?

Familiar heaviness pressed my chest, dulling my newfound hope. I saved my notes and pushed my phone aside.

CHAPTER TWENTY-SEVEN
Detonation

"Thanks for this." Isabelle popped into my office brandishing an A4-sized piece of white paper I had printed.

I glanced up from the document I edited at the computer and smiled.

"I like having hard copies." She tucked her monthly payslip into her pants pocket.

"Anytime."

"Maybe I should invest in a printer."

"Or you can use the work one." Which reminded me, I needed to print my "decisions document" which I had completed last night so I could simultaneously pace my bedroom, read the questions, and talk on my mobile when I called the adoption agency tomorrow morning.

Isabelle laughed. "Considering my place's small and would rarely use a printer, you're probably right. Bossman won't mind."

She was right. Keanu was an accommodating supervisor. How many bosses picked up their pregnant employee for work?

"Thanks again. By the way, how's the shoulder? Enjoying your newfound freedom?"

"Still sore but much better. It's nice having full use of my left hand." I had fulfilled the required number of days to restrict my movement with the sling.

"I'm glad, but make sure you take it easy. No stressful movement."

"I know."

Isabelle tapped the door frame. "Have a great night."

"You too." I opened my work email, where I had emailed

myself the document in question, and sent the file to the printer. The last thing I needed was someone seeing all the crazy stuff going through my thoughts.

I exited my office and almost walked into Mr. Everton.

He caught my right elbow and steadied me. "You all right?"

I chuckled. "Thanks for catching me, especially now I'm well and truly in beached-whale territory." Thirty-five weeks of my pregnancy had passed, and I still agonised over whether to keep the baby, let alone name the poor thing.

Mr. Everton released my elbow and stepped backward. "Do you have a moment?"

"Of course." How could I say no to the big boss? "Your office or mine?"

He nodded toward my open doorway.

I trundled back behind my desk and onto my comfy swivel desk chair. My lower back twitched with relief.

Mr. Everton overfilled the seat in front of my desk.

"How can I help you, sir?"

He furrowed his brow. "My wife's turning fifty next month, and I want to organise a special night for her."

"Great! Here at Benanu's?"

He nodded.

I opened the events file and started a new entry. "Did you have anything in particular in mind? Were you wanting to use the new private dining room?" Keanu started work with a renovation team last week to repurpose one of the oversized storage rooms near the kitchen.

"Will it be ready by July eighteen?" His eyes flickered. "I've left the reno logistics to Keanu so I'm … out of the loop."

I squinted at my boss. Was he struggling to let go of the responsibilities Keanu often begged to take on?

"Do you know, or should I speak to my son?"

"Let me check my emails." Knowing Keanu, he would have emailed me the timeline last week. I scrolled past a heap of unread email and opened one from Keanu. "Yes, it should be finished by July ten."

"Good." Mr. Everton drew his brows together. "Do you have time now to discuss it?"

"Sure."

We spent the next twenty minutes discussing what he wanted arranged for his wife's surprise birthday party.

"I'll make sure we have a capable team rostered." All the staff knew work shifts would be rejigged on dates the private dining room was booked until each member of the team had experienced the added workload. Keanu toyed with the idea of offering Isabelle a permanent server position for the room once bookings were consistent. A deserved pay rise too.

"Thanks." Mr. Everton stood.

My desk phone rang.

He nodded and exited my office.

I scooped the handset and rested it against my ear. "Tara speaking."

"Tara Roberts. You never called." A gruff, deep male voice spoke.

"Um, okay? Who's this?"

"It's Roger Fulton. You never gave me your mobile number."

The Tribune job! How had I forgotten about it?

"Di said things are complicated for you at the moment."

I huffed a dry laugh. "You could say that. But I'm sorry I never let you know my answer, truly I am."

"After you fainted, I figured it might be a while until you're able to take on anything extra."

"I'm afraid so." I cleared my throat. "I suppose that means I should decline—"

"How about we table this conversation until, say"—a moment passed—"September? October?"

My tight chest loosened. "Really?"

He grunted. "Like I said back in May, you've a clear, relatable voice, and I think you'd be an asset to the team."

"Thank you, sir."

"I'll call you in a few months. All the best." His rough voice disappeared, and a long beeping sound filled my hearing.

Had I imagined a conversation with Diana's boss? I stared at the earpiece in my hand, dazed. A slow grin spread across my face, and giddiness bubbled inside my chest.

I shook my head, chuckled, and closed the document for Mrs. Everton's birthday shindig. My email to myself filled the screen, and I squeaked. The printer! I "sprang" from the wheeled desk chair, lost my balance, and caught myself against the desk. My pulse roared. *Slow down before you hurt yourself!*

After several deep breaths, I power-waddled along the hallway to the small office supply slash printer room opposite Keanu's office and rifled one-handed through the printouts waiting to be claimed. Where was it? I neatened the documents into a straight pile and flipped each page. My hand tremored the more pages I turned until I reached the final page. What had happened to my printout? I rubbed my temple. Maybe the print job had failed?

A shadow filled the doorway behind me.

I turned, and my stomach dropped.

Keanu clutched papers to his chest, his expression dark and stormy. "Looking for this?"

Oh, fruitcake.

"In my office. Now."

I grimaced at his brittle tone.

Keanu's jaw flexed, and he stormed across the hallway.

Had he read my document? *Please, Lord, let him have only skimmed it.* I clenched the bench top beside me and heaved tight breaths. Not that skim-reading would make a difference. That blasted document had every thought and plan splattered across it.

"Tara!"

I startled and bolted across the hallway on unsteady legs. "Y-yes?"

Keanu hunkered at his desk, his dark eyes burning through my face. "Please close the door."

"I'd prefer to leave it open." So others could see where he stashed my body after this disastrous conversation.

"Close. The. Door." Keanu's words were calm. Too calm.

I whispered a too-late prayer, closed the door, and dropped to the chair in front of his desk.

He slid papers across his neat desk and pointed to the top section.

I glanced down and read the words near his large, rigid finger. Adoption options. No doubt about it. This was my document.

"Adoption?" Keanu's tone softened. Had I detected a quaver in his voice?

I met his gaze and sucked in a breath. All the fire had disappeared from his eyes and been replaced with … deep sadness?

"And what's this about Chicago? Y-yer leaving?" He cleared his throat.

"I'm … not sure yet. I'm working out what I should do." Why did he look almost … devastated?

"How can ya consider giving up the baby?" His jaw flickered, and a firmness re-entered his eyes. "Because Alannah sucked at parenting?"

I widened my eyes.

"Don't use her failings as an excuse to give up."

The nerve! What did he know? I gritted my teeth and leaned forward. "What gives you the right to speak about me or my mum like that?"

"I'm saying it like I see it." He narrowed his eyes.

"Well, I don't particularly care for whatever it is you think you know. I'll decide for myself." Why had I confided in him on umpteen different occasions? Ugh!

"Scared people make foolish decisions."

I bristled. "I beg your pardon. I'm not scared." *Liar.*

Keanu shook his head. "Why contemplate adoption then?"

I blustered a frazzled breath. "Because there're plenty of families desperate for children, and I can fill a need."

"Ba-bow." Keanu pressed an imaginary buzzer on his desk. "Try again."

My heart clanged, and I gripped both arms of the seat. My left shoulder twinged. "How dare you."

"Tell me the truth."

"I've told you the truth!"

He shook his head. "Say it."

My chest heaved with every breath.

"Say it."

I rocked slightly on the chair.

Keanu's gaze drilled into mine. He leaned closer. "Say. It."

"I don't want to be a single mother!" I stood, wheezing, and paced. My fingers itched to smack his handsome face.

Keanu stood and rounded the desk. "Then don't do it alone."

"How, Mr. Smarty-Pants? Isaac's gone!" I thrust my right arm in a wide arc.

"But yer friends are still here. Di, her family." He stepped close enough to punch. "Me."

"You?" I furrowed my brow. "You already do too much." My upcoming midwife appointment popped into my brain.

He reached out his hand, frowned, and dropped his arm to his side. "I could do more." Had his voice dropped?

"I can't expect that from you. Or Di and Victoria." I sighed. "I need to know I can parent this child without scarring it."

"You are brave," he whispered. "A brilliant mum-to-be."

My throat thickened, and heat tickled my eyes.

"I wanna do more. Help in any way." His throat bobbed. "In every way."

Huh?

"Not that I'm doing it for this reason, because I'm not, but I know it was a big thing when ya decided to date Isaac and—"

"What thing?" What did our conversation have to do with my dating Isaac? "What're you talking about?"

"I went to a men's event at church with Matt."

What? I scrunched my face.

"I know I'm hard-headed, but … I felt accepted there. Was thinking of attending a Sunday meeting when I'm not working."

"You're … going to church?" When had this happened? And why tell me now?

"Yeah. And I thought maybe …" He rubbed his bearded chin and shrugged.

"You thought what?" My palms dampened, and my mind clouded. What was he saying?

"Stay in Tellarine. Raise the baby here and … let me be involved."

"Involved? How?" My pulse raced.

Keanu touched my chin with his thumb. "Anyhow. I know ya don't need me or anyone else to raise a kid because yer more than capable, but … I …"

My heart beat like it would smash through my ribs and fly from my body.

"Stay. For me."

My lungs squeezed. I gripped the back of the chair. Stay for him? As in …? I sucked in a rapid breath. Did he …? *No, not possible.* Then why now? Was this some weird sense of duty he felt compelled to offer?

"Say something." Keanu's intense gaze raked across my face.

Say something? What the heck was I meant to say or do? This was leagues worse than a pity date. My breaths shortened, and I gripped the chair back tighter, ignoring the sting in my shoulder.

Keanu drew his brows together.

Take a chance, my stupid heart begged. It could take a hike for all I cared. How could he ask to be involved now? My fiancé had dumped me not even a month ago, and this heavy lump of a kid was due next month. I had enough decisions to make!

"Tara?"

"Are you insane?"

Keanu's eyes widened.

"Do I look stupid?" White spots dotted my vision.

"What? No!" His brows dipped farther. He reached across and grabbed my elbow. "Are you okay?"

I shook away his warm touch. "I … I need to go home."

"But—"

"I'm not feeling well, and I'm going home." I stepped toward the closed door and gripped the handle with shaking hands, my back to Keanu.

"I've wanted to say this for a long time," he said, his voice gravelly.

Not possible. Keanu was smarter than that.

I exited his office on wooden legs and escaped down the hallway, bumping my shoulder hard against my office door frame. I fumbled with my computer mouse and shut down my desktop, then stuffed my things in my tote bag stashed under my desk. When would my hands stop shaking? And what was I meant to do now?

I dashed through Benanu's with my head down and gaze to the carpet, avoiding everyone, desperate to evade the walls closing in on me. *Breathe!* I spilled out the exit in the frigid air and blazed in the direction of home.

Home? Was Tellarine home anymore? With Isaac gone, this building pressure from everyone telling me to make a decision was doing my head in. I blinked away tears and searched my surroundings. The last thing I wanted was to step in front of another oncoming vehicle.

I pushed aside the image of Keanu's dark eyes but failed. His almost desperate request bounced inside my skull. How could he put such pressure on me? I checked for traffic and waddled across the road. Why would he make an offer as though he cared? He had said less than ten words to me since my engagement, and had withheld any facial expression resembling a smile. And what about his admission a few months ago of not wanting to fill his spare room with a family anytime soon?

An unbidden thought jabbed my heart, and my lungs screamed. I grasped a nearby white picket fence. Did he know how my dumb heart craved him? Was he using this knowledge against me? Exploiting my weakness?

I palmed my wet cheeks and scurried up my street. A sharp, deep pang for my mum oscillated in my chest cavity. Even with our ups, downs, and in-betweens, Mum had always been available for me. Practical in action when things were tough.

Terrified Tara sparked her greatest mothering achievements.

My disused, dejected car caught my eye as I hustled along the driveway. Despite our differences, Mum would take me in without question. Could I last the seventy-five-minute trip to Swan Hill? Should I? Driving one hundred and ten kilometres was no small feat.

But what was the alternative? Living in a town which reminded me of Isaac and trying to live up to everyone's expectations while working for a man I held strong, juxtaposed feelings for? Was staying worth risking another mental breakdown?

I fought my front door open with my tremoring hands and collapsed on the couch. The telltale signs of another panic attack washed over me, and I counted my breaths with closed eyes. Shaking chills. Teetering anxiety. Numbness. Walls closing in. Accelerated heartbeat and a barrage of heat.

A weak cry escaped my lips, and I rocked on the couch, my baby secured underneath my palms.

My long-term distress was not worth suffering a life in Tellarine.

I sucked in a breath, whispered a prayer, and set my plan in motion.

CHAPTER TWENTY-EIGHT
Runaway

I slammed my car boot, securing my suitcase bursting with baby-related things and maternity clothing, and slid behind the steering wheel with great difficulty. How did overly pregnant women manage to drive? After adjusting my seat and mirrors, I buckled and chanted "you can do it!" inside my frenetic mind, and slowly reversed down the driveway. Gravel crunched under the tyres, echoing my snapping nerves.

My body pounded at every pulse point, my head resounding with blood-induced thumping. I pulled onto the deserted street and stopped outside a tiny grey weatherboard home four houses away.

"Don't give up," I whispered in a husky, stilted voice. "You *are* doing this."

The engine idled, its mechanical tune serenading my harried neurons.

I fumbled with my phone resting in the cup holder and reread the message I had drafted to Keanu.

Me: THANK YOU FOR YOUR SUPPORT THE LAST FEW MONTHS. I'VE DECIDED I CAN'T STAY. I'M TENDING MY RESIGNATION, EFFECTIVE IMMEDIATELY, AND STAYING WITH MY MUM. ALL THE BEST.

I scrunched up my face, brushing away tears. What an impersonal farewell, but what else could I do? Stay and obliterate my heart? I could never stay with a man duty-bound to look after me and my child, no matter the compelling, unknown reason. Or, God forbid, a ploy to use my feelings against me.

My clenched jaw vibrated, and I eased my gritted teeth. At least Isaac had been honest when he pursued me. Although his honesty had dried up the moment his family reappeared.

Now was not the time to dwell on the men complicating my thoughts. I pressed Send, switched off my phone, and returned the handset to the cup holder. Time to focus on the monumental task at hand.

"Please, God, help me get to Mum's safely." I gripped the steering wheel, checked the mirrors, and drove in the opposite direction of Benanu's, toward Robinvale-Sea Lake Road.

How had my life dipped into this cavernous valley? Each boulder-sized choice I needed to decide pushed its weight on my chest. Heavy and sobering. I blinked away wetness, focusing my mind and eyes on the road ahead and not the things I fled.

Several kilometres down the minor highway, leaden clouds gathered in the darkening sky. I ignored my jackhammering chest and tightened my hold. My fingers numbed.

Tall eucalypts interspersed with squat shrubbery danced and convulsed along the kerbless road. A strong gust of wind battered the side of my car and swilled amber dirt across the windscreen. My arms ached from my firm grip on the wheel, my left shoulder lanced with sharp prickles. *Keep going, you've made it this far!*

The skies opened, and heavy, fat raindrops splattered the windshield. Shudders drilled along my spine. I flicked the window wipers into action, pressed my back against the seat, and relaxed my injured shoulder.

The dashboard clock glowed bright in the dimmed light. Twenty heart-stopping minutes down, far-too-many-minutes-to-survive to go.

Keanu's despondent expression overshadowed all my thoughts, and I swallowed a sob. Heat built in my chest and eyes. I squinted through steady rainfall and intermittent swiping wipers, desperate to dispel the incoming internal storm.

A hot, pressurised bubble floated up my oesophagus, and I gurgled a cry. Why had I fallen into Isaac's bed? What if Intoxicated Tara had instead chosen Keanu, then where would I be? *Not pregnant*, a voice whispered. Keanu would have picked up on the signs of my inebriated state, driven me to Diana's, and tucked me into the guest bed.

But I *was* pregnant, and my child was fathered by someone else. Tears tracked my cheeks. Someone unwilling to pull his head out of the sand long enough to talk to me about his child's future. A man leaving me with the burden of care, an encumbrance my friends seemed to think I could manage well on my own. But my mind and upbringing begged to differ. After the example my mum had set, would I manage motherhood any better?

No, you wouldn't, my beaut—

"Shut up!" I heaved rapid, slurpy breaths. "You have no power over me because I have the mind of Christ."

Scripture sprang to my mind. I muttered sections of verses I recalled, blinking and palming my wet eyes while hurtling at high speed down the narrow, sealed road. Anxious driving and snotty crying were not a safe—or attractive—mix, but with each Scripture I recalled, my heartrate notched lower, my mind geared for my arrival in Swan Hill.

Old memories of Mum and me resurfaced. Mum grinning at my attempted Mother's Day breakfast of burnt toast and spilled orange juice. Baking choc chip cookies, side by side, in her tiny kitchen. Snuggling in bed tucked securely beside Mum, her arm around my back, her breaths fluttering my hair. Kisses to my knees and elbows after acquiring another battle scar in the backyard.

Tight hugs, soothing back rubs, and whispers of hope after my earth-shattering trauma and consequent abortion. Mum had held the husk of my existence together.

My throat swelled. Mum had screwed up plenty, but there were also many moments she had been just who I needed when I needed her. Could I do the same for my growing bundle?

My breaths slowed, and my snotty waterworks trickled to a trifling drip. I steadied my pulsating, heavy arms and willed myself to Mum's place.

A little over an hour later, thanks to the atrocious weather, I pulled into Mum's driveway and killed the engine. Tiny reverberating tremors antagonised my exhausted body, and I closed my eyes. "Thank You, God."

I rested for what seemed like hours although—if the clock was still to be trusted—three minutes had passed. Gathering energy, I grabbed my tote bag and phone and exited the vehicle. My jelly-like legs wobbled with each uncertain step to the front door, and I sagged with my right shoulder propped against the wall.

The deadbolt clicked, and Mum swung the wooden door wide. "Tara."

A fresh batch of tears streamed from my scratchy eyes.

"Oh, love. C'mere." Mum enveloped me in her arms and pulled me indoors. She escorted me to the worn floral-patterned couch and rocked me in time to her hummed tune.

Her comfort was exactly what I needed.

"You look gorgeous, by the way." Mum's voice was soft, free from the strain of our previous conversation six weeks earlier. "Pregnancy suits you."

"Thanks." I blotted my face with a tissue.

"Did you get my birthday card last month?"

I furrowed my brow. "No?"

"That makes sense. I figured you'd have made contact after my peace offering."

I stared at my mother, her features soft and oozing love. Had I held tight to the hurt when she had hoped to reconcile weeks ago?

She touched my hand. "Perhaps the card was lost—we all know how hopeless Australia Post can be at times—but you've a smart mother. I saved a copy of the Amazon gift card code in case something went amiss."

"Thanks, Mum." I melted against her side, warmth pooling in my chest.

"But I *am* sorry to have missed so much of your pregnancy. I knew I should've called you sooner, and I'm sorry, love."

"It's okay." I closed my eyes and breathed in her floral scent.

"Will I get to meet your man soon?"

I stiffened.

Mum nudged me upright and away from her. She caught my gaze with her luminous blue eyes. "Or is he the reason for your tears?"

I blew out a breath. "He's reunited with his wife and son."

Mum blinked. "He's married?"

I nodded. "He was told she died several years ago—"

Mum swore under her breath.

"She was pregnant at the time, so now Isaac has an instant family." No need for us to fill the void in his heart.

"Oh, love." She grasped my fingers. "So, what's the plan now?"

I shrugged. "I'm toying with so many plans I—"

"Will you tell me about them? Later?" Mum's eyes beseeched mine. "Sometimes it helps you process possibilities when you bounce ideas off someone else."

I had trusted Mum for as long as I could recall, and she had never failed me. "Later sounds good."

"For now, I think you should take a nap."

I smiled. Ever the mother.

Mum led me to my old bedroom and assisted me under the covers. If she could jump into "mum mode" at the drop of a hat, maybe I could too.

"How'd you go?" Mum placed a steaming mug of herbal tea on the kitchen table and sank onto the dining chair opposite me.

My stomach cramped with a Braxton Hicks contraction. I dropped my mobile phone on the table, grimaced, and lifted my right pointer in a "give me a moment" gesture. Was it me, or were these abdomen-tightening sessions firmer and longer than a few weeks ago? I breathed through the squeezing sensation.

"Another Braxton Hicks?"

I nodded and exhaled.

Mum placed her palm on my belly and scrunched her nose. "I don't envy you."

My muscles eased, and I slouched against the seat back. "Sorry."

"Don't apologise. It's getting to the pointy end of the deal, and"—she pulled a face like a kid staring through a toy store window and shrugged—"I'm excited!"

"Me too." A mere week and a half had passed, but my entire perspective had shifted since leaving Tellarine. Seeing Mum in action fuelled my hopes that maybe I could raise this kid. The beautiful hand-crafted wooden bassinet and pile of tiny baby rompers Mum bestowed on me helped nurture my contemplative thoughts about how I could manage this single-mother gig.

Mum blew ripples in her scalding drink. "So? What did they say?"

Oh, yeah. Talk about baby brain! I glanced at my mobile phone before returning her gaze. "Swan Hill District Health contacted

Robinvale and had my patient details transferred, so I'm officially in the care of the midwives here."

"Fabulous! When're you booked in for a check-up?"

"Tomorrow morning, if that's okay?" Mum was working afternoons at the café this week, but if she had plans, I could work around it. The hospital was five minutes away, so worst-case scenario I could catch a taxi or the twenty-three-minute-long bus journey.

"Tomorrow morning's perfect. Did you mention how your practice contractions have ramped up since you arrived?"

I nodded. "They'll check everything's okay, but I was reassured it's to be expected."

"And you've one more week until baby has the green light to arrive?"

I chuckled. "Yeah. Once we reach the thirty-seven and a half milestone, baby can arrive anytime."

"So you could be holding a squeaky bundle of joy in less than a fortnight?" Mum's face softened.

"I could." I sipped my tea, imbibing hot liquid as warmth flowed through my veins. The baby was almost here, and I was far from panicked.

My phone vibrated.

Mum nodded to the handset. "Has Diana confirmed her visit? Did you tell her earlier she's more than welcome to stay the night if it's easier for her?"

"Yeah, I mentioned it when I called this morning." I might be a little forgetful at the moment, but my best friend's birthday was etched in my brain. I unlocked my phone, glanced at the messages, and clutched my rounded belly.

Keanu. The day I fled Tellarine he had called four times and sent twelve texts without one amusing name. Not that I had known he tried to contact me until I switched my phone back on the following day. Another three days passed, with seven additional texts, before I read each message filled with concern for my safety. His final SMS—a desperate plea to send an "I'M OKAY" reply so he knew I was "ALIVE AND NOT DEAD IN A GUTTER"—seemed as though he were genuinely worried, but interpreting tone was impossible via text.

Once I confirmed my existence with a two-word reply, I dealt with Diana's justified explosion.

Keenie: IT'S NOT THE SAME HERE WITHOUT YOU. LET ME KNOW WHEN YOU PLAN TO RETURN TO WORK AFTER SIGMUND IS BORN.

I furrowed my brow. Had I imagined quitting? I mulled and typed my response.

Me: BUT I QUIT? I DON'T KNOW IF I'M COMING BACK.

Keenie: YOUR JOB'S STILL HERE AND WILL BE INDEFINITELY. CALL IT A FAITH DECISION. I'M LEARNING STUFF WITH MATT, JON, AND MR. J.

A faith decision? Since when did he speak Christianese?

I was far from fluent in the language, so how could he know how to speak it? My reoccurring thoughts of Keanu knowing my harboured crush snuck back into my swirling mind, and oxygen fled from my lungs. Was it a game to him? To make me think he wanted to be part of my life? Pain lanced my chest.

No. Keanu would never stoop so low.

I shifted on the chair and sipped my cooling beverage, my gaze glued to the phone. Why would Keanu attend church and learn about God's way of doing things with the guys if not for a prank? Had he been serious when he said he felt accepted at church? And was he truly anticipating my return?

"Is that Diana?" Mum stood and deposited her mug in the sink.

"No, it's … Keanu." I pursed my lips.

Mum's eyes twinkled. "He's a nice young man."

How would she know? "But … you've never met?"

She filled the sink with hot water and a squeeze of washing detergent. "We've spoken on the phone."

"When?" And what had they talked about?

"I called Benanu's the weekend before you went overseas. I'd been trying to chase you up about your storage plans—because you seemed to avoid answering that question—and he said he was covering it. He was a little cool toward me, but polite, and by the end of the conversation I'd extracted a laugh from him, so I figured that was a win."

I stared at my mother and shook my head.

"Okay, time for you to put your feet up while I prepare dinner." Mum grabbed my tea and ushered me to the couch.

"But I can help. I'm not useless."

She patted my shoulder and smiled. "You might as well take

advantage of this peace and quiet while you have it."

"Fine."

Mum chuckled, handed me the TV remote, and exited the lounge room.

The baby kicked and shifted, his or her movements strong but restricted. How much more space did my petite torso contain for this growing baby? Let alone my thinning skin! One more stretch, and I feared my belly might split like a pair of over-washed too-tight yoga pants.

The consensus was this baby would be on the bigger side if I went over forty weeks. One midwife in Robinvale had suggested the baby would be rip-roaring big before the forty-week mark. Words no first-time mother wanted to hear.

I palmed my belly and smiled when a small blunt object pushed against my fingers.

My phone buzzed with Diana's ringtone.

I swiped the screen. "Happy birthday again, gorgeous lady."

"Thanks! And thanks again for your gift. I think Jonathan blushed when he saw it, but you know it's a little hard to tell with his darker complexion."

I smirked. "Have you tried it on?"

Diana's laughter trickled over the phone line. "I was wearing it when he arrived home after work. He tripped and fell over the couch."

I snorted, my cheeks sore from grinning.

"I laughed so hard."

"I bet you did." Nothing like coming home to your wife clad in lingerie inappropriate for public consumption. "Did he enjoy your birthday gift?"

She lowered her voice. "He's napping on the couch, exhausted. Enough said."

I burst out in gut-shaking laughter. Ow.

"So. I've got good news and bad news."

"Oh?" I brushed my hand over my maternity pants.

"Good news is I can visit and will probably stay the night!"

"Yay! And the bad news?"

Diana sighed. "It won't be until late next week."

"That's okay. I'll keep my legs closed until after your visit." If only it were that easy to keep a baby inside. Since arriving in Swan

Hill, I had focused my research reading about the birth process and early days of rearing a newborn. Several times I shut my internet browser and concentrated on something else before my blood pressure rose.

She snort-giggled. "Thanks for the vivid image, Tar. If that were possible, Victoria might've stayed pregnant a few extra months to widen the age gap between Jasmine and Elijah."

"If it were possible, I suspect many first-time mothers would opt for decade-long pregnancies to avoid the inevitable." An extension sounded good to me.

Diana's lilting laughter smoothed the jagged edges of my increasing nervousness about the baby's impending exit.

"I'm glad you're okay with a delay. I'll message you potential dates tomorrow once I get my article submitted. Roger sends his regards."

I smiled. "He hasn't gone missing yet?"

"Huh?"

"Under all that paper on his desk."

Diana chuckled. "I've threatened to file everything away, but he says it's organised in a way he can find everything he needs."

A rumbling motorcycle buzzed along the road, vibrating the lounge window.

"Okay, I'd better go," Diana said. "Will message. Love you."

"Love you too, birthday girl." I settled against the couch cushions with my feet elevated, thankful for my persistent friends and my take-charge mum.

CHAPTER TWENTY-NINE
Benefaction

Someone knocked at Mum's front porch.

I heaved myself off the couch, trotted to the entryway, and opened the door. A blast of mid-July frigid air chilled my cheeks. "So good to see you."

Diana enveloped me, her body—covered head to toe in purple woollen garments—pressed to mine. "You're looking great."

I leaned away and peered past her arm. "Where's your car?"

"Long story." She grasped the handle of a purple-and-black wheeled suitcase.

I stepped backwards and allowed her into the warmth.

Diana shrugged out of her scarf, beanie, and gloves.

"Come dump your stuff in my room. It'll be like old times." I lumbered down the hallway and plopped onto my unmade bed. It seemed like forever since Diana and I had shared a room at the Morgans' in South Yarra.

Diana dropped her belongings at the foot of the spare bed, scrounged through her handbag, and perched on the edge of the mattress. "My car played up this morning, hence my text that I'd be later than planned."

"That sucks. How'd you get here?"

"Keanu offered to drive me, which didn't surprise me since he's been insisting I check up on you." Diana widened her eyes. "Not that I hadn't wanted to visit without his harassment."

My pulse clattered. Had Keanu been here and not even stopped to say hi? Not that I blamed him for dropping Diana off and running. My limited communication these past few weeks spoke volumes.

"But I got him to drop me at Robinvale Station, and I caught a bus."

I pressed my hand to my chest, where my heart had drooped. No Keanu.

"It was actually pretty easy since your local bus is two streets away. If I'd known it'd be so simple, I might've caught a bus sooner. Gives me time to write while I travel."

"Well, you made it here in one piece."

Diana removed an envelope from her coat pocket and met my gaze with serious eyes.

My breath stalled. "What's that?"

"Is it more comfortable for you here or on the couch?"

Why would my comfort matter? I scrunched my face. "I guess the couch if you want to sit closer?"

She nodded, assisted me off the bed, and followed me to the lounge room.

I propped myself on the couch and patted the neighbouring cushion. "What's going on?"

Diana lowered to the seat. "This was delivered with Benanu's mail last week. Keanu gave it to me." She handed over the envelope.

I flipped it over and furrowed my brow. An unfamiliar loopy script with my name and Benanu's address was scrawled across the front. Who was it from?

"We think we know who might've sent it."

We? "Who?"

She nodded at the paper in my hands. "Open it."

I squinted at her impassive face, sighed, and ripped the top open. A single piece of folded paper rested inside. I inhaled a shaky breath, extracted and unfolded the paper.

Tara,

I'm not sure how or what to say.

I darted to the name at the bottom of the page and gasped. Isaac.

"Thought so," Diana whispered.

So his radio silence had ended with a Dear John—or in this case, Dear Jane—letter? I clenched my jaw and fought the fire sizzling through my veins.

Diana touched my fisted hand on my lap. "Want me to read it to you?"

I flexed my jaw. "No. I can do this."

"You can."

I turned to my friend. "But you can read it as well."

She nodded and squeezed my hand.

I blinked my heated eyes and read from the top of the page.

Tara,

I'm not sure how or what to say. I've stared at this blank sheet of paper for hours and still don't know what to write. Is "I'm sorry" enough? I don't know, but I'll say it anyway.

Sorry for breaking my promises (and maybe even your heart?). I'm gutted by this crazy turn of events, but elated to have another chance with Heidi.

I won't give them up again, so this is goodbye.

I'll be uncontactable from here on out. We're relocating overseas for a fresh start, and I leave our child in your capable hands.

Heidi and I talked long and hard about what we should do for Mini Roberts. Apart from suggesting you leave my name off the birth certificate if you can, I've enclosed a cheque. It's the entirety of my savings account. Use it however you see fit for you and the baby's future.

Take care,

Isaac.

He had completely opted out of our child's life. I blinked back tears and rubbed at the stabbing pain near my heart. But could I blame him after I pushed him into a corner the last time we spoke?

Diana grabbed the envelope, peeked inside, and withdrew a small piece of paper. Her eyes boggled.

"What?" I pinched the paper from her fingers. A bank cheque. I searched the page and spluttered. "Sixty thousand dollars?"

Diana leaned closer. "Sixty-three thousand, four hundred and twenty-two dollars to be exact. Seems he *did* clear out his savings."

I pressed my trembling lips together and stared at the cheque. Sixty thousand dollars would be a decent deposit for a small country home for baby and me. Or approximately eight years of payments at the inexpensive Tellarine bungalow I still rented.

Diana touched my shoulder. "You could use a little for your immediate needs, then invest the rest for future university fees."

"I could do a lot with it. But it's not much when you consider it's meant to cover eighteen years of our kid's life." Better than a kick in the head.

She quirked her lips. "Roughly … three and a half thousand dollars per year. Not much when you consider the cost of living, but—"

"At least it's something. I can be thankful for that." I glanced through the kitchen archway to the microwave clock. "Want to go for a walk? The ANZ bank is about twenty-five minutes by foot."

"Or we can catch the bus?"

I nodded. "It might take just as long because of the out-of-way route it takes."

"But at least there's less chance you'll conk out on me." Diana stood and reached out for my hand.

"You talked me into it." I chuckled and lumbered from the couch with her assistance.

"Bathroom stop first." Diana ducked down the hallway.

I wandered to my bedroom and contemplated the latest chapter close in my life. After rummaging through my chest of drawers for my black scarf and beanie, a sudden realisation whacked me between the eyes. All of my anger and resentment toward Isaac had fizzled away. I donned my winter coat and knitwear and grabbed my tote bag and keys, my heart lighter than it had been in a long while. I could forgive him and retain my peace.

"Goodbye, Isaac." I tucked his letter and cheque in my tote bag and whispered my thanks to God for the surprise outcome.

CHAPTER THIRTY
Nascence

A dull back ache woke me from my sleep. I dug my fingers against the sore spots in my lumbar area and squinted, bleary-eyed, at my bedside clock. Almost six in the morning. Maybe I stirred when Mum left for work minutes ago?

Diana's side-lying elongated frame filled the spare bed underneath a pile of blankets, her even breathing evident by the gentle rise and fall of her shoulder.

Pain radiated through my lower back and around my front. I clutched my belly and breathed through another Braxton Hicks contraction. Were they getting stronger?

The soreness eased, and I relaxed against the pillows. More sleep would be advantageous now I was a day shy of thirty-eight weeks. Mum seemed determined for me to prioritise rest, and Diana had sided with her when the usual discussion about my resting came up at dinnertime last night.

I closed my eyes and drifted off to sleep.

Sharp, brutal biffs punched my lower torso, and I sucked in a breath. What was that? I opened my eyes and focused on the clock. Six fifty-two. I waited out the back-dampening pain until it abated, levered myself upright, and plodded to the toilet. The cool bathroom tiles soothed my hot feet.

Maybe a drink of water would help. I trekked to the kitchen, reached for a glass, and hissed. Another Braxton Hicks? I grappled the edge of the kitchen benchtop and breathed through the vice-like pressure around my abdomen and back. Sweat beaded across my forehead and under my arms.

Could this be it? The gut-and-back compression dissipated, and my legs wavered. I shook my head, counted my breaths, and released the bench edge. *Don't be such a lightweight, Tara.*

I filled the drinking glass and sipped the refreshing water. The last thing I wanted was to be one of those oversensitive first-time mothers who failed to discern the difference between real and false labour. No thanks. After the birth stories I had heard and recently read online, my pain was bearable. Nothing like true, excruciating labour pain. Probably my womb flexing its muscles for use on another day. Go uterus!

I grabbed the blanket from the back of Mum's armchair, wiggled about—why was it such a struggle to find a comfortable position?—and lay on my side under the blanket. Before I managed to fall asleep, another wave of not-quite-agonising contractions erupted. I breathed through the pain and waited for sweet relief. Exhaustion overwhelmed me, and I napped on and off.

Diana yawned and plopped onto the couch beside me.

I stirred and stared at her through my half-lidded eyes.

"Morning."

"What time is it?" I suppressed a yawn.

"It's almost eight." She furrowed her brow and pressed her palm to my forehead. "You okay? You're clammy but not burning up."

"Just a little discomfort. Nothing bad." Kinda.

"Discomfort?" Diana straightened. "Just the usual tightening sensations?"

I nodded and breathed through another round of gut compression, clutching my thigh underneath the blanket. Would I survive the birth if this was pre-labour pain? No wonder the few women I had spoken with about childbirth opted for an epidural.

Diana's dark eyes widened, and any signs of sleepiness erased. "Your face says otherwise. Maybe we should call the hospital and chat with one of the midwives."

I panted through the agony.

"What's the number?" Diana leapt from the couch and steamrolled into the kitchen. "Found it!"

I closed my eyes. Thank God Mum was organised and kept important information on the fridge door.

Diana shook my shoulder.

I glanced up at her concerned expression. She offered her phone to me. "They want to speak to you."

Had I dozed? I grabbed the handset. "Hello?"

"Tara, it's Fleur Duggan, a midwife at Swan Hill Maternity. I saw you last week?"

"Yes, I remember." Her reassuring smile had calmed me the moment we met.

"Your friend tells me you're experiencing more pain than usual?"

"Uh huh."

"How far apart are the contractions?"

I wrinkled my nose. "I haven't been counting, but I've had a lot since I woke just before six."

"Hmm." Something shuffled on Fleur's end of the line. "You're thirty-eight weeks tomorrow, correct?"

Another round of abdomen crushing flooded my body, and I gritted my teeth.

"Tara?"

I grunted and panted. What a flattering conversationalist.

"Are you having a contraction now?"

"Y-es." My strained voice sounded weird.

"Your friend said you'd just finished a contraction when she called not five minutes ago."

My stomach softened. I leaned forward and wiped perspiration from my neck. Gross.

"I think it'd be a good idea to get your bag and come in," the midwife said.

Come in? As in "you might be in labour" come in? But that meant I might give birth today! Was I ready to face the journey ahead? Had I been in La-La-Land the past week, thinking I could raise a tiny person? How could I after I had snuffed out my last child's chance to live?

I stood and swayed, suddenly lightheaded.

Diana clasped my elbow. "You okay?"

I caught my breath, waited for the slight spinning to cease, and nodded. I pushed the accusatory thoughts aside and gripped the phone closer to my ear. "My mum's using the car."

"Did she say you should go to the hospital?" Diana whispered.

I nodded again and shifted on my feet.

Fleur cleared her throat. "There's no one nearby who can drop you off?"

"No." The only neighbour I knew was old little Mrs. Dendy, and she had looked five-hundred years old when I was ten.

"Hmm." More shuffling echoed over Fleur's side of the phone line. "I'll arrange for an ambulance, but it might take fifteen to twenty minutes, okay?"

"Okay." What other choice did I have? Hopefully she was wrong and this was false labour.

"I'll see you soon." Fleur disconnected the call.

I kneeled on the carpeted floor and rested my head on the couch seat. Another contraction rippled through me, and I moaned as pressure built at the base of my spine. Whoa.

Diana rubbed my lower back and thrust my water bottle to my lips.

I slurped a mouthful and enjoyed the chilled sensation filling my chest but wished I could shake the restlessness overtaking my body. Maybe this *was* labour? Had I messed up the birth like everything else in my life? *Help me, please, God.* Once my muscles relaxed, I rocked on my heels, grasped the couch, and stood.

A sudden jolt and downshift of baby weight caught me off guard.

Diana's eyes widened. "What is it?"

"I think …" I gasped. Additional movement seemed baby was far too close to the exit zone.

"Is it normal for your belly to have … shifted?" Diana stared at my abdomen, and her mouth slackened. "The bulge has moved south."

"Nor-mal." I trudged the carpeted lounge room in sluggish steps, my hormone-laden limbs unable to stand still. A midwife at the antenatal class in Robinvale had said my body would know what to do when labour commenced, but the picture in my mind differed from this odd experience of my body taking charge. Literally. I wanted to press Pause and nap on the couch, but my limbs zinged with untapped energy.

Diana sank to the couch and watched my slow gait.

On my fourth mild trek around the coffee table, my head buzzing with too many thoughts, another squeezing contraction rooted my legs in place. I dug my toes into the plush carpet.

Diana sprang to her feet and reached for me.

I grabbed hold of my friend's forearms and groaned. The pain flinching my healing left shoulder did not compare to the torture strangling my pelvis. A peculiar sensation shuddered through me before warmth rushed down my legs, soaking my bare feet.

Diana squeaked and stepped backward so she still supported me but protected her feet from being soused with my bodily fluid.

Great. Mum was going to kill me for ruining her carpet. I lifted onto my toes, the carpet squidgy underfoot, while lingering pain pulsated my uterine walls.

"Can you stand on your own?"

I grunted a nod.

Diana disappeared into the kitchen, carried a chair to the tiled front entry, and escorted me to the hard-bottomed seat. "I'll call your mum. Where's your bag?"

"In m-my car." What a perfect day to lend my wheels to Mum.

"Sit here and … cross your legs!"

I huffed a weary laugh and closed my eyes. Despite my still, seated pose, my stomach tossed. Good grief, nausea too?

Diana rushed away. Minutes later she deposited my tote bag at the front door. "I popped your phone, wallet, phone charger, keys, drink bottle, and a hoodie in there."

"Thanks," I whispered.

"Where does your mum keep towels?"

I nodded toward the hallway. "Linen cupboard … n-near the bathroom."

"Thanks." Diana powered down the hallway and returned with a heap of towels. She handed me one and disappeared into the lounge room.

I held the towel to my chest and rested my chin on the soft fabric. Oh to sleep for a week. Could a woman sleep full stop after having a baby? Or would I be an exhausted wreck until my child reached adult years? I had struggled to sleep for weeks after my last baby's demise. Memories of the procedure tortured my mind, and something pinched in my chest. Different circumstances but my sleep suffered.

How was I to resolve this pull to the past while living in the present and planning for the future? Could I face my new baby when my heart was swamped in betrayal? My regret ran deep, the pain of my decision stabbing my heart. Still.

Even though I knew I never had the strength to raise *his* baby. Could I have birthed the child and given the baby to another family to raise? Why had Mum never suggested adoption back then?

An image of me smiling and baking cookies with a curly-haired child filled my mind. I caught my breath and rubbed my tummy. Would I have a girl or a boy? And why had I never allowed myself to ponder this question? Because of what I did to their older sibling?

I shook my head and mentally pulled Scripture to mind. Bible promises for the broken and repentant soul. The tractor beam of sorrow needed its connection severed. I whispered a prayer and cast my thoughts toward a hopeful future.

What would I name my baby? Isaac and I had thrown a few ideas around, but I had laughed off many of his suggestions, especially the floral ones. I assumed Petal, Pansy, Daffodil, Belladonna and Azalea were humorous offerings. Much like the silly names Keanu and I had sent each other.

How could I have left such an important decision off my mental to-do list for so long? What kind of mother would I be when I never prioritised essential deliberation over my baby's name?

When had I jumped back on the merry-go-round in my head? *Help. Please, God.*

Diana kneeled beside me armed with fresh grey trackie daks. "Your mum will meet us at the hospital. Let's get you out of your wet pants."

"Sorry." I lifted my bum, not caring my friend was about to get an eyeful of my birthday suit.

"Don't apologise. I'm relieved I'm here to help. What would you've done if I weren't here?"

I shuddered to think what might have happened. What was still to happen.

Diana stripped my wet pyjama pants and undies, wiped my legs with a towel, and slipped on fresh underwear with a crazy-thick maternity pad. She leaned closer, hoisted my feet into the soft tracksuit material, and pulled the pants to my knees.

The familiar cramping clawed through my womb. "Wait." I grabbed Diana's shoulder and squeezed, shocked by new internal sensors triggering an impulse to push. No. Not yet! My insides tossed.

"Breathe like we practised last night." My friend coached me through the overwhelming contraction.

I breathed, in and out, eyes squeezed shut. Where were the ambos? Would I give birth at Mum's front door? Shivers slid along my spine and shuddered my limbs. My chest tightened, and I firmed my grip on Diana's shoulder. "Sorry." Tears pooled behind my eyelids.

Diana touched my knee, a gentle squeeze, and clucked her tongue. "No apologising."

Why had I not trusted myself when I knew my discomfort differed from previous practice contractions? Were my instincts broken? Was I irreparable?

I glanced at my beautiful never-had-a-baby-but-still-a-perfect-helper bestie and lowered my head. Why did anyone bother with me? How could anyone care?

Keanu's dark eyes filled my mind, and I whimpered. I had thoroughly messed up my life. My eyes stung.

Diana touched my chin.

I met her gaze.

She smiled at me, her cocoa eyes oozing with love. "You're going to be okay."

I palmed my stomach. Soon my life would be consumed with everything baby. Could I do this?

Should I do this?

"You're going to be a brilliant mum, but first you need to pop this baby out." Diana rubbed my shoulder. "Can I suggest whatever urges and sensations you feel, we breathe through these contractions until the ambos arrive? It might feel impossible, but I think you can do it."

"'Kay." My friend believed in me, and the Lord was on my side, so what else did I need? Other than to stop wavering. I exhaled a breath. "C-can you pray?"

"You bet!" Diana scavenged my bag, inserted my water bottle between my shaky hands, and prayed her heart out.

I quaffed water with my eyes closed. The refrigerated liquid cooled my insides while her faith-filled words soothed my overcharged emotions.

The sound of a vehicle engine vibrated outside the house, followed by quick footsteps, and firm raps on the door.

Diana ushered a paramedic into the house.

A semblance of lightness lifted my heavy shoulders. Thank the good Lord for the cavalry!

"Tara? How're you doing?" The well-built twenty-something brunette woman approached.

I glanced at my half-up, half-down pants. So not a good look. "Please, g-get me out of here."

Diana stepped out of the way of another paramedic wheeling a stretcher bed. "Her water's broke about ten or so minutes ago. She's been breathing through serious contractions."

"Was the fluid clear?"

"Yes."

My stomach churned. *Please, Jesus, let me deliver this baby with the hospital midwife.* Bile burned the back of my throat.

The paramedics whispered to each other. "Gravida," "vitals," and "expedited" floated to my fuzzy hearing before they rounded on me.

The female paramedic touched my arm. "Let's get you secured on the stretcher, and we can check your vitals in transit."

I nodded, leaned against her for support, and lay on the soft bed.

Moments later, they wheeled me into the ambulance, Diana not far behind.

The female paramedic wrapped a blood pressure cuff around my arm and slipped a baby monitor over my belly.

Another contraction reared its ugly head.

Diana grabbed my hand. "Breathe and squeeze. Don't worry if you break any fingers, I'll get them patched up at hospital."

I crushed Diana's hand and breathed through tears, my back and pelvis screaming, desperate to reach the hospital in one still-pregnant piece. My mind emptied through the agony, a welcomed hiatus on all thinking. I focused on my breaths, my pinched sides and lungs, and the stifling band of torment rippling across my torso.

"Well done, Tar. Another one over." Diana handed me my water bottle.

"We're about two minutes out," the paramedic behind the wheel called from behind me.

I cheered internally and sipped a toast to my sexless future. Curse you, drunken sexual encounter! Although my Jesus-led morals now steered me toward future husband-only sex, sex was an emphatic "no" here on out. No temptation was worth ripping my body apart like this. Well, unless I married and my hubby was dedicated to raising babies with me, but the likelihood of marriage seemed farfetched. Plus, what decent man would marry a woman who killed her first baby? Scratch that, what decent man would marry me knowing *none* of my secrets, let alone all of them?

"Your blood pressure's stellar considering the strain you're under," Twenty-Something said. "Baby seems content too."

I closed my eyes and enjoyed the few painless minutes my drained body offered before another onslaught of midsection mashing squeezed my son or daughter closer to their wailing exit.

Diana whispered prayers and kissed my forehead.

I was going to be a mother within the hour, no matter how undeserving I might be. *Sweet Jesus, help me.*

The ambulance shuddered to a halt, and someone shuffled nearby. The vehicle door clicked, and cool air filtered into the confined space.

"You can follow after us," the male paramedic said before my stretcher bed jolted and shifted nearer the cold.

Flashes of light permeated through my closed eyelids. I pressed against the mattress to extract all the warmth I could find, thankful to be strapped to the jouncing bed.

Moving leaves and birdcalls were replaced with echoed footsteps, a squeaky wheel, and foreign medical language.

Someone touched my shoulder.

I opened my eyes in a bright white hallway within the hospital.

The female paramedic smiled at me. "An orderly will take you through to Maternity. All the best."

"Thanks," I whispered. Contraction number fifty-four million steamrolled me, and I gritted my teeth with a groan. I deserved all the pain my body threw my way.

Diana grabbed my hand.

"Let's get moving," a man with a deep voice said above my head.

I breathed and squeezed against the almighty force barrelling my baby closer to my arms while the man pushing my bed moved through the hospital corridors like a maniacal supercar driver navigating corners at the Nürburgring Grand Prix.

Diana jogged beside me, her hand slipping in my grasp.

My butt cheeks and pelvic floor ached from clenching against my body's demands to release the baby. Something warm and squishy pressed against my backside, and I prayed it was fluid—any bodily liquid or waste product would do—than a baby limb.

We bounded into the maternity ward, and I released a strangled cry.

"You made it!" Fleur's brilliant smile and calm demeanour tranquilised my raging panic to a more manageable level of anxiety. "Let's get you settled in room three."

Between Race Car Driver Wannabe, Fleur, and Diana, they managed to shift me and my baby monitor from one bed to the other.

"You look ready to pop," Fleur said with a smile. She slipped on disposable gloves and opened a plastic-wrapped bag which contained a myriad containers, tools, and things I had little interest in.

"She's been holding back for several contractions." Diana lifted my water bottle to my lips.

"Let's take a look." Fleur removed my tracksuit pants and underwear with assistance from Diana. "Baby is crowning. You've done remarkably, Tara."

Go me. I offered a weak smile.

"When the next contraction hits, I want you to push."

I grunted.

"I'd like to get you on your knees so we have the full force of gravity on our side."

Diana and Fleur rotated me onto my side, supporting my back and hips until I rested on my knees and elbows, limbs splayed and posterior aimed heavenward.

What a pretty picture I made.

"Am I late?" Mum's harried voice echoed in the room.

Awesome, Mum. Perfect timing. I rested my cheek against the pillow at my head.

"Right on time, Grandma," Diana said.

"How you doing, love?" Mum leaned close and kissed my temple, her perfume wafting under my nose.

"You've raised a brave lady." Fleur rubbed my lower back. "She's pushing with the next contraction."

"Oh." Mum hissed air and leaned against the bed so her face was near mine. "I'm so proud of you."

My vision misted, and I closed my eyes. My lower body tensed, and I turned my face into the pillow. Maybe I should suffocate myself and be done with it.

"Time to push." Fleur's firm hand pressed against the band of pain encompassing my waist.

I flexed my jaw, grunted, and pushed downwards. My knees dug into the mattress and the pillow muffled my growls. The unrelenting pressure dragged a scream from my burning lungs. Was my backside on fire? I gritted my teeth and gurgled.

"You're doing great," Fleur said from somewhere behind me.

The pressure eased, but the burning discomfort remained.

"Baby's head's out. Push to release the shoulders." Fleur's confidence fuelled my waning efforts.

Within seconds, a wet whooshing sound resonated, and the pelvic pressure extinguished like a released water valve. I collapsed forward, the top of my head bearing the brunt of my weight, and gulped air. Moisture trickled down the backs of my quaking legs.

Someone rubbed my shoulder, and I turned my sweaty head.

Mum grinned at me with glassy eyes. "Well done, Mummy."

Mummy.

She helped me lie on my side.

The quavering squawk of a newborn reverberated the room.

Unworthy mummy.

"Congratulations!" Fleur beamed and glanced between my mum and my friend. "Can you help Tara onto her back? It'll be easier to deliver the placenta and snuggle her son."

A son? Did I deserve the responsibility? Tears stung my eyes.

Diana and Mum helped me turn onto my back.

"Here's your little boy." Fleur tucked the towel-clad baby against my chest.

I stared at his puffy red face and breathed in his sweet scent.

Unworthy.

Fleur's eyes softened. "Did you opt for the oxytocin shot to accelerate placenta delivery?"

"Yes." Anything to speed up this process and rest. Everything hurt.

"He's gorgeous." Diana beamed beside me with damp eyes.

"He's got your eye shape." Mum slipped the towel edge from my son's head.

Fluffy tufts of dark hair covered his head. How had two blondes created a dark-haired child?

I watched the off-white wall ahead. What would my first child have looked like? Me? Or *him*?

"How about we see if bubs will feed? It'll help your uterus contract." Fleur helped position the baby in my arms.

I stared at the little human. What was I meant to do with a baby? *God, why had you entrusted this innocent to me?*

He nuzzled my chest, his tiny mouth wide and searching.

The midwife angled his little head. "Often newborns need extra time to—"

I hissed.

"He attached well! Good on you, little man," Fleur cooed.

For the love of all things holy! Did this kid have a vacuum in his head?

"You're a natural, Mummy." Fleur smiled, grabbed something, and jabbed a syringe in my thigh.

I flinched. Was everyone plotting against me? I glanced around the room filled with happy smiles and pleasant chatter. A clear baby bassinet and blue blanket. Vibrant life. How did I belong here?

Before long, the midwife gently tugged on the umbilical cord—which gave me a squirmy feeling in my gut—and a meaty-looking pile of jelly-flesh flopped out. She inspected and prodded the placenta.

Nice career choice.

I wrinkled my nose and stared at the suckling baby with perfect, albeit swollen, features. His petite hand palmed my chest and tickled me with his tiny fingers.

"What will you call him?" Mum asked.

I furrowed my brow, the returning heaviness clouding my mind. What *would* I name him?

"Many parents wait several days after the birth to choose a name," Fleur said. "The government only needs the child registered within sixty days of birth, so you have time. There's no pressure to have a name the moment bub arrives."

God bless Fleur.

"Want some more water?" Diana extended my bottle toward my lips.

"Please." I gulped several mouthfuls.

Fleur arranged some things on a small trolley. "You'll need to drink lots of water if you plan to breastfeed."

Feeding. Another important decision I had researched but avoided choosing an option. Formula bottles were easier for someone else to feed the baby, but breastfeeding would make financial sense. So long as I produced enough milk for the baby's needs.

Fleur cleared away the birth mess and inched closer. "Do you mind me checking the impact zone? From my vantage point, I think you might need a few stitches."

I winced. "Do whatever you need to do."

Fleur smirked. "Don't worry, I'll dose you with plenty of local anaesthetic."

I pushed aside my multiplying concerns, doubts, and fears, and glanced at Diana while the midwife poked around. "Nothing awkward about this, hey?"

Diana chuckled. "What're besties for?"

"How about we get some photos of you and Mr. Handsome?" Mum pulled her phone from her jacket pocket. "Daphne will be beside herself."

Oh yeah. Communicating baby news to family and friends. I rubbed at the slight ache in my right temple. "Can you send the pic directly to Jae too? I don't want her getting second-hand info from Aunt Daphne."

"Of course, love." Mum snapped a few pictures, grinned at her phone screen, and tapped a message.

Fleur readjusted the end of the bed and manoeuvred a set of metal stirrups. "Just need to get your legs in these. Can you scoot forward?" She positioned them—and then me—into place.

Diana brushed her fingers over Mr. Handsome's hair. "Would you like me to get your phone? Or do you want me to message anyone from home?"

Home. Where was my home now the baby was here? "I …" My throat clogged.

"I messaged Jonathan and Victoria earlier for them to pray, but I didn't tell anyone else. Can I message Sam and Keanu?"

The post-birth high-on-love-hormones part of my heart broke through the heavy fog of indifference clogging my cottony head and screamed "Yes!" I nodded against my better judgement.

"Want me to say anything in particular?"

Something stung down below, and I flinched.

"Sorry, sometimes it's better to just jab the anaesthetic without warning," my evil midwife said. "You need about three stitches. Another incoming jab."

I winced.

"I'll warn you before I start sewing you up."

Great. What a joy this birth thing had turned out to be.

Diana snapped a photo of me and bubs. "Want to smile?"

I offered a barely there lift of my lips. Take it or leave it.

She scrunched her lips and clicked another photo. "What did you want me to say to … them?"

I pulled a face. Sorry for freaking out? I wish you were here but am glad you cannot see me now? My son has similar hair colouring to you?

My son. Air disappeared from my lungs.

Diana quirked an eyebrow. "How about I say Mum and baby are doing well …"

Not sure "doing well" was true.

"We'll have more info once you're patched up?"

I widened my eyes. "Don't mention the patched-up bit."

"Why? Guys know where babies exit the female body." Diana pressed her upturned lips together.

"I don't want you drawing attention to that." To me.

"They'll be thinking it regardless." Fleur chuckled. "Okay, can you feel this?"

I waited for the painful needle prick. A mild semi-tugging caught my attention.

"Nothing?"

"Just a weird tug?"

"But it doesn't hurt?"

"No."

"Perfect." Fleur donned a pair of spectacles and ducked low.

"Totally not awkward," Diana whispered.

I watched the baby sleep against my breast, my breaths quickening with the knowledge I was all he had in this world.

CHAPTER THIRTY-ONE
Disillusioned

"He's perfect." Victoria cuddled my napping two-day-old nameless son on Mum's couch and grinned at the new grandmother beside her.

"Isn't he." Mum leaned close and stroked her forefinger along his cheek. "I'm shocked how smitten I am of him."

The last forty-eight hours had revealed a softness I never knew Mum possessed.

I readjusted the recliner cushions padding my back and rear end and pressed my lips together. How long until I could sit like a normal human or pee without discomfort?

"I miss their gorgeous smell," Victoria said. "It's the smell of love and merited achievement."

Or the smell of regret and sorrow. No matter how long I held the baby, my heart stabbed for his lost sibling.

"Don't get any ideas." Diana approached from the kitchen and handed me a glass of water.

Victoria chuckled. "For you or me?"

Diana's cheeks flushed a soft pink.

"Nicholas had the snip years ago."

Diana scrunched her nose. "TMI."

I glugged my water and observed the two older women cluck over the newborn baby.

Diana lowered to the armchair beside me. "You're never going to be short of helpers. What with the related and adopted grandmothers, the favourite aunt"—she pointed to herself—"and others at church."

All I needed to do was revive my dying heart and dive into

motherhood.

"Do you need another ice pack?" Diana whispered.

"Not yet, thanks." Whichever amazing individual had discovered the wonders of post-birth ice-packed sanitary pads was worthy of a Nobel Prize.

"I think Mr. Handsome is stirring," Mum said.

What purpose did I serve other than to feed and change the beloved grandchild?

The baby whined like a kitten and flexed his little arms over his head.

I yawned, my exhaustion debilitating.

Victoria stood and delivered the baby into my arms. "How about you feed him while your mum and I get some lunch. My treat."

"Sounds great." I slipped into autopilot, unclipping my feeding bra, and let the little sucker at it.

Mum and Victoria exited through the front door.

"Are you okay? You've been a bit … out of it." Diana pressed her lips together.

"I'm peachy." My chest tightened, and my eyes pricked with tears.

She kneeled in front of my chair. "You must be drained with all that broken sleep. Do you want me to stay longer and help?"

I wiped my wet eyes. "What could you do? I'm the one-stop-baby-needs shop."

She lay a hand on my knee. "I can get baby from his bed when he cries, deliver him to you, burp him and change him, and put him back to bed."

How could I burden my friend with tasks I was meant to do?

Diana widened her smile. "You can get extra rest and not worry about anything but your recovery."

Spending more time thinking seemed like the worst idea in the world. I shook my head. "Your hubby misses you. And it's not fair to Victoria to drive all this way to not take you home as planned."

She appraised me with searching eyes. "I'm really happy to stay."

Why could I not just accept her help and be done with it? What was wrong with me?

"When's Jaelle calling?" Diana glanced at her phone.

"Just before dinner." I had yet to speak face-to-face with my cousin—or as close as one could via the internet—since giving birth, but I had received an Amazon box filled with blue outfits and lacy breastfeeding bras this morning.

"Victoria wants to head off around five-ish so we can be home for dinner." Diana met my gaze. "But you ask me to stay, and I will."

I brushed my finger along Mr. Handsome's soft hand which clutched my bra and pulled my hand away. "If I had a husband waiting at home for me, I'd be home for dinner too."

Diana tilted her head. "Keanu's been messaging me constantly about you."

If he knew the mess inside my brain, he would stop caring.

"I think he's apprehensive to message you because he doesn't want to step wrong."

I wiped another tear from my cheek.

"He'd be a great influence in Mr. Handsome's life if you let him, as will Jonathan, Dad, Matt, and even Sam."

I stared at the little boy who would grow up with a mother who had never lived with a father or brothers of her own. A little boy deprived of his father. Was I able to mother this boy like he deserved? What hope did I have raising a kid with all my baggage? *Lord, I need Your peace. And sleep. Oodles of sleep.*

"You've already seen Keanu work his magic on my little sister and brother."

Surrounding the baby with strong, compassionate men would set him off to a good start in life. Having a mother who cared would be even better.

"Maybe I'll message him." Maybe not. Keanu was a night owl, so he might be up during one of the night feeds … should I want to message him in the future.

"And don't forget to message me too. I can always send you Jonathan's roster so you know when he's on nights and might have a moment to message."

I raised a brow. "Am I that desperate to need to chat with your husband in the middle of the night?"

Diana shrugged. "I've seen a sleep-deprived Victoria sprawled on her lounge room floor in tears over a fictional TV character, so anything's possible."

I tapped the baby's shoulder until he mimicked feeding again. "Yeah, I might get desperate, so send me the roster."

♥ ♥ ♥ ♥ ♥ ♥ ♥

Someone shook me awake.

I squinted at Mum with burning eyes.

"You asked me to wake you when Jae calls." Mum pointed to my open laptop on the end of my bed, the screen facing away from me.

"Thanks." My voice rasped.

"Mr. Handsome's sleeping sound in the lounge."

I pulled myself upright and peeked around Mum. The bassinet was not in its usual location.

"I'll keep him as long as you need, love." Mum passed me the laptop and exited the room, closing the door behind me.

I slipped the laptop onto my lap, yawned, and unmuted the screen.

"Aren't you a woman of leisure," Jaelle said with a smirk.

I glared at my cousin and ran my fingers through my bed hair. "You would be too if you squeezed a human out of your bits."

Jaelle winced. "How're you doing? What with the bruising—"

"Tearing." I growled.

Her wince deepened to a grimace.

"And the heaviest period I've bled in my lifetime." Was it payback because I enjoyed a menstrual-free nine months? How was this fair to women?

My cousin shuddered. "I'm sorry it's not been a barrel of laughs for you."

"Hardly." I rubbed my tired eyes.

"But is the payoff worth it? To have a warm, squishy, adorable little baby to love?"

"It's …" I shrugged.

"Not what you expected." Jaelle's gaze into the webcam intensified.

"No," I whispered. The waves of guilt pounding me the moment I tried to connect with the baby were draining my sanity.

"It's okay, TarTar. Things don't always go the way we hope, but you're tough. You'll get through this."

I blinked away tears. "Will I?"

"Of course. There're people with you who have your back.

Aunt Alannah's loving her new granny gig, and I'm sure Diana's happy to pitch in." Jaelle lifted her hand, palm outstretched, as though to touch my screen and caress my face. "And when I accumulate some more leave, I'm visiting for a week or two."

I wiped my fingers along my wet cheek. "I'd like that."

"But for now, do you need some name ideas? Although he's definitely a Mr. Handsome, I'm not sure the Victorian Births, Deaths and Marriages Registry will allow the name."

I puffed a half-hearted laugh. "True."

"What kind of name are you thinking? Modern? Classic?" She scrunched her nose. "Maybe Biblical? Which're probably also classic names."

I tapped the laptop edge. "I want something uncommon but nothing outrageous. Maybe with a nice meaning?"

Why had Isaac and I not treated the name game with more importance? Even when Keanu had exchanged weird names with me, he had been focused and attentive. Interested. An unseen fist punched at my chest.

"What?" My cousin's voice woke me from my internal musing.

I shook my head. "Nothing."

"Didn't look like nothing to me." She furrowed her brows. "Maybe you should connect with someone who can help you work stuff out … decipher your thoughts."

Who could fulfill such a role?

"When's the last time you saw your therapist?"

I stared at the screen. "It's been a long time."

She leaned forward. "It might help?"

I scrubbed my face with my hands. "Maybe it'll be easier if I get more sleep. All my research says parents are off kilter the first few months of parenthood." Forget a month, could I survive the week like this?

"Then let people help you." Jaelle bounced on her seat, her curls jolting around her face. "Let your mum fuss over you and Mr. Handsome. And anyone else who volunteers."

Why had I told Diana to go home this afternoon? I ground my back molars. I had to figure my mess out.

Jaelle widened her eyes. "I saw you at your worst, remember?"

I nodded, my gaze dropping to the keyboard.

"Please let us help you so you don't end up back there."

My vision blurred. The last thing I wanted was to return to that nightmare. I nodded.

"I'll check back on you in a few days. Get some rest."

"Thank you." I blew my cousin a kiss.

She caught it with a flourish of her hand. "Anytime. Love you."

"Bye." I exited the chat portal, closed my laptop, and sank back under the covers.

CHAPTER THIRTY-TWO
Reconnecting

Baby lamb-like bleats woke me from sleep, and I blinked in the dark room. I glanced at the clock—the sole, dull light in my bedroom—relieved I had slept four hours, and stumbled toward the bassinet at the end of my bed before Mum woke to help. "Shoosh, you."

Three-day-old-baby cries were louder than one-day-old-baby cries.

I picked up the warm, little person, returned to my bed, and positioned my tender backside in a wall-leaning, seated position. My eyes adjusted to the darkness. "You need to be quieter so Grandma can sleep. No point waking us both."

His cries intensified, and his no-longer-puffy face reddened.

"Hold your horses, desperado." I yawned, pulled my phone closer, and latched the nipple torturer to my chest.

Mr. Handsome settled into his colostrum-rich snack.

I stared at my phone. Two past two. Would he be awake? I sent Keanu a message before I could talk myself out of it.

Me: HEY. ANY CHANCE YOU'RE AWAKE LIKE ME?

My heartrate accelerated. What was I doing? I held my breath and monitored the screen.

Keenie: BREASTFEEDING MY BABY? NO.

I choked back laughter, my chest shaking enough to disturb the little drinker.

Bubs fussed at my breast with an upset mewl.

I resettled him and returned to my phone.

Keenie: STARING AT THIS *INSERT SWEAR WORD* SPREADSHEET? YES.

Me: What spreadsheet? Can I help?

Maybe I could be of more use than a food factory to an infant.

Keenie: Next quarter projections Dad wants by end of week.

Keenie: Might call Di since my Number One is off hugging a baby.

Number One. Why did his incidental remark heat my cheeks?

Keenie: How are you and Cletus?

I stifled a yawn.

Me: Exhausted.

Keenie: I bet. Can I help in any way?

I smiled at the screen.

Me: Want to change and burp Mr. Handsome?

Keenie: Would love to. Be there in an hour. ;-)

What would my life be like opening the door to a man like Keanu? Trusting him to support and help me? I pushed away the tempting thought. Exhaustion must be weakening my defences.

Keenie: Milk come in yet?

I squeaked a laugh, which disturbed the little mister, if his flailing arm was any indication. "You're okay." I clipped my bra, switched his tiny body from resting in the crook of my left arm to my right, unclipped the other side of my bra, and positioned my son.

He latched on like the pro he was.

Me: You reading your app again?

Keenie: Maybe.

I grinned at the screen like a crazy, sleep-deprived, emotional yo-yo of a lady.

Me: Not yet. I hear it feels like your boobs are going to explode, so I'm not looking forward to that since everywhere else already exploded.

Keenie: You're a human IED.

Me: Sums it perfectly.

I had missed this banter. So much.

Keenie: Picked a name yet?

I stared at the screen. Why did his question not grate against my nerves like the previous times I had been asked the exact same question by others over the last three days? And why did I want to be honest with him? What was it about Keanu that kindled a deep sense of safety?

Me: Not Yet.

I looked at the little boy in my arms—falling asleep on the job—and brushed his cheek with my finger. Three days old and still unnamed. I sighed.

He released his suction hold, eyelids fluttering, and a crazy-clown gassy faux-smile stretched across his mouth.

"Burp time." I yawned, hoisted him against my shoulder, and rubbed his back in small circles. What would I name this floppy-headed, teeny ball of squish?

Mr. Handsome puffed a tame burp. His breaths evened.

I extracted myself from the warm covers, tucked the little mister in his bassinet, and resettled in bed without inflicting more pain on my battle-weary body.

Keenie: Need ideas? Ichabod Roberts has a nice ring to it.

Me: Maybe you should think of serious name contenders. You know, names for a child destined for places other than therapy.

I yawned again.

Me: Time for me to sleep. Chat later.

I plugged my phone back in the charger as it vibrated with another message.

Keenie: Will do. Sweet dreams.

If I slept long enough to dream, most of my problems would be solved.

Keenie: Can you snap me another pic of Horatio? Need to see if my name ideas still match him.

I leaned over my slumbering week-old baby and fought against the whirlpool of messy feelings overflowing my head and quickening my heartbeat. My son was not only without a name—yes, I was a terrible mother—but his sleeping features triggered thoughts of my would-be preschooler.

My throat closed, and my eyes watered. I sniffed, snapped a photo, and dropped to my bed.

Me: Pretty much the same photo I sent two days ago with a different outfit.

Same old, same old. I rubbed my tired face and rotated my achy neck. Familiar dark, weighted tentacles gripped my shoulders, and Jaelle's warning echoed in my ears.

Please let us help you so you don't end up back there.

My anxiety levels had increased, along with my wayward thoughts. And the guilt. No matter how much sleep I grabbed, the shadows gripped tighter. Maybe she was right.

I laced my sneakers and slipped from my bedroom.

"He sleeping?" Mum smiled from where she stood in the kitchen.

I nodded.

Her brows dipped low, and she rounded the bench. "You okay, love?"

"Do you mind if I go outside for some fresh air?"

"Of course not. I'll keep an eye on Mr. Handsome." She rubbed my arm.

"Thanks, Mum." My chest clamped.

"That's what I'm here for." She beamed, lowered her arm, and returned to the kitchen.

I wandered outdoors and along the front path, breathing in cool air and lavender. Five hundred metres down the road, I stopped at a vacant block and retrieved my phone.

Call her. You can do this.

I scrolled my contacts and dialled her number.

"Doctor Braithwaite's office, Carolyn speaking," said an unrecognisable voice.

"Uh, hi." I cleared my throat. "My name's Tara Roberts—"

"Hello, Tara. How can I help you?" Carolyn sounded kind.

"I, ah, was a patient? B-but haven't seen Dr. Braithwaite ... f-for a while." My hands shook, and I pressed the phone closer to my face. "I wondered ... could I speak with her? Please."

"Of course, Tara." She clicked and typed. "Do you mind if I put you on hold for a moment?"

"Yes, sure, that's fine." I walked along the edge of the path and the muddy plot of land, turned at the neighbouring house, and paced along the same straight path until I reached the next house.

The cool breeze nipped at my hoodie neckline, and I flipped the black cotton-terry hood over my unkempt hair. What would my uni friends think of this dishevelled version of me?

"Tara, it's good to hear from you. How are you doing?" Dr.

Braithwaite's soothing voice resonated.

"I'm … not doing so great," I whispered.

"And that's okay. What's happening with you at the moment?"

I retraced my steps along the path, drawing cooled air into my tight chest. "I have a week-old son."

"Congratulations. You must be exhausted."

"Yeah."

"Was this a planned pregnancy?"

"No. But different circumstances to last time." Thank God.

"And is the father involved? Or are you doing this alone?" Dr. Braithwaite's questions inferred so much more than she asked. She knew my fears, my hang-ups, and everything in between.

"Alone."

"I see."

"But it was going to be a partnership … until it wasn't." How could I begrudge Isaac his family?

"And what prompted you to call me?"

"I feel … guilty." I slowed my pace and stared up at the overcast sky. "How can I be a mother when …"

"What do you think about when you look at your baby?"

I braced against a cold wind chilling my legs through my maternity jeans. "His baby."

"Do you think of him too?"

I shook my head. "Not really. Just the baby."

Dr. Braithwaite tapped a computer keyboard. "Are you able to come in and see me this week?"

"I'm back at Mum's." Too far from Melbourne.

"Right." Something shuffled. "I could refer you to someone local?"

There was no way I was going to see the local therapist who I visited immediately after my trauma. She and I had not clicked.

"Or we can book in a telehealth video call? Would you feel comfortable doing so at home?"

A telehealth video call? The wonders of technology amazed me. "I could book a time when I know Mum's home so she can watch the baby."

"Excellent. How about I send you back to Carolyn so she can book a time and update your details?" A smile brightened Dr. Braithwaite's reassuring voice.

"Thank you." I turned in the direction of home.

"Talk soon."

"Bye." I confirmed my information with the receptionist, booked a meeting for tomorrow afternoon while Mum was home, and checked the letterbox.

My phone beeped several times.

Unknown: HELLO, TARA, CONFIRMING YOUR TELEHEALTH APPOINTMENT WITH DR. BRAITHWAITE TOMORROW AT 14:00 ONLINE. PLEASE CLICK THE FOLLOWING LINK AT YOUR APPOINTMENT TIME.

Keenie: XAVIER SPENCER

Keenie: YOU WANTING A MIDDLE NAME? BOTH WORK AS FIRST NAMES, BUT THE ABOVE ORDER SOUNDS BEST.

A middle name too? Too much thinking. I tucked my mobile away, yawned, and opened the front door.

"Feeling a little better?" Mum met me in the entryway. "He's still asleep in your room."

I padded into the lounge room and drooped on the couch. "I booked an online appointment with Dr. Braithwaite for tomorrow afternoon."

Mum stood in the archway between the lounge and kitchen, nodding more times than necessary. "When do you need me?"

"The appointment's at two o'cloc—"

"Perfect time for me to take a walk after the early afternoon feed."

"Thanks." My eyes stung. We both knew the walls were thin in this old house.

Mum smiled at me. "Nap or cuppa?"

I melted against the couch cushion and closed my eyes. "Nap then cuppa?"

Mum's soft laughter faded through the kitchen archway.

CHAPTER THIRTY-THREE
What's in a Name?

I guided my sporty black-and-orange three-wheeled pram over a crack in the footpath and sucked in lungfuls of crisp August air. Early afternoon sunshine warmed my skin as I trailed the tree-lined residential street. The new month held promise with its long-forgotten patches of blue sky.

Swan Hill was humungous compared to Tellarine but still boasted the quaint feel of a country town. Compared to the outer suburbs of Melbourne, this neighbourhood looked like Sticksville.

My cup of tea.

Mr. Handsome wiggled in his bassinet enclosure, sighed, and returned to his dreamworld. He remained unnamed—to my dismay—but there had been greater issues to deal with during the last three weeks since his arrival.

I had attended five telehealth sessions with Dr. Braithwaite in the past fortnight. She thought it imperative to focus on the essentials—my mental stability and managing ways to limit stress and maximise sleep. The appointments offered me perspective while unravelling the chaos in my head, and the breastfeeding-safe medication Sertraline, which Mum's GP prescribed a week ago, notched my anxiety down a level or two while facilitating restful sleep. My therapist reminded me pregnancy, birth, and surviving daily life with a newborn was stressful for those with robust, trauma-free minds, let alone someone like me.

Keanu and Diana had said something similar last week. Maybe God was trying to tell me something.

I pulled the pram shade cover over the baby, opened the little see-through panel, and rested my phone on the canopy. I needed to reread Keanu's message from this morning.

Keenie: HERE'S A NAME YOU MIGHT LIKE? BEEN HOLDING IT BACK BECAUSE IT'LL CRUSH ME IF YOU HATE IT. ;-) WHAT ABOUT KAI?

My hands had trembled when I first read his message. I had never heard the name until I worked at Benanu's and had only glanced it once when working on a payroll issue for Mr. Everton.

Kai was Keanu's middle name.

I stared at his message, heart thumping. Was this a casual name offering a guy with a common name like Joshua or Daniel might give? Or was there more to his message?

We had discussed around thirty potential names via text. Should I treat this like all the others? Unfortunately, I had another problem. I loved the name Kai. The more I peeked at the sleeping baby in the pram—*my* sleeping baby—the name resonated. Kai Roberts.

Kai Everton.

I huffed at the ridiculous thought and reprimanded my stubborn heart. Keanu and I could be friends but nothing more. I was a hot mess, and he was … not.

But you're getting better every day.

I silenced the whispers and sidled along a walking path into Barry Steggall Park.

Preschool-aged children played on the colourful equipment, running between play areas with delighted cries. Some adults supervised, a few pretended to supervise while glancing at their mobile phones more than their minors, and a few brave souls climbed the equipment with their kids.

I spotted a vacant canvas-covered picnic table near a roped climbing frame and walked in its direction, whispering a prayer, capturing the fleeting thought about my lost preschooler.

Forgive yourself.

I parked the pram and plopped on the wooden bench seat. My stamina had improved since my son ripped his way out of my body, but I had a long way to go before I walked—let alone jogged or, heaven help me, ran—several kilometres without passing out.

Mr. Handsome slept without stirring, his blanket rising and falling with each of his breaths.

I allowed myself a moment to gaze and grieve like Dr. Braithwaite suggested. No one could undo what had been done to my first baby, but I had been in a dark place. The sole light to shine in my broken world had been Diana and her suggested uplifting songs. Now I shared a relationship with Jesus—even if I seemed to have a habit of pulling away during difficult times … *sorry, Lord*—there was hope for this baby. For my ability to mother him. And a kindled hope in my heart to forgive myself and move forward.

But moving forward did not mean I would spend the rest of my life with a wonderful guy. I smiled down at the tiny head poking from the blankets. Other than this little guy.

"It's a lovely day, isn't it?"

I glanced up and eyed a weathered, elderly woman with cropped grey hair and a wooden cane drop to the end of the bench seat. I cracked a polite smile. "Yes, it's nice when winter switches on the sun."

She chuckled a husky laugh. "It's good for old and young bones."

I nodded and turned to observe my son.

She leaned closer and peeked into the pram. "What a darling. Boy or girl?"

"Boy."

"Ah, I remember the early days with my boy, Darryl. Such sweet bonding moments."

Bonding moments for some. I strained to keep a smile on my lips.

She reached out and touched the pram blanket covering my baby.

I stared, wide-eyed. If she woke him …

"A good boy too, sleeping for his mummy." She leaned back and rested her hand on her knees. "How old?"

I relaxed my shoulders. "Three weeks."

"He a good feeder?"

Did all elderly strangers ask such personal questions? "Ah, yes."

"My Darryl had quite the suction."

Talk about too much information.

"What's the dear little fella's name?"

I fisted my hands in my lap and begged my voice to remain steady. Calm.

"I hope it's not one of those age-old beloved names with newfangled spelling to confuse those with common sense?"

I sucked in a steadying breath. "I'm, ah, still working on his name."

The old woman straightened.

I dropped my gaze to the concrete path.

She tutted. "Guess you're not Greek or Jewish, or one of those Eastern religious types, or you'd have shamed your family by not naming the poor boy yet."

I squeezed my fists tighter. My vocal cords froze.

"But I guess that's to be expected in this lazy, selfish time we live in. No respect for the ways of old." She stood and approached the pram.

I stiffened, adrenaline pumping through my veins.

"Shameful. Hope you get named soon, son." She tutted and wandered away.

Blood pounded between my ears. I gripped the pram handle, jolting the frame by accident, and counted my breaths.

Lazy. Selfish. Shameful. The words bounced around my head, and I fought back tears. Was I selfish to have focused on "fixing me" instead of devoting my waking hours naming my son?

When would I do better? Be better?

My phone vibrated on top of the pram.

I slipped the handset off the canopy with shaky hands and unlocked the screen.

Di-Di: Just thinking of you, my wonderful friend and beautiful mother of my favourite nephew. Is the weather good over your way too? Hope you're having a fabulous day filled with the tangible presence of our Lord and Saviour.

Tears dribbled down my cheeks, and I swiped my palms across my face.

My phone chimed again.

Di-Di: Was humming this tune this morning and thought of you.

I double-checked my sleeping baby, clicked the YouTube link, and lowered the media volume on my phone. Blanca's *How Much More* played. I held the bottom edge of my mobile against my ear and listened to the upbeat track, more tears trickling my cheeks.

God loved me more than the birds He fed and the flowers He watered. His love for me—and my baby—was greater than the love other men and women on earth blessed with children had for their babies. God's heart was for me, even in my weakness and lack. My indecision.

I covered my mouth with my free hand and sobbed. My vision flooded with tears as the lyrics ministered to me. What would I do without the Lord? And Diana? Warmth overflowed in my chest. I dropped my phone in my lap, sniffled, and wiped my fingers across my eyes and nose.

A young man holding hands with a toddling youngster walked nearby, his eyes regarding me. He raised his brows and slowed.

I smiled, shook my head, and wiped my damp fingers against my thighs.

He passed by with a smile and a nod.

Mr. Handsome squeaked a "I'm beginning to wake, Mummy, so get ready!" noise.

"Let's go, little man." I pocketed my phone, unlocked the pram brake, and wandered home, my mind clear for the first time in a long time.

Fifteen minutes later, I trundled through Mum's front door.

Mr. Handsome whimpered, the beginning of his usual "feed me already!" routine.

"You're back!" Mum approached, pushed the pram cover back like an accordion, and hoisted her crying grandson into her arms. "Have a nice walk?"

"Yes and no." I manoeuvred the pram to my bedroom and propped it in the corner under the window near my old school desk.

"Yes and no?" Mum rocked the baby in the doorway.

"Had some things on my mind." I slipped past Mum and walked to the lounge room.

Mum's footsteps padded behind me. "Oh?"

"Then an old woman told me in not so many words what a terrible mother I am for not naming my child yet." I grabbed the baby and settled on the recliner.

"What? What old woman?" Mum's fiery eyes tracked my movements.

"Just a stranger making conversation." I positioned my son and gritted my teeth when he latched on to drink. The maternal health nurse said last week the discomfort would ease over time.

"But to be so rude?" Mum huffed a breath.

I shrugged.

Mum strode to the kitchen, poured me a tall glass of water, and placed it on the nearby side table.

"Thanks."

She lowered to the neighbouring armchair. "Have you progressed in the name department?"

I pursed my lips. "Maybe. I want to look up the origins of a particular name."

"Which name?" Mum yanked her phone from her pocket. She peered at me with wide, pleading eyes.

When had my relationship with Mum relaxed? Once upon a time she had forced her way into every decision. Now she hinted her interest without pushing me to make choices.

I smiled at her. "Kai."

She furrowed her brow. "K-Y?"

I scrunched up my face. "No. K-A-I."

"Oh, that's a much nicer way to spell it." Mum typed on her screen.

Maybe-Kai pulled back, spraying milk in his face, and spluttered.

I plugged the leak with my breast pad and set him upright, patting his back as he coughed and gasped.

"Is Mummy shooting milk too fast for you, love?" Mum crooned a besotted smile at her grandson.

He squirmed, belched like a sailor, and hiccupped.

Oh man. I rested bubs against my stomach to wait out the interruption. Newborn hiccups were cute the first time, but the second, third and twentieth time? A tiresome ten-minute wait. The stamina of such a tiny body hiccupping for an extended period of time amazed and frustrated me.

"Kai. Hmm." Mum hummed and scrolled. "Did you know Kylo is a variation of Kai?"

Kylo? "Like Kylo Ren, Darth Vader's emo grandson?"

"That's where I heard the name!"

I snorted a laugh, my chest vibrating Mr. Handsome's hiccupping back.

"Apparently it's a popular name worldwide. Kai, not Kylo." Mum scratched her cheek. "With varying meanings depending on which culture you defer to."

"Like what?" I brushed my son's uber-soft hair with my fingers. His ears were soft too.

"Let's see. It means 'warrior' in some European nations but also 'keeper of the keys' … of earth, I assume, to the Scandinavians, Greeks, and Welsh." Mum pursed her lips and squinted. "Or that might be the African meaning? This website is confusing."

"So it means 'warrior' and something about keeping earth's keys." Not much to go by yet. "Anything else?"

"It means 'shell' in Japanese and 'sea' in Hawaiian culture."

Hawaiian culture.

"This website lists other complementary names," Mum said. "Oh! Did you know Keanu means 'the breeze' in Hawaiian?"

The breeze and the sea. Keanu was like a refreshing sea breeze on a warm summer's afternoon teasing my senses. Inviting. Welcoming.

Mum lowered her head and eyed me. "Have you gravitated toward a Hawaiian-inspired name for any particular reason?"

My cheeks warmed. "You just listed a bunch of countries. It's popular in lots of places."

"But it's very complementary to one particular gentleman's name." She raised her brow and smiled.

My pulse tripped, and I slowed my breaths. "Maybe."

"Was it one of his suggestions?"

I nodded.

"It's his best yet. 'Kai' has more … character."

"It's his middle name," I blurted.

"What?" Mum gazed at my hiccup-free child.

Why had I opened my big mouth? I shifted my son into feeding position. "How about we try again."

"Whose middle name? Keanu's?"

Mr. Handsome attached and drank without a hitch.

If I named my son Kai, Mum was bound to find out. "Yeah."

"Oh." Mum dragged her voice like she uttered a fifteen-letter word.

I pulled a face and met Mum's gaze. "Is that a bad thing?"

"No. Not at all. But …" She touched my arm. "It might come across as meaning more … unless you want it to mean more."

Did I? The name grew on me more with each passing minute. "He didn't say it was his middle name. I saw it once. At work."

"Hmm."

Lord, what should I do?

"Speaking of work, have you entertained any thoughts for what you want to do?"

What I want to do?

"You're still renting the little place in Tellarine, right?"

I nodded.

"And after what you said a few weeks ago, I assume you still have a job?"

"Right." My voice croaked.

Mum glanced out the lounge room window. "I don't intend kicking you out at any stage, but I wonder if your place is here or … there?"

I exhaled a loud, long breath. "I'm not sure yet." Not while I still recovered.

"And that's perfectly all right." Mum squeezed my hand with a smile and stood. "How about I make us a cuppa?"

"Thanks, Mum." I gazed down at my son guzzling milk and permitted a moment of deliberation for our future.

CHAPTER THIRTY-FOUR
Off-Limits

"Tara! Your phone's blowing up here on the table!" Mum's voice travelled through the kitchen window to her small backyard.

"Okay! I'll be in soon!" I smiled at my son where he lay beside me on the large patchwork rug. "Your gran can exaggerate sometimes, kiddo."

He rested on his stomach for his designated dose of "tummy time" with eyes wider than usual. The little guy had become more alert as the weeks passed. Before long he would be a month old. Where had the time gone?

I slid my forefinger along his soft, tiny fist bunched near his chin. This afternoon was the first time I had enjoyed a quiet moment with him. A perfect day of parenting and weather—two in a row, to be exact. Could I be exiting the dark tunnel at long last? I leaned across and kissed his squishy cheek, his newborn scent warming my insides.

My son deserved a mother willing and able to care for him.

Mr. Handsome blinked his sleepy eyes in the waning late-afternoon sun.

"C'mon, let's go inside." I bundled him against my chest, covered him in the blanket, and trod across the uneven grass into the house.

"Not sure who wants your attention, but they sound keen." Mum turned toward us where she stood at the kitchen sink and grinned. "He about ready for a nap?"

"Yeah, he's getting sleepy after all that exercise." I kissed the top of my son's soft hair.

Mum clasped her gloved hands together. "You two look gorgeous bundled up like that. You really are an amazing mother."

"Thanks."

"I'm almost done here." She removed her gloves and nodded to the lounge room. "Why don't you pull the bassinet in there and take an hour or so to yourself? I can keep an eye on him while I make dinner."

If I moved back to Tellarine, how was I going to juggle all things mothering plus the usual domestic duties?

Mum stepped closer. "What's up, love?"

"How did you do it all?" I glanced around the room, a home I had lived in for a long stretch of my growing-up years. "How am I going to do it all?"

Mum escorted us to my room and unlocked the bassinet casters. "First off, you know I didn't do it all. I dropped the ball a lot."

Fair point.

"Don't make that 'I feel bad you know I know' face." Mum chuckled and dropped a nappy, a portable waterproof change mat, and wipes in the bassinet then wheeled it down the hallway.

I grabbed a tiny blue terry-towel Bonds *Wondersuit* and followed her.

Mum set the nappy change items on the couch and extracted my son from my grip. "Secondly, you'll be a wonderful mum because you want to be."

I kneeled beside the couch and offered my finger to be squeezed by bubs.

"You care enough to want to do the right thing." Mum slipped Mr. Handsome out of his boat-themed onesie and changed his nappy. "You've made me realise how I messed up so many things when it came to you … and yet you're still here, allowing me to be part of your life."

My throat clogged. "I'd love you regardless."

She blinked her glassy eyes. "I know, and I love you too. I mightn't've said it enough, but I hope to fix that from now on."

We redressed the droopy-eyed youngest Roberts and tucked him in bed.

Mum wrapped me in a brief hug. "Okay, take a rest now, love."

"Thank you." I grabbed my phone from the kitchen and settled on my bed with a yawn. A nap might be in order.

I unlocked my phone and furrowed my brow. Why were there five unread SMSs in my text thread with Keanu? My pulse skittered, and I opened the thread.

Keenie: SHOULD I BE NERVOUS YOU DIDN'T REPLY TO YESTERDAY'S SUGGESTION LIKE YOU USUALLY DO? OR THIS MORNING'S MORE COMMON NAME OFFERING?

Keenie: WAS YESTERDAY'S NAME AS HORRIBLE AS I'M IMAGINING YOU THINK IT IS? AND NOW I'VE BEEN EXCOMMUNICATED?

Keenie: HAVE I MESSED UP SOMEHOW?

Keenie: DID YOU RECEIVE MY MESSAGES?

Keenie: SILENCE IS GOLDEN UNLESS YOU'RE CHECKING YOUR PHONE EVERY FIVE MINUTES LIKE A DESPERATE TWEEN.

I giggled at the screen. Had Keanu switched brains with the aforementioned tween? I peered at the time and pressed the Call button.

Keanu's number rang less than three seconds. "Tara."

Tingles shivered along my spine at the gentle tone in his voice. "Hey."

"It's good to hear your voice." Keanu's words sounded huskier than usual.

"You too." Could he hear my rapid heartbeat?

"Gimme a moment." The phone line muffled.

I lay flat on my back along the bed.

The background noise on his end of the line disappeared. "Hey."

"Hey," I whispered.

"Wasn't sure what happened. If I'd done something wrong."

"No. I just had to think."

"About?"

"The name." I tapped my fingers on the bedspread.

"Kai?"

"Yeah." Should I tell him I know it's his middle name?

"Like it?" Had I heard a waver?

"It's … perfect."

"Really?" The huskiness in his voice returned.

"Yeah." I groaned. "But I need to think of a middle name now."

Keanu's laughter echoed loud and clear.

I loved his laughter. Could friends love the sound of another friend's laugh?

"I have a confession to make."

I smirked. "That it's your middle name?"

"How'd y'know?" I imagined Keanu's dark eyes now wide and intense.

I wished we were having this conversation in person. "I did a payroll job for your dad a while back."

"Makes sense." The phone connection crackled. "Ya still wanna use it even knowing this?"

"I do." I stiffened. What a terrible phrase to use right now. "Yeah, maybe."

He cleared his throat. "I'll, ah, keep that in mind when I think of middle names."

"Cool, cool." Ugh, so not cool.

"Otherwise, ya doing well?"

"Pretty good."

"Good."

Yeah, good. I played with the edge of my windcheater hem. "I guess you must be coming up to dinner rush, so I won't keep you any longer."

"Right, yes, okay."

I rolled to my side. "See you when I see you?"

"See ya when I see ya, Tar."

"Bye." I ended the weird conversation, flopped against the pillow, and tried to catch a little shuteye in spite of my thundering pulse and heightened senses. But my mind had other ideas.

Thoughts of Keanu stretched out on his stomach across his carpeted office floor, attention zoned in on my son like I had seen him play with Diana's little brother. Keanu at his desk, my son balanced on his lap typing nonsense at his computer. Keanu holding my son securely on his shoulders as he walked about Benanu's, gleeful laughter ringing.

"Stop it." I gritted my teeth. Why was my heart and mind so cruel to me? Could these dysfunctional parts of my soul not understand that Keanu could be nothing more than a friend?

But why? My heart whispered. *Why was he off-limits?*

"Because …" I rolled off the bed and stared at the clothes I had rifled through and discarded on the floor this morning. "It's just not … possible." I lowered to the carpet and crossed my legs.

But he asked you to stay.

I grabbed a pair of maternity jeans Victoria had lent me, folded it, and placed it at the end of my bed. I needed clothing which fit my new body shape. My oversized T-shirts worked if I had leggings or fitted pants, but all I had packed were maternity clothes. Why had I been short-sighted? Now I had lost a decent portion of pregnancy weight—a lot of my fat had relocated to my ginormous milk-makers—I had to peg the waistband of my trousers. But the peg system was unreliable and popped at the most inopportune time, like baby and my trip to the supermarket yesterday morning. The check-out lady probably thought I was a weirdo grabbing at my hips every few seconds.

Victoria's borrow pile grew. I folded each precious item with painstaking care and allowed my mind to wonder. To ponder. Keanu had asked me to stay, but his motivation was unclear. And asking him *now* what he had meant seemed too frightening a prospect.

I reorganised the rest of my scant wardrobe into "wearable," "bearable," and "unsuitable" piles, slid the wearable items back into my drawers, shoved the unsuitable clothing into a plastic bag, and stared far too long at the clothes I wished not to wear but needed to wear if I wanted to cover my backside in public.

Did I have enough money to buy a few necessary items? I tucked Victoria's garments into a cloth bag and perched on the side of my bed.

Mum knocked on my door.

"Come in."

She poked her head through the small gap and grinned. "Your milkman needs you."

"Funny." I grabbed Victoria's bag of clothes and popped them near my tote bag.

Mum opened the door wider. "You been busy instead of resting?"

"Yeah. I need to get some new clothes because"—I pointed to the bag of too-big clothes—"these maternity ones aren't cutting it."

Mum nodded toward Victoria's bag. "What's this one?"

"Things I borrowed from Victoria. Didn't want to confuse them in case I donate the others."

Mum crossed her arms. "Maybe we can drop them with her when we pick up more clothes from your place?"

"What?"

A gurgling cry pierced the air.

"Let's visit Tellarine." Mum stepped back and disappeared down the hallway.

Visit Tellarine? I stared at Victoria's clothes. It was a cheaper option by far, but was I ready to return, even if for a visit?

Somehow I knew I would never be one hundred percent ready to see Keanu.

CHAPTER THIRTY-FIVE
Coming Home

"Can you please pull over?" I peered at the bush scenery through the windscreen and slowed my breathing.

"Everything okay, love?" Mum glanced at me with wide eyes and flicked on my car's turning indicator.

"We're twenty minutes out from Tellarine, and I feel ready to drive." Dr. Braithwaite told me a few sessions ago to choose moments and be intentional when facing specific fears. Driving was a small concern on my long list of issues, and this was a safe environment to test myself.

Mum slowed and pulled onto the shoulder of the single-lane highway, tyres crunching over the dirt-gravel surface, and parked. She unbuckled and turned toward me. "You sure?"

Not really. "I need to start somewhere."

She nodded. "You do."

I unbuckled, opened the passenger door, and muttered prayers as I rounded the car and filled the driver's seat.

Mum settled in the passenger seat. "Take it slow if you need, there's no time pressure."

I gave her the ghost of a smile, readjusted the mirrors, and glanced at the rear seat. The mirror positioned above my son's car seat reflected his gorgeous slumbering features.

"Still sleeping?" Mum asked.

"Yeah." I focused ahead on the task at hand, repositioning my seat. *Please, Lord, help me overcome this tiny hurdle.* I had driven without trepidation many times before and would do it again.

After checking and rechecking the rear-view and right-side mirrors, I pulled onto the deserted road and accelerated until the vehicle reached the speed limit.

"How you feeling?" Mum clasped her hands together in her lap.

I concentrated on the road and multitasked an internal assessment. Heartrate steady? Check. Pulse calm and muted? Check. Eyesight and hearing unobstructed? Check and check.

"Tara?"

Hands and arms unwavering? Check and … hmm. My arms were a little tense, but taut muscles versus losing the plot seemed like a win to me.

"Love?" Mum's voice carried the edge of fear.

"What?" I shimmied my shoulders and relaxed against the seat back.

"I asked how you were feeling? Do you need me to drive?"

I smiled at Mum before returning my attention to the road. "Sorry, no. Was triaging myself, and other than stiffness in my upper arms, I'm feeling great."

"Really?" Did I detect hope in Mum's tone?

"Yeah, really." *Thank you, God, for this victory.*

Twenty-three minutes later, I pulled up in front of Diana's ancient metal fence.

"House number nine? My favourite number." Mum grinned at Diana's hinged metal gate enclosing the shrubby garden. "It's such a quaint house."

"There're plenty of quaint houses in this neighbourhood." Warmth for this little country town pooled in my chest.

"Maybe I should see if there are any houses for sale." She opened the door and slipped from her seat.

Any houses for sale? My heartbeat thudded. Would Mum consider moving closer if I decided to move back to town? What would that be like? To have her around the corner? I waited for the icy sting of dread or the heat of annoyance to fill my chest. Nothing.

"You coming?" Mum leaned into the back row and unclipped her grandson.

I exited the vehicle and commenced the ridiculous task of emptying a gazillion things from the car boot. How could a teeny person need so much stuff? I unfolded the pram, inserted and secured the pram bassinet, then shoved my tote bag, several baby blankets and extra cloth nappy burp rags in the underneath pram storage compartment. I slung the overstuffed nappy bag over my shoulder, grabbed Victoria's maternity clothes, and slammed the boot.

"Ready, pack horse?" Mum hugged my baby close to her chest.

"Yeah, you can pop him in."

Mum cooed and smiled as she tucked the little man into the pram. "You go ahead. I can push."

I awkwardly unlocked the cold metal gate, bounded along the path, up the stairs, and knocked on the front door.

The sound of clomping elephants, grunting, giggles, and squeaks heightened inside the house.

I stepped back.

The wooden door opened wide, and Jonathan and Diana tussled in the opening.

"I won!" Diana shrieked and cackled.

"Tara? Can you help?" Mum called from the bottom of the verandah steps.

Oh yeah. Stairs and prams were a sucky mix.

Jonathan strode toward Mum, snagged both sides of the pram, and lifted that puppy up the stairs like an oversized cardboard box filled with airy compostable white packing peanuts.

"Oh." Mum's eyes widened.

I smirked and dumped my bags inside the house beside the doorway.

"Don't you dare touch that baby!" Diana brushed past me and pulled her grinning husband away from the pram. "I won."

"What's going on?" Mum grabbed the pram handles and narrowed her eyes at my friends.

Diana elbowed a now-laughing Jonathan against the wooden slats of the house. "We raced to the door for the first baby hug."

That explained the ruckus.

I gestured for Mum to push the pram past the crazies, assisted her indoors, and faced my beaming, red-faced friends. "Must you be so weird around an overprotective grandmother? You'll both get a turn." Talk about clucky!

Diana wrinkled her nose. "Sorry." She pulled me against her side for a quick hug and linked our arms, then interlocked her other arm with Jonathan's. "We'd better behave, or we might be banned from baby cuddles."

Jonathan raised a smirky eyebrow. "Once I change into my

uniform, Grandmama will beg me to hold her grandson."

I snorted. "You're not wrong. I think Mum was checking out your guns before."

"He's a nice package, isn't he?" Diana fluttered her lashes at her husband.

He leaned closer to his wife. "I'll give you a nice packa—"

"I'm right here, guys." Sheesh. Married couples. "Go have sex on your own time. Today's about me."

"It sure is," Jonathan said.

Diana chuckled and leaned closer. "I've missed you."

We entered the house without the iconic *Wizard of Oz* skipping or theme song and closed the wintery air outside.

I flopped on the couch beside my stiff-backed mother, who held my son. "The Harrises have promised to be on their best behaviour."

"If you say so."

"How about formal introductions?" I grabbed my son from Mum's arms.

Mum acquiesced. "I've met your friends, remember?"

Diana lowered to the vacant space beside me. "And I've seen Mr. Handsome twice now."

Jonathan kneeled on the floor at his wife's feet.

"But you've never been officially introduced." I lifted my son's arm until it extended toward Diana and Jonathan. "Auntie Di and Uncle Jon, this is Kai Stephen Roberts."

"Kai Stephen. What a wonderful name." Diana reached out with her thumb and forefinger, and shook Kai's chubby hand.

"Pleased to meet you, Kai." Jonathan brushed his palm over Kai's socked foot.

Mum nudged my shoulder. "When did you decide on a middle name?"

"It came to me last night. Now I can fill out that blasted government paperwork."

Diana smiled when Kai grasped her finger and squeezed. "Will you list Isaac as the father?"

I shrugged. "It's all done online, so I'll see if it's possible to skip that section or not. If I can skip it, I'll skip it."

"I was a little apprehensive you might've named him Kai Isaac," Mum said.

"The thought crossed my mind." I would tell Kai about his

biological father when he was old enough to understand, and go into more detail when he was older, but our chapter with Isaac was over. "But no. One significant name is enough."

Nervous tingles shot through my gut. What would Keanu do when I told him Kai's name?

I passed Kai to Diana.

Jonathan leaned against his wife and grinned at my son.

"You planning to show him off at Benanu's while you're here?" Diana fingered the tufts of hair on Kai's head.

"Maybe." Fresh tingly bubbles fizzed in my no-longer-flat stomach.

"Victoria will be here for lunch. We could pop out between lunch and afternoon rush and visit. Leave the grandmothers to chat?"

"That sounds like a lovely idea," Mum said. "Vicki's great company, and it might be better if I visit your workplace another time."

I stared at my Mum. Maybe she was right. It might be awkward if Mum came along and met Keanu for the first time when there were unresolved things between my boss and me.

"What do you think?" Diana kissed Kai's head.

"Yeah, okay. Let's drop by for a quick visit." I watched my best friend and her husband dote over my son, and a pang stirred in my chest.

I had barely stepped through the threshold of Benanu's when a shrill "Ohmygoodness!" rose above the clang of cutlery against ceramic and chattering patrons.

Isabelle squealed and rushed from behind the bar.

"Eager," Diana whispered behind me.

I hoisted Kai into a cradled position.

Isabelle beamed at my son and wrapped an arm around my shoulders. "He's the cutest little scrumptious thing I've ever seen."

Kai batted his long lashes, stared up at my friend slash co-worker, and gurgled.

If humans could melt, Isabelle would have puddled at the welcome mat.

Diana nudged us forward. "How about we get out of the doorway."

We ambled toward the bar where Dominic polished glasses. "Welcome back, Tara."

I handed Kai to Diana and slouched on a bar stool. "Moving up in the world?"

Dominic nodded. "Bossman's been teaching me a few tricks now he's busier with office stuff."

Guilt needled my chest, and I rubbed my ribs. "Has he hired any office help?"

"He's had a few people through for interviews, but between him, Mrs. Everton, Isabelle, and Diana, they've been covering all the important things."

I turned and eyed my friend, who held Kai tight while Isabelle fawned over him. "Since when have you been working here again?"

Diana shrugged. "I just came in a couple of times, mostly to show Mrs. E a few things."

Nice to know Keanu's mum was willing to jump in and help when needed.

I caught Dominic's gaze and ignored the butterflies upsetting my digesting lunch. "Is the Bossman in today?"

He nodded toward Isabelle. "Think so. Ask Iz. She's been looking after his calendar."

Isabelle nudged my shoulder. "You two talking about me?"

"Always." Dominic flashed a grin, his intense gaze drilling into his colleague's face.

Isabelle's cheeks coloured with pink.

Oh.

"Um, yeah. He's in a meeting at the moment, but"—Isabelle checked the wall clock across the room—"they should be finishing up."

"Thanks." I glanced at the staff-only entry.

"Can I still carry him?" Diana asked.

I nodded.

Dominic slid from behind the bar and opened the door. "Don't be a stranger."

"I won't." I smiled knowing my words were true. My heart was answering the call from Tellarine to return home.

Diana and I ambled along the hallway, where we waved at

passing kitchen staff.

Mrs. Everton approached with a wide grin. "It's lovely to see you!" She embraced me with a floral hug and peered at Kai in Diana's arms. "He's beautiful. What's his name?"

I pressed a hand against my topsy-turvy stomach. "Kai Stephen."

Mrs. Everton whipped her head up to face me, and her side fringe shifted over her eye. She brushed aside blonde strands with her fingers. "Kai?"

I pursed my lips. "Yes."

Her eyes seemed to sheen, and she blinked. "A perfect name for a perfect boy."

"Thank you."

She touched Kai's little fingers. "Does my son know?"

"I strongly hinted at liking the name but didn't confirm it."

Diana widened her eyes. "I thought you told him?"

I shook my head.

"Wow. Okay."

Mrs. Everton glanced down the hallway in the direction of Keanu's closed office door. "We can look after this little guy should you need a moment with my son, can't we, Diana?"

Diana clapped Kai's hands together. "Definitely."

A sudden realisation dawned on me. My son's name was the middle name of the man my heart was hung up on, not my son's father's name. And now the mother of the man my heart craved knew I had chosen his name … and encouraged me to steal a private moment to talk with her son.

Was this more serious than I imagined? *Could it be, please, God?*

Keanu's office door opened, and two men exited the room.

Pastor Davidson? What was the senior pastor of Tellarine Christian Church doing here?

"Tara! Lovely to see you." Pastor Davidson beamed and approached me. "This your little one?"

My breath hitched when Keanu's dark eyes zeroed in on me. His hair and beard were scruffier than normal, but his ironed white business shirt and navy tie looked professional.

"Yes, isn't he the cutest?" Diana bounced my son in her arms.

Keanu seemed transfixed on my face.

My airways constricted and my cheeks heated. How was his gaze so … potent?

"What's your name, young man?" Pastor Davidson chuckled beside Diana and Mrs. Everton.

I heaved a breath. My ribcage seemed two sizes too small for my body.

Keanu glanced at my son.

I opened my mouth and squeaked.

"Kai. This darling boy's name is Kai." Mrs. Everton's pitch matched my mother's besotted tone.

Keanu inched closer, his unreadable eyes aimed over everyone else's heads straight at me.

My heart pounded.

"It was a pleasure seeing you all." Pastor Davidson smiled at our little group and turned to Keanu. "Thank you once again for your generosity. I'll see you Friday evening."

Keanu shook the pastor's hand. "I'll be there to help set up."

I stood stock-still, anchored to the hallway carpet. What was going on?

"Keenie, love? I think Tara needs to sit down." Mrs. Everton beamed up at her son. "Why don't you escort her to sit in your office for a moment? Diana and I can watch Kai."

Keanu engulfed my clothed elbow with his enormous hand and lightly tugged me along the hallway to his office.

My elbow burned with his touch. Would I go up in smoke if he touched my skin? *Don't think about him touching your skin!* Heat flooded my cheeks.

Keanu led me to the chair opposite his desk. "Mind if I close the door?"

Words escaped me. I flopped onto the warm seat and shook my head.

He turned his back to me and closed the door, sighed, and rested his forehead on the solid wood panel.

"You okay?" My vocal cords croaked.

"I'm composing myself," he said, his words muffled against the door.

"What's un-composing you?" I whispered.

"Even I know that's not a word." He turned and aimed his tortured eyes at me.

I straightened in the chair so I could gather more oxygen in my lungs. Had someone turned the air off? A drip of perspiration slid down my neck.

"His name's Kai?" he whispered.

"Kai Stephen." I glanced at the wall in the direction of where we had stood in the hallway. "What was that all about? Your meeting with Pastor Davidson and … the other part."

Keanu rubbed his hand across his chin. "Benanu's is assisting the church with at-cost catering for a few key events over the coming months."

At-cost price? "And Friday?"

"Men's meeting."

"Y-you still attend church?"

He nodded. "Every Sunday I'm not needed here."

I stood and stepped close enough to touch him.

He heaved a breath.

I reached out on tiptoes and touched his chin. "But you've skipped seeing the barber."

Keanu closed his eyes. "I need a haircut."

"You do." I lowered my hand and stood flat on my feet.

He lifted his eyelids and peered down at me. "I'm sorry I blew up the last time we saw each other."

I pressed my palms on my thighs. "I'm sorry too. But …" I dropped my chin and stared at the buttons on his shirt.

"But what?" His voice was soft, gentle.

"Why did you ask me to stay?"

"What do y'mean?"

I stiffened my back and lifted my head. I could do this. "What was the reason you asked me to stay? Were you genuine in your request, or … were you using my feelings against me?"

He stepped closer, the toe of his shoe less than a step from mine. "I'd never do that."

A weight I had no idea I carried lifted from my shoulders. "Was my position in this office the sole motivator for your heartfelt plea? 'Cause you'd miss my shining work ethic?"

"No."

"And pity for the rejected and desperate heavily pregnant woman wasn't a factor?"

His nostrils flared. "Never."

"Then why?" My words were barely audible to my ears.

"A Tara-less life seemed like …an unbearable thought." He touched my elbow. "And I was right."

"Were you?" My sight blurred, and I blinked away tears.

He pulled me against his firm chest.

I rested my ear against his pounding heart.

"Uh huh. A Tara-and-Kai-less life isn't for me." He rested his huge hand against my back and swirled small circles near my spine.

Heat trickled through my torso. I prayed I would not float away. "Unfortunately, you'll have to live a bit longer without me."

He harrumphed.

I smirked. "Unless you can talk my mum into moving closer."

His hand on my back stilled. "Is that a possibility?"

"I think so."

"Done."

I closed my eyes and breathed in his familiar scent.

Keanu resumed my mini backrub. "How long are y'staying?"

"Once I collect some clothes from the bungalow, we'll head home." Daytime driving was something I could work on, but night drives would need to wait a while longer.

"I'll make time for a haircut before y'next visit."

I leaned back and tilted my head up. "What if I visited tomorrow?"

His brown eyes sparkled with hazel shards. "Then I'd be a liar."

"I won't be here tomorrow, so you're off the hook." I stepped from his embrace. "I'd better make tracks."

He clicked his neck and nodded. "Can I give my namesake a hug?"

"Of course."

Keanu opened the door and checked the hallway. "Mum and Di are still yacking."

I trailed beside my friend—were we more than friends now? Closer friends?—and caught Diana's attention. "The big fella wants a little fella hug before we go."

Mrs. Everton clasped her hands at her chest.

Diana offloaded my son into Keanu's arms.

I snapped a photo of Keanu smiling at my tiny baby in his thick arms and thanked God for the hope of new beginnings and faithful friends.

CHAPTER THIRTY-SIX
A Culmination of Good Things

"You think she'll get it?" I unwrapped another fancy vase and handed the weighty glass to my non-vertically challenged friend.

"With her café experience, I can't see how they won't want her." Diana stretched and deposited Mum's vase on the top shelf of the built-in wall unit in Mum's new lounge-dining room.

"I hope so." I retrieved the final paper-clad vessel and kicked the empty cardboard box to the centre of the large room.

Diana grabbed and positioned the crystal vase. "You still on for dinner tomorrow?"

"We a—"

My phone shrieked from the coffee table on the other side of the room.

"Sorry." I dashed across the aged psychedelic carpet and gazed at the screen. Kim from Mother's Group. "Hey, Kim."

"Have I caught you at a bad time?" Kim's timid voice rang clear through my earpiece.

"Not at all. What's up?"

"I'm in Robinvale picking up Delilah's special formula and noticed the pharmacy have a super special on Huggies nappies. Less than half the price I pay at the supermarket." Her voice wavered. "Would you like a box?"

"Sounds like a bargain, so count me in!" Although I had purchased a large box on my last grocery shop, nappy sales in my preferred disposable brand were rare.

"Great. Is Kai in size two infant nappies like Delilah?"

"I just moved him up to size three." My almost four-month-old son had turned into quite the rolly-polly boofa baby.

Kim's soft laughter trickled over the phone line. "I forget he's bigger than my petite princess. Okay, I'll get you a box and bring it to Group on Wednesday."

"Thanks. Text me the cost, and I'll transfer money to you."

"Will do, bye."

"See ya." I disconnected and placed my phone on the coffee table.

"That one of your Mother's Group ladies?" Diana slid a knife along the top of another cardboard box.

I helped her unload Mum's bell collection. "Yeah. Kim, the quiet one with the doll of a daughter." Our mother's group was a church outreach group I helped run with another mum at church. Most of the women were unchurched, and many were single mothers. I enjoyed our weekly conversation and morning tea.

"When're Jae and Paul visiting? Was it the end of November or the beginning of December?"

I grinned and shoved a Keanu-hand-sized ceramic bell painted with tulips into the display cupboard. "She called last night. They'll be here from November twenty-five through to December seventeen! We're having an early Christmas here in Tellarine."

"Awesome! Make sure you tell Victoria because they've got the best house for entertaining if you end up getting the gang together." Diana pulled more bells from the box and unwrapped them.

"I'll have a think and chat with Jae. She's starting to show, so by the time they're here at the end of the month, she'll probably have popped." Seemed my cousin unknowingly started her pregnancy when I ended mine.

"Is she still stressing about it all?"

"Think so." I chuckled and shoved the empty box away.

Diana pulled a small, heavy box closer. "This'll be my last, and then I'll have to head off."

"Already?"

"Yeah, need to give myself ample time to primp for the big date." Jonathan and Diana's first wedding anniversary had occurred two days earlier.

I positioned a small, clear glass bell beside a smaller brass ringer. "And this is just for the anniversary, not a joint thing for Jon's birthday?"

Diana shook her head. "Tomorrow night's the birthday celebration."

"I'll do my best to be on time, but with this deadline Roger gave me, I might run a little late. Can't disappoint the boss." Working with the gang at The Tella Tribune for the past three weeks had been more fun than I had anticipated. Researching, analysing, and writing tapped into a part of my brain I had missed using.

"I totally understand. I'll be waking early to submit my piece."

A sudden prickling warmth overcame my chest, and I sucked in a breath. Was it feed time already? "What's the time?"

Diana yanked her phone from her pocket. "Almost four."

No wonder my letdown reflex kicked in! I was almost an hour past Kai's usual afternoon feed. "Where's—"

The front door opened, and Kai's soft snorty-cry filled the air.

My milk manufacturing plant kicked into high gear, and I grimaced. "In here!"

Keanu wheeled the pram into the room. "Sorry I'm late. After we walked Alannah to Benanu's, we got caught up playing at the park, didn't we, mate?"

Diana chuckled. "Playing with whom?"

I strode across the room and unclipped my unhappy son from his seat. "It's okay. I kinda forgot until …"

"Till what?" Keanu asked.

I hoisted Kai onto my hip. "My boobs sent out a Bat Signal."

Diana choked back a laugh.

Keanu smirked. "Glad to heed the call."

I settled on the couch and freed one of my overfilled girls. "Avert your eyes."

Keanu turned his back and pushed the empty pram to the corner near the front window.

I guided Mr. Hangry-Pants to my sore, bulging milker.

His blue-grey eyes widened, and he gulped like a heavyweight champion.

"You can turn around. He's on and not choking." Thank the Lord. Spluttering and coughing followed by a bout of hiccups was the likely outcome of drinking from a bursting bosom a month ago.

Keanu sank to the couch and slid his arm around my back. "Kai's a lady magnet. All the toddlers giggled when he slid down the slide."

Slid down the slide? I peered at my boyfriend and spoke through gritted teeth. "I hope you're joking."

He rubbed my shoulder. "I held him the entire time, like a handsome hand puppet."

Lucky.

"He giggled each time he went down. Had us all in stitches with his infectious laugh."

Diana "aww-ed" and pressed her palm to her chest.

Totally clucky. I brushed my fingers through Kai's soft hair and turned to Keanu. "Think Jon'll knock her up tonight?"

"Tara!" Diana's cheeks bloomed with an attractive shade of pink.

Keanu smirked and pulled me closer to him. "Tonight. Tomorrow night. Sometime soon."

Diana gathered her belongings. "And on that note, I'm off."

"We're great at naming babies," Keanu said.

I held back a laugh. "Totally. I can forward Keanu's list if you like?"

"Very funny." Diana leaned and kissed Kai's head. "But do keep it handy."

I widened my eyes and stared at my bestie. "Are you …?"

The front door squeaked open, and Mum entered the room. "There's my boy!" She smiled at Diana and Keanu.

"I'll see you tomorrow." Diana blew us kisses and left the room.

She had better spill her beans—if there were beans to spill—when I saw her next.

"How'd you go, Mum?" I covertly detached Kai, slipped my breast pad and bra into position, and set him upright.

"Burp time?" Keanu slid his arm from behind me and reached for the baby.

"Yes." I turned back to Mum.

She dropped to the vacant cushion beside me. "I think I did okay. Akamu said Emma or Keanu would call later this week."

"Probably me." Keanu rubbed Kai's back in soothing circles.

Was it possible to be jealous of an infant?

"Mum's winding down her involvement now that Number One's back next week."

Number One. My cheeks warmed at his affectionate nickname and tone, and I snuck a furtive glance at the man I loved. Despite not having said those three sacred words, I knew deep down he was my Mr. Right.

Mum smoothed her business skirt over her knees. "And you're sure you two won't mind working with me? I applied at the Italian restaurant and the new Indian place, but … there's just something about Benanu's."

I smiled. "Yeah. There is. And I've no issue—"

Kai let loose a frog-like belch and smiled.

"Good boy!" Mum and Keanu said.

I chuckled and reached for my son. The things tiny humans did to warrant praise.

"Round two?" Keanu kissed Kai's head and relinquished his hold on him, then slid his arm behind my back.

"Yep. Close your eyes." I unclipped and released my rock-hard breast with a wince.

Mum pulled a face. "How're you going to get him onto that?"

I inspected the situation and deduced Kai would not be able to latch on. "The maternal health nurse suggests I express a little milk when I'm engorged like this."

Kai fussed in my lap.

"I'll get you on soon, hungry hippo. Give me a second to prime the pump."

Keanu cleared his throat.

"I'll get a milk bag." Mum dashed off to the kitchen.

I glanced at my boyfriend with his eyes squeezed shut and a pained expression on his face. "You doing all right?"

"My imagination's running wild. Think it's worse hearing what's going on than seeing." His voice was gravelly and low.

Tendrils of heat danced in my abdomen. "I disagree. It'd be much worse seeing."

"You're probably right." He leaned closer. "Busy on Friday? Let's go to the city registry office and elope so I'm allowed a backstage pass to all the feeding sessions."

I elbowed his side. "Funny. Even if we wanted to, we couldn't. You need to lodge notice of your intention to marry a month before the wedding." I discovered this fun fact when engaged to Isaac. No shotgun Vegas-style weddings in Australia!

"Spoilsport." Keanu leaned closer and nuzzled my ear. The guy had decent aim with his eyes shut.

"Here you go!" Mum traipsed in the room with a milk storage bag and the bag holder which attached to the manual breast pump.

"Thanks." I nudged Keanu back, balanced Kai in my lap, and set the milk catching station. "Can you be ready to grab this, Mum? I'm trying not to trigger a letdown, but if it does, I want to get him on fast."

Mum nodded and poised her hands nearby.

I gently pressed my desperate-to-be-drained boob and gritted my teeth. The pressure was reminiscent of when my milk came in months ago.

Milk dribbled into the bag building to a pitter-patter against the thin plastic. I massaged until it seemed Kai would be able to latch on with comfort and shifted my baby into optimal feeding position. The telltale tingling of stimulated milk flow burned in my chest. "Now!"

Mum grabbed the bag while I fumbled Kai into place.

The little guy's eyes widened a split second before he closed them and gulped.

"All good?" Keanu asked.

"Yep." I rotated my sore neck.

Mum stood. "I'll get this into the freezer. We've a lovely collection now for when you return to work."

Keanu rubbed my neck with his warm fingers. "I thought Kai was going to work too?"

"Not on Tuesdays. I have him all to myself." Mum grinned from the doorway and disappeared.

"She babysitting?" His deft fingers pried all the tension from my body.

"Mmm hmm."

Keanu growled and nipped my ear. "Don't make those sounds."

I checked Kai was fine, then turned to Keanu. "Kiss me."

A mischievous smile slipped to his yummy lips. "Thought I was."

I licked my lower lip.

His hot mouth covered mine in a slip-slide of wet, hungry kisses. The guy knew how to wield his lips, which triggered all the other inappropriate thoughts in my brain.

Maybe …

Kai pulled off, squeaked, and cried between intermittent

coughs.

I wrenched my lips from Keanu's perfect face and gasped.

Kai's face was covered in milk, and my body was shooting milk across the room.

I scrambled with my bra to cover the leak with my breast pad. Freaking Keanu exciting my body with a kiss and setting off another letdown.

Keanu emitted a strangled noise, grabbed Kai, and set to burping the drowned kid.

My cheeks heated, and I stared at my boyfriend. "You saw that, didn't you?"

His wide eyes watched the patch of carpet where milk had landed. "It's better than a Nerf gun or water pistol. Y'sure I can't use those babies the next time I go paintballing with the guys? They won't know what hit them."

I burst into laughter. "Not a chance, bucko."

"Was worth a try."

I rubbed my son's back where he lay on Keanu's broad chest and drank in the cosy scene.

What had I done to deserve this blissful life? My mum and I were no longer at war, and the issues in my head were clearing with each passing day. I had an adorable son, supportive family and friends, and a keeper of a boyfriend.

Thank you, God, for loving me despite my past, my hang-ups, and my failings.

I stared at the man who held my overflowing heart in his gigantic hands, and the words spilled over before I could stop my mouth. "I love you," I whispered.

Keanu's dark eyes shined, and he gifted me with one of his secret smiles. "I know."

I snuggled against his side, wrapped my arm around my son, and smiled. My fractured mind was healing in the hope of tomorrow.

AUTHOR'S NOTE

Thank you for traversing Tara's arduous journey with me. She started whispering the finer details of her story while I reworked *Wounded Soul* in 2021, so I jotted and stashed away those ideas despite my "Diana tunnel vision". When my focus shifted to Tara earlier this year, I unearthed my notes and buckled in for a rough ride.

Tara pulled a myriad of emotions from me while I wrote, prayed, rewrote and edited her story, but she also released my (often hidden) sass and quick wit. Allowing this side of me to roam the pages was more enjoyable than I imagined, and the writing process flowed better than I thought possible. Brandishing my growing confidence in my abilities helped too!

My sincere apologies if the labour, birth and post-birth scenes were difficult to read. I wanted Tara's experiences to be raw and real. Childbirth is an intimate event, and often the people around the birthing mother are unaware of her thoughts and feelings along the journey. I drew from the thick archives of stories I'd heard over the years, along with my personal pregnancy and birth memories with my five daughters, all of which held their own difficulties, highs and lows. In fact, I experienced false labour a week before my fourth daughter was born—something which embarrassed me since I'd laboured several times before!—so each pregnancy and birth, with its associated emotions, are incomparable to someone else's story. I hope you stuck with Tara as she pushed through hers.

Thank you for investing your time in reading *Fractured Mind*. The last book in *The Tellarine Series* will follow Belinda, Victoria's best friend. I suggest you stock up on tissues…

ABOUT THE AUTHOR

Sheridan Lee is an Australian writer with a penchant for true-to-life characters who triumph over adversity.

When she isn't singing along to her favourite Christian artists or watching Hollywood actors named Chris in superhero and Star Trek movies, Sheridan is reading or writing—with at least one of her five daughters lounging on her—and wishing the dirty laundry would clean itself.

Learn more about Sheridan and her books at www.sheridanlee.com.

SUBSCRIBE to Sheridan's newsletter (and receive The Tellarine Series prequel chapter as a gift): www.sheridanlee.com/subscribe

SHERIDAN'S BOOKS:

The Tellarine Series

Punctured Heart

Wounded Soul

Fractured Mind

Broken Spirit *(releasing 2023)*